總編嚴選

歷史名人堂

Hall of Fame

Featureflash / Shutterstock.com

目錄 Contents

商業大亨

民權領袖

美國文學大家

電影巨匠

英國文學大家

殞落巨星

體壇風雲人物

美國政壇領袖

藝術時尚鬼才

不朽音樂傳奇

Vocabulary Bank

1) **determination** [dɪˏtɝmə`neʃən] (n.) 堅毅，決心
Learning to play a musical instrument takes patience and determination.

2) **propel** [prə`pɛl] (v.) 驅策，推動
The man's debts propelled him to get a job.

3) **successively** [sək`sɛsɪvli] (adv.) 連續地，越來越
In the fall, the days get successively shorter.

4) **booming** [`bumɪŋ] (a.) 景氣好的，繁榮的 (n./v.) boom [`bum]
The man made millions in the booming real estate market.

5) **vast** [væst] (a.) 龐大的，鉅額的，遼闊的
The government spent vast amounts of money on the project.

6) **establish** [ɪ`stæblɪʃ] (v.) 創辦，建立 (n.) establishmant [ɪ`stæblɪʃmənt]
The university was established in 1926.

7) **enterprise** [`ɛntɚˏpraɪz] (n.) 事業，企業，公司
The Taiwan Power Company is a government enterprise.

8) **shift** [ʃɪft] (v./n.) 轉移，移動，轉變
Don't try to shift the blame onto me.

9) **facility** [fə`sɪləti] (n.) 設施，設備（此定義用複數 facilities）
Hotel facilities include a restaurant, bar and business center.

10) **diverse** [dɪ`vɝs] (a.) 多元的，不同的
San Francisco is a culturally diverse city.

11) **funding** [`fʌndɪŋ] (n.)（提供）資金、基金
The public radio station receives government funding.

進階字彙

12) **rags-to-riches** [rægz tu `rɪtʃɪz] (a.) 白手起家的，貧民致富的
Many women have been inspired by Oprah's rags-to-riches tale.

13) **self-made** [`sɛlf `med] (a.) 白手起家的
Silicon Valley is home to many self-made millionaires.

14) **superintendent** [ˏsupɚrɪn`tɛndənt] (n.) 主管，（機構、企業）負責人
All budget decisions are made by the organization's superintendent.

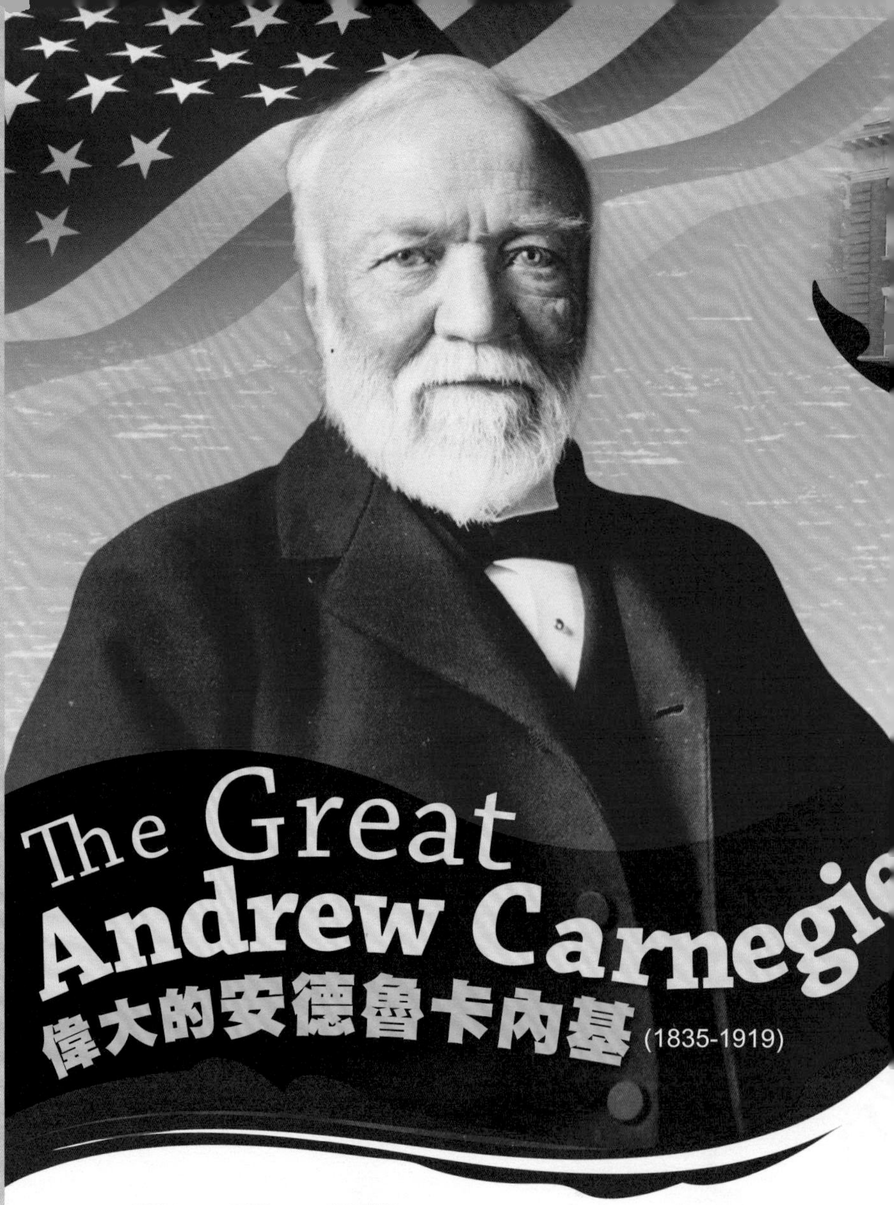

The Great Andrew Carnegie
偉大的安德魯卡內基 (1835-1919)

朗讀 MP3 1 單字 MP3 2 英文文章導讀 MP3 3

The life of Andrew Carnegie is a classic [12]**rags-to-riches** story. Born in 1835 into a poor Scottish family, he was truly a [13]**self-made** man. In order to seek a better life, Carnegie's father moved the family to America in 1848. They settled in Allegheny, Pennsylvania, where, at the age of 13, Carnegie got his first job in a cotton mill for just $1.35 a week. Even at this young age, he showed himself to be a hard worker with a love for learning and a passion for reading.

Carnegie's [1]**determination** and intelligence [2]**propelled** him into [3]**successively** better jobs. Hired as a telegraph operator by the Pennsylvania Railroad Company at the age of 18, he rose rapidly to the position o

©Wiki_Robert Lawton
©Wiki_CMU
內基圖書館之一，位於伊利諾州的 Macomb
Carnegie Mellon University 卡內基美隆大學

[14]**superintendent**. He also learned how to invest his money wisely in the [4]**booming** rail business. Later, he turned his attention to the steel industry, which made him a [5]**vast** fortune. He [6]**established** Carnegie Steel Company in 1891, and by the time he sold it to J.P. Morgan nine years later, it was the largest and most profitable industrial [7]**enterprise** in the world.

In his later years, Carnegie [8]**shifted** his focus from making money to spending it. He Ⓖdonated huge sum of money to create public [9]**facilities** in a [10]**diverse** range of fields. One example is the famous Carnegie Hall in New York. In addition to providing [11]**funding** for music and art, Carnegie's money was also used to establish many public libraries and educational institutions.

中 Translation

安德魯卡內基的一生是典型的貧民致富故事。一八三五年生於貧苦蘇格蘭家庭的他，是個真正白手起家的人物。為了追求更好的生活，卡內基的父親於一八四八年舉家搬到美國。他們落腳在賓州的阿列格尼市，十三歲的卡內基在那裡一家棉織廠找到第一份工作，週薪只有 1.35 美元。小小年紀的他，在此時他就已經展現出是個努力的員工，熱愛學習又對閱讀充滿了熱忱。

卡內基的堅定與智慧不斷將他推向一個比一個更好的工作。十八歲時，他受僱於賓州鐵路公司，擔任電報員，他快速升任主管職。他也學會如何明智地將錢投資於欣欣向榮的鐵路業。後來，他將注意力轉向鋼鐵業，賺了一大筆財富。他在一八九一年成立卡內基鋼鐵公司，等到九年後他把公司賣給 J.P. 摩根時，已經是世上最大且最賺錢的工業企業。

晚年時，卡內基把重心從賺錢移至花錢。他捐贈鉅額金錢，在各個領域建造公共設施。其中一個例子是紐約著名的卡內基音樂廳。除了提供資金贊助音樂和藝術，卡內基的錢也用於建造許多公共圖書館和教育機構。

Language Guide

卡內基贊助成立的機構

鋼鐵大王安得魯卡內基是史上第二富有的人，僅次於石油大王洛克斐勒 (John D. Rockefeller)，他們兩人與汽車大王亨利福特 (Henry Ford) 於十九世紀末、二十世紀初並列美國工業三巨頭。

卡內基在一八九九年發表的 *Wealth* 一文寫道：The man who dies thus rich dies disgraced.（死時身懷鉅富者得臭名。）他認為富有的企業家身負雙重任務，一為積聚財富，二為將財富用於慈善，唯行善才能讓生命有價值。從他三十三歲那年起，他開始將收入超過五萬美元（三十三歲時的年薪）的部分全數捐出。

直到去世為止，卡內基捐出了全部財富的九成（3.5 億美元），其中 1.25 億成立紐約卡內基有限公司 (Carnegie Corporation of New York) 繼續他的慈善事業，其他善款在他的出生地英國、生長地美國及其他英語系國家成立了多個教育相關的信託基金、超過三千座圖書館、卡內基美隆大學 (Carnegie Mellon University)、匹茲堡卡內基博物館 (Carnegie Museums of Pittsburgh) 等文教機構。由於熱愛音樂，他還捐款建造了七千座教堂管風琴 (church organ) 及名聞遐邇的卡內基音樂廳 (Carnegie Hall)。

Grammar Master

雙賓動詞：donate

雙賓動詞即後面可接兩個受詞的動詞，「賓」就是「受格」的意思。

主詞 人 物

例 Cindy **sent** me a letter.
辛蒂寄了一封信給我。

sent 為雙賓動詞，後面 me 和 letter 都是 sent 的受格。雙賓動詞基本句型除了例句提到的「主詞 + 雙賓動詞 + 人 + 物」也常把受格的「物」和「人」位置交換，但是中間要多個介系詞 to，表示「人」是「物」的接受者。

例 I **gave** a bouquet of roses **to** her.
我送了一束玫瑰花給她。（也可以說 I **gave** her a bouquet of roses.）

另外像是 donate、say、speak、describe、announce、introduce⋯⋯ 等雙賓動詞比較特別，一定要用「物 + 介系詞 + 人」的句型，不能在人後接物。

例 Many big corporations **donate** huge sums of money **to** political parties.
許多大公司都會捐大筆金錢給政黨。（不能說 Many big corporations **donate** political parties huge sums of money.）

The Road to Business Success
邁向成功之路

Vocabulary Bank

1) **industrialist** [ɪn`dʌstriəlɪst] (n.) 企業家，工業家
(v.) industrialize [ɪn`dʌstriəlaɪz] 工業化
John D. Rockefeller was the most powerful industrialist of his time.

2) **relevant** [`rɛləvənt] (a.) 有關的，切題的，有意義的
What you're saying isn't relevant to the discussion.

3) **subordinate** [sə`bɔrdənɪt] (a./n.) 下級的，次要的；下屬
Tom is happy in a subordinate role.

4) **lament** [lə`mɛnt] (v./n.) 悲嘆，痛惜
The couple lamented the death of their child.

5) **janitor** [`dʒænɪtɚ] (n.) 工友
Does your apartment building have a janitor?

6) **deprive (of)** [dɪ`praɪv] (v.) 剝奪
No child should be deprived of an education.

7) **overcome** [ˌovɚ`kʌm] (v.) 克服，戰勝
Paula was able to overcome her fear of flying.

8) **obstacle** [`ɑbstəkəl] (n.) 障礙，妨礙
There are many obstacles on the road to success.

9) **genius** [`dʒinjəs] (n.) 天賦，天才
The artist's genius was only recognized after his death.

進階字彙

10) **mogul** [`mogəl] (n.) 巨擘，大人物
Rupert Murdoch is the world's most famous media mogul.

11) **philanthropy** [fɪ`lænθrəpi] (n.) 慈善（行為、事業）
(n.) philanthropist [fɪ`lænθrəpist] 慈善家
Bill Gates has decided to devote the rest of his life to philanthropy.

12) **sage** [sedʒ] (a./n.) 睿智的；賢人
Peter never forgot the sage words of his grandfather.

13) **salutary** [`sæljəˌtɛri] (a.) 有益的，有益健康的
The island has a salutary climate.

14) **proactive** [pro`æktɪv] (a.) 主動的，積極的
Proactive employees are more likely to be promoted.

朗讀 MP3 4 單字 MP3 5 英文文章導讀 MP3 6

While Carnegie made his fortune as a steel [10]**mogul**, he is remembered today more for his [11]**philanthropy** than for his role as an [1]**industrialist**. He is also remembered for his writings and speeches on such subjects as world peace, democracy and education. He especially enjoyed talking to young people, and one of his most famous speeches, entitled *The Road to Business Success: a Talk to Young Men*, was delivered to students of the Curry Commercial College in Pittsburg, PA on June 23, 1885. Don't be fooled by the age of the speech (it was delivered nearly 125 years ago). Most of the [12]**sage** advice is still highly [2]**relevant** today. Let's see what he had to say.

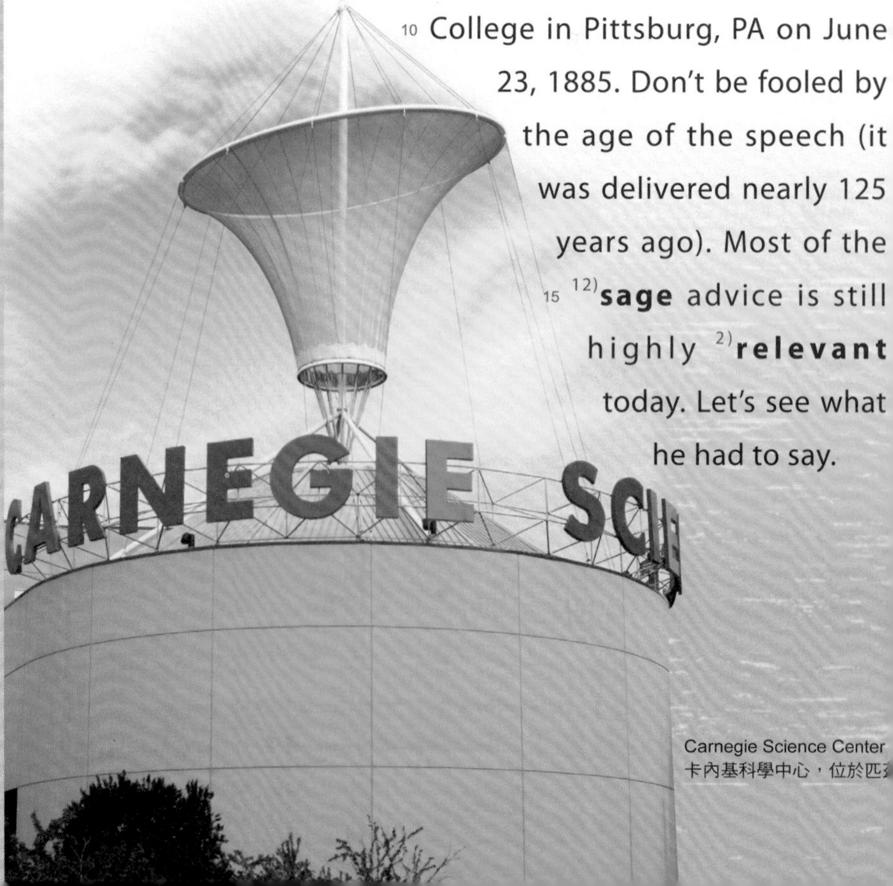

Carnegie Science Center
卡內基科學中心，位於匹

©Wiki_kinburn

Carnegie Hall 卡內基音樂廳，位於紐約市

In fitting with his own humble beginnings, Carnegie [G]starts off his speech by **1 making a case for** starting at **2 the bottom of the ladder** and working your way up. "It is well that young men should begin at the beginning and occupy the most [3]**subordinate** positions," he states. According to Carnegie, many of Pittsburgh's leading businessmen started out sweeping the offices they would eventually run. He [4]**laments** the fact that most offices now have full-time [5]**janitors**, thus [6]**depriving** new employees of "that [13]**salutary** branch of a business education." Those who are [14]**proactive**, however, can still find a way to [7]**overcome** this [8]**obstacle**. " But if by chance the professional sweeper is absent any morning, the boy who has the [9]**genius** of the future partner in him will not hesitate to **3 try his hand at** the broom," he says.

中 Translation

雖然卡內基以鋼鐵鉅子的身分致富，但他今日受到的懷念，卻是慈善家的身分，而不是企業家的角色。他有關世界和平、民主和教育等議題的著作與演講也深植人心。他特別喜歡與年輕人說話，他最有名的演講之一（講題為《邁向成功之路：對年輕人的談話》）就是一八八五年六月二十三日向賓州匹茲堡庫利商業專的學生發表的。不要被這篇演講久遠的年代給騙了（將近一百二十五年前發表），其中大部分睿智建言今日依然非常有用。我們來看看他說了什麼。

配合自己卑微的出身，卡內基的演講一開頭先說明從基層做起、力爭上游的重要性。他說：「年輕人應該從基層做起，擔任最低階的職位。」根據卡內基的說法，匹茲堡許多商業大老都是從打掃辦公室開始，後來這些辦公室都歸他們管。他感嘆現在大多數辦公室都有全職的工友打掃，因此剝奪了新員工學習「商業教育中這個有益環節」的機會。不過，積極的人還是可以想辦法克服這項障礙，他說：「如果碰巧哪天早上專業掃地工沒有來，具有未來合夥人潛質的年輕人就會毫不猶豫地試著拿起掃把。」

Tongue-tied No More

1 make a case for...
說明……的重要

make a/the case for... 裡的 case，是指在訴訟或爭論時提出的「論點，立論根據」。

A: What's your presentation going to be about?
你的簡報會以什麼為主題？

B: I'm going to make a case for increasing the marketing budget.
我會說明提高行銷預算的重要性。

2 the bottom of the ladder 基層

這邊的 ladder 是指需要一路往上爬的企業。the bottom of the ladder 即「企業基層」，相反的，「企業頂端」就是 top of the ladder。

A: Why don't you find a job at another company?
你為什麼不找別家公司的工作？

B: If I did, I'd have to start at the bottom of the ladder.
要是那樣，我就得從基層做起了。

3 try one's hand at sth.
著手嘗試

A: I'm thinking of trying my hand at a career in writing.
我考慮嘗試寫作工作。

B: Good luck with that!
祝你好運囉！

Grammar Master

start off ？還是 start out ？

start off 與 start out 在中文都是「開始」的意思，差別在於：

- start off 表示「從……某一部分開始接下來的動作」

例 Let's **start off** with a few questions from the audience.
我們一開始就先來讓觀眾提出一些問題。

- start out 表示「開始從事某職業或過某種生活」，帶有「一開始是 A 而後發展出 B」的語意

例 He **started out** as a salesman before entering politics.
他從政以前原是一名業務員。

朗讀 MP3 7 單字 MP3 8 英文文章導讀 MP3 9

Carnegie goes on to Ⓖrecommend that the students should aim high It's not enough to think of yourself as [1]**merely** a good employee, Carnegie advises. In order to **1 climb the corporate ladder**, workers need to think of all the ways they can help improve the company, especially [9]**in terms of** bringing in more money. He tells the students to have the attitude that their [10]**rightful** place in the business world is at the top, and that they should be the "king in their dreams" by taking charge of their careers. Employees must [2]**strive** to be far more than just average, Carnegie says; they need to be [3]**exceptional**—in that way, they can attract attention and get noticed by their superiors.

In addition to telling young men what they should do to [4]**ensure** a bright future, Carnegie also warns about the things they should avoid. Speaking of the dangers they would face on their upward path, he [11]**admonishes** "The first and most [12]**seductive**, and the destroyerof most young men is the drinking of [5]**liquor**." Carnegie also speaks out against [6]**speculation**. Rather than gamble their money on risky investments, he says, people should [7]**pursue** hard work and focus on one particular

Vocabulary Bank

1) **merely** [ˋmɪrli] (adv.) 僅僅，只有
(a.) mere [ˋmɪr]
Jim was merely a child when his parents died.

2) **strive** [straɪv] (v.) 努力，奮鬥
My parents taught me to strive for success.

3) **exceptional** [ɪkˋsɛpʃənəl] (a.) 優異的，特殊的
Yo-Yo Ma is an exceptional cello player.

4) **ensure** [ɪnˋʃʊr] (v.) 確保，保證
Companies are required to ensure the safety of their products.

5) **liquor** [ˋlɪkɚ] (n.) 酒，尤指白蘭地、威士忌等烈酒
Does that restaurant have a liquor license?

6) **speculation** [͵spɛkjəˋleʃən] (n.) 投機，投機買賣
It's important to know the difference between investing and speculation.

7) **pursue** [pɚˋsu] (v.) 從事，追求
Allen wants to pursue a career in real estate.

8) **conventional** [kənˋvɛnʃənəl] (a.) 慣例的，普通的，傳統的
The professor encouraged his students to challenge conventional thinking.

進階字彙

9) **in terms of** [ɪn tɝmz əv] (phr.) 對於，以…來看
In terms of box office, the movie was a big success.

10) **rightful** [ˋraɪtfəl] (a.) 正當的，當然的
The stolen car was found by the police and returned to its rightful owner.

11) **admonish** [ədˋmɑnɪʃ] (v.) 告誡，責備
The teacher admonished the student for being late.

12) **seductive** [sɪˋdʌktɪv] (a.) 誘惑的，性感的，有魅力的
The woman gave the man a seductive look over her shoulder.

©Wiki_kilnburn

Dunfermline 卡內基的出生地，位於英格蘭

©Wiki_ Newkai

卡內基圖書館之一，位於西北大學 (Syracuse University)

field. In other words, people need to find the area that best suits their talents, and then constantly strive to improve. Although [8]**conventional** wisdom says **2** **don't put all your eggs in one basket**, Carnegie suggests the opposite. Just make sure to watch that basket very closely, he tells the students.

中 Translation

卡內基接著建議學生應該目標遠大。光是把自己定位為好員工是不夠的，卡內基如此建議學生。要在公司一步步升遷，員工必須想盡一切能協助改進公司的方法，尤其是如何讓公司有更多收入這方面。他告訴學生該有的態度是，自己應該位居商場頂端才對，應該主宰自己的事業，做「自己夢想的國王」。員工必須努力達到遠高於平均之上，卡內基說，他們必須出類拔萃，這樣就能吸引上司的注意並獲得青睞。

除了告訴年輕人該如何做才能確保前途光明，卡內基也針對應該避免的事情提出警告。說到他們一路向上路途中會面對的危險，他告誡他們：「第一個也是最具誘惑力、足以毀掉大多數年輕人的就是酗酒。」卡內基也大聲地反對投機生意。他說與其將錢押注在高風險的投資上，人們應該努力工作並鎖定某個領域。換句話說，人們必須找出最適合自己天分的領域，然後持續努力進步。雖然一般認為是不要把雞蛋放在同一個籃子裡，但是卡內基卻持相反意見。他告訴學生，只要非常仔細看緊這個籃子就沒問題。

若有疑問請來信：eztalkQ@gmail.com

內基圖書館之一，位於約州的 Gloversville

Tongue-tied No More

1 climb the corporate ladder 升官，升職

climb the corporate ladder 字面上的意思是「爬企業梯子」，但其實指的是在公司裡的層層位階，也就是升官、升職的意思。

A: How come you work so late every day?
你怎麼每天都工作到很晚呢？

B: You have to put in lots of overtime if you want to climb the corporate ladder.
如果想升官，就必須加很多班啊！

2 put all one's eggs in one basket 孤注一擲

這句就是家喻戶曉的「把雞蛋全放在同一個籃子裡」，因為要冒著全軍覆沒的危險，因此常常用於否定句，叫人不要如此。

A: I'm just applying to one university—Harvard.
我只申請一間大學 —— 哈佛。

B: You shouldn't put all your eggs in one basket.
你不該把雞蛋全放在同一個籃子裡。

Language Guide

此卡內基非彼卡內基！

聽到「卡內基」，許多人會想到專攻人際溝通及潛力開發的卡內基訓練，其創辦人戴爾卡內基（Dale Carnegie，1888-1955）曾任業務員及演員，一九一二年於紐約的基督教青年會開辦成人的溝通課程，為日後遍佈全球訓練機構的濫觴。戴爾卡內基這位當代著名演說家也是一位暢銷作家，《卡內基溝通與人際關係》(*How to Win Friends and Influence People*) 為其代表作。

Grammar Master

「建議」的表達法

「建議他人作某事」有以下兩種不同的用法：

- recommend/suggest + 動名詞

例 We strongly **recommend** reporting the incident to the police.
我們強烈建議這件事要報警處理。

- recommend/suggest + (that) + 人 + (should) + 原形 V

例 He **recommended** that I should buy a more powerful computer.
他建議我買台性能好一點的電腦。

請注意第二個用法，recommend/suggest 後接的是原形動詞。在表示「建議」的句型中，should 常被省略，以避免語氣太過強硬。

Vocabulary Bank

1) **modest** [ˋmɑdɪst] (a.) 不太大（多、顯眼的），適度的
It's hard to support a family on such a modest salary.

2) **pledge** [plɛdʒ] (v.) 承諾給予，許諾
Donors have pledged millions in aid for victims of the earthquake.

3) **charity** [ˋtʃærəti] (n.) 慈善，慈善事業
(a.) charitable [ˋtʃærətəbəl]
John gives 15% of his annual salary to charity.

4) **donation** [doˋneʃən] (n.) 捐獻，捐款
(v.) donate [ˋdonet]
The charity is funded by private donations.

5) **cash register** [kæʃ ˋrɛdʒɪstɚ] (phr.) 收銀機
The robber demanded all the money in the cash register.

6) **stock** [stɑk] (v.)（商店）進貨，理貨
The clerk stocked the freezer with ice cream.

7) **expense** [ɪkˋspɛns] (n.) 支出，開支
Rent is my biggest monthly expense.

8) **paper route** [ˋpɛpɚ rut] (phr.)（小孩）送報紙的工作
Did you have a paper route when you were a kid?

9) **pool** [pul] (v.) 集合（資金、資源等）
We pooled our money to buy a birthday present for Dad.

10) **embark (on)** [ɪmˋbɑrk] (v.) 開始，著手進行
We're embarking on a new project next month.

進階字彙

11) **tycoon** [taɪˋkun] (n.)（企業）大亨
The tycoon left his entire fortune to charity.

12) **tax return** [tæks rɪˋtɝn] (phr.) 報稅單
Have you filed your tax return yet?

13) **deduct** [dɪˋdʌkt] (v.) 扣除，減免
How much does the company deduct from your paycheck each month?

14) **lucrative** [ˋlukrətɪv] (a.) 賺錢的，有利可圖的
Real estate investing can be very lucrative.

© 達志 / UPI PHOTO

Warren Buffett
華倫巴菲特

朗讀 MP3 10 單字 MP3 11 英文文章導讀 MP3 12

A man gets up at six in the morning, prepare breakfast, packs a lunch, gets in his car and drives to the office just like he's done every day for over half a century. He lives in a mid-sized, five-bedroom house bought for a [1]**modest** $31,500 in 1958, when homes were still affordable. Sound unusual? Not really. But here's where the story gets interesting. In 2007, this same man [2]**pledges** $30.7 billion to [3]**charity**, making it the largest single [4]**donation** in history. Who is this person? He's Warren Buffett. Called the "Oracle of Omaha," he **1 breaks the mold** when it comes to business [11]**tycoons**.

Warren Buffett was born on August 30th, 1930 in Omaha, Nebraska. As a boy, he worked in his grandfather's corner store, running the [5]**cash register**, [6]**stocking**

shelves and ⓖkeeping the front sidewalk swept clean. It was during this time that young Warren started to **2 cut his teeth** in business. In 1943, at the age of 13, he filled out his first income [12]**tax return**, [13]**deducting** his watch and bicycle as business [7]**expenses** for his [8]**paper route**. Two years later, Warren [9]**pooled** his savings with a classmate to buy a pinball machine. Placing it inside a neighborhood barbershop, he [10]**embarked** on what would prove to be one of the most [14]**lucrative** investing careers of our era, or any other. A little over 60 years later, Warren Buffett would be worth $62 billion. He'd also be the richest person in the world.

中 Translation

有個男人在清晨六點起床，準備早餐，把午餐包好，坐進車子，開車前往辦公室，一如他半個世紀以來每天的例行公事。他住在一個中等坪數，有五個臥房的屋子，是一九五八年以區區三萬一千五百美元買來的，當年住家還在一般人買得起的價格。聽來非比尋常？不盡然，但故事有趣的地方在後頭。二〇〇七年，這個男人承諾捐出三百零七億美元用於慈善，創下史上最大單筆捐款紀錄。這個人是誰？他是華倫巴菲特。被喻為「奧馬哈先知」的他，打破了商業大亨的既定形象。

華倫巴菲特在一九三〇年八月三十日出生於內布拉斯加州的奧馬哈。他小時在祖父的街角小店工作，負責收銀、貨物上架及維持店前人行道清潔。小華倫就是在那段時間開始學習做生意。一九四三年，年僅十三歲的他便首度申報所得稅，把他購買手錶和自行車的費用列為送報工作的營業支出扣除。兩年後，華倫拿存款和同學合資買了一台彈珠台。他把機器放置在住家附近的理髮店，展開我們這個年代——或任何年代皆是——最有賺頭的投資生涯之一。六十多年後，華倫巴菲特的身價高達六百二十億美元，也成為世界首富。

Language Guide

Omaha 奧馬哈

奧馬哈是內布拉斯加州 (Nebraska) 的最大城，位於美國密蘇里河畔 (Missouri River)，被譽為「通往西部的門戶」(Gateway to the West)。

本文多次提及巴菲特的中西部背景，美國中西部多為北歐後裔（即斯堪地那維亞人，Scandinavian），承襲祖先出身貧寒的刻苦精神著稱。巴菲特生活儉樸，在投資時不碰不了解的產業（如科技類股），專門購入逢低價的優質公司股票（既要價廉也要物美），也被認為是中西部樸實、節儉傳統的體現。oracle 有「先知，聖賢」的意思，最早是指古希臘的先知，因為他們了解神意，可以給人們忠告。巴菲特因為投資準確，所以被人稱為 Oracle of Omaha。

Tongue-tied No More

1 break the mold 打破既定模式

mold [mold] 是「模型，鑄模」，引申為「既定模式」，而 break the mold 就是「打破窠臼」的意思。

A: That band's music is so creative and unique.
那個樂團的音樂很有創意又獨一無二。

B: Yeah. They really break the mold.
是啊，他們真的打破了既定模式。

2 cut one's teeth 從…獲取經驗

除了有「獲取經驗」的意思之外，也有「開始從事」的意思。

A: How did you get your start as a reporter?
你怎麼開始當記者的？

B: I cut my teeth working at a local paper.
我是在一家本地報社工作開始的。

Grammar Master

keep 的用法

動詞 keep 的意義與用途很廣，常見的有：

- **keep (+ sb./sth.) + adj./adv.**
  表示「保持某種狀態」

例 You should **keep** calm during an earthquake.
地震來襲時應該保持冷靜。

- **keep + 動名詞 (v-ing)**
  表示「繼續（做某事）」

例 Mike **kept** interrupting the professor during class.
麥克在課堂上一直打斷教授。

常見需與動名詞連用的動詞還包括 consider（考慮）、admit（承認）、delay/postpone（延期）等。

例 Paula once **considered** going to live in another country.
寶拉曾考慮到他國居住。

Vocabulary Bank

1) **ultimate** [ˋʌltəmɪt] (a.) 極致的，終極的
Hawaii is the ultimate vacation destination

2) **textile** [ˋtɛkstaɪl] (n./a.) 紡織品；紡織的
The textile factory exports most of its products.

3) **stake** [stek] (n.) 股份，股本
The CEO owns a large stake in the company.

4) **outright** [ˋaʊtˋraɪt] (adv.) 全部地，一次付清地
They couldn't afford to buy the car outright.

5) **downturn** [ˋdaʊn͵tɝn] (n.)（經濟）衰退
Michael lost his job in the economic downturn.

6) **mock** [mɑk] (v.) 嘲諷，嘲笑
His older brother mocked him for being bad at sports.

7) **insider** [ˋɪn͵saɪdɚ] (n.) 內部人士，消息靈通的人
According to company insiders, the deal is likely to be approved.

8) **bubble** [ˋbʌbəl] (n.)（資產）泡沫
Many investors lost all their money in the stock market bubble.

進階字彙

9) **frugality** [fruˋgæləti] (n.) 節儉，樸素
(a.) frugal [ˋfrugəl]
The Scots are famous for their frugality.

10) **bank** [bæŋk] (v.)（在銀行）存錢，（和銀行）往來
You should bank your paycheck before you have the chance to spend it.

11) **gourmet** [gʊrˋme] (a./n.) 美食的；老饕，美食家
Phil took his girlfriend to a gourmet restaurant on Valentine's Day.

12) **weather** [ˋwɛðɚ] (v.) 平安度過（風暴等），承受住
The politician was able to weather the scandal.

13) **dotcom** [ˋdɑtˋkɑm] (n./a.) 網路公司（的），也可寫作 dot-com
Brad worked at a dotcom in the late '90s.

口語補充

14) **has-been** [ˋhæs͵bɪn] (n.) 過氣的人事物
He used to be a big star, but now he's just a has-been.

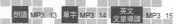

朗讀 MP3 13 單字 MP3 14 英文文章導讀 MP3 15

From the start, Warren Buffett has mixed a strategy of value investing—buying good companies that are cheap—with a Midwestern sense of [9]**frugality**. While most investment professionals live and work in major financial centers like New York and London, Buffett decided to open a small office in his hometown. When asked about his life in Omaha, Buffett replied: "Really getting to do what you love to do everyday—that's really the [1]**ultimate**." At 31, he'd already [10]**banked** his first million, thanks to the success of his various investment partnership. That same year, Buffett started ⓖbuying up shares in a New England [2]**textile** firm, Berkshire Hathaway. This company would become the foundation of the Buffett empire, and turn many investors into millonaires.

Over the years, Warren Buffett's Berkshire Hathaway has bought large [3]**stakes** in a number of important American companies. These include the Washington Post Company, GEICO, ABC and Coca Cola. He also bought a little-known [11]**gourmet** chocolate company [4]**outright** for $25 million in 1972. Today, See's Candies is worth 15 times that much and has stores all over the world. Berkshire Hathaway has successfully [12]**weathered** many market [5]**downturns**. During the tech boom of the late '90s, Buffett was [6]**mocked** for claiming he couldn't find value in [13]**dotcom**

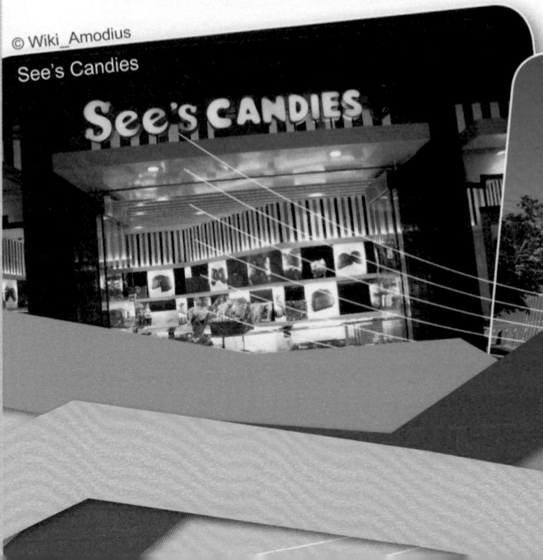

companies. [7]**Insiders** started to **1 write him off** as a [14]**has-been**. A few years later, however, Buffett had the last laugh. The [8]**bubble** burst in 2000, wiping out $5 trillion in the market value of technology companies.

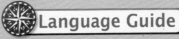

中 Translation

從一開始，華倫巴菲特就把中西部的節儉觀念結合上價值投資策略——買股價低的好公司。多數投資專業人士都在紐約和倫敦等主要金融中心居住及工作，巴菲特卻決定在家鄉開一間小辦公室。被問及在奧馬哈的生活時，巴菲特回答：「每天都確實去做你熱愛的事——真是棒極了。」三十一歲時，拜多次合夥投資成功之賜，他已經賺到人生第一個百萬美元。同年，巴菲特開始購買新英格蘭一家紡織公司「波克夏哈薩威」的股份。這家公司後來成為巴菲特帝國的基石，也讓許多股東躋身百萬富豪。

多年下來，華倫巴菲特的波克夏哈薩威公司已經買下數家重要美國公司的大量股份，其中包括華盛頓郵報公司、蓋可保險公司、美國廣播公司（編註：American Broadcasting Company 的縮寫）和可口可樂。他也於一九七二年以兩千五百萬美元買下一家不知名的高級巧克力公司所有股份。如今，「喜思糖果」的市價翻了十五倍，分店遍及全世界。波克夏哈薩威已成功度過多次股市衰退。在九〇年代晚期的科技熱潮期間，巴菲特因聲稱看不出網路公司的價值而備受奚落，業內人士開始將他貶為過氣人物。然而幾年後，得意的人是巴菲特。網路泡沫在二〇〇〇年破滅，科技公司有五兆美元的市值蒸發殆盡。

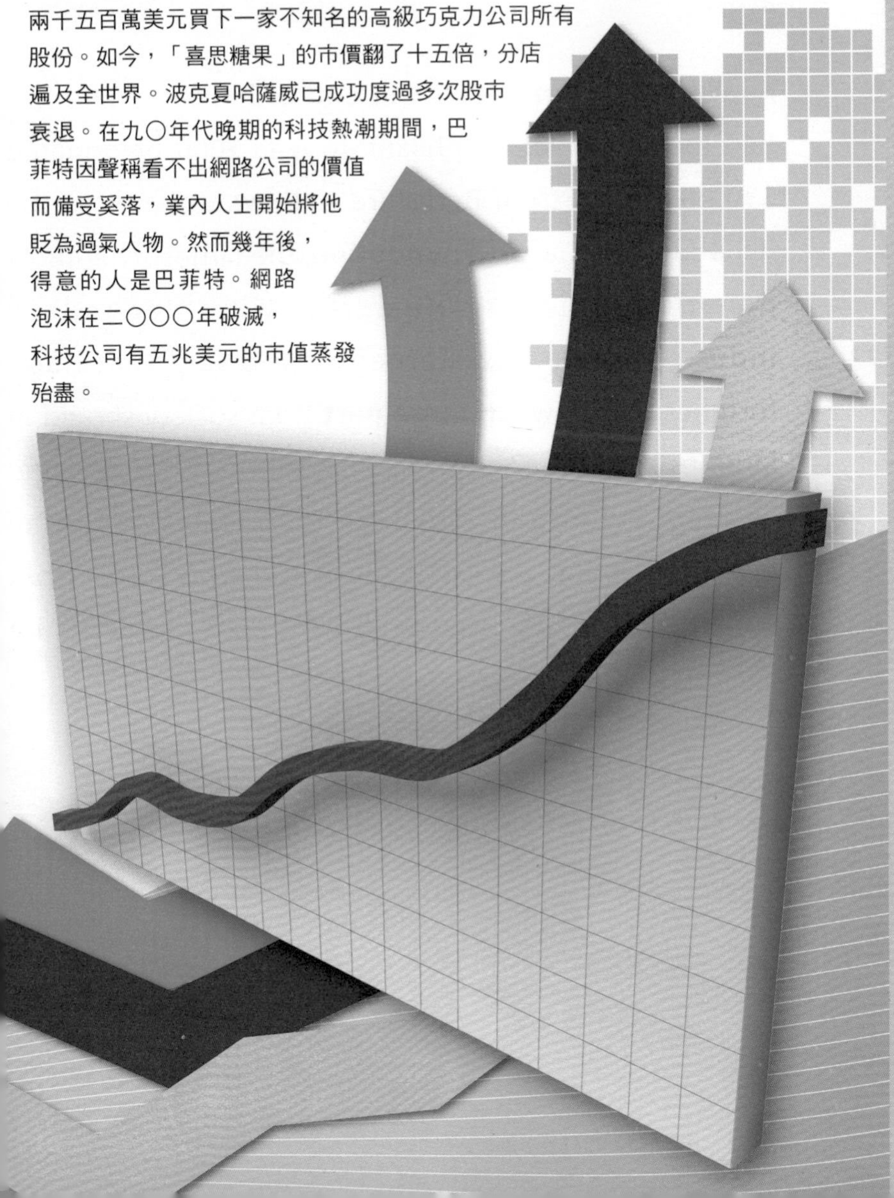

Language Guide

investment partnership 合夥投資

相較於以個人資金投入股市的散戶，合夥投資的作法是集合家族成員或是合夥人的資金，以能達到請專業顧問操盤來增加獲利機會的規模經濟 (economies of scale)，還能分攤成本並共享大額投資才有的稅賦優惠。

GEICO 美國雇員保險公司

GEICOG 是一家保險公司，全名為 overnment Employees Insurance Company。一九九六年時被巴菲特旗下的波克夏哈薩威 (Berkshire Hathaway) 買下全部股份，成為其子公司。其實巴菲特早在一九五一年就開始投資 GEICO。時年二十二歲，還在哥倫比亞大學念 MBA 的巴菲特發現，GEICO 捨棄保險業務員，改以直接郵寄保單的方式，針對財務穩健且個性保守的公務員、軍人及事故率低的用車人推銷保險，成本上極具優勢，於是一舉「大量」買進，只是當年投資金額不過一萬美元出頭（還是分四次投資），就占了他個人資產的一半以上。隔年獲利百分之五十了結的決定，讓巴菲特接下來二十年後悔不已，因為那些持股要是擺上二十年，總市值將變成一百三十萬！

一九七六年，GEICO 因保單定價錯誤導致財務危機，瀕臨破產，當時已是大富翁的巴菲特仍看好這家公司的競爭優勢，陸續大量買進該公司股票，直至一九九五年持股達到百分之五十一時，這些股票已為他賺進二十三億美元，巴菲特從此決定與這家公司長相廝守，再花二十三億美元把全部股份買下。

Tongue-tied No More

1 write sb./sth. off
對某人絕望，放棄努力

也可以說 write off sb./sth.。write off 字面上的意思就像中文所謂的「除名」，也就是死心了，不再將某人或某事列入考慮。

A: Can't he borrow the money from his parents?
他不能去跟父母借錢嗎？

B: No. They've already written him off.
不行。他們已經放棄他了。

Grammar Master

與 up 連用的動詞片語

副詞 up 有「光；盡」之意，因此 buy up 是指「全部買下」。其他類似的用法還包括 eat/drink up「吃／喝光」、clean up「徹底掃除」、use up「用盡」、dry up「乾涸；枯竭」等。

例
- Tom **bought up** all the red roses at the florist.
  湯姆把花店裡的紅玫瑰全買走了。
- Who **ate up** all the cookies?
  誰把所有餅乾都吃光了？
- You can't go out until you **clean up** this mess.
  你要把這一團亂完全收拾好才能出門。
- The river has **dried up**.
  河水已枯竭。
- Emma has **used up** all her sick days.
  艾瑪把病假都休完了。

Vocabulary Bank

1) **accumulate** [ə`kjumjə͵let] (v.) 累積，積聚
Mark's debts began accumulating after he lost his job.

2) **nevertheless** [͵nɛvəðə`lɛs] (adv.) 仍然，不過，然而
The plane crash was caused by a small, nevertheless fatal error.

3) **mansion** [`mænʃən] (n.) 豪宅
The streets of Beverly Hills are lined with mansions.

4) **fleet** [flit] (n.) 車隊，艦隊，機群
The company owns a fleet of delivery trucks.

5) **foundation** [faʊn`deʃən] (n.) 基金會
The billionaire established a foundation to support cancer research.

6) **legendary** [`lɛdʒən͵dɛri] (a.) 傳奇的，著名的
The steaks at that restaurant are legendary.

7) **in large part** [ɪn lɑrdʒ pɑrt] (phr.) 大部分，大多數
Gilbert's success is due in large part to his hard work and dedication.

8) **certainly** [`sɝtənli] (adv.) 無疑地，確實，必定
It certainly is hot outside today.

進階字彙

9) **indefensible** [͵ɪndɪ`fɛnsəbəl] (a.)（行為）無法辯解的
The murderer's crime was indefensible.

朗讀 MP3 16 單字 MP3 17 英文文章導讀 MP3 18

According to the Bible, "It is easier for a camel to pass through the eye of a needle than for a rich man to enter heaven." It's meant to [G]remind us that there is no glory in [1]**accumulating** vast wealth. [2]**Nevertheless**, Buffett's fortune continues to grow. Shares in Berkshire Hathaway are worth over $100,000, making them the most expensive on the New York Stock Exchange. And while he pays himself a very modest salary, his stake in Berkshire Hathaway is worth over $30 billion. But he doesn't live in a [3]**mansion** or own a [4]**fleet** of fancy cars. When Buffett spent US$10 million on a jet, he named it [9]**Indefensible**. Even after Wall Street almost destroyed the world's banking system in 2008, Buffett's reputation didn't suffer at all.

As Warren Buffett nears the end of his career, he has become known for his philanthropy. In 2006, he donated $30 billion worth of Berkshire Hathaway shares to the Bill & Melinda Gates [5]**Foundation**, the largest charitable donation in history. He agrees with [6]**legendary** industrialist Andrew Carnegie, who said that huge fortunes that flow [7]**in large part** from society should in large part be returned to society. This may not be good news for Buffett's children, but it [8]**certainly** is for the billions of people around the world who suffer from poverty and disease. And what will happen to Berkshire

New York Stock Exchange

Hathaway when he finally retires? At a recent annual company meeting, Buffett statethat he has no plans to retire anytime soon, and that he plans to work until six years after his death!

中 Translation

《聖經》上說：「駱駝穿過針眼，比富人上天堂來得容易。」這無非在提醒我們，累積鉅額財富不是光榮的事。但巴菲特的財富仍持續成長。波克夏哈薩威的股價超過十萬美元，成為紐約證券交易所的股王。而儘管他付給自己的薪水並不高，他持有的波克夏哈薩威股份價值卻超過三百億美元。不過他沒有住豪宅，也沒有名車車隊。巴菲特花一千萬美元購買一架噴射機時，他取名為「站不住腳號」。即便二〇〇八年華爾街幾乎完全摧毀全球金融體系之後，巴菲特的聲望仍然絲毫未損。

隨著華倫巴菲特的事業生涯步入尾聲，他開始以熱心慈善著稱。二〇〇六年，他捐了市值三百億美元的波克夏哈薩威股份給比爾及梅琳達蓋茲基金會，創下史上最高慈善捐款。他認同傳奇企業家安德魯卡內基的看法：大部分取自社會的鉅額財富，也應大部分回饋社會。這對巴菲特的子女或許不是好消息，但是對全球各地數十億飽受貧窮與疾病所苦的民眾肯定是一大福音。等到巴菲特最後退休時，波克夏哈薩威將何去何從？他在公司最近一場年度會議中指出，他沒有任何在近期退休的計畫，還說他打算去世後還要工作六年！（編註：引述巴菲特自己開的玩笑）

若有疑問請來信：eztalkQ@gmail.com

Language Guide

Bill & Melinda Gates Foundation 蓋茲基金會

簡稱 B&MGF 或 Gates Foundation，是全球最大的財務公開私人基金，由科技富豪比爾蓋茲及妻子梅琳達蓋茲創立。蓋茲基金會旨在全球普及醫療照護 (healthcare)、減少赤貧 (extreme poverty)，在美國廣泛提供教育機會、幫助更多人有能力使用資訊科技。

巴菲特於二〇〇六年捐出一千萬股波克夏 B 股 (Berkshire Hathaway Class B stock) 給蓋茲基金會時，設下三個條件：第一，比爾蓋茲或梅琳達蓋茲至少一人還在世，並實際參與會務；第二，這個基金會必須持續符合慈善機構的資格；第三，基金會每年必須將前一年波克夏 B 股持股獲利加上 5% 的淨資產捐出。

Grammar Master

remind 的用法

除了文中的 remind sb. that + 子句，remind of 和 remind about 也有「提醒某人某事」的意思，但其中略有些差異：

- **remind sb. of sth**：提醒某人過去發生的某事；因相似而使某人想起某事

例 That love song always **reminds** Laura **of** her first date.
那首情歌總是讓羅拉想起她第一次約會。

例 The landscape **reminds** Tracy **of** Ireland.
這裡的風景讓崔西想到愛爾蘭。

- **remind sb. about sth**：提醒某人必須做某事 (= remind sb. to v.)

例 Paul was glad that his wife **reminded** him **about** the meeting. He had completely forgotten about it.
保羅很高興他太太提醒他開會的事，他壓根兒忘了這件事。

Mini Quiz

1. Which of the following is NOT true about Warren Buffett?
   (A) He gained experience in business at a young age.
   (B) He lives and works in a major financial center.
   (C) He doesn't plan to leave most of his fortune to his children.
   (D) He has lived in the same house since the late 1950s.

2. He kept _________ me over and over, so I just turned off my phone.
   (A) called (B) call
   (C) calls (D) calling

3. If you hadn't reminded me _________ my appointment, I never would have remembered to go.
   (A) for (B) to
   (C) about (D) of

解答 1 (B) 2 (D) 3 (C)

Titan of Tech Steve Jobs

賈伯斯 劃時代科技巨人

© 達志 / UPI PHOTO

朗讀 MP3 19 單字 MP3 20 英文文章導讀 MP3 21

Born in February 1955, Steve Jobs was raised by [11]**adoptive** parents in Cupertino, California, a small city in what would later be Silicon Valley. Jobs became interested in [1]**electronics** at an early age. While working on a project in junior high, he called the president of Hewlett-Packard to ask for parts, and ended up with a summer job.

Entering Portland's Reed College in 1972, Jobs [2]**dropped out** after one semester, but stayed there for over a year, sleeping in friends' [3]**dorm** rooms and [12]**auditing** classes he found interesting. He then returned to California and got a job designing video games at Atari, but soon quit to seek [4]**enlightenment** in India and take [13]**psychedelic** drugs.

Back in Silicon Valley, Jobs ran into friend and fellow college dropout Steve Wozniac at a computer club meeting. Recognizing the commercial [5]**potential** of personal computers, the two founded Apple Computer on April Fool's Day, 1976. With money [6]**obtained** by selling

Jobs' VW bus, they [7]**assembled** the Apple I in his parents' garage. Their next PC, the Apple II, was a huge success, and the company began growing rapidly.

Jobs next led development of the Macintosh, the first affordable PC with a GUI and mouse. Nevertheless, he was fired by CEO John Sculley after a power struggle in 1985. Jobs kept busy over the next decade, though, founding NeXT Computer to build workstations and [8]**acquiring** Pixar, which later became the world's leading [9]**animation** studio.

When Apple bought NeXT in 1996, Jobs soon found himself back in charge of the company he co-founded. Under his leadership, Apple released a string of hits—including the iPod, iPhone and iPad—and transformed from a computer maker into a key player in the mobile revolution. [10]**Tragically**, Jobs, who had battled cancer for years, passed away on October 5, 2011. He was just 56.

Mini Quiz 閱讀測驗

What was the third computer produced by Apple?

(A) The Apple I
(B) The Apple II
(C) NeXT Computer
(D) The Macintosh

中 Translation

出生於一九五五年二月，史帝夫賈伯斯由養父母撫養長大，住在加州一座小城市庫柏提諾，位於後來的矽谷。賈伯斯年紀很小就開始對電子產品有興趣，國中做一項作業時，他打電話給惠普的總裁要一些零件，結果獲得了一份暑期工作。

一九七二年賈伯斯進入波特蘭的瑞德大學就讀，唸完一學期就休學，但是在那裡待了一年多，睡在朋友的宿舍房間，旁聽他有興趣的課。接著，他回到加州，到雅達利遊戲公司設計電玩遊戲，但不久就辭職遠赴印度追尋啟蒙、吃迷幻藥。

回到矽谷後，賈伯斯在電腦俱樂部的聚會上巧遇他的朋友、同為大學中輟生的史帝夫沃茲尼克。兩人體認到個人電腦商業化潛力無窮，於是在一九七六年愚人節創立蘋果電腦。靠著賈伯斯賣掉福斯小巴士的錢，他們在賈伯斯父母的車庫裡組裝出第一代蘋果電腦。他們推出的下一台個人電腦——第二代蘋果電腦——大獲成功，蘋果電腦也開始快速成長。

接下來，賈伯斯帶領開發出麥金塔電腦，第一台有GUI（圖形使用者介面）和滑鼠的平價個人電腦。儘管如此，他還是在一九八五年一場權力鬥爭後，被執行長約翰史卡利掃地出門。不過，接下來十年賈伯斯可沒閒下來，他成立NeXT電腦來生產電腦工作站，也收購皮克斯，後來成為全世界頂尖的動畫電影公司。

一九九六年蘋果買下NeXT，賈伯斯很快又重回領導他共同創立的公司。在他的帶領下，蘋果公司推出一連串轟動產品（包括iPod、iPhone 和iPad），並且從電腦製造商搖身一變，成為行動電子革命的要角。很不幸，與癌症奮戰多年的賈伯斯，在二〇一一年十月五日去逝，得年僅五十六。

V Vocabulary Bank

1) **electronics** [ɪlɛk`trɑnɪks] (n.) 電子科技，電子學，電器用品
The tech firm is hiring electronics engineers.

2) **drop out (of)** [drɑp aʊt] (phr.) 輟學
My parents would kill me if I dropped out of school.

3) **dorm** [dɔrm] (n.) 宿舍，全名為 dormitory [`dɔrmə͵tori]
Would you rather live in the dorms or rent an apartment?

4) **enlightenment** [ɪn`laɪtənmənt] (n.) 頓悟，開化
The ultimate goal of Buddhism is enlightenment.

5) **potential** [pə`tɛnʃəl] (n./a.) 潛力，可能性；潛在的，可能的
Going to university will help you reach your full potential.

6) **obtain** [əb`ten] (v.) 取得，獲得
The application form can be obtained online.

7) **assemble** [ə`sɛmbəl] (v.) 組裝，配置
IKEA furniture is easy to assemble.

8) **acquire** [ə`kwaɪr] (v.) 取得，收購
The present owners acquired the company for $50 million dollars.

9) **animation** [͵ænə`meʃən] (n.) 動畫
Japanese animation is becoming increasingly popular in the U.S.

10) **tragically** [`trædʒɪkli] (adv.) 悲慘地，不幸地
(a.) tragic [`trædʒɪk]
Mozart died tragically young.

進階字彙

11) **adoptive** [ə`dɑptɪv] (a.) 收養的
An adoptive family has been found for the orphan.

12) **audit** [`ɔdɪt] (v.) 旁聽
I audited a photography class last semester.

13) **psychedelic** [͵saɪkə`dɛlɪk] (a./n.) 迷幻的，幻覺的；迷幻藥
John likes to listen to psychedelic rock.

閱讀測驗解答 ❶ (D)

"You've got to find what you love."

賈伯斯給世人的三個故事

節錄自賈伯斯在史丹佛大學畢業典禮的演講
Steve Jobs' June 12, 2005 Stanford Commencement Address

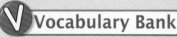

Vocabulary Bank

1) **calligraphy** [kə`lɪgrəfi] (n.) 書法
(v.) calligraph [`kælɪ͵græf] 寫書法
The poem was written in beautiful calligraphy.

2) **artistically** [ɑr`tɪstɪkli] (adv.) 藝術上，美術地
(a.) artistic [ɑr`tɪstɪk]
Not everyone is artistically talented.

3) **subtle** [`sʌtəl] (a.) 含蓄的，微妙的
The coconut milk gave the curry a rich, subtle flavor.

4) **fascinating** [`fæsə͵netɪŋ] (a.) 迷人的，極好的
(v.) fascinate [`fæsə͵net]
The movie had a fascinating plot.

5) **application** [͵æplə`keʃən] (n.) 應用，運用
Engineering is the application of science to practical problems.

6) **drop in** [drɑp ɪn] (phr.)（順便）拜訪
You're welcome to drop in anytime you're in the neighborhood.

7) **multiple** [`mʌltəpəl] (a.) 多重的，不只一個的
The secretary made multiple copies of the document.

進階字彙

8) **typeface** [`taɪp͵fes] (n.) 字體
What typeface will the book be printed in?

9) **typography** [taɪ`pɑgrəfi] (n.) 活版印刷術，字體設計、排版
Graphic designers should have a good understanding of typography.

10) **proportionally** [prə`porʃənəli] (adv.)（成）比例地，均衡地
(a.) proportional [prə`porʃənəl]Crime is proportionally higher in urban areas.

11) **font** [fɑnt] (n.) 字型，字體
If you use a larger font, the page will be easier to read.

朗讀 MP3 22 單字 MP3 23 英文文章導讀 MP3 24

Connecting the Dots 人生無不是的經驗

Reed College at that time offered perhaps the best [1]**calligraphy** instruction in the country. Throughout the campus every poster, every label on every drawer, was beautifully hand calligraphed. Because I had dropped out and didn't have to take the normal classes, I decided to take a calligraphy class to learn how to do this. I learned about serif and sans serif [8]**typefaces**, about varying the amount of space between different letter combinations, about what makes great [9]**typography** great. It was beautiful, historical, [2]**artistically** [3]**subtle** in a way that science can't capture, and I found it [4]**fascinating**.

None of this had even a hope of any practical [5]**application** in my life. But ten years later, when we were designing the first Macintosh computer, it all came back to me. And we designed it all into the Mac. It was the first computer with beautiful typography. If I had never [6]**dropped in** on that single course in college, the Mac would have never had [7]**multiple** typefaces or [10]**proportionally** spaced [11]**fonts**. And since Windows just copied the Mac, it's likely that no personal computer would have them. If I had never dropped out, I would have never dropped in on this calligraphy class, and personal computers might not have the wonderful typography that they do. Of course it was impossible to connect the dots

© Steve_Jobs_copyright_Acaben / flickr

looking forward when I was in college. But it was very, very clear looking backwards ten years later.

Mini Quiz 閱讀測驗

What does "Connecting the Dots" refer to?
(A) Because he was better with children than his wife
(B) Because it gave him time to write screenplays
(C) Because he couldn't find work as a filmmaker
(D) Because he gave up on his filmmaking dreams

中 Translation

那個時候，里德大學的書法課程大概是全國最頂尖的。校園內的每一張海報上、每個抽屜的標籤上，都是漂亮的手寫字。因為我休學了，不必正常上課，所以我決定去上書法課，學習手寫字。我學了serif與sans serif字體，學到在不同字母組合間變更字間距，學到字型藝術偉大的地方。字體藝術的美麗、歷史意義和微妙藝術感是科學無法捕捉的，我覺得很迷人。

我沒指望這些東西能實際應用在我的生活，不過十年後，當我們設計第一台麥金塔電腦時，那些東西全浮上我腦海，我們把這些東西都設計到麥金塔裡，那是第一台有漂亮字型的電腦。要不是我在大學時剛好去旁聽那一門課，麥金塔就不會有多種字體或間距比例相稱的字型了。又因為Windows 抄襲了麥金塔，不然個人電腦可能都不會有這些。要是我沒有休學，就不會剛好去旁聽那門書法課，個人電腦就可能不會有現在那些漂亮字體。當然，當年還在大學裡的我不可能高瞻遠矚把這些點滴預先串連起來，但十年後回頭看，一切就非常非常清楚。

Language Guide

college 和 university 的不同

這兩個字都是大學，只是 college 包含二年制的社區大學 (community college)，授予副學士的學位 (associate degree)，還有一般的四年制大學，授予學士學位 (bachelor's degree)，只有少部分的學校提供碩士學位。而 university 則提供碩士以上的學位，不只著重教學，也要從事研究計畫。

除此之外，四年制 college 與研究性大學的不同點在於，它常被稱為文理大學 (liberal arts college)，這種學校注重通識教育及全人能力，多數學生必須住宿，以便參與學校各項活動，發展人際關係。學校不以培養學生的單一學科專業、技職能力為考量，不會特別教授職場相關的實用課程。

Reed College 瑞德大學

賈伯斯只在瑞德大學上過一學期的課，但這所大學裡的課程卻啟發了蘋果教父的創意，他將書法課上傳授的內容用在麥金塔電腦，改變了個人電腦的樣貌。事實上，這所大學曾數次被選入全美十大文理大學，是間有名的私立學校。

瑞德大學創立於一九〇八年，位於奧勒岡州的波特蘭，是一所私立大學，學費含住宿費一年約一百六十七萬台幣。學生數有一千四百名，師生比為一比十。瑞德大學畢業生攻讀博士的比例很高，榮獲羅德獎學金（很難申請的世界級獎學金）的得獎人數更在所有全美的文理學院中排名第二。課程規畫中，大一必選希臘羅馬文學、歷史、藝術、宗教、哲學等學科，高年級則要研究文藝復興時代的文學、啟蒙時代、法國革命、工業革命、現代主義等主題。較特別的是，學校重視學生的學習情況，而非作業成績，所以大部分的考試和作業上只會有評語不會打上成績，不少學生畢業後，仍不知道自己的總成績分數。

閱讀測驗解答 ❶ (C)

朗讀 MP3 25 單字 MP3 26 英文文章導讀 MP3 27

Love and Loss 選你所愛，堅信不疑

I was lucky—I found what I loved to do early in life. Woz and I started Apple in my parents' garage when I was 20. We worked hard, and in 10 years Apple had grown from just the two of us in a garage into a $2 billion company with over 4,000 employees. We had just released our finest [1]**creation**—the Macintosh—a year earlier, and I had just turned 30. And then I got fired.

I was a very public failure, and I even thought about running away from the valley. But something slowly began to [9]**dawn on** me—I still loved what I did. The turn of events at Apple had not changed that one bit. I had been rejected, but I was still in love. And so I decided to start over.

Sometimes life hits you in the head with a brick. Don't lose faith. I'm [2]**convinced** that the only thing that kept me going was that I loved what I did. You've got to find what you love. And that is as true for your work as it is for your lovers.

Death 先知死，方知生

When I was 17, I read a quote that went something like: ""If you live each day as if it was your last, someday you'll most certainly be right." It made an [3]**impression** on me, and since then, for the past 33 years, I have looked in the mirror every morning and asked myself: "If today were the last day of my life, would I want to do what I am about to do today?" And whenever the answer has been "No" for too many days [4]**in a row**, I know I need to change something.

Remembering that I'll be dead soon is the most important tool I've ever [5]**encountered** to help me make the big choices in life. Because almost everything—all [6]**external** expectations, all pride, all fear of [7]**embarrassment** or failure—these things just [10]**fall away** in the face of death, leaving only what is truly important. Remembering that you are going to die is the best way I know to avoid the trap of thinking you have something to lose. You are already naked. There is no reason not to follow your heart.

Your time is limited, so don't waste it living someone else's life. Don't be trapped by [11]**dogma**—which is living with the results of other people's thinking. Don't let the noise of others' opinions [12]**drown out** your own inner voice. And most important, have the courage to follow your heart and [8]**intuition**. They somehow already know what you truly want to become. Everything else is secondary.

Mini Quiz 閱讀測驗

Why did Jobs make a habit of telling himself he'd be dead soon?

(A) Because it reminded him of what was most important
(B) Because he wasn't satisfied with his life
(C) Because he didn't want to make the big choices in life
(D) Because he felt that he had too much to lose

中 Translation

選你所愛，堅信不疑

我很幸運，年輕時就找到自己愛做的事。我二十歲時，跟沃茲尼克在我爸媽的車庫裡成立了蘋果電腦。我們很努力，十年後蘋果電腦從一間只有兩人的車庫變成一家有四千多名員工、市值二十億美元的公司，在那之前一年，我們才剛推出我們最棒的作品——麥金塔電腦——我也才剛滿三十歲。接下來，我就被解僱了。

我成了眾所皆知的失敗者，我甚至想要離開矽谷。但是我慢慢開始了解一件事，我發現我還是熱愛這個行業，絲毫不受蘋果電腦那件事的影響。雖然我被拒絕，可是我還在熱戀中，所以我決定從頭來過。

有時候，人生會用磚頭打你的頭。不要失去信心。我深深相信，唯一能讓我繼續向前的是：我愛我的工作。你得找出你的最愛，愛情上是如此，工作上也是如此。

先知死，方知生

十七歲時，我讀到一句話，好像是：「把每一天都當成生命最後一天，因為總有一天真的會是你最後一天。」這句話對我影響深遠，此後三十三年來，我每天早上都會照鏡子自問：「如果今天是此生最後一日，我今天即將要做的事是我想做的嗎？」每當連續太多天得到的答案都是「不是」，我就知道我必須有所改變了。

提醒自己快死了，是我在做人生重大決定時最重要的工具，因為一旦面臨死亡，幾乎每件事——外界期待、驕傲、害怕難堪或失敗——都會煙消雲散，只有真正重要的東西會留下。提醒自己快死了，是我所知可以避免畏懼有所損失的最好方法。既然已經赤條條、沒什麼好損失了，沒理由不順心而為。

你們的時間有限，所以不要浪費時間過著別人的生活，不要被教條給侷限——盲從教條就是活在別人思考的結果裡。不要讓別人的意見淹沒了你內在的心聲。最重要的是，要有勇氣去聽從你的內心和直覺，你的內心與直覺已冥冥中知道你真正想成為什麼樣的人，其他都是次要。 若有疑問請來信：eztalkQ@gmail.com

V Vocabulary Bank

1) **creation** [kriˋeʃən] (n.) 創作（品），產物
The artist's latest creations are on display at the gallery.

2) **convinced** [kənˋvɪnst] (a.) 堅信的
(v.) convince [kənˋvɪns]
The police remain convinced that the woman was murdered by her husband.

3) **impression** [ɪmˋprɛʃən] (n.) 印象，感想
What was your impression of Jennifer's boyfriend?

4) **in a row** [ɪn ə ro] (phr.) 連續
Michael was late to work two days in a row.

5) **encounter** [ɪnˋkaʊntɚ] (v./n.)（意外、偶然）遇見，遭遇（困境）
Laura was surprised when she encountered her ex-boyfriend at the mall.

6) **external** [ɪkˋstɝnəl] (a.) 外部的，外面的
You shouldn't judge people by their external appearance.

7) **embarrassment** [ɪmˋbærəsmənt] (n.) 難堪，尷尬
Vicky lowered her head to hide her embarrassment.

8) **intuition** [ˌɪntuˋɪʃən] (n.) 直覺
Sometimes it's best to trust your intuition.

進階字彙

9) **dawn (on)** [dɔn] (phr.) 頓悟，開始明白
It finally dawned on Richard that his wife wasn't coming back.

10) **fall away** [fɔl əˋwe] (phr.) 消失，消逝
When Dana practices yoga, all her worries fall away.

11) **dogma** [ˋdɔgmə] (n.) 教條，既定的信念
Don't let yourself be blinded by political dogma.

12) **drown out** [draʊn aʊt] (phr.)（聲音）壓過、淹沒（其他聲音）
The loud music drowned out our conversation.

閱讀測驗解答 ❶ (A)

Bill Gates
比爾蓋茲

朗讀 MP3 28 單字 MP3 29 英文文章導讀 MP3 30

In July 2007, Microsoft CEO Steve Ballmer made a [1)]**stunning** announcement: the number of PCs around the world running the company's popular Windows operating system would top 1 billion by the year's end. To put it another way, that would be more PCs running Windows than cars driving on the world's roads. Indeed, computers and cars have influenced the world in [2)]**comparable** ways—it's impossible to imagine modern life without either—and when it comes to computer software, the Henry Ford of the industry is without a doubt Microsoft [3)]**founder** and chairman Bill Gates. Throughout his [4)]**celebrated** career, he has [5)]**revolutionized** the way people work, learn, and even play. Now a billionaire many times over, Gates continues to change the world through his charity work. "Until we're educating every kid in a fantastic way, until every inner city is cleaned up," he says, "there is no [6)]**shortage** of things to do."

Although Bill Gates' vast fortune may [G]seem like the stuff of fairytales, his life isn't the typical rags-to-riches story. William Henry Gates III was born in Seattle, Washington on August 28, 1955 into a comfortable, upper-middle-class family. His father, William Jr., was a [7)]**prominent** lawyer, and his mother, Mary, was active

Vocabulary Bank

1) **stunning** [ˋstʌnɪŋ] (a.) 令人震驚的，令人嘆為觀止的，出色的
The team won a stunning victory in the championship.

2) **comparable** [ˋkɑmpərəbəl] (a.) 相似的，比得上的
The two applicants have comparable educational backgrounds.

3) **founder** [ˋfaʊndɚ] (n.) 創立者，創辦人
Jigoro Kano was the founder of judo.

4) **celebrated** [ˋsɛlə͵bretɪd] (a.) 著名的，馳名的
Mark Twain is one of America's most celebrated authors.

5) **revolutionize** [͵rɛvəˋluʃə͵naɪz] (v.) 徹底改變，變革
(n.) revolution [͵rɛvəˋluʃən]
Cell phones have revolutionized the way people communicate.

6) **shortage** [ˋʃɔrtɪdʒ] (n.) 短缺，匱乏
There is a shortage of affordable housing in the city.

7) **prominent** [ˋprɑmənənt] (a.) 卓越的，著名的
The conference was attended by many prominent scholars.

8) **enroll** [ɪnˋrol] (v.)（註冊）入學
How many students are enrolled at the college?

9) **exclusive** [ɪkˋsklusɪv] (a.) 嚴格限制（資格）的，排他性的
Membership in the exclusive VIP club is very expensive.

10) **academically** [͵ækəˋdɛmɪklɪ] (adv.) 學術上，學業上
(n.) academia [͵ækəˋdimɪə] 學術界，學術生涯
Academically successful students will have better career opportunities.

進階字彙

11) **avid** [ˋævɪd] (a.) 熱愛的，熱切的
Rick is an avid stamp collector.

12) **withdrawn** [wɪθˋdrɔn] (a.) 沈默孤僻的，內向的
Bob became depressed and withdrawn after his wife's death.

on the boards of local charities. An [11]**avid** reader as a boy, Gates showed promise at school at first, but his parents worried that he often appeared bored or [12]**withdrawn**. So they decided to [8]**enroll** him in the [9]**exclusive** Lakeside School, which they hoped he would find more [10]**academically** challenging. It was there, at the age of 13, that Gates first encountered computers.

中 Translation

二〇〇七年七月，微軟執行長史蒂夫鮑默爾做了一項驚人宣布：至該年年底，全球各地執行微軟知名視窗作業系統的個人電腦將超過十億部。換句話說：執行視窗的個人電腦將比在全球馬路上跑的車子還多。的確，電腦和汽車影響世界的方式雷同──我們無法想像現代生活缺少任何一者的樣子──而說到電腦軟體，該產業的亨利福特無疑是微軟創辦人兼董事長比爾蓋茲。在他顯赫的事業生涯中，他徹底改變了人們工作、學習，甚至玩樂的方式。現在，身價數百億的蓋茲透過他的慈善工作持續改變世界。「在我們能以最好的方法教育每個孩童之前，在每個內城（編註：inner city 市中心人口密集的貧民區）能揮別殘破之前，」他說：「我們不乏可盡力之事。」

或許比爾蓋茲龐大的財富看來宛如神話，他的人生卻不是典型的白手起家故事。威廉亨利蓋茲三世在一九五五年八月二十八日生於華盛頓州西雅圖一個優渥的中上階級家庭，父親威廉二世是頗有名氣的律師，母親瑪莉則活躍於當地慈善團體董事會。小時候就熱愛閱讀的蓋茲，剛開始就在上學時展現似錦前程，但他的父母擔心他時常顯得煩悶或孤僻，所以決定把他送去入學限制嚴格的湖畔中學，希望他會覺得那裡的課業較具挑戰性，而蓋茲就是十三歲時於該校首次接觸電腦。

Language Guide

Henry Ford 汽車大王亨利福特

亨利福特 (1863-1947) 是福特汽車公司 (Ford Motor Company) 的創辦人，他所發明的汽車一貫化組裝流程 (assembly line)，大量減少人力成本及加快生產速度最為人所稱道，對汽車得以量產功不可沒。福特汽車一九〇八年推出 Model T（福特 T 型車，常被暱稱為 Tin Lizzie、Flivver，或直接就叫它 T）是第一款價廉、省油、動力夠強的汽車，從此之後，汽車才開始成為實用的生活用品。

比爾蓋茲對電腦工業的貢獻，正如當年亨利福特對汽車工業的決定性影響，讓原本只有少數人能接觸的物品普及化，成為家家戶戶都用得到的商品，因此本文將比爾蓋茲比做電腦業的亨利福特。

Lakeside School 湖畔中學

湖畔中學是一所位於西雅圖哈勒湖 (Haller Lake) 附近的私校，據估計每年有四分之一畢業生進入長春藤盟校 (Ivy League schools)，百分之九十九的畢業生都能進入大學。比爾蓋茲及保羅艾倫當年就是用校內分時共享的電腦 (time-sharing computer) 設計井字遊戲軟體。

Grammar Master

seem 的用法

seem 有以下幾種不同用法

1. 當動詞，表示「看起來像，似乎」

例 He **seems** to have worked in marketing for many years.
他在行銷方面似乎有多年的工作經驗。

2. 當連綴動詞 (linking verb)，像 be 動詞一樣直接接形容詞在後面。常見的連綴動詞有：feel、look、smell、sound、taste、seem、become、run 等等。

例 The kids **ran** wild when their parents were away.
父母一不在，那些孩子就開始撒野。

3. 另外，連綴動詞還可接 like，然後再加名詞或子句。

例 Skydiving at night doesn't **seem like** a good idea.
夜間跳傘似乎不是個好主意。

朗讀 MP3 31 單字 MP3 32 英文文章導讀 MP3 33

While in the eighth grade, Gates wrote his first computer program, a tic-tac-toe game in BASIC that allowed users to match [1]**wits** with an early General Electric model. A few years later, Gates launched Ⓖhis first business [2]**venture**, Traf-O-Data, with fellow Lakeside student Paul Allen. Their creation, which [3]**analyzed** data from roadway traffic counters, earned around twenty thousand dollars for the young software designers. After graduation, Gates attended Harvard University, where his parents hoped he would begin preparing for a career in law. But the [10]**allure** of the computer [4]**lab** proved too strong. He spent more time there than he did in class, and in 1975 dropped out after only a year and a half. [11]**Swapping** academia for business, Gates joined Allen in New Mexico, where he was working at the time, and soon after the pair founded Microsoft.

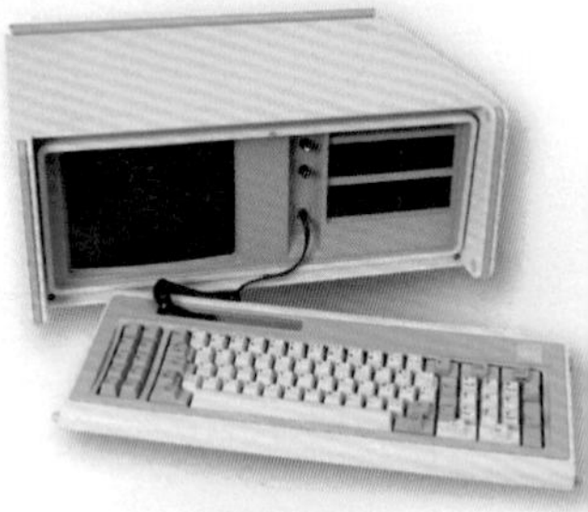

Microsoft moved to its present home in Bellevue, Washington in January 1979, and true to its name, the company started developing software for microcomputers, or today's PCs. In the early days, Gates not only took responsibility for [12]**overseeing** company operations, but was also involved in writing software [5]**code**. In [6]**partnership** with IBM, Gates led the development

Vocabulary Bank

1) **wits** [wɪts] (n.) 智力，機智，match wits 即「鬥智」
The chess match was a battle of wits.

2) **venture** [ˋvɛntʃɚ] (n.) 新創事業，投資事業
The business venture ended in bankruptcy.

3) **analyze** [ˋænə͵laɪz] (v.) 分析
The scientists analyzed the fossil to determine its age.

4) **lab** [læb] (n.) 研究室，實驗室，檢驗室是 laboratory [ˋlæbrə͵tori] 的簡稱，computer lab 即「電腦中心」
Are your tests back from the lab yet?

5) **code** [kod] (n.) 以程式語言撰寫一段程式碼，代碼
Who wrote the code for this program?

6) **partnership** [ˋpɑrtnɚ͵ʃɪp] (n.) 合夥關係，合作
The two companies formed a partnership to develop the product.

7) **release** [rɪˋlis] (v./n.) 推出，發表，發行
The company will release its new product next week.

8) **retail** [ˋritel] (a./n.) 零售的；零售（業）
Our products are only sold in retail stores.

9) **interact** [͵ɪntɚˋækt] (v.) 互動，互相影響
In small classes, students can interact more with their teachers.

進階字彙

10) **allure** [əˋlʊr] (n.) 魅力
The actor couldn't resist the allure of the stage.

11) **swap** [swɑp] (v.)（以…）交換
Can I swap seats with you?

12) **oversee** [͵ovɚˋsi] (v.) 管理，監督
Martha was hired to oversee the sales department.

13) **forefront** [ˋfor͵frʌnt] (n.) 領導地位，龍頭地位
Martin Luther King, Jr. was at the forefront of the civil rights movement.

of MS-DOS (Microsoft Disk Operating System), which propelled the company to the [13]**forefront** of the industry in the early '80s. Then, in 1985, Microsoft [7]**released** the first [8]**retail** version of the popular Windows operating system, forever changing how people [9]**interact** with their computers.

中 Translation

八年級時，蓋茲用 BASIC 寫出他第一道電腦程式：讓使用者與早期奇異電腦鬥智的井字遊戲。幾年後，蓋茲和他湖畔中學的同學保羅艾倫首度創業：Traf-O-Data 公司。他們的作品可以分析道路交通量計數器收集來的數據，替這兩位小小年紀的軟體設計師賺進約兩萬美元。畢業後，蓋茲赴哈佛大學就讀，他的雙親希望他能開始準備走法律的路。但結果電腦中心的誘惑實在太強烈，他花在那裡的時間比在課堂還多，一九七五年，他在哈佛讀了一年半後就退學了。從學術轉往商場，蓋茲赴新墨西哥州找在這裡工作的艾倫，不久兩人便成立微軟。

微軟於一九七九年一月遷至華盛頓州貝爾維的現址，而且一如其名，該公司開始為微型電腦（也就是今天的個人電腦）研發軟體。草創初期，蓋茲不僅負責監管公司營運，也實際參與軟體程式碼的撰寫。與 IBM 合作，蓋茲帶頭開發出 MS-DOS（微軟磁碟作業系統），在八〇年代初期將公司推到軟體業龍頭地位。接著，一九八五年，微軟推出廣受歡迎視窗作業系統的第一零售版，永遠改變人們與電腦的互動方式。

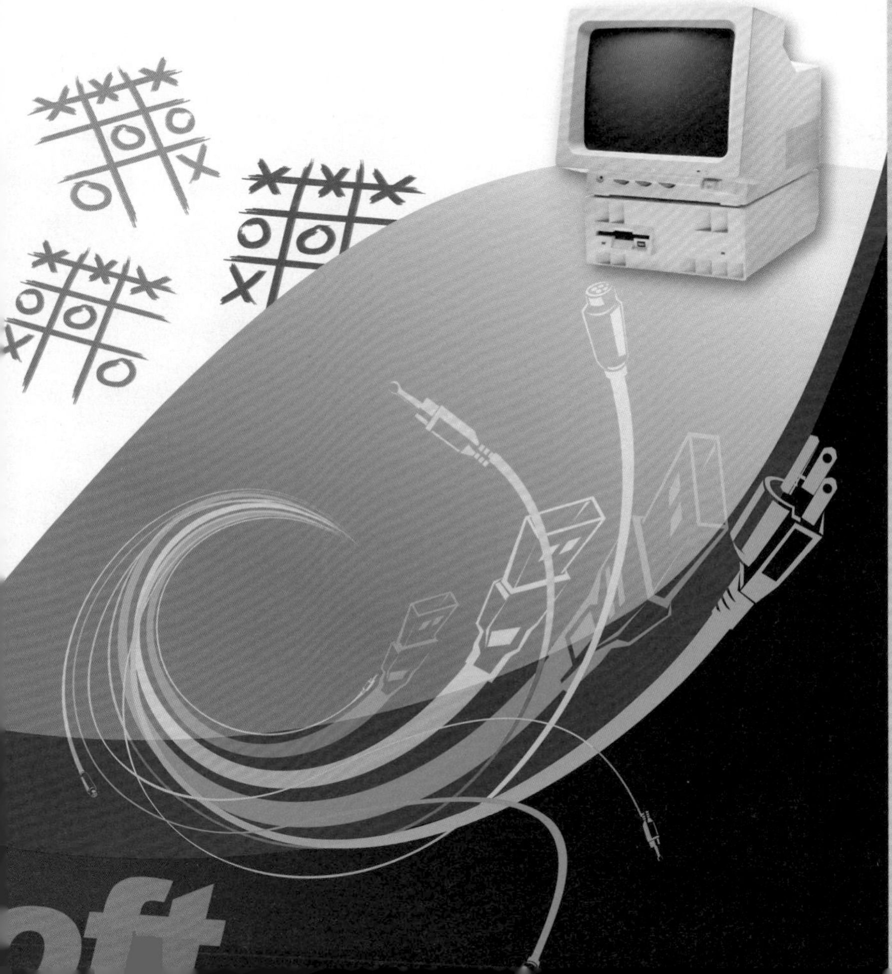

Language Guide

tic-tac-toe 井字遊戲

這是一種雙人玩的紙筆遊戲 (pencil-and-paper game)。雙方在井字格 (3×3 grid) 中輪流以圈叉劃記，一般由打叉開始，三格連成一線者獲勝。

BASIC 培基程式語言

BASIC 是 Beginner's All-purpose Symbolic Instruction Code（初學者全功能指令代碼）的縮寫。BASIC 是在一九六四年由 John George Kemeny 和 Thomas Eugene Kurtz 兩人所開發。在此之前，幾乎所有電腦運算功能都必須由電腦科學家及數學家撰寫專用程式，而 BASIC 程式語言的目的，就是要讓非主修科學的學生也能夠學習使用。

初期電腦業巨擘

文中提到的奇異公司（General Electric，縮寫為 GE）和 IBM（International Business Machines 的縮寫）是一九六〇年代的主要電腦公司。當時市場有一種說法：一家獨大的 IBM 是 Snow White（白雪公主），跟著七家小公司 Seven Dwarfs（七矮人），GE 就是其中一家。GE 於一九七〇年代將電腦部門賣給七矮人之一的 Honeywell 公司之後，IBM 就不再是白雪公主，而被稱為 Big Blue（因其商標為藍色，故被稱為藍色巨人）。

traffic counter 是啥？

文中提到 Bill Gates 念高中時和同學 Paul Allen（以及 Paul Gilbert）創辦的 Traf-O-Data 公司，主要業務是在分析 traffic counter 的資料。traffic counter 是一種立在馬路邊的電子儀器，儀器上連接能偵測車輛經過的裝置，如雷達、氣壓偵測器、地下壓電器等，記錄到的車流資料會回傳到立在路邊的 traffic counter 儲存下來，最後要交給專業人士判讀，作為交通建設的參考數據。

MS-DOS 作業系統

MS-DOS (Microsoft Disk Operating System) 是一系列 DOS 作業系統中最常被運用的一支，在一九七九年由 Microsoft 公司設計並取得著作權，是八〇及九〇年代個人家用電腦 (personal computer) 最主要使用的作業系統。

Grammar Master

同位語用法

同位語皆為名詞（片語、子句），用來補充或加以敘述前面之主詞或受詞。通常同位語的前後會有逗點區隔，例如本文中的句子，Gates launched his first business venture, Traf-O-Data, ... 這裡的 Traf-O-Data 指的就是 his first business venture「他的首度創業」。

例 My brother went out on a date with Wendy, **the girl next door,** last night.
我弟弟昨晚跟鄰家的女孩溫蒂約會。

朗讀 MP3 34 單字 MP3 35 英文文章導讀 MP3 36

As a rule, it's hard for an [1]**entrepreneur** to build a business empire without stepping on a few toes, and Bill Gates is Ⓖno exception. He's well known for his no-[2]**nonsense**, and at times [12]**confrontational** style of management, and his actions have landed the company in [13]**hot water** more than once. Microsoft has been widely [3]**criticized** for its anti-[4]**competitive** practices over the years, most [5]**notably** for pressuring computer makers to ship their products with Windows [6]**installed**. This practice caused many software designers to cry [7]**foul** and resulted in antitrust suits by both the U.S. government and the EU, both of which Microsoft lost. Nevertheless, with Gates in charge, the company has managed to weather these storms.

Long one of the world's richest men ([8]**ranked** no. 1 in 14 of the past 16 years), Gates announced that he was

© 達志 / UPI PHOTO

Vocabulary Bank

1) **entrepreneur** [ˌɑntrəprəˋnɝ] (n.) 創業者，企業家
Silicon Valley has the highest concentration of entrepreneurs in the world.

2) **nonsense** [ˋnɑnsɛns] (n.) 胡說，胡鬧
I've had enough of your nonsense!

3) **criticize** [ˋkrɪtɪˌsaɪz] (v.) 批評，指責
(n.) criticism [ˋkrɪtɪˌsɪzəm] 評論
The police were criticized for not preventing the riot.

4) **competitive** [kəmˋpɛtətɪv] (a.) 競爭性的，有競爭力的
The company has a strong competitive advantage.

5) **notably** [ˋnotəbli] (adv.) 值得一提，特別，尤其
(a.) notable [ˋnotəbl]
There have been many layoffs, most notably in the manufacturing sector.

6) **install** [ɪnˋstɔl] (v.) 安裝，設置
We're having an air conditioner installed tomorrow.

7) **foul** [faul] (n.)（比賽）犯規，cry foul 即「喊冤」
The player was removed from the game for committing too many fouls.

8) **rank** [ræŋk] (v./n.) 排名，把…評等
Our university's law program is ranked fourth in the country.

9) **devote** [dɪˋvot] (v.) 將…奉獻給，致力於
Mother Teresa devoted her life to helping the poor.

10) **enhance** [ɪnˋhæns] (v.) 提高（價值），增進（品質）
The government is working to enhance water quality.

11) **generosity** [ˌdʒɛnəˋrɑsəti] (n.) 慷慨，大方
We'd like to thank everybody who donated money for their generosity.

進階字彙

12) **confrontational** [ˌkɑnfrʌnˋteʃənəl] (a.) 對抗的，敵對的
(n.) confrontation [ˌkɑnfrʌnˋteʃən] 衝突，對質，對抗
Stan's confrontational attitude made him hard to get along with.

口語補充

13) **hot water** [hɑt ˋwɔtɚ] (phr.) 麻煩，險境
You'll be in hot water if the teacher catches you cheating.

leaving his day-to-day duties as Microsoft chairman in June 2006 to 9)**devote** more time to philanthropy. The Bill and Melinda Gates Foundation, which Gates heads along with his wife Melinda and close friend Warren Buffet, is the largest charitable organization in the world. Each year, the foundation funds projects focused on combating disease, improving educational opportunities, and 10)**enhancing** information technology both at home and abroad. It should come as no surprise that Gates, who was so successful in earning money in his first career, has proven equally good at giving it away in his second. His 11)**generosity** continues to change the world.

中 Translation

一般而言，企業家很難不踩著別人的腳來建立商業帝國，比爾蓋茲也不例外。他以直接了當、不惜正面衝突的管理風格著稱，而他的作為不只一次讓公司陷入困境。長年來，微軟一直因其反競爭的壟斷做法飽受批評，特別是施壓電腦製造商內建視窗作業系統出貨。這種做法讓許多軟體設計公司高喊不公，也使美國政府和歐盟對微軟提出反托辣斯的訴訟，微軟雙雙敗訴。儘管如此，在蓋茲掌舵下，微軟還是安然度過這些風波。

長期名列全球首富之一（過去十六年有十四年名列第一），蓋茲在二〇〇六年六月宣布卸下微軟董事長的日常職務，以便投入更多時間於慈善事業。以蓋茲與妻子梅琳達和摯友華倫巴菲特為首的「比爾及梅琳達蓋茲基金會」是世界最大的慈善組織。每一年，基金會都會資助國內外著眼於對抗疾病、提升教育機會和改善資訊科技的計畫。毫不意外地，在生涯第一階段賺錢賺得如此成功的蓋茲，已在第二階段證明他同樣擅長捐錢。他的慷慨將繼續改變世界。

若有疑問請來信：eztalkQ@gmail.com

Language Guide

antitrust 反托辣斯

antitrust 是 anti-（表示「反」的字首）加上 trust 組成的字。trust 是指公司、企業之間的串連，以避免因彼此削價競爭互蒙其害，而企業聯手控制價格的結果，就是消費者遭殃。antitrust law（反托辣斯法）就是要杜絕企業獨佔或聯合壟斷，在台灣稱之為「公平交易法」。

Grammar Master

no exception 也不例外

exception 中文是「不包括在內的人（或物），例外」，be no exception 是英文中常見的慣用語，表示「（人或物）都不例外，都一樣的意思」。

例 There are **no exception** to the dress code.
服裝規定大家都一樣。

Mini Quiz

1. Which of the following is NOT true about Bill Gates?
   (A) He no longer works at Microsoft full time.
   (B) He had a middle-class upbringing.
   (C) He dropped out of college in his freshman year.
   (D) He has gotten Microsoft in trouble before.

2. In the article, the author compares computers with ________.
   (A) education
   (B) automobiles
   (C) modern life
   (D) Henry Ford

3. Margaret ________ very quiet today.
   (A) looks like
   (B) seems
   (C) feels like
   (D) sounds

4. Ellen's first husband, ________, died in a plane crash.
   (A) is Roger
   (B) was Roger
   (C) Roger's
   (D) Roger

5. My diet allows me to eat any fruit ________ bananas.
   (A) beside
   (B) other
   (C) except
   (D) apart

解答 1 (C) 2 (B) 3 (B) 4 (D) 5 (C)

Vocabulary Bank

1) **movement** [ˋmuvmənt] (n.)（思想、社會等）運動
The feminist movement began in the 19th century.

2) **influential** [ˌɪnfluˋɛnʃəl] (a.) 有影響力的，有支配力的
The reporter got a job at an influential newspaper.

3) **tirelessly** [ˋtaɪrlɪsli] (adv.) 不屈不撓地，不知疲倦地
The organization has fought tirelessly for women's rights.

4) **philosophy** [fɪˋlɑsəfi] (n.) 哲學，生活的信條（或態度）
(a.) philosophical [ˌfɪləˋsɑfɪkəl]
There aren't many career options for philosophy majors.

5) **contribution** [ˌkɑntrəˋbjuʃən] (n.) 貢獻
The chemist received an award for his contributions to science.

6) **dub** [dʌb] (v.) 給予…封號
Elvis was dubbed the King of Rock 'n' Roll.

7) **epic** [ˋɛpɪk] (n./a.) 史詩，史詩般的作品；史詩般的
That channel plays all the old Hollywood epics.

8) **senior** [ˋsinjɚ] (n.) 較年長者，老年人
Carol's twin sister is five minutes her senior.

9) **vow** [vaʊ] (n./v.) 誓言，誓約；發誓
The couple wrote their own wedding vows.

10) **alcohol** [ˋælkəˌhɔl] (n.) 酒，酒精
(n.) alcoholism [ˋælkəhɔˌlɪsm] 酗酒
The restaurant applied for a license to serve alcohol.

11) **practice** [ˋpræktɪs] (n.)（醫生、律師等專業人士的）執業，事業
Dean joined his father's legal practice after graduating from law school.

進階字彙

12) **devout** [dɪˋvaʊt] (a.) 篤信宗教的，虔誠的
Maria comes from a family of devout Catholics.

13) **promiscuity** [ˌprɑmɪsˋkjuəti] (n.) 亂交，雜交（超過一個以上的性伴侶）
Most religions discourage promiscuity.

14) **bar** [bɑr] (n.) 律師業
Richard graduated from law school but never passed the bar exam.

Gandhi

印度精神領袖 甘地

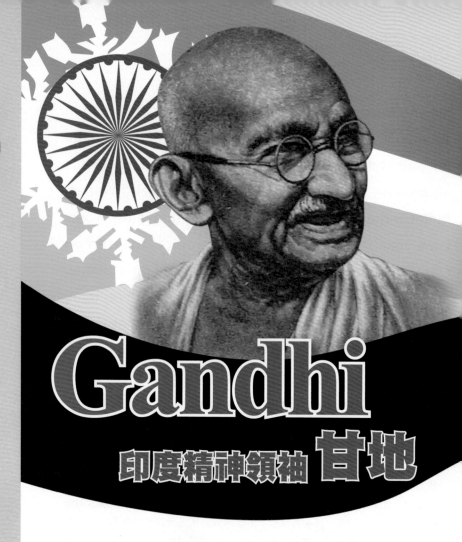

朗讀 MP3 37 單字 MP3 38 英文文章導讀 MP3 39

"You must be the change you want to see in the world These are the words of Mohandas Gandhi, the founder c the Indian independence [1]**movement** and one of the mos [2]**influential** figures of the twentieth century. Ⓖ Throughout hi life, Gandhi worked [3]**tirelessly** to bring change to India an improve the lives of his fellow Indians. His [4]**philosophy** c nonviolent resistance, or *satyagraha*, not only won Indi independence from Great Britain, but also influenced othe great civil rights leaders like Martin Luther King, Jr. an Nelson Mandela. So important were Gandhi's [5]**contribution** that the Indian poet Rabindranath Tagore [6]**dubbed** hir Mahatma, which means "great soul," and he is remembere fondly as the Father of India, or "Bapu" by his people.

Mohandas Karamchand Gandhi was born in Porbanda India on October 2, 1869. As a young boy, he enjoye

cting out stories from the great Indian 7)**epics**. At the age f 13, according to custom, he married Kasturbai Makhanji, who was one year his 8)**senior**. In 1888, shortly before his 9th birthday, Gandhi went to England to study law at University College London. Following a 9)**vow** he made to his mother, a 12)**devout** Hindu, he gave up meat, 10)**alcohol** and 3)**promiscuity** while abroad. Gandhi was admitted to the 4)**bar** in June 1891 and returned to India, only to learn that is mother had died during his absence. After failing to stablish a successful law 11)**practice** in his home country, e decided to accept a contract with an Indian firm in South Africa in 1893.

中 Translation

要改變世界，先改變自己。」這是穆漢達甘地的名言，他是印度獨立運動的創始人，也是二十世紀最具影響力的人物之一。終其一生，甘地不遺餘力地致力為印度帶來改變，改善印度同胞的生活。他的非暴力抗爭理念，或稱不合作主義，不僅讓印度脫離英國獨立，也影響了世上其他偉大的民權領袖，如小馬丁路德金恩和曼德拉。甘地的貢獻是如此重要，使得印度詩人泰戈爾稱之為「聖雄」，即「偉人」之意，而他也被印度人民視為印度國父，或 Bapu（父親），永遠懷念。

穆漢達卡拉姆昌德甘地在一八六九年十月二日生於印度波港。小時候，他喜歡拿印度偉大史詩的故事來演戲。十三歲時，他依習俗娶了大他一歲的卡絲圖芭伊瑪康姬。一八八八年，就在他十九歲生日前夕，甘地前往英國的倫敦學院大學修習法律。他的母親是虔誠的印度教徒，為了遵守他對母親發過的誓，甘地在國外期間戒絕肉、酒和雜交。甘地在一八九一年六月取得律師資格後回到印度，才得知母親已在他離家期間過世。由於未能於祖國順利執業，他在一八九三年決定接受南非一家印度事務所的聘用合約。

Language Guide

satyagraha
非暴力抗爭及不合作主義

satyagraha [səˋtjɑgrəhə] 是梵文 (Sanskrit)，satya 是「真理」(truth)，agraha 是「堅持」(firmness) 的意思。satyagraha 指的是「非暴力抗爭」(nonviolent resistance)，是由甘地所提倡的一種哲學思想，也是他帶領印度爭取獨立時所採行的方式。

甘地的非暴力抗爭及不合作主義也影響了後來的民權運動 (civil rights movement) 人士，如南非的曼德拉與美國的馬丁路德金恩。而實行非暴力抗爭及不合作主義的人則被稱為 satyagrahi。

對甘地來說，satyagraha 的意義遠遠超過所謂的「消極反抗」(passive resistance)，他說過：

" Truth (satya) implies love, and firmness (agraha) engenders and therefore serves as a synonym for force. I thus began to call the Indian movement *satyagraha*..."

「真理 (satya) 有愛的含義，而堅持 (agraha) 能讓力量落實，因而成為了力量的同義詞。因此，我開始將印度的獨立運動稱為 satyagraha……」

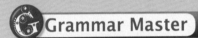

Grammar Master

throughout 的用法

throughout 當介系詞，有「遍及、貫穿」的意思，另外，它也可以當作副詞使用。

- throughout 當介系詞，後接名詞，可置於句首或句中，也可以用 all through 表示

例 He lived in the small house **throughout** his life.

= **Throughout** his life, he lived in the small house.

= He lived in the small house **all through** his life.

他終其一生都住在這棟小房子。

- throughout 當副詞（通常用在句尾），有「處處」的意思

例 The apartment is carpeted **throughout**.

這間公寓整間都鋪了地毯。

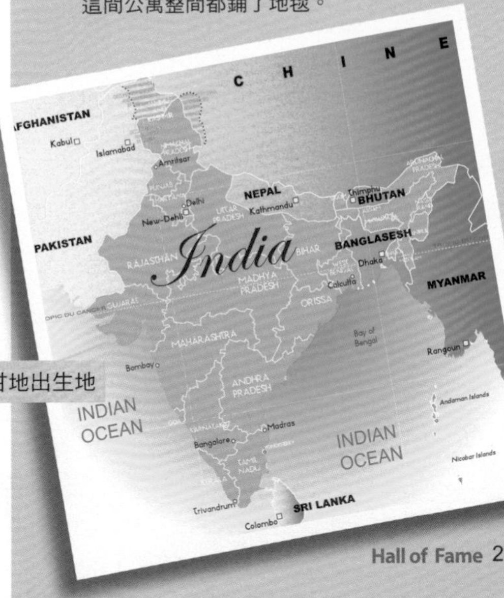

Vocabulary Bank

1) **discrimination** [dɪ͵skrɪmə`neʃən] (n.) 差別對待，歧視，偏袒
Japanese Americans were victims of discrimination during World War II.

2) **valid** [`vælɪd] (a.)（法律上）有效的，合法的
It's illegal to drive without a valid driver's license.

3) **in light of** [ɪn laɪt ʌf] (phr.) 鑑於，根據
It was necessary to review the policy in light of recent developments.

4) **status** [`stætəs] (n.) 地位，身分
Luxury cars are status symbols.

5) **register** [`rɛdʒɪstɚ] (v.) 登記，註冊
You have to register before you can vote.

6) **urge** [ɝdʒ] (v.) 力勸，催促
The captain urged passengers to stay calm.

7) **landlord** [`lænd͵lord] (n.) 房東，地主
The landlord decided to raise our rent.

8) **desperate** [`dɛspərɪt] (a.) 危急的，嚴重的
The villagers live in desperate poverty.

9) **rural** [`rurəl] (a.) 鄉間的，農村的
The typhoon caused heavy flooding in rural areas.

進階字彙

10) **magistrate** [`mædʒɪs͵tret] (n.) 地方法官、執法官
Everyone rose when the magistrate entered the courtroom.

11) **opt** [`ɑpt] (v.) 選擇，挑選
The couple opted to rent a movie instead of going out.

12) **expatriate** [ɛks`petriət] (a./n.) 移居國外的；移居國外者，常簡稱為 expat [`ɛks͵pæt]
Most of the foreign reporters hang out at the expatriate bar.

13) **levy** [`lɛvi] (v.) 徵收，徵稅
The government plans to levy a new tax on imported goods.

口語補充

14) **boot (off/out)** [but] (v.) 趕走
The man was booted off the plane for causing a disturbance.

朗讀 MP3 40 單字 MP3 41 英文文章導讀 MP3 42

It was during his time in South Africa that Gandh experienced the [1]**discrimination** that would begin tc shape his philosophical and political beliefs. ⒼOnce he wa [14]**booted** off a train for refusing to move from his first-clas seat even though he had a [2]**valid** ticket. He also refused a court [10]**magistrate**'s order to take off his turban. [3]**In light o** this racist treatment, Gandhi began to question the [4]**status** of Indians in the British Empire, and [11]**opted** to stay on in South Africa to organize the large [12]**expatriate** community there. In 1906, an act was passed requiring all Indians tc [5]**register** with the government. When Gandhi [6]**urged** hi fellow Indians to resist peacefully, even if this meant being jailed or beaten, his philosophy of *satyagraha* was born.

After returning to India in 1915, Gandhi joined the Indiar National Congress and became involved in the home rule movement. He continued to promote *satyagraha* by assisting poor farmers in resisting unfair taxes [13]**levied** by their British [7]**landlords**. He organized the cleanup of villages and the construction of schools and hospitals. Concerned by the [8]**desperate** state of many [9]**rural** communities, he workec

甘地的房間和紡車 © http://www.flickr.com/photos/chromatic_aberration/

o rid them of alcoholism, discrimination against the untouchables" (India's lowest social class) and *purdah* (the ractice of keeping women separate from men). One famous ymbol of his nonviolent struggle against British rule was is spinning wheel, or *khadi*. Gandhi encouraged all Indians ot to buy British-made cloth and instead make their own lothes from thread they spun themselves.

Translation

地就是在南非期間遭到差別待遇，才開始塑造出他的哲學和政治信念。有一次儘管他有效票，仍因拒絕離開頭等艙座位而被趕下火車。他也拒絕地方法官要他摘掉頭巾命令。有鑑於這些種族歧視待遇，甘地開始質疑印度人在大英帝國的地位，並選擇繼留在南非把為數眾多的印度移民組織起來。一九〇六年，南非通過一項法律，要求所印度人和政府登記。甘地呼籲印度同胞就算會被捕入獄或遭到毆打也要以和平方式抗，不合作主義的哲學於焉誕生。

一九一五年回到印度後，甘地加入印度國大黨，也參與自治運動。他繼續推動不合作運，協助貧困農民抵制英國地主強徵的不公平賦稅。他發起村莊大掃除，以及學校和醫的興建。由於擔心許多農村社區的危急情況，他致力協助他們脫離酗酒、對「賤民」印度最低社會階層）的歧視和深閨制度（讓女人與男人分處二室）。他對抗英國政權的暴力抗爭有個著名的象徵：他的紡車，或稱 khadi。甘地鼓勵所有印度人拒買英國製布料，改用他們自己紡的線來縫製衣物。

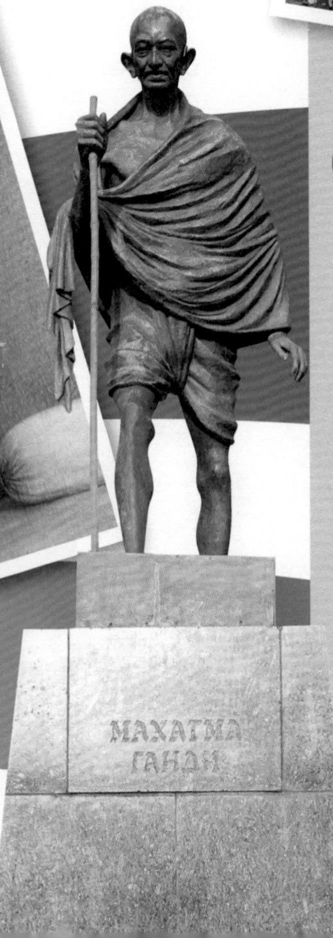

Language Guide

untouchables 種姓制度

在這裡的 untouchables 指的是印度種姓制度 (caste system) 中的「賤民」，也就是社會階級最下層的人，賤民的來源不可考，有可能是來自南亞不同人種的混雜。賤民的英文又稱為「達利特」(Dalit)。Dalit 的詞源 (etymology) 來自於馬拉地語 (Marathi language)，有「被壓迫、迫害」的意思。對印度的上層階級來說，賤民代表著軟弱、貧窮與羞恥。

達利特大多為勞力工作者 (manual laborer)，能做的工作包括清潔廁所與排水溝、清除垃圾、宰殺牲畜或是皮革製作等。因此達利特被認為是骯髒的，並且這種骯髒還會經由接觸傳染給別人。當年甘地追求印度獨立時，其中一項訴求就是要廢除種姓制度，甘地將達利特稱為「神之子」(Children of God)，即使印度已經制定憲法和法律禁止種姓制度和種姓隔離，但是在印度許多地方，達利特依然遭到社會歧視。

Dalit

Grammar Master

once 的用法

- once 當副詞：表示「曾經」，放在名詞之前

例 Spain was **once** a powerful nation.
西班牙曾是個強國。

也可以像本單元此句（文中第 3 行）一樣，將 once 放在句首。

- once 當連接詞：表示「一旦……，就……」
  句型：Once S. + V.., S. + V....
  = S. + V... once S. + V....（once 前不加逗號）

例 **Once** you pass the exam, you'll receive your diploma.
= You'll receive your diploma **once** you pass the exam
你只要通過考試，就能得到文憑。

- once 表示「次數」的時候，翻譯為「一遍、一次」，多放於句尾

例 Kathy has only been to Disney World **once**.
凱西只去過一次迪士尼樂園。

Vocabulary Bank

1) **advocate** [ˋædvə͵ket / ˋædvəkɪt] (v./n.) 提倡，擁護；提倡者，擁護者
Both candidates in the election advocate tax reform.

2) **boycott** [ˋbɔɪ͵kɑt] (v./n.) 抵制，杯葛
People were urged to boycott the company's products.

3) **treason** [ˋtrizən] (n.) 叛國罪，危害國家罪
The spy was caught and executed for treason.

4) **intensify** [ɪnˋtɛnsə͵faɪ] (v.)（使）加強，增強，加劇
(a.) intense [ɪnˋtɛns] 激烈的，極度的
The tropical storm intensified into a typhoon.

5) **on behalf of** [ɑn bɪˋhæf ʌf] (phr.) 代表
I'm proud to accept this award on behalf of my colleagues.

6) **undertake** [͵ʌndɚˋtek] (v.) 進行，從事
You should think carefully before undertaking this difficult task.

7) **fast** [fæst] (n./v.) 禁食，齋戒
During Ramadan, the daily fast lasts from sunrise to sunset.

8) **grant** [grænt] (v.)（尤指正式或法律上）同意，准予
American women were granted the right to vote in 1920.

9) **harshly** [hɑrʃli] (adv.) 嚴厲地，嚴峻地
(a.) harsh [hɑrʃ]
I think drunk drivers should be punished harshly.

10) **extremist** [ɪkˋstrimɪst] (n.) 極端主義者，激進份子
The bombing was carried out by a right-wing extremist.

11) **mourning** [ˋmɔrnɪŋ] (n.) 哀悼，哀痛
(v.) mourn [ˋmɔrn]
The whole town is in mourning after the school shooting.

進階字彙

12) **noncooperation** [͵nɑnko͵ɑpəˋreʃən] (n.) 不合作
The president faced noncooperation from the opposition party.

13) **stint** [stɪnt] (n.) 從事某項工作（或活動）的時間
The soldier served two stints in Iraq.

14) **cornerstone** [ˋkɔrnɚ͵ston] (n.) 基石
Honesty is the cornerstone of any successful relationship.

朗讀 MP3 43 單字 MP3 44 英文文章導讀 MP3 45

During the early 1920s, Gandhi [1]**advocate** [12]**noncooperation** with British rule in India, which include [2]**boycotting** British goods, schools and law courts, an refusing titles and honors. He was arrested and charge with [3]**treason** in March 1922, and served two years of hi six-year sentence, just one of his many [13]**stints** behind bars Then, in 1928, calls for Indian independence [4]**intensified** In what became known as the Salt March, thousands joine Gandhi in resisting a tax on salt by marching 241 miles t the sea to make their own salt. Gandhi continued his effort [5]**on behalf of** the untouchables throughout the 1930s [6]**undertaking** many [7]**fasts** and hunger strikes, although h had yet to win *swaraj*, or complete individual, political an spiritual independence for India.

This would change, however, with Great Britain's entry into World War II. Gandhi refused to support Britain's figh for democratic freedom when such freedom was denied t India. He drafted the Quit India resolution, which became the [14]**cornerstone** of a new movement. Gandhi and hi

甘地與尼赫魯

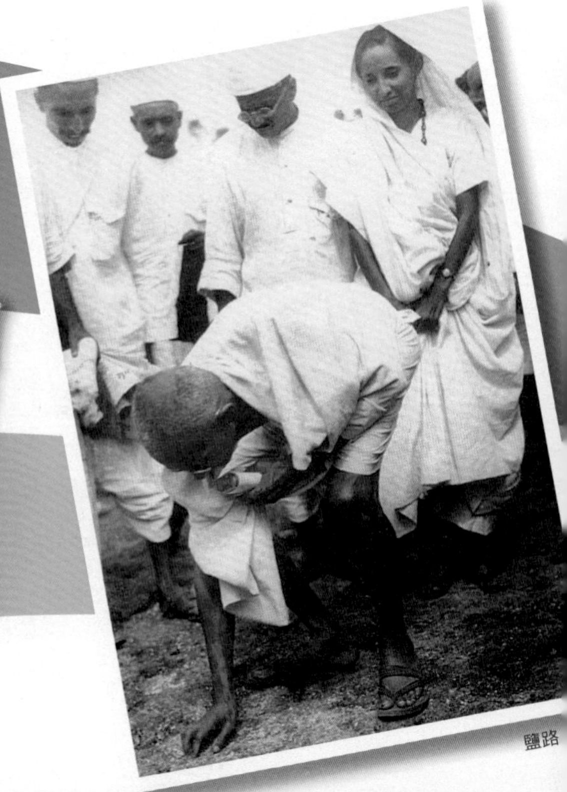
鹽路

upporters stressed that they would only support the war fort if India were [8]**granted** immediate independence. While e authorities cracked down [9]**harshly**, (G)this time it was clear at independence was near. Two states—one for Hindus ndia) and one for Muslims (Pakistan)—would be created, ut this victory would come at a great cost. Gandhi was ssassinated on January 30, 1948 by Hindu [10]**extremists,** nd the country went into [11]**mourning**. In the words of waharlal Nehru, India's first prime minister, "Our beloved ader, Bapu as we called him, the father of the nation, is no ore."

Translation

九二〇年代初期，甘地提倡對英國統治的不合作運動，包括杯葛英國商品、學校和法，並拒絕官祿和榮銜。他在一九二二年三月遭到逮捕，被控叛國罪，服了六年徒刑的兩年，而這只是他多次入獄的其中一遭。一九二八年，印度獨立的呼聲愈益高漲。在來被稱為「鹽路長征」的遊行中，數千人和甘地一同步行兩百四十一哩到海邊自己製，以抵制鹽稅。整個一九三〇年代，甘地持續為賤民付出努力，進行多起禁食與絕食議，但他仍未替印度贏得 swaraj(編註：梵文中自治獨立的意思)，即個人、政治與精上的完全獨立。

過，隨著英國加入第二次世界大戰，情況有了轉變。既然英國不給予印度自由，甘地拒絕支持英國為民主自由而戰的戰鬥。他起草《退出印度》決議書，成為一項新運的基礎。甘地和他的支持者強調，除非印度立刻獲准獨立，否則他們不會支持戰事。然執政當局採取嚴厲鎮壓，但這一次，獨立之期顯然不遠矣。英屬印度將分成兩個家——信奉印度教的印度，以及信奉回教的巴基斯坦，但勝利的代價極高。甘地在九四八年元月三十日被印度教極端份子暗殺身亡，印度舉國哀悼。印度首任總理尼赫在悼文中寫道：「我們摯愛的領袖，我們口中的父親，祖國之父，不在人世了。」

有疑問請來信：eztalkQ@gmail.com

甘地陵寢

Language Guide

Quit India 退出印度運動

由甘地發起，印度在英國殖民時代一個重要的公民運動，目的是逼迫英屬印度政府願意談判，讓印度能夠快速獨立。draft 是「草擬」之意，這裡在說甘地草擬了退出印度運動的決議書 (resolution)。因為甘地的要求和杯葛，即使政府強力鎮壓 (crack down)，印度獨立仍然成功在望。

India-Pakistan Partition 印巴分治

印度教徒和回教徒一直以來互不信任，英屬印度在大英帝國統治結束後，分裂成以印度教 (Hindu) 為主的印度，和回教 (Muslim) 的巴基斯坦 (Pakistan)。這場宗教分裂造成近一千兩百二十五萬人流離失所，傷亡者則高達十萬至一百萬不等。甘地試圖提倡兩邊和解，引起不滿，因而被印度教極端主義份子暗殺。

Grammar Master

虛主詞 it 的用法

文中第二十二行 ...it was clear that independence was near. it 只是虛主詞，真正的主詞為 independence was near，若將句子還原，則會變成：

- It was clear that independence was near.

= That independence was near was clear. (X)

像第二句這樣的句型反而不如第一句用虛主詞 (it) 表示來得清楚明瞭。

用虛主詞 (it) 代替 that 子句（名詞子句）這類用法，在英文文章中常常出現。

句型：It is/was ＋形容詞＋ that ＋主詞＋動詞 ...

It：虛主詞；that ＋主詞＋動詞 ...：真正主詞（也是這句話真正的重點）

例 It was obvious that Roger was lying.
羅傑很顯然是在說謊。

Mini Quiz

1. Which of the following is true about Gandhi?
   (A) He founded the Indian National Congress
   (B) He married an older woman.
   (C) A poet named him the Father of India.
   (D) He was born in the 18th century.

2. __________ you learn how to ride a bike, you never forget.
   (A) Already
   (B) Ever
   (C) Once
   (D) Before

3. Tracy remained calm __________ her visit to the dentist.
   (A) thorough
   (B) thoroughly
   (C) through
   (D) throughout

解答 1 (B) 2 (C) 3 (D)

Vocabulary Bank

1) **upbringing** [ˋʌp͵brɪŋɪŋ] (n.) 養育，扶養
Did you have a strict upbringing?

2) **minister** [ˋmɪnɪstɚ] (n.) 牧師，神職人員，pastor [ˋpæstɚ] 則是「（基督教）本堂牧師」
The minister at our church is retiring next year.

3) **unrest** [ʌnˋrɛst] (n.) 不安，動盪
There are rumors of unrest in the border region.

4) **activist** [ˋæktəvɪst] (n.) 運動人士，活躍人士
Dozens of human rights activists were arrested at the march.

5) **tension** [ˋtɛnʃən] (n.) 緊張（局勢），張力 (a.) tense [ˋtɛns]
Experts are worried about increasing tension on the Indian-Pakistan border.

6) **supreme** [səˋprim] (a.) 頂級的，最高等的，Supreme Court 即「最高法院」
Ali Khamenei has been Iran's supreme leader since 1989.

7) **declare** [dɪˋklɛr] (v.) 宣告，宣布
Maria was declared winner of the debate contest.

8) **unconstitutional** [͵ʌnkɑnstəˋtuʃənəl] (a.) 違反憲法的
New York's death penalty law was ruled unconstitutional.

9) **demonstration** [͵dɛmənˋstreʃən] (n.) 抗議，示威
The president stepped down after nationwide demonstrations.

10) **unleash** [ʌnˋliʃ] (v.) 引發，使爆發，突然釋出
The president's assassination unleashed violent protests.

11) **clash** [klæʃ] (n./v.) 發生衝突，衝突
A deadly clash between government troops and rebel forces left hundreds dead.

進階字彙

12) **clergy** [ˋklɝgi] (n.)（統稱）神職人員
The couple hopes that their son will enter the clergy.

13) **doctorate** [ˋdɑktərɪt] (n.) 博士學位
How long did it take to complete your doctorate?

14) **theology** [θiˋɑlədʒi] (n.) 神學，宗教理論
The professor is an expert in Catholic theology.

15) **culminate** [ˋkʌlmə͵net] (v.) 達到高潮，告終
The years of research culminated in an important scientific discovery.

Martin Luther King, Jr.

美國民權領袖 金恩博士

朗讀 MP3 46 單字 MP3 47 英文文章導讀 MP3 48

Martin Luther King, Jr. is one of America's Ⓖmost well-known civil rights leaders. Born in Atlanta, Georgia on January 15, 1929, he had a strong religious [1]**upbringing**. Under the influence of his father, who was a [2]**minister** in the African American Baptist church, King also decided to enter the [12]**clergy**. After receiving a [13]**doctorate** in [14]**theology** from Boston University in 1955, King returned to the South and became a pastor in Alabama.

The 1950s were a time of [3]**unrest** as civil rights [4]**activists** challenged racial segregation laws. In 1955, King led a boycott of segregated buses in Montgomery, Alabama. The boycott lasted for over a year, and [5]**tensions** became so great that his house was bombed. Eventually, the United States [6]**Supreme** Court [7]**declared** Alabama's segregation laws [8]**unconstitutional**.

While King was a firm believer in non-violence, civil rights actions became more intense in the 1960s. In 1963, [9]**demonstrations** in Alabama turned violent as local white police officers [10]**unleashed** dogs and water cannons on protesters. The [11]**clashes** resulted in the 1964 Civil Rights Act. Demonstrations [15]**culminated** in

the famous march on August 28, 1963, in Washington, D.C., where, from the steps of the Lincoln Memorial, King delivered his famous "I Have a Dream" speech.

That same year, King received the Nobel Peace Prize. Over the next few years, King continued to push for equality. He was assassinated on April 4, 1968, while assisting a garbage workers' strike in Memphis, Tennessee.

中 Translation

小馬丁路德金恩是美國最知名的民權領袖之一。一九二九年一月十五日出生於喬治亞州亞特蘭大，他在虔誠的宗教環境中被撫養長大。他的父親是非裔美國人浸信會教堂牧師，在父親的影響下，金恩也決定成為神職人員。在一九五五年獲得波士頓大學神學博士學位後，金恩回到美國南方，在阿拉巴馬州擔任牧師。

五〇年代是民權運動人士挑戰種族隔離法律的動盪時代。一九五五年，金恩在阿拉巴馬州蒙哥馬利帶頭抵制公車種族隔離制。這項抵制持續了一年多，緊張局勢一觸即發，導致他的房子遭到炸彈攻擊。最後，美國最高法院宣布阿拉巴馬州的種族隔離法違憲。

雖然金恩堅信非暴力主義，但公民權利行動在六〇年代變得更激烈。一九六三年，阿拉巴馬州的示威運動在當地白人警察發動狗和水柱對付抗議者之後，演變成暴力事件。這些衝突促成了一九六四年的《民權法案》。示威運動最後在 一九六三年八月二十八日著名的華盛頓特區遊行達到最高潮，那時，在林肯紀念堂的台階上，金恩發表了他著名的「我有一個夢想」演說。

同年，金恩獲得諾貝爾和平獎。接下來幾年中，金恩繼續推動平權。他在 一九六八年四月四日被暗殺，當時他在協助田納西州孟菲斯的垃圾工人進行罷工。

Language Guide

種族隔離法與民權運動（一）

美國一直到第二次世界大戰結束，都還是個實行「種族隔離法」(racial segregation [ˌsɛgrɪˋgeʃən] laws) 的國家。戰後十年間，美國黑人爭取平等自由的民權運動團體受到政府鎮壓，只能在法院進行鬥爭。由於美國法院偏袒種族主義，黑人轉向呼籲國際重視此問題。為改變美國在國際上的形像，美國最高法院於一九五四年做出「公立學校實行種族隔離教育是不平等的」之判決。

由於訴諸法律的進度太過緩慢，黑人不再寄望於修法，轉而靠自身的力量。一九五五年，黑人女性帕克斯在阿拉巴馬州蒙哥馬利市 (Montgomery) 的公車上拒絕讓座給白人，因而被捕入獄。當時還很年輕的馬丁路德金恩博士領導全城五萬黑人拒搭公車長達一年，迫使公車的種族隔離規定取消，開啟了美國黑人摧毀種族隔離制度的希望。

Grammar Master

most + adj.

形容詞可分為「原級」、「比較級」、「最高級」三種

	句 型
原級	S + be V + adj.
比較級	S + be V + adj.(er) / more adj. + than...
最高級	S + be V + the adj.(est) / the most + adj.

比較級用在兩個名詞間做比較的情況，而最高級則是一名詞與一群體間的比較，簡單的說就是「最……」的意思。

最高級常用句型

- 最高級 + in 地點：
  Tokyo is the busiest city **in Japan**.
- 最高級 + 形容詞子句：
  David is the most generous person **I have ever known**.
- 最高級 + of all：
  The students in my class are great, but Nina is the best **of all**.
- one of + 最高級 + 複數名詞 （+單數動詞）：
  Ice cream is **one of** the most popular **treats** among children.

Has Martin Luther King's Dream Come True? 平權夢想成真？

Vocabulary Bank

1) **startling** [ˋstɑrtəlɪŋ] (a.) 令人吃驚
The team of scientists made a startling discovery.

2) **racism** [ˋresɪzəm] (n.) 種族主義，種族歧視
(n.) race [ˋres] 種族，人種
(n.) racist [ˋresɪst] (a.) 種族歧視的，種族主義的
Racism is still a problem in many countries.

3) **passionately** [ˋpæʃənɪtli] (adv.) 有熱忱地，熱情地
(a.) passionate [ˋpæʃənɪt]
Caroline believes passionately in women's rights.

4) **contrast** [kənˋtræst] (v.) 對比，對照
My assignment is to write a paper contrasting Islam and Christianity.

5) **fail** [fel] (v.) 辜負（期望）
If I drop out of college, I'll feel like I failed my parents.

6) **constitution** [͵kɑnstɪˋtuʃən] (n.) 憲法
The U.S. Constitution guarantees freedom of speech.

7) **guarantee** [͵gærənˋti] (v./n.) 保證，擔保
Freedom of speech is guaranteed by law.

8) **cash** [kæʃ] (v.) 把（支票、匯票等）兌現
Where can I get this check cashed?

9) **distract** [dɪˋstrækt] (v.) 使分心
Loud music distracts me when I'm studying.

朗讀 MP3 49 單字 MP3 50 英文文章導讀 MP3 51

The election of Barack Obama to the Presidency of the United States is a historic event. It's even more [1]**startling** when you realize that only 50 years ago, many African Americans couldn't vote . So, is [2]**racism** dead? Are people from different races truly equal? Has Martin Luther King's dream come true? Let's take a look at his famous "I Have a Dream" speech and see how many of his dreams have been realized.

On August 28, 1963, Martin Luther King, Jr. spoke [3]**passionately** to 250,000 people from the steps of the Lincoln Memorial in Washington, D.C. In his speech, King [4]**contrasted** the American dream with the sad reality in which many black Americans lived. ©He talked about how the American dream had [5]**failed** black Americans, comparing the [6]**Constitution** to a check that had been written out to every American—a check that [7]**guaranteed** equality and opportunity, but that hadn't been [8]**cashe** yet, a check that would give black Americans "th riches of freedom and the security of justice."

© 達志 / UPI PHOTO

King rejected talk of gradual change. He even warned against it, claiming it was like a drug that [9]**distracted** people from their goals. Instead, he talked of how he wanted America to be. He described the way he wanted all Americans to live. Here are some of his visions:

中 Translation

歐巴馬選上美國總統是一個歷史性的大事。如果你想到，許多非裔美國人不能投票才只不過是五十多年前的事，那歐巴馬的當選就更叫人吃驚了。所以，種族主義結束了？不同種族的人真的平等了？馬丁路德金恩的夢想已經成真了？讓我們來檢視他著名的演說「我有一個夢想」，看看他的夢想有多少已經實現。

一九六三年八月二十八日，小馬丁路德金恩在華盛頓特區林肯紀念堂的台階上對著二十五萬人激昂演說。在他的演說中，金恩將美國夢與許多美國黑人可悲的生活現實進行對比。他談到美國夢背棄了美國黑人，並將憲法比喻為開給每個美國人的支票，這張支票保證會有平等和機會，但尚未兌現，這張支票保證將提供美國黑人「豐足的自由和正義的保障」。

金恩拒絕接受逐步改變的論調，他甚至警告反對，宣稱那就像會讓人遠離目標的毒品。取而代之的是，他談到他所憧憬的美國，他描述了他所期待的到的美國人生活方式。以下是他的一些願景：

Language Guide

種族隔離法與民權運動（二）

一九五七年，馬丁路德金恩博士帶頭組成南方基督教領袖會議 (Southern Christian Leadership Conference, SCLC)，將民權運動推廣到美國南部的各個生活角落。一九六〇年，北卡羅萊納州格林斯伯勒市 (Greensboro) 有四位黑人大學生進入一間餐廳，遭到白人服務員斥離，四個大學生靜坐不動，此舉獲得美國南部廣大黑人學生響應，進而發展成大規模靜坐，最後有將近兩百個城市取消餐廳隔離制。美國民權運動持續發燒，一九六一年迫使南部各州取消州際公車上的種族隔離制。

一九六三年，金恩博士在南部種族隔離極嚴重的伯明罕組織示威遊行 (Birmingham campaign)，要求取消全市隔離制，示威群眾受到殘酷鎮壓，上篇文章中警察放狗咬人、用水柱驅離的行為，就是在此次行動中發生。最後該市的種族隔離制全部取消。

Grammar Master

分詞構句（表承接上句）

本句還原為：

He talked about…, and **he** compared…

當主詞相同，可去掉後句的連接詞和主詞，並把動詞改為 Ving，變為…

He talked about…, **comparing**…

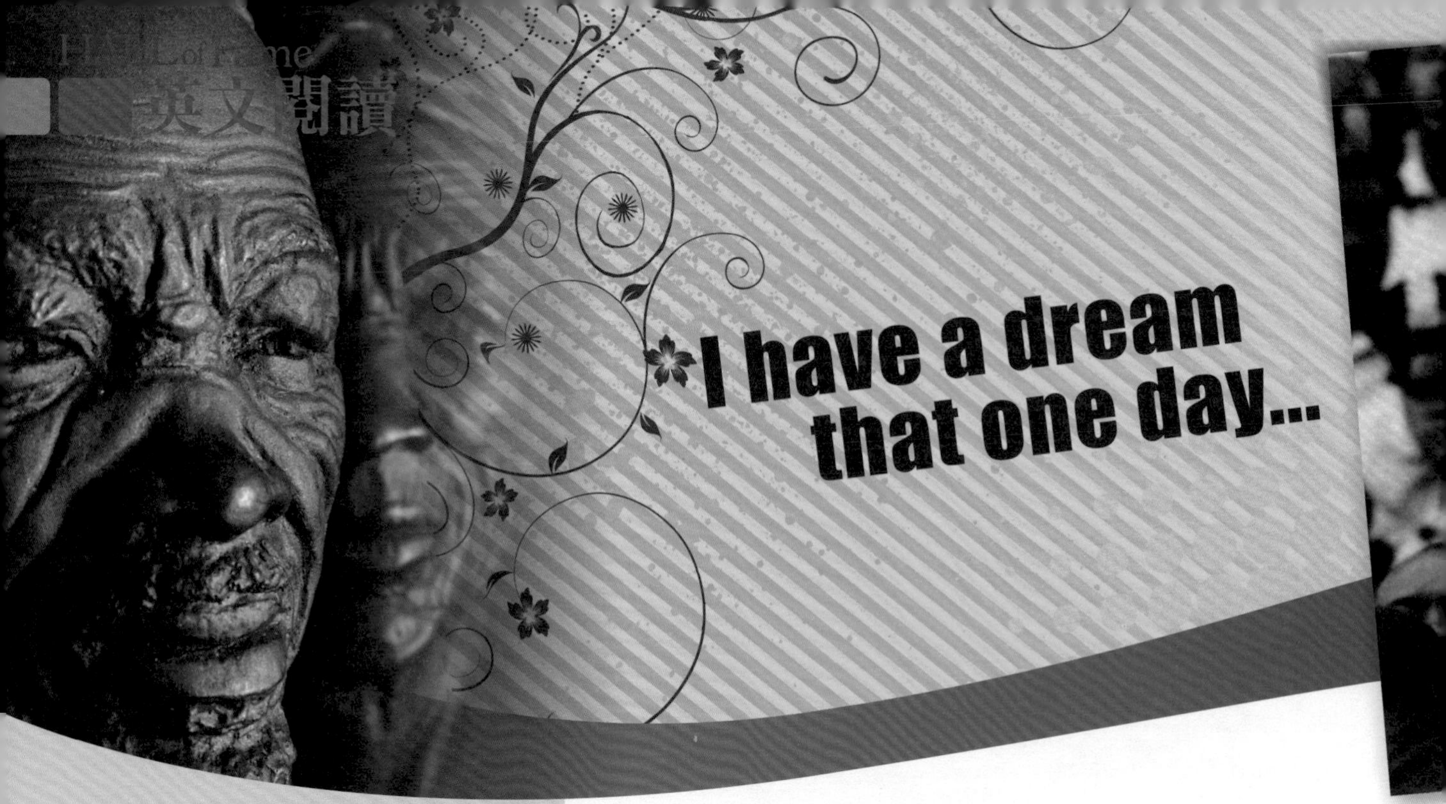

I have a dream that one day...

Vocabulary Bank

1) **brotherhood** [ˋbrʌðɚ͵hʊd] (n.) 手足之情，四海一家的信念
Last Sunday, our pastor talked about the importance of brotherhood.

2) **transform** [trænsˋfɔrm] (v.) 改變，改觀
Technology has transformed the way we live and work.

3) **oasis** [oˋesɪs] (n.)（沙漠中的）綠洲
The travelers filled their canteens at the oasis.

4) **proportion** [prəˋporʃən] (n.) 比例，比率
A large proportion of Americans are overweight.

5) **content** [ˋkɑntɛnt] (n.) 內容
The film contains adult content.

6) **appointment** [əˋpɔɪntmənt] (n.) 任用，指定
His appointment as ambassador to Spain has been confirmed.

進階字彙

7) **harmoniously** [hɑrˋmoniəsli] (adv.) 和諧地
(a.) harmonious [hɑrˋmoniəs]
Good employees must be able to work harmoniously with others.

8) **sweltering** [ˋswɛltərɪŋ] (a.) 熱得難受的，悶熱的
The pool is always crowded on sweltering summer days.

9) **fitting** [ˋfɪtɪŋ] (a.) 適當的，合適的
The writer finally came up with a fitting ending to his novel.

10) **almighty** [ɔlˋmaɪti] (a./n.)（常用大寫）全能的（神）
Let us pray to Almighty God.

朗讀 MP3 52 單字 MP3 53 英文文章導讀 MP3 54

"I have a dream that one day on the red hills of Georgia the sons of former slaves and the sons of former slave owners will be able to sit down together at a table of 1)**brotherhood**." This does happen now. People from all races interact 7)**harmoniously** all over America.

"I have a dream that one day even the state of Mississippi, a desert state, 8)**sweltering** with the heat of injustice and oppression, will be 2)**transformed** into an 3)**oasis** of freedom and justice." The Civil Rights Act of 1964 forced all states to treat all races equally. However, many are still concerned that the 4)**proportion** of African American men in jail is significantly higher than that of other racial groups.

"I have a dream that my four children will one day live in a nation where they will not be judged by the color of their skin but by the 5)**content** of their character." The election of Barack Obama and the 6)**appointment** of other African Americans to important positions, as well as the achievements of black actors,

© 達志 / UPI PHOTO

artists and business people show that people of all races are able to succeed.

So perhaps it's 9)**fitting** to end with the following quote from King's famous speech: "Free at last! Free at last! Thank God 10)**Almighty**, we are free at last!"

中 Translation

「我夢想有一天，在喬治亞的紅山上，昔日奴隸的兒子能夠和昔日奴隸主的兒子會坐在同一張桌子，共敘兄弟情誼。」現在這已經發生，全美國各種族的人都能和諧互動。

「我夢想有一天，甚至連密西西比州——不公不義和壓迫的熱浪叫人悶熱難受的荒漠之州——也會變成自由和正義的綠洲。」一九六四 年的《民權法案》強制規定各州種族平等。然而，許多人擔心，非裔美國男子入獄的比例明顯高於其他種族這一事實。

「我有一個夢想，我四個孩子有一天會生活在一個不是以皮膚顏色，而是以品格優劣作為評判標準的國家裡。」歐巴馬的當選以及其他非裔美國人被任命擔任要職，還有黑人演員、藝人和商人的成就，在在說明所有種族的人都能成功。

因此，也許以下面這句引用自金恩著名演說的話來做結束很適合：「終於自由了！終於自由了！感謝萬能的主，我們終於自由了！」

REV. MARTIN LUTHER KING. JR.
1929 — 1968
"Free at last. Free at last.
Thank God Almighty
I'm Free at last."

Language Guide

種族隔離法與民權運動（三）

民權運動勢力從此迅速擴大， 八月二十八日更集結二十五萬人向華府進軍（March on Washington，即文中所說的 the famous march)，同時部分黑人展開以暴制暴的鬥爭，終於在一九六四年迫使詹森總統 (Lyndon Johnson) 簽署《民權法案》(Civil Rights Act)。但上有政策，下有對策，南部各州仍用各種手段阻撓黑人選民登記。金恩博士於是前往極端種族主義的阿拉巴馬州塞爾馬市推動黑人選民登記運動，並於一九六五年三月冒著被恐嚇暗殺的風險發起另一次行動，向阿拉巴馬州首府蒙哥馬利市進軍。最後美國政府終於在全球輿論壓力下，於八月要求國會通過《選民登記法》。

《民權法案》及《選民登記法》實際上未能完全消弭美國南部的種族隔離制度與歧視，長期的紛擾反而挑起美國北部的種族歧視情緒。一九六八年三月，金恩博士發起另一次「貧民進軍」（亦稱「窮人運動」），途經田納西州孟菲斯市 (Memphis) 時，不幸被種族主義分子槍殺。

為什麼要說 the red hills of Georgia?

金恩博士在演說中提到 the red hills of Georgia，應該是要作為美國初期的殖民及奴役制度的象徵。

紅山山脈 (Red Hills) 位於美國東南部，橫亙喬治亞州西南及佛羅里達州北部。這個地區的原住民是古印地安人 (Paleo-Indians)，十六世紀成為阿帕拉契印地安人 (Apalachee Indians) 的棲息地，阿帕拉契族因遭白人殖民者屠殺、奴役及感染外來疾病而幾乎滅絕。十八世紀塞米諾族（Seminole）在此定居，同一段期間，一批從南卡羅萊納州及喬治亞州逃離的黑奴也來到這個地區。十九世紀初白人殖民者將紅山地區開闢為棉花田，大量蓄奴種植棉花。南北戰爭 (the Civil War) 結束之後，這片地區又成為北方富商的畜牧地。

Vocabulary Bank

1) **resident** [ˋrɛzɪdənt] (n.) 居民
Most of the residents of the town are Hakka.

2) **midst** [mɪdst] (n.) 當中，中間
The country is in the midst of a severe recession.

3) **mistake (for)** [mɪˋstek] (v.) 把…誤以為，誤解
People often mistake me for my brother.

4) **admirer** [ədˋmaɪrɚ] (n.) 愛慕者，崇拜者
Jim is only one of Stacey's many admirers.

5) **equality** [iˋkwɑləti] (n.) 平等
Women are still struggling for equality in the workplace.

6) **clan** [klæn] (n.) 家族，宗族
The two clans have been at war for centuries.

7) **expel** [ɪkˋspɛl] (v.) 使退學，開除
Anyone caught cheating on the exam will be expelled.

8) **eventually** [ɪˋvɛntʃuəli] (adv.) 最後，終究
Allen and Grace plan to get married and have children eventually.

9) **correspondence** [͵kɔrəˋspɑndəns] (n.) 通信，函授（課程）
The university offers a number of correspondence courses.

10) **league** [lig] (n.) 聯盟，聯合會
The League of Nations later became the United Nations.

進階字彙

11) **fraternity** [frəˋtɝnəti] (n.) 友愛，手足之情
The Olympic Games help promote fraternity among nations.

從階下囚到總統
尼爾森曼德拉
Nelson Mandela
From Prisoner to President

非洲民族議會 (ANC) 的

朗讀 MP3 55　單字 MP3 56　英文文章導讀 MP3 57

On June 23, 1990, hundreds of thousands of Bosto [1]**residents** turned out on this beautiful summer's day t welcome a true hero to their city. The man of the hour wa in the [2]**midst** of an eight-city U.S. tour, and while no roc star, it was easy to [3]**mistake** him for one with the crowds c [4]**admirers** cheering his name and wearing T-shirts with hi face on them. Nelson Mandela, the world's most celebrate freedom fighter, who had been released from prison in hi native South Africa only months before, had come to shar his message with America. Thanking Bostonians for the support, he said, "Together, we have turned the wheel c history in favor of the forces fighting for liberty, [5]**equalit** and [11]**fraternity** for all."

Nelson Mandela was born on July 18, 1918 in Transke South Africa. He is often called "Madiba," the name of hi Thembu [6]**clan**, but it was actually one of his school teacher Ⓖwho gave him the English name Nelson. After his fathe Henry died when he was nine, he was raised by the chief c the Thembu people, Ⓖwhom he was expected to succee one day. Mandela enrolled at Fort Hare University, bu

© 達志 / UPI PHOTO

vas soon [7]**expelled** after leading a student strike in 1940. le [8]**eventually** completed his B.A. by [9]**correspondence** hrough the University of South Africa, at which point he entered law school. Mandela joined the African National Congress (ANC) in 1943, and founded the ANC Youth [0]**League** a year later.

Translation

一九九〇年六月二十三日，成千上萬波士頓居民在這個豔陽高照的夏日聚集，為的就是要歡迎一位真正的英雄蒞臨他們的城市。這位風雲人物正在美國八座城市進行訪問，雖然他不是搖滾巨星，但很容易讓人誤以為他是，因為大批仰慕者高呼他的名字、身上穿著印有他臉孔圖樣的 T 恤。尼爾森曼德拉這位世界上最有名的自由鬥士，幾個月前才從他祖國南非的監獄中釋放出來，特地來此向美國分享他的理念。他感謝波士頓人對他的支持，並說：「齊心協力，我們已將歷史巨輪推往為全人類的自由、平等和博愛而戰。」

尼爾森曼德拉於一九一八年七月十八日出生於南非的川斯凱。他常被稱為「馬迪巴」，這是他所屬的騰布族名，但他的英文名字「尼爾森」其實是學校老師幫他取的。九歲時，父親亨利過世之後，他由騰布族人的族長扶養長大，期待他有朝一日能接班。曼德拉進入福特哈爾大學就讀，但在一九四〇年率領一次學生罷課活動後旋即被退學。最後他在南非大學以函授方式完成學士學位，他也是在這個時候進入法學院。曼德拉於一九四三年加入非洲民族議會黨 (ANC) ，一年後成立該黨的青年聯盟。

Language Guide

法國大革命的口號

文中曼德拉對波士頓居民說的那段話，引述自法國大革命的精神：自由 (liberty)、平等 (equality) 與博愛 (fraternity)。其中 fraternity 一詞字面上的解釋為「兄弟情、友愛」，英解則為 feelings of friendship and mutual support between people，也就是一群人彼此友誼和互相支持的感覺，因此中譯為「博愛」。

Grammar Master

who 和 whom 的不同用法

關係代名詞代替人的用法中，主格 who 與受格 whom 最容易混淆，分辨方法如下：

- 關係代名詞後面若是動詞，使用主格 who。

例 Anyone **who** trespasses will be punished severely.
違規者將會遭受嚴厲懲罰。

- 關係代名詞後面若是名詞，使用受格 whom。

例 My grandfather, **whom** I greatly respected, passed away last year.
我尊敬的爺爺去年過世了。

以文中第 19 行這句為例：..., __ he was expected to.... 關係代名詞後接代名詞 he ，所以用受格 whom。

但其實 whom 現在只會出現在正式文章中，且兩者的區分也不那麼明顯。

囚禁曼德拉近十八年的羅賓島監獄

Vocabulary Bank

1) **initial** [ɪˋnɪʃəl] (a.) 最初的，初步的
(v.) initiate [ɪˋnɪʃi͵et] 創始，開始
According to initial reports, several people were injured in the accident.

2) **spur (on)** [spɝ] (v.) 鞭策，鼓勵
The thought of winning first prize spurred the contestants on.

3) **counsel** [ˋkaʊnsəl] (n.) 諮詢，忠告
The president followed the counsel of his advisors.

4) **opposition** [͵ɑpəˋzɪʃən] (n.) 反對（派），對抗
(v.) oppose [əˋpos] 反對，對抗
(n.) opponent [əˋponənt] 對手，反對者
The proposed law faces strong opposition.

5) **campaign** [kæmˋpen] (n.)（社會）運動，活動
The government announced a campaign against drunk driving.

6) **harass** [həˋræs] (v.)（不斷）騷擾，攻擊
The employee was fired for harassing a coworker.

7) **protester** [ˋprotɛstɚ / prəˋtɛstɚ] (n.) 抗議者
Hundreds of protesters gathered in front of the White House.

8) **ban** [bæn] (v./n.) 禁止，取締
The city is considering banning smoking in restaurants.

9) **imprison** [ɪmˋprɪzən] (v.) 監禁，使入獄
The terror suspects were imprisoned without trial.

10) **renounce** [rɪˋnaʊns] (v.)（聲明）放棄，拋棄
Gandhi renounced the use of violence.

11) **negotiate** [nɪˋgoʃi͵et] (v.) 協商，談判
The government refuses to negotiate with terrorists.

進階字彙

12) **solidify** [səˋlɪd͵faɪ] (v.) 鞏固，加強
Support for the new policy is solidifying.

13) **underprivileged** [͵ʌndɚˋprɪvəlɪdʒd] (a.) 貧困的，社會地位低下的
There are scholarships available for underprivileged students.

14) **trumped-up** [ˋtrʌmpt͵ʌp] (a.) 編造的，捏造的
The political prisoner was convicted on trumped-up charges.

15) **acquit** [əˋkwɪt] (v.) 宣告無罪，無罪釋放
The defendant in the case was acquitted of all charges.

朗讀 MP3 58 單字 MP3 59 英文文章導讀 MP3 60

Mandela's [1]**initial** involvement in politics was [2]**spurred** on by the pro-Afrikaner National Party's victory of 1948. Throughout the 1950s, Ⓖinfluenced by Gandhi's nonviolent resistance movement, he worked tirelessly to [12]**solidify** the ANC's anti-apartheid platform. Mandela also established the country's first black law firm with his Fort Hare classmate Oliver Tambo, and together they provided free legal [3]**counsel** to many [13]**underprivileged** black South Africans. In 1956, his political activities led to his arrest along with 150 fellow [4]**opposition** leaders on [14]**trumped-up** charges of high treason. The trials lasted four years, and although the accused were all [15]**acquitted**, the opposition began to disagree on the best way to oppose National Party rule.

In 1960, the ANC initiated a [5]**campaign** to protest pass laws, which the apartheid government used to enforce segregation and [6]**harass** its opponents. On March 21 between five and seven thousand people surrounded a local police department in the township of Sharpeville near Johannesburg. The outnumbered police opened fire, killing 69 [7]**protesters** in what became known as the Sharpeville Massacre. In response, Mandela founded Umkhonto we Sizwe, or "Spear of the Nation," the ANC's military wing, and launched sabotage campaigns against the government which in turn [8]**banned** the group and arrested its

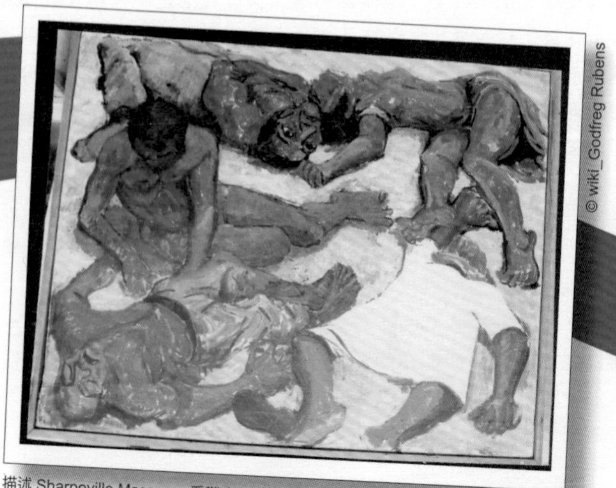

描述 Sharpeville Massacre 受難者的畫作

eaders. In 1964, Mandela was given a life sentence and **imprisoned** on Robben Island, where his fame grew both in South Africa and abroad. While in prison, Mandela turned to self-study and educating his fellow prisoners. He famously refused a conditional release if he [10]**renounced** armed struggle, stating, "Only free men can [11]**negotiate.**"

Translation

親荷裔南非人的國民黨在一九四八年大選獲勝，曼德拉深受刺激，於是開始涉足政治。整個一九五〇年代，在甘地的非暴力抗爭運動影響之下，他努力不懈地加強鞏固 ANC 反種族隔離政策的黨綱。同時，曼德拉和他在福特哈爾大學的同學奧利佛坦波也一同開設南非第一家黑人法律事務所，共同為許多弱勢的南非黑人免費提供法律諮詢。一九五六年，他所從事的政治活動使他遭到逮捕，連同一百五十位反對黨領袖也被莫須有地冠上叛國的指控。這項審判歷時四年，雖然被告全部無罪釋放，但是反對黨對於該用什麼方式對抗國民黨統治最為合適，開始有了歧見。

一九六〇年，ANC 發起抗議通行法的活動，實行種族隔離的政府就是用這項法律來執行種族隔離以及騷擾反對者。同年三月二十一日，鄰近約翰尼斯堡的夏普威爾小鎮一個地方警局，被五千到七千名民眾團團圍住。人數比較少的警方對民眾開火，造成六十九名抗議者死亡，此事件後來稱為夏普威爾屠殺。為此曼德拉成立了「民族之矛」，也就是 ANC 的軍事組織，發起對抗政府的破壞活動，結果該組織被政府禁止，其領導人也遭到逮捕。一九六四年，曼德拉被判無期徒刑，監禁在羅賓島，他的名聲因此在南非與海外傳了開來。在獄中，曼德拉開始自修，並教育同窗獄友。他最有名的就是拒絕了有條件的釋放，條件是他要放棄武裝抗爭，他說：「只有自由的人才能討價還價。」

曼德拉與奧利佛坦波

Language Guide

apartheid 種族隔離政策

apartheid [ə`pɑr͵taɪt] 是南非（荷蘭）語 (Afrikaans) 中「隔離」的意思，字典一般翻譯成「（南非的）種族隔離」或「種族隔離政策」(segregation [͵sɛgrɪ`geʃən])。南非的白人政府於一九四八年到一九九九年實行種族隔離政策，後來經曼德拉的努力才將該政策廢止、並解除黨禁。apartheid 不僅僅是一種「政策」，這個字在一定程度上，代表了南非長久以來的社會狀態。然而，南非後期的白人政府卻總是避談這個字，強調他們是在發展一種基於民族自覺等概念的「多種族主義」multinationalism。

pass laws 通行法

南非早年施行的通行法是對於非白人極不人道的一項法律，這項法律規定黑人不能與白人同車、日落後不能滯留在白人居住的城市，黑人離開居住地區時必須帶著通行證，任何沒有通行證而擅自移動的黑人，下場就是被逮捕入監。推動這項法律的正是執行南非種族隔離政策最力的政治人物——維沃爾德 (Hendrik Frensch Verwoerd)，他甚至還推動一項群居法 (group areas act)，將黑人的活動區域限制在「獨立黑人家邦」bantustan，以確保他們遠離政治核心。

之後發生的夏普維爾屠殺事件」(Sharpeville Massacre [`mæsəkə]) 也是起因於民眾反對通行法的抗議活動，但南非警方竟在毫無預警下，對手無寸鐵的示威者開槍，總共造成六十九人死亡，約一百八十人受傷。

一九九四年南非舉行不分種族的民主大選，曼德拉當選南非首位黑人總統的三個月後，便將三月二十一日這一天定為南非的人權日 (Human Rights Day)，紀念當時犧牲的民眾。

Grammar Master

分詞構句

分詞構句可以使文章看起來更有變化，讀起來更有深度，例如第 3 行開始的這句，可以還原為以下兩個句子：

1. **He** was influenced by Gandhi's nonviolent resistance movement.（原句前半部）
2. **He** worked tirelessly to solidify the ANC's anti-apartheid platform.（原句後半部）

兩句主詞相同的句子，可用連接詞來連接，也可以將第一句的主詞刪除，因為第一句是被動語態，所以要用過去分詞 influenced，而第一句中的 was 可以直接省略，再將**兩句中間用逗號連接**，就可以完成分詞構句囉！

例 **The country** is blessed with abundant natural resources and **the country** has attracted traders and explorers for centuries. → 簡化為分詞構句

= Blessed with abundant natural resources, **the country** has attracted traders and explorers for centuries.
這國家幸運地擁有豐沛的自然資源，幾世紀以來吸引商人和探險家絡繹不絕。

Vocabulary Bank

1) **harbor** [ˋhɑrbɚ] (v.) 心懷，懷有
Many people harbor suspicions about the leader's motives.

2) **injustice** [ɪnˋdʒʌstɪs] (n.) 不公，不義
Native Americans have suffered many injustices.

3) **ally** [ˋælaɪ] (n.) 同盟者，同盟國
Germany and Japan were allies in World War II.

4) **poll** [pol] (n.)（多為複數）投票所，投票
Polls will be open until 8:00 p.m. on election day.

5) **woo** [wu] (v.) 勸誘，爭取
The party tried to woo voters with promises of tax cuts.

6) **corporation** [͵kɔrpəˋreʃən] (n.) 股份（有限）公司，企業，multinational corporation 即「跨國企業」
Karen plans to work for a large corporation after she graduates.

7) **presidency** [ˋprɛzədənsi] (n.) 總統任期、職權、職位
The author is writing a book about the Clinton presidency.

8) **bid** [bɪd] (n.) 申請（比賽等的）主辦權，投標
Chicago's bid for the 2016 Olympics was unsuccessful.

9) **remark** [rɪˋmɑrk] (v./n.) 談到，說；言辭，評論
Morgan remarked that Diana looked like she'd lost weight.

10) **reign** [ren] (v./n.) 盛行，統治
(a.) reigning [renɪŋ] 統治的，稱霸的
The queen reigned for over 60 years.

進階字彙

11) **oppressor** [əˋprɛsɚ] (n.) 壓迫者，壓制者
(v.) oppress [əˋprɛs] 壓迫，壓制
(n.) oppression [əˋprɛʃən]
The people rose up and fought against their oppressors.

12) **dwell (on)** [dwɛl] (v.) 老是想著，停留在
It's not healthy to dwell on things you can't change.

13) **uprising** [ˋʌp͵raɪzɪŋ] (n.) 起義，暴動
The uprising was put down by government troops.

14) **instrumental** [͵ɪnstrəˋmɛntəl] (a.)（對完成某事）很有幫助的
The coach was instrumental to the team's success.

朗讀 MP3 61 單字 MP3 62 英文文章導讀 MP3 63

Despite serving nearly 28 years in prison, Mandela didn' [1]**harbor** any bitterness towards his [11]**oppressors** after hi release in February 1990. He stated that since he had a jol to do—namely, establishing a free and democratic Soutl Africa—there was no time to waste [12]**dwelling** on pas [2]**injustices**. The ban on the ANC now lifted, Mandela movec directly from his cell to the negotiating table, where h worked with President F.W. de Klerk to plan South Africa' first free elections. For successfully ending apartheid, thes unlikely [3]**allies** shared the Nobel Peace Prize in 1993. Anc five short months later, South Africans of all races went t the [4]**polls** together for the first time, electing Mandela th country's first black president.

During Mandela's time in office, he took on the difficul task of improving living conditions in the poor blacl townships, long the center of violent [13]**uprisings** agains the former government. He also [5]**wooed** multinationa [6]**corporations** that had pulled out of South Africa to return Although he stepped down from the [7]**presidency** in 199 and retired from public life, Mandela continues to serve his

© wiki_Paul Mannix

曼德拉位於羅賓島監獄的第五號牢房

曼德拉與戴克拉克

eople through the Nelson Mandela Foundation. Among s goals is working to educate the public about HIV/AIDS, hich claimed the life of Mandela's son in 2005. Most ecently, he was [14]**instrumental** in South Africa's successful **bid** for this summer's FIFA World Cup. He once [9]**remarked**, et freedom [10]**reign**. The sun never set on so glorious human achievement." Ⓖ Nor has the world seen many gures as glorious as Nelson Mandela.

Translation

管在監獄中待了將近二十八年，曼德拉在一九九〇年二月被釋放後，卻對迫害者有心存怨念。他說因為有正事要做——也就是建立自由民主的南非——所以沒有間可以浪費在回想過去的不公不義。如今 ANC 的禁令解除，曼德拉直接從牢房坐談判桌，與總統戴克拉克共同規劃南非首次自由選舉。由於成功終結了南非的種隔離制，這兩位最難想像的盟友於一九九三年共同獲得諾貝爾和平獎。短短五個之後，南非所有種族首次一起走進投票所，選出曼德拉擔任南非首位黑人總統。

德拉在位期間，他肩負起改善貧窮黑人區生活條件的艱鉅任務，這些地區長久以一直是對抗前政府的暴力起義中心。他也爭取撤離南非的跨國企業重回南非。雖他於一九九九年卸任，從公職生涯退休，但仍繼續透過尼爾森曼德拉基金會服務民。基金會的目標之一，就是致力於教育大眾有關 HIV/AIDS 的知識（編註：HIV luman Immunodeficiency Virus) 人類免疫缺陷病毒，俗稱「愛滋病毒」；AIDS cquired Immunodeficiency Syndrome) 愛滋病，或譯作「後天免疫缺乏症候群」，是染 HIV 的末期表現），曼德拉的兒子二〇〇五年就是死於愛滋病。近年，多虧有他，非成功取得今年夏季世界盃足球賽的主辦權。他曾經說過：「讓自由為王。對於人類此光輝的成就，太陽的光芒將永不會停止照耀。」像尼爾森曼德拉這般榮耀的人物全世界也很少見。 若有疑問請來信：eztalkQ@gmail.com

© fstockfoto/shutterstock.com

2010 世界盃足球賽

Language Guide

Robben Island 羅賓島

Robben 在荷蘭語中意指「海豹」seal，因早期歐洲航海者在島上捕食海豹而得名，位於開普敦的北方，面積約六平方公里。羅賓島在一九六〇年到一九九一年期間關過上千名因為爭取自由、人權而入獄的政治犯（多為有色人種），故又名「鎖住自由的監獄島」，曼德拉就在這裡被囚禁長達十八年。

如今羅賓島已成為是南非著名的旅遊勝地。一九九七年元旦正式成為對外開放的博物館，裡面的導遊有一些甚至是曾經被關在這裡的政治犯，最值得一看的就是當年囚禁曼德拉的第五號牢房。羅賓島在一九九九年被聯合國教科文組織宣布為世界遺產。

Grammar Master

nor 的倒裝用法

nor「也不」，本身就有否定的意味，當 nor 放在句首時，其後句型要倒裝。其他類似用法的字還有：never、hardly、seldom。

例 Not all women are attracted to successful men. **Nor** are all men afraid of successful women.
並非所有女人都會被成功的男人所吸引，也並非所有男人都害怕成功的女人。

例 **Never** had the traveler seen such a spectacular sight.
遊客從未目睹如此壯觀的景致。

Mini Quiz

❶ According to the article, which of the following is true about Nelson Mandela?
(A) He was sentenced to 28 years in prison.
(B) He became the country's first black lawyer.
(C) He was expected to serve as chief of his clan.
(D) He was given the name Nelson at birth.

❷ Formal letters are often addressed "To ________ It May Concern."
(A) Who
(B) Which
(C) That
(D) Whom

❸ Barely ________ his speech when someone started coughing loudly.
(A) the speaker had started
(B) had the speaker started
(C) had started the speaker
(D) started the speaker had

解答 ❶ (C) ❷ (D) ❸ (B)

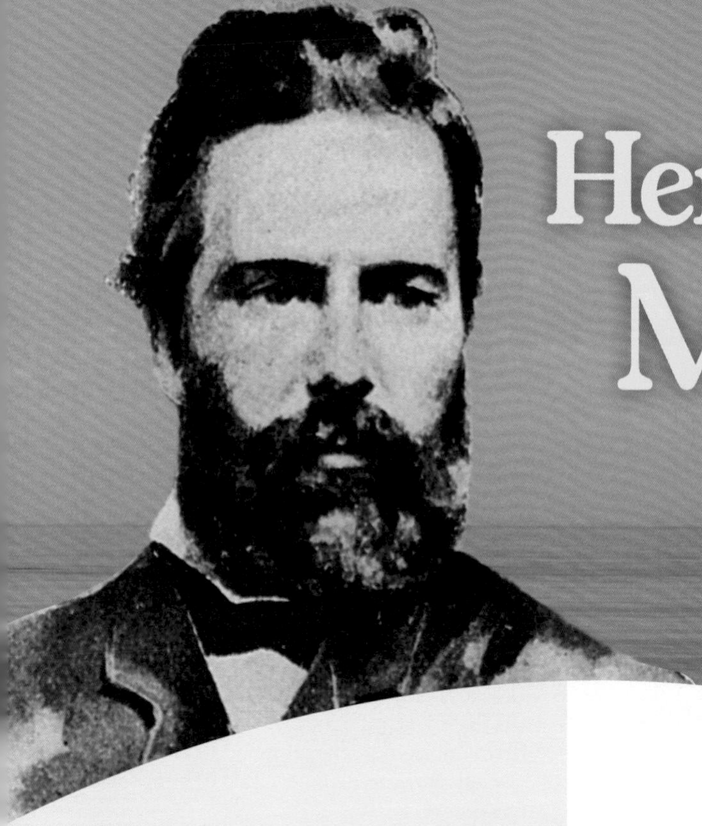

Herman Melville's Moby Dick

梅爾維爾 白鯨記

Vocabulary Bank

1) **masterpiece** [ˋmæstɚˏpis] (n.) 傑作，名作
Many feel that the Mona Lisa is da Vinci's masterpiece.

2) **in search of** [ɪn sɜtʃ əv] (phr.) 尋找
Thousands of people came to California in search of gold.

3) **happen (to)** [ˋhæpən] (v.)（偶然）發生，碰巧
I happened to meet an old friend at the post office.

4) **incredible** [ɪnˋkrɛdəbəl] (a.) 不可思議的，難以置信的
It seems incredible that nobody saw the economic crisis coming.

5) **gather** [ˋgæðɚ] (v.) 猜想，推測
I gather that you're new here.

6) **essay** [ˋɛse] (n.) 短文，論文
Mike got an A on his English essay.

7) **inspiration** [ˏɪnspəˋreʃən] (n.) 靈感，啟發
(v.) inspire [ɪnˋspaɪr]
Many poets seek inspiration from the natural world.

進階字彙

8) **ram** [ræm] (v.) 猛烈撞擊
The drunk driver rammed into a telephone pole.

朗讀 MP3 64 單字 MP3 65 英文文章導讀 MP3 66

One of the greatest [1]**masterpieces** of American literature was written in 1851 by an author named Herman Melville. The novel is about a group of sailors who travel together on a whaling ship called the Pequod. They're [2]**in search of** a giant white sperm whale named Moby Dick—which also [3]**happens** to be the name of Melville's book. Now before we learn about the story behind this [4]**incredible** adventure, let's get to know its author a little better.

Herman Melville was born on August 1, 1819 in New York City. His parents were Allan and Maria Gansevoort Melvill (Maria added an "e" to "Melvill" after her husband died). As you've probably [5]**gathered** by now, Herman Melville is known mainly for his writing. He not only wrote novels, but also [6]**essays**, short stories and even poems. But would it surprise you to find out he was also a sailor? It's true! What's also true is the story from which Melville got the idea for Moby Dick. That story, of the real-life

whaling ship, the Essex, which was [8]**rammed** and sunk by a large sperm whale in 1819, was well-known among sailors of Melville's time, and it provided his [7]**inspiration** for Moby Dick.

中 Translation

美國文學最偉大的傑作之一，在一八五一年問世，作者是名為赫爾曼梅爾維爾的作家。這部小說講述一群水手的故事，他們乘坐一艘名為「裴廓德」的捕鯨船一起航行，尋找一條名為「莫比迪克」的巨大白色抹香鯨——這碰巧是梅爾維爾這部鉅作之名。現在，在我們進一步探知這個不可思議的冒險故事之前，且讓我們稍加了解它的作者。

赫爾曼梅爾維爾在一八一九年八月一日生於紐約市。他的雙親是艾倫及瑪麗亞甘瑟福爾特梅爾維爾（瑪麗亞於丈夫去世後，在原姓氏 Melvill 的字尾多加了一個 e。）你應該已經猜到，赫爾曼梅爾維爾主要以寫作聞名。他不僅寫小說，也寫散文、短篇故事，甚至詩。但，一旦得知他也是水手，你是否感到驚訝？這是千真萬確的！同樣確有其事的是梅爾德爾撰寫《白鯨記》的靈感來源。捕鯨船「艾克賽斯號」在一八一九年遭到一頭大抹香鯨撞沉的故事，在梅爾維爾時代是每個水手耳熟能詳之事，而它也成了梅爾維爾撰寫《白鯨記》的靈感來源。

Language Guide

與海洋有關的文學作品

與海洋有關的文學作品不勝枚舉，像是本篇介紹梅爾維爾的《白鯨記》(一八五一)、海明威 (Ernest Hemingway) 的《老人與海》The Old Man and the Sea (一九五二)、畢爾羅逖 (Pierre Loti)《冰島漁夫》An Iceland Fisherman (一八八六)……等等都是這個文類出色的作品。這個文類之所以自成一格，是因為「海洋」這個意象有著神祕、深不可測的特質，反映出人類面對大自然時各種極端的人性反應，讓作品充滿無限的可能性和想像空間。

《白鯨記》是美國史上第一部史詩級作品，美國近代作家威廉福克納 (William Faulkner) 說「看完會讓我有『真希望這是我寫的』那種感受的作品，就是《白鯨記》了。」其崇高地位可見一斑。海洋文學其實可以追溯到荷馬 (Homer) 的希臘史詩《奧得賽》(The Odyssey)(約西元前八世紀)。同樣都是面對海洋的神祕力量，奧得修司 (Odysseus) 的驕傲和《白鯨記》船長艾伯 (Ahab) 的狂妄、不服輸有異曲同工之處，因此也有人說《白鯨記》就是一部「美國奧得賽」。

whaling 捕鯨業

是以捕獲鯨魚做為糧食或是做為其他商業用途的行業，早期捕鯨業船隻的速度無法追捕到大型鬚鯨 (baleen whale)，因此以游速較慢的抹香鯨 (sperm whale) 和露脊鯨 (right whale) 為主要。抹香鯨是世界上最大型的齒鯨，也是所有鯨類中潛水最深、最久的一種。十九世紀末，蒸汽船讓早期無法獵捕的大型鯨魚成為目標。捕鯨業的蓬勃發展使得鯨魚數量銳減，後在英國劍橋成立國際捕鯨委員會 (International Whaling Commission, IWC)，希望在維持捕鯨業正常營運之餘也能讓鯨魚維持穩定的數量。

The Essex 艾賽克斯號

艾賽克斯號於一八一九年從美國麻州南塔克特島 (Nantucket) 出海捕鯨，卻遭到一頭抹香鯨襲擊沈船，艾賽克斯號因而出名。在發生船難之後，僅存的船員為求生存分食罹難同伴的血肉以及與大海搏鬥的真實過程，都讓人印象深刻。這個船難事件也　發梅爾維爾寫出《白鯨記》這本經典小說。

朗讀 MP3 67 單字 MP3 68 英文文章導讀 MP3 69

The main characters—Ishmael, Ahab, and Starbuck—are sailors aboard the Pequod. The ship is on a whaling trip, but Ahab, the ship's captain, is after one whale [1]**in particular**: Moby Dick. Why? Because years earlier Moby Dick bit off one of his legs. Ahab wants [2]**revenge**. Starbuck, the first [3]**mate**, doesn't think revenge on a whale is right, because whales don't know right from wrong. At the end of the story, Ahab throws his harpoon at Moby Dick and [4]**accidentally** gets dragged into the ocean, where he drowns. Moby Dick also rams the Pequod, causing it to sink. Because of Ahab's [5]**quest** for revenge, everyone drowns except for Ishmael.

Moby Dick teaches us about revenge and [10]**obsession**. Ahab, an obsessed and angry man, doesn't care about other people. His only concern is killing a whale—a whale who didn't hurt him on purpose. In the end, Ahab's obsession and anger [6]**overcome** him. The whale Moby Dick is a symbol for the ocean and nature. The ocean is powerful yet [11]**unthinking** ; it can kill people

Vocabulary Bank

1) **in particular** [ɪn pɚˋtɪkjəlɚ] (phr.) 特別，尤其
Are you looking for anything in particular?

2) **revenge** [rɪˋvɛndʒ] (n./v.) 報仇
The man swore revenge for his brother's murder.

3) **mate** [met] (n.)（商船的）高級船員
first mate 即「大副」；second mate 即「二副」
The second mate was in charge of navigation.

4) **accidentally** [͵æksəˋdɛntəli] (adv.) 意外地，不小心地
(a.) accidental [͵æksəˋdɛntəl]
Robin accidentally deleted his report and had to rewrite it.

5) **quest** [kwɛst] (n.) 探索，追尋
Iran refuses to give up its quest for nuclear energy.

6) **overcome** [͵ovɚˋkʌm] (v.) 壓倒，使無力
The dead soldier's parents were overcome with grief.

7) **motive** [ˋmotɪv] (n.) 動機，目的
What was the man's motive for killing his wife?

8) **mysterious** [mɪsˋtɪriəs] (a.) 神祕的，使人摸不透的
The young man died under mysterious circumstances.

9) **perspective** [pɚˋspɛktɪv] (n.) 角度，觀點
You should try to see things from my perspective.

進階字彙

10) **obsession** [əbˋsɛʃən] (n.) 著迷，縈繞於心的慾望
(a.) obsessed [əbˋsɛst]
Tim teased his sister about her Hello Kitty obsession.

11) **unthinking** [ʌnˋθɪŋkɪŋ] (a.) 無思想（能力）的，不動腦筋的
How could you make such an unthinking decision?

12) **illogical** [ɪˋlɑgɪkəl] (a.) 悖理的，不合邏輯的
It's illogical to feel guilty about your parents' divorce.

without reason, and doesn't have [7]**motives** of its own. It would be [12]**illogical** to seek revenge on the ocean, just as it's illogical to seek revenge on a whale. Moby Dick can also be seen as a symbol for the [8]**mysterious** power that controls the world—God to some, fate to others. From this [9]**perspective**, Ahab's failure in his quest represents the limits of human knowledge and power.

中 Translation

故事主角——以賽馬利、艾伯和史塔巴克——是裴廓德號上的水手。這艘船正展開一場捕鯨行程，但船長艾伯卻特別追逐一頭鯨：莫比迪克。為什麼？因為多年前，莫比迪克咬斷他的一條腿。艾伯想復仇。大副史塔巴克不覺得報復一頭鯨是對的，因為鯨不會分辨是非。故事最後，艾伯把他的魚叉擲向莫比迪克，卻意外被拖入海中，不幸溺斃。莫比迪克也撞擊裴廓德號，使它沉沒。由於艾伯尋仇，除了以賽馬利以外，船上每個人都溺死了。

《白鯨記》教導我們復仇與執迷。執迷不悟、滿懷忿恨的艾伯不在乎其他人的死活。他一心只想殺掉一頭鯨——一頭不是故意要傷害他的鯨。最後，艾伯的執迷和憤怒讓他一敗塗地。白鯨莫比迪克是海洋與大自然的象徵。海洋力量強大但沒有思想；它殺人不需要理由，本身也並無動機，報復海洋是不合邏輯的，就如同向一隻鯨尋仇一般不合邏輯。莫比迪克也可以看成是控制世界的神祕力量——對某些人來說代表上帝，對其他人來說則是命運。從這個觀點來看，艾伯追尋後的挫敗表示了人類知識和力量的有限。

Language Guide

Starbuck 史塔巴克

《白鯨記》中的大副——史塔巴克和星巴克(Starbucks)究竟有什麼關聯？這因為星巴克的創辦人對《白鯨記》情有獨鍾，不過一開始並不是要用這位大副的名字當做品牌名稱，而是故事中的船號——裴龐德號 (Pequod)，但因為這個名字不夠順口，因此改為故事中這位愛喝咖啡的大副。星巴克的創辦人在的名字後方加了 s，為的就是期許所有的員工都能像史塔巴克一樣，對咖啡和工作充滿熱愛。雖然咖啡在這部作品中並不是主要的意象，但其背景和人物的連結著實替這個咖啡品牌增添了一道文藝光環。

Vocabulary Bank

1) **controversial** [ˌkɑntrəˋvɝʃəl] (a.) 有爭議的
Gun control is a very controversial subject.

2) **take place** [tek ples] (phr.) 進行，舉行，發生
The movie takes place in 19th century England.

3) **abolish** [əˋbɑlɪʃ] (v.) 廢除，取消
The citizens fought to abolish the unfair law.

4) **narrate** [ˋnæret] (v.) 敘述，作旁白
(n.) narrator [ˋnæretɚ] 敘述者，旁白者
The series is narrated by a famous actor.

5) **raft** [ræft] (n./v.) 木筏，橡皮艇；泛舟
Many Cubans come to America on wooden rafts.

6) **civilize** [ˋsɪvəˌlaɪz] (v.) 使文明，教化
The goal of the missionaries was to civilize the natives.

7) **manage (to)** [ˋmænɪdʒ] (v.) 設法做到，能應付（困難）
How did you manage to finish that task so quickly?

進階字彙

8) **runaway** [ˋrʌnəˌwe] (a./n.) 逃跑的；逃跑者
(phr.) run away [rʌn əˋwe] 逃跑
The charity runs a shelter for runaway children.

9) **unlikely** [ʌnˋlaɪkli] (a.) 意想不到的，不太可能的
Steve and Cindy make an unlikely couple.

10) **homemade** [ˋhomˋmed] (a.) 自製的
Is this cake homemade?

11) **abusive** [əˋbjusɪv] (a.) 惡行惡語的，虐待的
A decade ago abusive teachers were more common than now.

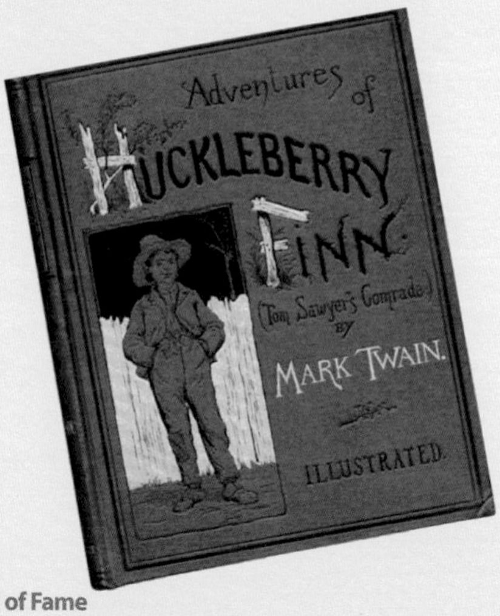

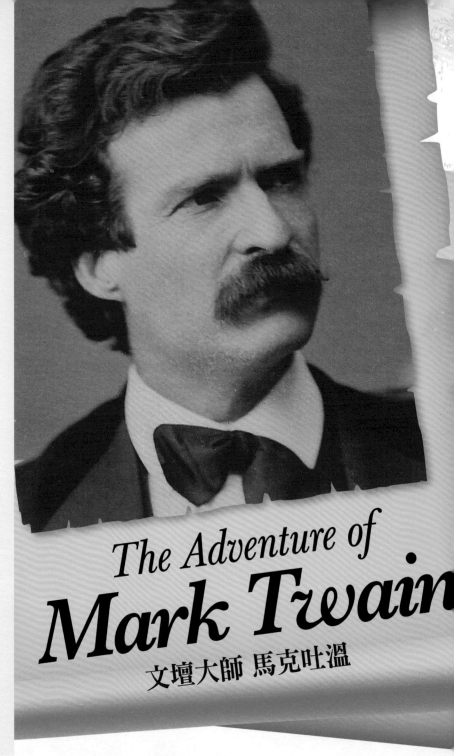

The Adventure of Mark Twain
文壇大師 馬克吐溫

朗讀 MP3 70 單字 MP3 71 英文文章導讀 MP3 72

Have you ever heard of Samuel Longhorn Clemens? No? Well, it's a good bet that you know who he is. He's more commonly known as Mark Twain, one of America's most famous authors. He was born on November 30, 1835 in a small town in Missouri, and you may not be aware that before Twain became a writer, he was a printer, a steamboat pilot and a miner! But he's most famous, of course, for his stories and novels. His most popular book is *The Adventures of Tom Sawyer*, and his most [1]**controversial** and historically meaningful book is The Adventures of Huckleberry Finn.

What's so special about *The Adventures of Huckleberry Finn*? Published in 1885, its main characters are Jim, a [8]**runaway** slave, and Huckleberry Finn, a young boy who runs away from home and helps Jim escape to freedom. The story [2]**takes place** in Missouri in 1835, thirty years before slavery was [3]**abolished** in 1865. Huck Finn [4]**narrates** the adventures he has with Jim and the friendship that develops between the [9]**unlikely** pair as they float down the Mississippi River in a [10]**homemade** [5]**raft**. As the story opens, Huck escapes from his guardians, Miss Watson and Miss Douglass, who want to [6]**civilize** him. However, Huck's drunk and [11]**abusive** father captures him and locks him away in a cabin in the woods. Huck [7]**manages** to escape again by faking his own death, and moves to nearby Jackson Island in the Mississippi.

中 Translation

你聽過山繆爾朗洪克萊門斯嗎？沒有？我敢打賭你一定知道他是誰，他比較為人熟知的名字是馬克吐溫，美國最著名的作家之一。他在一八三五年十一月三十日出生於密蘇里州一個小鎮，你或許不知道，在成為作家之前，他曾當過印刷工、汽船駕駛和礦工！但他最出名的當然是他的故事和小說。他最受歡迎的作品是《湯姆歷險記》，而最受爭議也最具歷史意義的一本書則是《哈克歷險記》。

《哈克歷險記》有何特別之處？本書出版於一八八五年，主人翁包括逃跑的奴隸吉姆和協助吉姆奔向自由的蹺家小男孩哈克。故事發生在一八三五年的密蘇里，距一八六五年廢除奴隸制度還有三十年。哈克敘述他和吉姆的冒險，以及這兩位看似不搭軋的夥伴划著自製木筏沿密西西比河而下期間發展出的友誼。故事一開始，哈克逃離想教化他的監護人華生小姐和道格拉斯小姐。但是，哈克酒醉施暴的父親逮住他，把他鎖在樹林裡的一間木屋，哈克裝死成功逃了出來，搬到附近密西西比河中的傑克森島。

JIM AND THE GHOST.

Language Guide

The Adventures of Tom Sawyer 湯姆歷險記

在本書中，作者將密西西比河 (Mississippi River) 的自然生活，描繪的像個樂園一般。聰明又俠義的主角湯姆，和幾個少年男女是如何逃過耿直、勤勉但囉唆的波莉阿姨 (Aunt Polly) 的鞭子？又怎樣逃老師的懲罰？他們發揮孩子氣的機智，在大人的苦笑中快樂的過日子。內容雖然頑皮，但夾雜不少對當時社會風俗的諷刺，所以作為成人的讀物也依然吸引人。

故事發生在十九世紀美國密西西比河地區，主角人物湯姆是個活潑調皮、愛幻想又富有冒險精神的男孩，因父母雙亡與弟弟一同被波莉阿姨收養。個性不受拘束的湯姆，不愛上課、喜歡與好友哈克 (Huckleberry Finn) 一起胡鬧。某日湯姆和哈克無意在山洞內發現了印第安喬 (Injun Joe) 私藏的金幣因而一夕致富，卻也因此展開一連串更驚奇的歷險故事。

馬克吐溫筆下那個充滿機智、勇於犯難的湯姆，早已成為美國人天真樂觀、開朗豪邁性格的代表人物，藉由如電影「法櫃奇兵」(*Raiders of the Lost Ark*) 少年版的冒險旅程，作者鋪陳出形形色色善惡冷暖的人間浮世繪，所有大人小孩的思維、情緒、邏輯，無不栩栩如生地呈現出來。這部小說主要是以馬克吐溫的家鄉為背景，藉由小主角的童年純真，襯托出成人社會中的現實與不公平，所以在童趣中帶著些許深意。

slavery 奴隸制度

美國奴隸制度從早期的英屬殖民時期就存在，到正式立國後仍然繼續。十八世紀已經有些州通過法律禁止蓄奴，但南方由於採棉業興盛需要人力，還是支持蓄奴。因為對奴隸制度的立場不同，美國漸漸分裂成對立的自由州 (free states) 和蓄奴州(slave states)，最後演變成南北戰爭 (Civil War)。南北戰後美國國會簽署《美國憲法第十三條修正議案》(Thirteenth Amendment)，才正式廢除美國奴隸制度。但是黑人在各方面還是常處於弱勢，也常遭到歧視。大多人認為馬克吐溫是反對奴隸制度，在《哈克歷險記》(*The Adventures of Huckleberry Finn*) 中就可看出，書中對原來為奴隸的黑人角色 Jim，有正面的刻畫，是主角忠實而溫暖的朋友。

Vocabulary Bank

1) **endure** [ɪn`dʊr] (v.) 忍受，持續
I can't endure your awful singing any longer!

2) **dilemma** [dɪ`lɛmə] (n.) 進退兩難，困境
The government is faced with the dilemma of raising taxes or cutting services.

3) **warm-hearted** [`wɔrm`hɑrtɪd] (a.) 親切的，好心腸的
Sally wants a husband who is honest and warm-hearted.

4) **intelligent** [ɪn`tɛlədʒənt] (a.) 聰明的，有才智的
Dolphins are very intelligent creatures.

5) **largely** [`lɑrdʒli] (adv.) 大部份，主要地
The local economy is based largely on agriculture.

6) **revolutionary** [ˌrɛvə`luʃəˌnɛri] (a.) 革命（性）的，完全創新的
The scientist made a revolutionary discovery.

7) **perception** [pɚ`sɛpʃən] (n.) 認知，看法
There is a public perception that the government is incompetent.

8) **occupy** [`ɑkjəˌpaɪ] (v.) 占有（時間、空間地位等）
The company's office occupies the fifth floor of the building.

9) **literature** [`lɪtərəˌtʃɚ] (n.) 文學，文學作品
(a.) literary [`lɪtəˌrɛri] 文學的，文藝的
Donna studied French literature in grad school.

進階字彙

10) **confide (in)** [kən`faɪd] (v.) 向（某人）吐露祕密，與（某人）交心
If I confide in you, will you promise not to tell anyone my secret?

11) **a.k.a.** [`e`k`e] (phr.) 又名，也稱做，為 also known as 的縮寫
Cassius Clay, a.k.a. Muhammad Ali, is one of the greatest boxers of all time.

朗讀 MP3 73 單字 MP3 74 英文文章導讀 MP3 75

It's there on Jackson Island that Huck meets Jim, Miss Watson's slave. Jim [10]**confides** in Huck that he ran away because Miss Watson was going to sell him to a place where he would [1]**endure** even harsher conditions. This creates a [2]**dilemma** for Huck: should he return Jim to Miss Watson or break the law by helping him escape? At first, Huck thinks he's doing something wrong by helping Jim. In those days, slaves were considered property and not people. However, as Huck spends more time with Jim, he comes to realize that Jim is kind, [3]**warm-hearted**, and just as human as a white person.

Back in 1885, many people were extremely racist. It was common for whites to **1** **look down on** blacks, believing they were less [4]**intelligent** and [5]**largely** inferior. The Adventures of Huckleberry Finn was [6]**revolutionary** because it shows that one's skin color doesn't determine one's character. In the story, Jim, a black slave, is a good person, but some of the white characters, such as Huck'sfather, are bad. The story questioned the [7]**perceptions** white people had of African Americans. This made a lot of people angry at the time the book was published. In fact, for

©scatterkeir/flickr.com

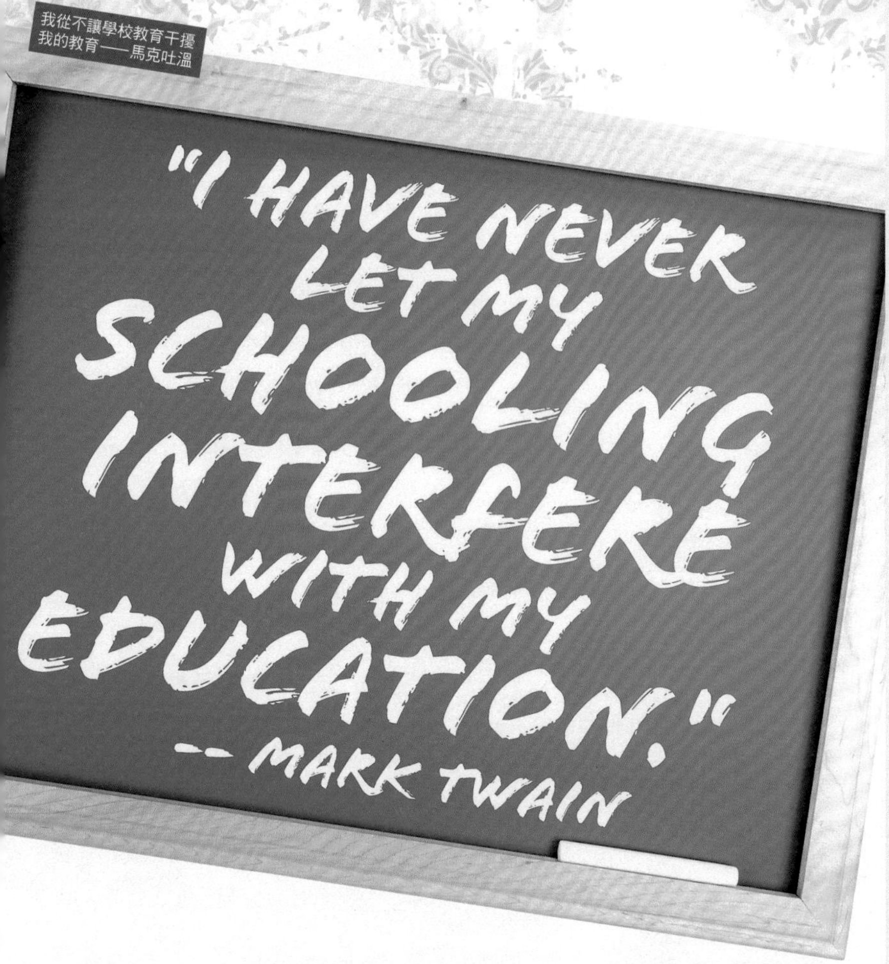
我從不讓學校教育干擾
我的教育——馬克吐溫
"I HAVE NEVER
LET MY
SCHOOLING
INTERFERE
WITH MY
EDUCATION."
-- MARK TWAIN

a time it was even banned from some public libraries. Even though the book made people angry, it greatly influenced many people's ideas about slavery and race. Given the important place Huckleberry Finn [8]**occupies** in American [9]**literature**, it's not hard to see why Samuel Clemens, [11]**a.k.a.** Mark Twain, is so famous!

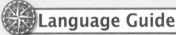

中 Translation

哈克就是在傑克森島上遇到吉姆——華生小姐的奴隸。吉姆向哈克透露，他會逃跑是因為華生小姐要把他賣掉，在那裡他得忍受更嚴酷的環境。這讓哈克陷入兩難：他該把吉姆送還給華生小姐，還是違法協助他逃跑？起初，哈克認為自己幫助吉姆是不對的。在那個年代，奴隸被視為財產而不是人。然而，在與吉姆朝夕相處之後，哈克逐漸了解吉姆是個善良、熱心的人，跟白人一樣有人性。

在一八八五年，很多人都有嚴重的種族主義者。白人普遍瞧不起黑人，認為黑人的智慧較低，是次等人種。《哈克歷險記》顛覆了傳統，因為它證明膚色不會決定人格。在故事裡，黑奴吉姆是個好人，但一些白人角色，例如哈克的父親，就非善類。這個故事質疑了白種人對非裔美國人的看法，書出版之後，許多人因此火冒三丈，事實上有一段時間甚至被一些公立圖書館拒於門外。儘管這本書引起人們憤怒，卻大大影響了許多人對奴隸和種族的想法。從《哈克歷險記》在美國文學占有如此重要的地位，就不難看出為什麼山繆爾克萊門斯（即馬克吐溫）這麼出名了！

Tongue-tied No More

1 look down on 輕視，瞧不起

look down 原意是「往下看」，「往下看著……」要說 look down + at + sb./sth.。look down 可引申為「輕視，瞧不起」的意思，可說 look down + on + sb./sth.，或 look down your nose + at sb./sth.。

A: Why does Karen look down on Lisa?
凱倫為什麼瞧不起麗莎？

B: Because Lisa doesn't have a college education.
因為她沒有大學畢業。

Language Guide

African American 非裔美國人

African American 是美國人口中的黑人，是指從撒哈拉以南非洲 (Sub-Saharan Africa) 移居美國的人民。從十六世紀開始，非洲黑人被英國送去美國做奴隸。在美國獨立之後，非洲黑人的奴隸身分並沒有被改變。十九世紀的南北戰爭，他們在名義上擺脫了奴隸的身分，卻沒有獲得真正的自由。終於到了一九五〇、六〇年代，他們展開一連串的民權運動，認同自我，爭取平等，不再認為自己的膚色代表低等，因而提出「black people」 和指美國黑奴後代的「negro」(在西班牙語中意思為黑色)區分。後來為了更具有歷史含義，因此以「African American」表示移民美國的非洲人來稱呼他們。

筆名 Mark Twain 的來由

mark twain 意思是標記二噚深（也就是 mark number two），噚 (fathom) 在古英文中的本意是兩臂之長，後引申用為長度單位，大約三百七十公分。Mark Twain 是水運領航員的專業術語，表示水深二噚寬是輪船可以安全通過的最小範圍。這個筆名來自於克萊門斯早年的水手生涯。在一八八三年的作品——《密西西比河上的生活》(*Life on the Mississippi*) 裡頭，克萊門斯提到這個筆名其實並不是出自於他的想法。筆名其實是從密西西比河上的老船長艾賽亞賽勒斯 (Isaiah Sellers) 而來的，老船長喜歡將他熟知的水文知識和船舶生活情況發表在報章雜誌上，並在文章的最後簽上 Mark Twain。在接到這位老船長的死訊時，克萊門斯才正開始在報社工作，需要一個筆名，克萊門斯便將這個筆名繼承下來，終身所用。

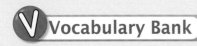

Vocabulary Bank

1) **recall** [rɪˋkɔl] (v.) 回想，想起
I can't recall the last time I had a meal this good.

2) **superficial** [ˌsupɚˋfɪʃəl] (a.) 膚淺的，表面的
Nick always seems to date pretty but superficial women.

3) **practically** [ˋpræktɪkli] (adv.) 幾乎，差不多，實際上
We were practically the only people in the restaurant.

4) **lyric** [ˋlɪrɪk] (n.) 歌詞（固定用複數 lyrics）
Do you know who wrote the lyrics to this song?

5) **anthem** [ˋænθəm] (n.) 頌歌，國歌，聖歌
Do you know the words to our college anthem?

6) **banner** [ˋbænɚ] (n.) 旗幟，橫幅
The soldier at the front of the parade carried a banner.

7) **detective** [dɪˋtɛktɪv] (n.)（私人）偵探，警探
My little brother likes to read detective stories.

8) **coin** [kɔɪn] (v./n.) 創造（新詞彙、說法）；錢幣
Do you know who coined the term "yuppie"?

進階字彙

9) **extravagant** [ɪkˋstrævəgənt] (a.) 奢侈的，浪費的，（價格）過高的
Shelly likes to give extravagant gifts.

©Penguin Group

© Saint Paul Public Lib

F. Scott Fitzgerld's Gatsby — Was He Really So Great?
費茲傑羅《大亨小傳》

朗讀 MP3 76 單字 MP3 77 英文文章導讀 MP3 78

"Whenever you feel like criticizing anyone, just remember that all the people in this world haven't had the advantages that you've had." This is the advice from his father that Nick Carraway [1)]**recalls** at the beginning of *The Great Gatsby*, F. Scott Fitzgerald's most famous novel. Nick is the story's narrator, and for the most part he manages to follow this advice. Readers, however, are usually less successful. The story, set in 1920s America, involves characters so **shallow** and [2]**superficial** that they [3]**practically** beg for criticism.

F. Scott Fitzgerald is widely considered to be one of the greatest American writers of the 20th century. Born in 1896 to Irish-Catholic parents in St. Paul, Minnesota, he was named after distant cousin Francis Scott Key, who wrote the [4]**lyrics** to the U.S. national [5]**anthem**, "The Star-Spangled [6]**Banner**." Fitzgerald himself got an early start to his writing career by publishing a [7]**detective** story in his school paper at the age of 12.

A poor student, Fitzgerald left Princeton in the middle of his senior year to fight in World War I. After the war, he wrote short stories for magazines, many of which are still quite popular today. Scott, as he was known, married his wife Zelda in 1920. Hardly a match made in heaven, the couple's relationship was complicated by Fitzgerald's heavy drinking and Zelda's mental illness. For brief periods, though, the couple lived an [9]**extravagant** lifestyle typical of the Jazz Age—a term [8]**coined** by Fitzgerald himself.

中 Translation

「每當你想批評別人，請記得不是世上每一個人都有你掌握的優勢。」這是史考特費茲傑羅最著名的小說《大亨小傳》開場時，尼克賈拉威所回憶父親的忠告。尼克是故事的敘述者，大多時候他都盡力遵照父親的訓示，但讀者通常比較沒辦法做到。這本以一九二〇年代美國為背景的故事，裡頭的角色膚淺又表面，幾乎招來全面的批評。

史考特費茲傑羅被公認為二十世紀最偉大的美國作家之一。一八九六年出生於明尼蘇達州聖保羅市，雙親為愛爾蘭天主教徒，他的名字是取自遠房表親法蘭西斯史考基伊，也就是美國國歌〈星條旗〉作詞人。費茲傑羅很早就開啟寫作生涯，十二歲便在校刊上發表一則偵探故事。

念書不認真的費茲傑羅，在普林斯頓念到大四時，輟學去參與第一次世界大戰。戰後，他替雜誌寫短篇小說，其中許多至今仍廣受歡迎。被稱為史考特的他，於一九二〇年娶了薩爾達為妻。這對夫妻完全稱不上天作之合，由於費茲傑羅的酗酒和薩爾達的精神疾病，兩人的關係困難重重。但這對夫妻曾數度短暫過著「爵士年代」典型的奢華生活——爵士年代是費茲傑羅自創的名詞。

Language Guide

Irish-Catholic 愛爾蘭天主教徒

愛爾蘭宗教衝突始自於十六世紀的宗教改革，英國脫離天主教 (Catholicism)，改奉新教 (Protestantism)，但愛爾蘭人仍信仰天主教，因此雙方衝突不斷。英國人為了守住統治權，大舉鎮壓天主教徒。十九世紀時，愛爾蘭的環境狀況非常惡劣，主食馬鈴薯歉收，造成「大饑荒」(the Great Famine)，約一百萬人餓死，政府救災無效，迫使許多走投無路的愛爾蘭人紛紛移民美國。

"The Star-Spangled Banner" 星條旗

《星條旗》是詩人弗朗西斯 (Francis Scott Key) 在美國一八一二年戰爭中，看見美軍英勇抵抗敵軍的所做出的詩，後以約翰史密斯 (John Stafford Smith) 作的曲子為配曲。一九三一年正式成為美國國歌 (national anthem)，常和《永遠的星條旗》(The Stars and Stripes Forever) 搞混。

The Jazz Age 爵士時代

十九世紀末期，爵士樂漸漸興起。第二次世界大戰 (WWI) 後，爵士樂已從紐奧良 (New Orleans) 傳出，成為美國新藝術的一支。因此用 jazz 這個字來代表同時期，一次大戰後至經濟大蕭條 (the Great Depression) 前美國經濟最輝煌的黃金時代，又稱做咆哮的二〇年代 (the Roaring Twenties)。工業革命帶動起來的繁榮經濟，一夜致富發橫財在這個時代不再是夢，美國人開始過度浪漫地嚮往新時代，奢侈享樂變成生活宗旨，炫耀性消費成為時代潮流。一九二九年華爾街 (Wall Street) 股市突然宣告崩盤，美國陷入經濟大蕭條，戰後迷失的一代受到突然夢醒的墜落感，咆哮時代就此終結。

Vocabulary Bank

1) **pursuit** [pɚ`sut] (n.) 追蹤，追求
The bank robbers were caught by the police after a high-speed pursuit.

2) **arrogant** [`ærəgənt] (a.) 傲慢的，自大的
It's arrogant to think you're smarter than everybody else.

3) **moral** [`mɔrəl] (n.) 道德倫理
Parents should teach their children good morals.

4) **unfortunately** [ʌn`fɔrtʃənɪtli] (adv.) 遺憾地，可惜
Unfortunately, I won't have time to do any sightseeing while I'm in Paris.

5) **suspicious** [sə`spɪʃəs] (a.) 多疑的，可疑的
The villagers are very suspicious of strangers.

6) **unworthy** [ʌn`wɚði] (a.) 不值得的，不配得到的
The politician was unworthy of the people's trust.

7) **affection** [ə`fɛkʃən] (n.) 愛，情感
George has a deep affection for his parents.

8) **mistress** [`mɪstrɪs] (n.) 情婦
Many wealthy men have mistresses.

9) **admiration** [͵ædmə`reʃən] (n.) 欽佩，佩服
The teacher earned the admiration of his students.

10) **sincerity** [sɪn`sɛrəti] (n.) 誠意，真誠
Why do you doubt my sincerity?

11) **deserve** [dɪ`zɝv] (v.) 應受（賞罰）
I hope that killer gets the punishment he deserves

進階字彙

12) **socialite** [`soʃə͵laɪt] (n.) 社交名流
Most New York socialites live in Manhattan.

13) **lavish** [`lævɪʃ] (a.) 鋪張的，奢華的
Celebrities often have lavish weddings.

朗讀 MP3 78 單字 MP3 79 英文文章導讀 MP3 80

The Great Gatsby is the story of Jay Gatsby's [1]**pursuit** of the love of his life, the [12]**socialite** Daisy Buchanan. Separated by World War I, Gatsby returns to find Daisy already married to Tom Buchanan, an [2]**arrogant** millionaire with more money than [3]**morals**. After making his own fortune by illegal means, Gatsby moves into a mansion across the bay from the Buchanans. With his [13]**lavish** weekly parties, he's soon the center of attention, even though nobody seems to know anything about him. Over the course of a summer, Gatsby tries to win back Daisy's love.

[4]**Unfortunately**, the course of love is never smooth. Daisy's crowd soon becomes [5]**suspicious** about the source of Gatsby's wealth, and Daisy herself proves to be [6]**unworthy** of Gatsby's [7]**affection**. Towards the end, she **1** **sits idly by** as her husband blames Gatsby for the death of his [8]**mistress**, Myrtle, who Daisy herself has accidentally killed.

There are few characters in the story worthy of [9]**admiration**. George Wilson, Myrtle's simple, hardworking husband, is one. Yet even he can't get a break. Despite his

[10]**sincerity**, his wife doesn't love him; and because of his poverty, she doesn't even respect him. He does, however, earn a little respect, and plenty of pity, from readers. That's more than can be said of most of the novel's characters, who probably [11]**deserve** more criticism than one book can hold. And that, in addition to the advice Nick receives from his father, may be another reason why the narrator doesn't even try.

中 Translation

《大亨小傳》是傑伊蓋茲比追求畢生所愛（社會名流黛西布坎南）的故事。因一次世界大戰分隔兩地，蓋茲比回鄉後發現黛西已經嫁給湯姆布坎南——一個有錢但沒什麼道德的傲慢富翁。蓋茲比以非法手段致富後，搬進布坎南家海灣對岸的豪宅。每星期都舉辦奢華派對的他，很快就成為矚目焦點，儘管似乎沒人知道他的來歷。整個夏天，蓋茲比都在試著贏回黛西的芳心。

可惜，求愛過程老不順利。黛西那夥人很快開始懷疑蓋茲比的財富來源，而事實也證明黛西並不值得蓋茲比傾心。最後，她只是呆坐著聽任丈夫將情婦蜜托之死歸咎於蓋茲比，但其實是黛西誤殺的。

故事中沒有多少角色值得推崇，喬治威爾森是一個，他是蜜托的丈夫，純樸又努力工作，但連他也難逃命運捉弄。雖然誠懇老實，妻子卻不愛他，甚至嫌他窮而不尊重他，不過他的確贏得了讀者些許的敬重以及滿滿的同情，這已經比小說裡大多數罄竹難書的角色好多了，所以，除了因為父親早有忠告之外，這或許也是這位敘述者根本懶得批評人的原因。

Tongue-tied No More

1 sit/stand idly by 袖手旁觀

idly [ˋaɪdlɪ] 是形容詞「懶散地，閒散地，無所事事地」。一個人「閒散地坐／站在一旁」，在英文中衍生的意義就是「袖手旁觀」。

A : Did you read the article about the famine in West Africa?
你讀了那篇有關西非飢荒的報導嗎？

B : Yeah. How can governments stand idly by when so many people are suffering?
有啊。那麼多人在受苦，政府怎麼可以袖手旁觀？

Language Guide

費茲傑羅與太太

一九二〇年出版第一本書——《塵世樂園》(This Side of Paradise) 就榮登暢銷排行，費茲傑羅嚐到名利雙收的滋味。同年便馬上與富家女友賽爾妲 (Zelda Sayre) 結婚。

一九二五年，費茲傑羅出版他的嘔心力作《大亨小傳》，儘管這本書被後世作家讚譽為二十世紀經典小說的第二名，但是當時的銷量並不好。為了維持奢靡的生活開銷，費茲傑羅開始為報章雜誌撰寫小說、短文，以賺取高額稿費。只是對他來說，為了賺錢而寫出的粗糙作品，他自己都非常痛恨。同時，賽爾妲與他的感情開始出現裂痕，在外面有其他的感情。費茲傑羅最痛苦的三〇年代就此展開，賽爾妲因精神崩潰而住進療養院，並在療養院度過餘生。高額的醫療費用以及女兒的學費壓得費茲傑羅喘不過氣。後來他便開始為好萊塢編劇，並著手《最後一個影壇大亨》(The Love of the Last Tycoon) 這本長篇小說。一九四〇年，他因心臟病發而猝死，當時《最後一個影壇大亨》初稿只完成四分之三，隔年他的好友才將其遺作出版。

《大亨小傳》雖不是描述自己的故事，卻也真切地道出他的人生寫照。費茲傑羅夫婦在美國經濟最輝煌的咆哮年代裡，天天過著奢侈放縱的派對生活，無法在同一處所居住超過一年的他們，居無定所，到處去旅行，也因為這樣的生活方式，他們被稱為爵士時代的王與后，也是那個時代中真實的文化縮影。

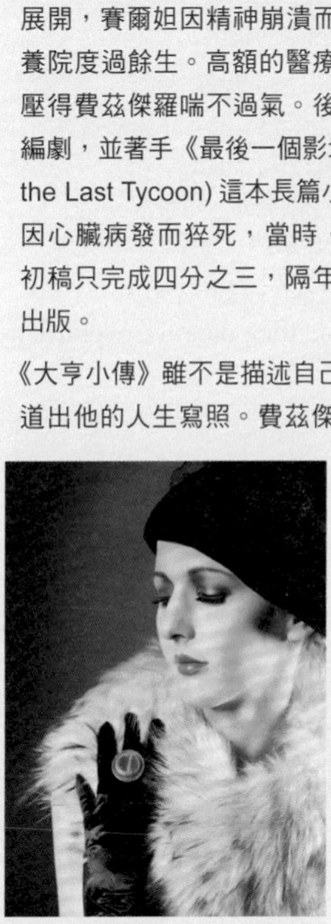

Vocabulary Bank

1) **slum** [slʌm] (n.) 貧民窟
The slum has no electricity or running water.

2) **entertainer** [ˌɛntɚˋtenɚ] (n.) 表演者，藝人
Many famous entertainers have appeared on the talk show.

3) **alcoholic** [ˌælkəˋhɔlɪk] (n.) 酒鬼，酗酒者
Most alcoholics begin drinking at an early age.

4) **abandon** [əˋbændən] (v.) 放棄，拋棄
It is illegal to abandon or abuse a pet.

5) **strain** [stren] (n.) 沈重的壓力，（身心的）緊張狀態
The strain of losing his job was too much to bear.

6) **breakdown** [ˋbrekˌdaʊn] (n.) 精神崩潰，體力衰竭
The woman had a nervous breakdown after her husband left her.

7) **commit** [kəˋmɪt] (v.)（下令）把…送進（醫院、監獄）
Dale's parents had him committed after he tried to kill himself.

8) **orphanage** [ˋɔrfənɪdʒ] (n.) 孤兒院
We donated clothes and toys to the local orphanage.

9) **odd** [ɑd] (a.) 臨時的，不固定的
Peter was only able to find odd jobs during the recession.

10) **production** [prəˋdʌkʃən] (n.) 戲劇演出
The Drama Department is putting on a production of Hamlet this fall.

11) **comedy** [ˋkɑmədi] (n.) 喜劇
(n.) comedian [kəˋmidiən] 諧星，喜劇演員
(a.) comedic [ˋkɑmədɪk] 喜劇的
(a.) comic [ˋkɑmɪk] 喜劇的，滑稽的
Kelly likes to watch Jim Carrey comedies.

12) **convince** [kənˋvɪns] (v.) 說服
The kids convinced their parents to let them have pizza for dinner.

進階字彙

13) **troupe** [trup] (n.)（演員等表演者）一團、一班
The acting troupe is performing a Shakespeare play.

14) **acrobat** [ˋækrəˌbæt] (n.) 雜技演員
Did you see the acrobats perform at the circus?

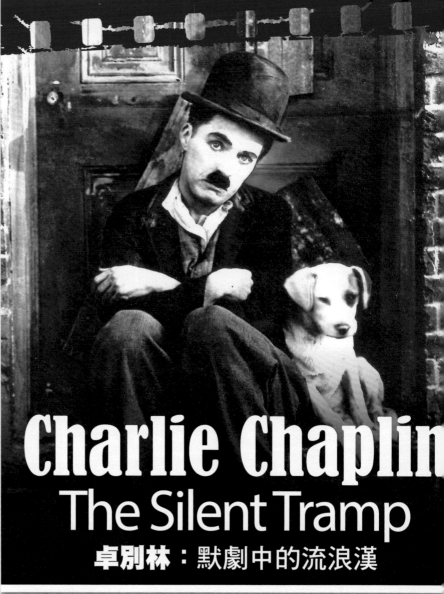

Charlie Chaplin
The Silent Tramp
卓別林：默劇中的流浪漢

© 達志 / UPI PHOT

朗讀 MP3 82 單字 MP3 83 英文文章導讀 MP3 84

On April 16, 1889, Charles Spencer Chaplin was bor in a London [1]**slum** to music hall [2]**entertainers** Charle and Hannah Chaplin. Although his father enjoyed modes success as a singer, Charlie didn't have an easy childhooc Charles Sr. was an [3]**alcoholic**, and [4]**abandoned** the famil when Charlie was just three, leaving Hannah to raise hin and his older half-brother Sydney on her own. Hannal was able to support them for a while with her singing but soon began having problems with her voice. Wher she lost her voice in the middle of a show one evening the stage manager called the five-year-old Charlie, whc he'd heard singing earlier, onto the stage to finish th performance. Unfortunately, Hannah's voice never returned and the [5]**strain** led to a mental [6]**breakdown**. She was [7]**committed** to a mental hospital, and the brothers spent the rest of their childhoods in and out of poorhouses and [8]**orphanages**.

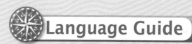

Determined to follow his parents onto the stage, Charlie joined the Eight Lancashire Lads, a clog dancing [13]**troupe**, when he was eight. But his stint as a dancer didn't last long, and he was forced to work [9]**odd** jobs to make ends meet. Charlie got his break as an actor in 1903, playing a small role in a West End [10]**production** of *Sherlock Holmes*. Meanwhile, Sydney had become a performer in Fred Karno's [11]**comedy** company. He [12]**convinced** the former [14]**acrobat** to hire his brother, and within two years he was one of Karno's most popular comedians. This gave Charlie the chance to tour the United States with the company, and during a show in New York he caught the eye of comedy director Mack Sennett.

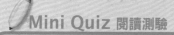

Mini Quiz 閱讀測驗

Which of the following is NOT true about Charlie Chaplin?

(A) He toured the U.S. with a comedy company.
(B) Both of his parents were singers.
(C) He convinced Fred Karno to hire his brother.
(D) He wasn't a dancer for very long.

中 Translation

一八八九年四月十六日，查理史賓賽卓別林出生於倫敦的一個貧民窟，父母親為音樂廳的藝人查爾斯卓別林和漢娜卓別林夫婦。雖然父親是個小有名氣的歌手，但查理的童年並不好過。老查爾斯是個酒鬼，在查理三歲的時候拋棄了家庭，留下漢娜獨力撫養他和他同母異父的哥哥席尼。剛開始漢娜還能靠唱歌撫養他們，但不久後她的嗓子就開始出現問題。某天晚上她表演到一半時完全失聲，稍早聽過查理唱歌的舞台經理便要五歲的查理上台完成表演。不幸的是，漢娜的嗓子再也恢復，這樣的打擊導致她精神崩潰，最後她被送進精神病院，兩兄弟就在進出救濟院和孤兒院中度過童年。

查理決心要跟隨父母的腳步走上舞台，八歲時加入了蘭開夏八少年劇團，一個木屐舞團。但他的舞者生涯並沒有持續太久，還被迫去打零工來餬口。一九〇三年，查理好運降臨，在倫東西區上演的《夏洛克福爾摩斯》舞台劇中飾演一個小角色。此時，席尼已經在佛瑞德卡諾喜劇劇團表演，他說服這位雜技演員雇用他的弟弟，不到兩年查理已經是卡諾劇團裡最受歡迎的諧星之一，這讓查理有了和劇團一起巡演美國的機會，並且就在紐約的一場演出中，他吸引了喜劇片導演麥克塞納特的目光。

Language Guide

music hall 音樂廳表演

music hall 除了可以用來指娛樂表演的場地，也可指十九世紀中期至二十世紀中期流行於英國的一種娛樂表演。這種形式通常融合了時下流行的歌曲與喜劇，或是特技雜耍表演。音樂廳表演源自於沙龍酒吧 (saloon bar)，讓觀眾繳交入場費來欣賞歌唱、跳舞、或是戲劇表演。music hall 不同於其他戲院之處在於，觀眾的座位通常都會圍繞著一張張桌子，讓觀眾在欣賞表演之餘還可以喝酒或是抽菸。興建於一八五二年的坎特伯里音樂廳 (Canterbury Music Hall) 被視為是第一個正規的音樂廳，而創建者 Charles Morton 也被譽為音樂廳之父 (Father of the Halls)。

poorhouse 救濟院

poorhouse 也可被稱為 workhouse，通常是由政府建立，目的是提供窮困的人一個生活的地方。從查爾斯狄更斯 (Charles Dickens) 在作品中所描述的救濟院來看，早期救濟院的貧民或孤兒並不見得會獲得公平對待，也有強制勞動或體罰的狀況發生。十九世紀到二十世紀初期，美國的救濟院常坐落農場中，這種形式被稱為 poor farm，主要是提供年長者或行動不便者居住，健康狀況許可的人必須要種植穀物或是打掃等。

The West End 倫敦西區

倫敦西區是位於英國倫敦西區的劇院區，共約有四十家劇院，有劇院天地 (*Theaterland*) 之稱，與美國百老匯 (Broadway) 齊名。在西區上演時間最久的音樂劇為《悲慘世界》(*Les Misérables*)，上演最久的非音樂劇則是著名推理作家阿嘉莎克莉絲蒂 (Agatha Christie) 的《捕鼠器》(*The Mousetrap*)，已有五十九年的歷史。

解答 (C)

Vocabulary Bank

1) **debut** [deˋbju] (n./v.) 處女秀，首度演出
The singer made her debut on a TV talent show.

2) **memorable** [ˋmɛmərəbəl] (a.)
(adv.) memorably [ˋmɛmərəbəli] 難忘的，值得的
The singer gave a memorable performance at the charity concert.

3) **outfit** [ˋaut͵fɪt] (n.) 全套服裝
Shannon bought a new outfit to wear to the party.

4) **salary** [ˋsæləri] (n.) 薪資
It's hard to support a family on such a low salary.

5) **artistic** [ɑrˋtɪstɪk] (a.) 藝術的，美術的
The boy showed artistic talent at an early age.

6) **elaborate** [ɪˋlæbərɪt] (a.) 製作精巧的，裝飾華麗的
Michael Jackson was famous for his elaborate outfits.

7) **touching** [tʌtʃɪŋ] (a.) 感人的，動人的
The director's latest film is a touching love story.

進階字彙

8) **slapstick** [ˋslæp͵stɪk] (a./n.)（以喧鬧、肢體語言為主的）鬧劇（的）
The comedian is famous for his slapstick routines.

9) **baggy** [ˋbægi] (a.) 寬鬆而下垂的，袋狀的
Teenagers these days like to wear baggy clothes.

10) **bumbling** [ˋbʌmblɪŋ] (a.) 笨手笨腳的，糊里糊塗的
The bumbling player got taken out of the game.

11) **good-hearted** [ˋgud ˋhɑrtɪd] (a.) 好心腸的，仁慈的
The little boy was adopted by a good-hearted couple.

12) **vagrant** [ˋvegrənt] (n.) 流浪漢
Vagrants often sleep on the park benches.

13) **entice** [ɪnˋtaɪs] (v.) 誘使，慫恿
The store cut prices to entice shoppers.

14) **pathos** [ˋpeθɑs / ˋpeθos] (n.)（文學、音樂等作品）激起憐憫、同情的因素
Dickens makes effective use of pathos in his novels.

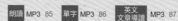

朗讀 MP3 85 單字 MP3 86 英文文章導讀 MP3 87

Sennett was so impressed by Charlie's performance as a comic drunk that he offered him a one-year, $150-a-week contract at Keystone Studios. And so he moved to California in 1913 and began his silent film career. While Charlie's first appearance in the [8]**slapstick** comedy *Making a Living* was forgettable, his next film, *Kid Auto Races at Venice*, marked the [1]**debut** of his most [2]**memorable** character. When Sennett asked him to dress in a comedy [3]**outfit**, Charlie started borrowing things from the other actors: a derby, tight coat, [9]**baggy** pants, cane, and shoes so big he had to wear them on the wrong feet to keep them from falling off. The Tramp was an instant hit with audiences, and Charlie was soon writing and directing his own films. By the end of his year at Keystone, he'd made over 30 comedy shorts, starring as the [10]**bumbling** but [11]**good-hearted** [12]**vagrant** in most of them.

©Gertjan R. / comm

[13]**Enticed** by a [4]**salary** of $1,250 a week—one of the highest in the world at the time—Charlie signed with Essanay Studios in 1915. Given more [5]**artistic** freedom, he added depth and [14]**pathos** to his comedy in films like *The Tramp*, widely regarded as his first classic. Just a year later,

Charlie left Essanay for Mutual Film, which paid him $670,000 to make 12 films. His Mutual comedies—like *One A.M.* and *Easy Street*—with their sharp humor and [6]**elaborate** sets, turned him into an international star. In 1917, Charlie built his own studio and signed a million dollar contract with First National, which gave him the resources to make classics like *The Kid*, a [7]**touching** story about slum life inspired by his own childhood.

Mini Quiz 閱讀測驗

What was Charlie Chaplin's most memorable character?

(A) The Vagrant
(B) The Tramp
(C) The Kid
(D) The Comic Drunk

中 Translation

塞納特對查理表演的喜劇式醉漢大為驚豔，他提出一份週薪一百五十元、與基石電影公司簽訂一年的合約。於是查理在一九一三年搬到加州，開始他的默劇生涯。雖然查理在螢幕處女作《謀生之路》這部鬧劇中的演出令人印象不深，但他在下一部電影《威尼斯兒童賽車》奠定了他最令人難忘的角色形象。塞納特要求他穿著喜劇服裝，查理便開始向其他演員借道具：圓頂禮帽、緊身外套、大寬褲、拐杖和一雙大到必須左右腳反穿才不會掉的鞋。「流浪漢」一角立刻風靡觀眾，不久後查理也開始寫劇本和執導自己的戲。與基石一年的合約將盡時，他已經製作了超過三十部喜劇短片，大多數都是扮演笨手笨腳但內心善良的流浪漢。

一九一五年，在週薪一千兩百五十美元的誘惑下（當時全世界最高的週薪之一），查理和艾森奈電影公司簽下合約。擁有更多的創作自由，查理在《流浪漢》（一般公認是他第一部經典之作）等片中加進了深度與感傷，短短一年後，查理離開艾森奈電影公司，進入共通電影公司，共通付他六十七萬美元拍攝十二部電影。他在共通所拍攝的作品——例如《凌晨一點鐘》和《安樂街》——有犀利的幽默和精心設計的場景，讓他成為國際巨星。一九一七年，查理成立自己的攝影棚，並與第一國家電影公司簽訂百萬美元的合約，給他資源創作出許多經典作品，例如《孤兒流浪記》，一部以他自身童年為靈感來源的感人貧民窟故事。

Language Guide

Kid Auto Races at Venice
《威尼斯兒童賽車》

在片長十一分鐘的《威尼斯兒童賽車》這部電影中，卓別林是加州一場兒童賽車比賽的觀眾。但卓別林卻製造了許多麻煩，像是妨礙比賽的進行或是阻擋攝影師的拍攝。這部電影是在一場真正的兒童賽車比賽拍攝，所以卓別林是真的在一場賽車觀眾前拍戲。而卓別林經典的「流浪漢」(The Tramp) 形象首度在這部電影出現，是默片時代的重要象徵。

The Kid《孤兒流浪記》

《孤兒流浪記》是卓別林自編、自導自演的作品，也是他第一部長片。故事描述未婚媽媽 Edna 埃德娜因為生活困苦，決定把她的新生兒放進一台轎車中， 希望孩子能有更好的生活。不料這台轎車遭竊，孩子也被竊賊丟棄。再度以流浪漢形象演出的卓別林收留了這個嬰兒。孩子就這樣一天天長大，偶爾丟幾顆石頭打破別人的玻璃，好讓卓別林可以靠著修補玻璃來賺錢。而此時，孩子的生母成為巨星，想要找回當年遺棄的孩子。孩子也被醫生發現不是卓別林的親生兒子而強制送到孤兒院，但還是被他搶了回來藏身在廉價旅館。之後，旅館老闆發現這就是 Edna 懸賞要找的孩子，便把孩子送回她身邊。卓別林相當失落，但一覺醒來後如願與 Edna 母子團聚。這個作品被視為是他自己的童年寫照，內容也正如電影開頭提到的，是一部笑中帶淚的喜劇片 (A comedy with a smile—and perhaps a tear)，也成為一九二一年第二賣座電影。

解答 (B)

Vocabulary Bank

1) **distribution** [ˌdɪstrə`bjuʃən] (n.) 經銷，配銷
Who owns the distribution rights to that product?

2) **feature** [4] (n.)（電影）長片，正片，亦作 feature motion picture/film
The Sugarland Express was Steven Spielberg's first feature film.

3) **cameo** [`kæmɪˌo] (n.) 客串演出
Several famous actors make cameo appearances in the film.

4) **critical** [`krɪtɪkəl] (a.) 評論的，批評的
(n.) critic [`krɪtɪk] 評論家，批評家
The band's first album was a critical success.

5) **financial** [faɪ`nænʃəl] (a.) 財務的，財政的，金融的
(adv.) financially [faɪ`nænʃəli]
There's a rumor that the company is having financial difficulties.

6) **box-office** [bɑks `ɔfɪs] (n.) 票房（收入）
The movie did better at the box office than expected.

7) **professional** [pr `fɛʃənəl] (a.) 專業的，職業的
Cynthia wants to be a professional musician.

8) **carry over** [`kæri `ovɚ] (phr.) 從某領域、狀態延續到另一個領域、狀態
The man's success in business carried over into his political career.

9) **divorce** [dɪ`vors] (n./v.) 離婚
I hear that Mark's wife wants a divorce.

10) **nasty** [`næsti] (a.) 難處理、忍受的，惡劣的，惡意的
The nasty weather kept us indoors all day.

11) **playwright** [`pleˌraɪt] (n.) 劇作家
Shakespeare is England's most famous playwright.

12) **outrage** [`aʊtˌredʒ] (v./n.) 激怒；憤怒
(a.) outrageous [aʊtˌredʒəs] 離譜的，不合理的
The public was outraged by the policeman's murder.

13) **communist** [`kɑmjəˌnɪst] (n./a.)（常為大寫）共產黨員，共產主義者；共產黨的
Many Indonesian communists were killed in the 1960s.

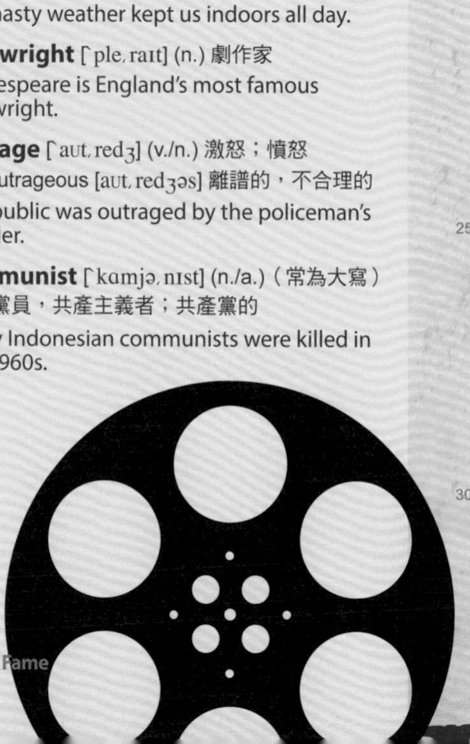

朗讀 MP3 88 單字 MP3 89 英文文章導讀 MP3 90

In 1919, Charlie got together with fellow Hollywoo stars Mary Pickford and Douglas Fairbanks, and director W D. Griffith, to found the United Artists film [1]**distributio** company. Now that he had complete creative control, h focused his efforts on [2]**feature**-length films. *A Woman i Paris* (1923), a romantic drama in which Charlie only had [3]**cameo** role, was followed by *The Gold Rush* (1925), his mo successful silent comedy, and *Circus* (1928), which wo him his first Academy Award. When talkies took over in th 1930s, Charlie decided to keep the Tramp silent, afraid h would lose international audiences if he began talking i English. Nevertheless, his [4]**critical** and [5]**financial** succes continued with *City Lights* (1931), his most moving comedy and *Modern Times* (1936), his comic [14]**critique** of industria society. Charlie's first talkie, *The Great Dictator* (1940), whic made fun of Hitler and the Nazis, was his biggest [6]**box-offic** success.

Unfortunately, Charlie's great success in hi [7]**professional** life didn't [8]**carry over** into his persona life. His first three marriages, all to young actresses (th first two were just 16 years old), ended in [9]**divorce**. Nex a brief relationship with another actress resulted in [10]**nasty** [15]**paternity** suit. When he finally married 18-yea old Oona O'Neil (daughter of [11]**playwright** Eugene O'Neil) a the age of 54, her father was [12]**outraged**, and never spoke t her again. And the arrival of the Cold War added to Charlie' troubles. Long suspected by the U.S. government of being [13]**communist**, he was denied reentry to the country after trip to England in 1952. Charlie spent the rest of his life in small town in Switzerland with Oona and their eight childrer

Mini Quiz 閱讀測驗

Which film did Charlie play a small part in?

(A) *The Gold Rush*
(B) *The Great Dictator*
(C) *Modern Times*
(D) *A Woman in Paris*

中 Translation

一九一九年，查理和同為好萊塢明星的瑪莉畢克佛、道格拉斯費爾班克斯及導演戴維沃克格里菲斯，成立了聯藝電影發行公司。這時查理有了完全的掌控權，便全心投入於劇情長片。一九二三年的愛情電影《巴黎婦人》，查理只有客串一角；接著一九二五年的《淘金記》是他最成功的默片喜劇；一九二八年的《馬戲團》則讓他贏得了第一座奧斯卡。等到有聲電影在一九三〇年代開始出現時，查理決定繼續讓流浪漢保持沈默，他擔心如果他開始說英文會失去國際間的觀眾。儘管如此，他名利雙收式的成功仍不間斷，一九三一年的《城市之光》是他最動人的一部喜劇；一九三六年的《摩登時代》是他用喜劇方式批判工業社會。一九四〇年的《大獨裁者》，是查理的第一部有聲電影，他揶揄希特勒和納粹，是他票房成績最好的一部。

不幸的是，查理職業生涯上的成功並沒有延續到他的私人生活。他的前三段婚姻，都是娶了年輕女演員（前兩任妻子只有十六歲），皆已離婚收場。接著，他和另一位女演員的短暫戀情最後還因為查理是否為生父而鬧上法庭。最後，他在五十四歲那年娶了十八歲的烏娜歐尼爾（劇作家尤金歐尼爾之女），尤金歐尼爾大為光火，從此再也沒和女兒說過話。接著冷戰的到來更讓查理困難重重。美國政府長期懷疑他是共產主義者，在一九五二年他到英國之後就被美國政府拒絕入境。查理和烏娜及八個孩子在瑞士一個小鎮度過餘生。

若有疑問請來信：eztalkQ@gmail.com

進階字彙

14) **critique** [krɪˋtik] (n./v.) 批評，評論
The article was a critique of the government's foreign policy.

15) **paternity** [pəˋtɝnəti] (n.) 父子關係，父親的義務，paternity suit 即「鑑定父子關係的訴訟」
The paternity test proved that the man was the girl's father.

Language Guide

The Gold Rush《淘金記》

一九二五年的《淘金記》也是卓別林自編、自導自演的默劇電影，故事描述由卓別林飾演的淘金者來到阿拉斯加，誤打誤撞闖進了逃犯拉森 (Larsen) 的小屋，不久壞天氣也讓另一位淘金者吉姆 (Big Jim) 躲進屋裡。當拉森外出覓食時，卓別林飾演的淘金者因為受不了飢餓而把自己的鞋子煮來吃，而吉姆則因太過飢餓而把卓別林看成一隻雞，進而拿起刀槍攻擊他。在一陣混亂中，一隻熊闖進小屋成了他們的食物。他們分道揚鑣之後，拉森和吉姆因為金礦而起了爭執，拉森把吉姆打昏後卻因雪崩而掉落山谷。卓別林則來到一個小鎮並邂逅了舞女喬治亞，並與失憶的吉姆重逢，兩人再度結伴尋找金礦，經歷一番千辛萬苦之後，兩人終於如願以償成了大富翁，在回鄉的船上卓別林也與喬治亞重逢而有圓滿結局。此片於一九九二年被美國國家電影保護局 (National Film Registry) 收藏於美國國會圖書館 (Library of Congress)，也被美國電影學會 (American Film Institute) 列為百大電影之一。

The Great Dictator《大獨裁者》

《大獨裁者》是卓別林第一部有聲電影，被視為影射希特勒，反法西斯主義 (fascism) 與納粹主義 (Nazism)，是他最賣座的作品。

卓別林在劇中一人分飾兩角，一是猶太理髮師，他因傷在醫院待了二十年，出院時才發現 Tomainia 這個國家已經被殘暴的獨裁者迅科 (Hynkel)，也就是卓別林的另一個角色所統治，此時猶太人受到嚴重的迫害。之後在一次偶然下，理髮師與他以前曾幫助過的官員休茲 (Schultz) 相遇，並打算一起推翻迅科政權，卻不幸被抓進集中營 (concentration camp)。就在休茲與理髮師逃走時，士兵將理髮師誤認為訊科而將他帶去演講，反而真正的獨裁者被當作逃犯抓了起來。理髮師在發表的演說中提及廢除反猶政策及提倡民主，迎向本片的高潮。

電影拍攝期間，因美國政治情勢原採姑息主義，不願參與歐洲事務，故本片一開始不受重視，直到後來太平洋戰爭暴發，德國對美國宣戰，美國也於珍珠港事件後正式參與二次大戰，這部諷刺希特勒的影片才逐漸受到好評。

解答 (D)

Orson Welles
A Man of Many Talents
奧森威爾斯
多才多藝的大師

© Carl Van Vechten / commons.wikimedia.org

Vocabulary Bank

1) **famed** [femd] (a.) 有名的，負盛名的
The English city of Bath is famed for its Roman baths.

2) **pianist** [`piənɪst / pɪ`ænɪst] (n.) 鋼琴手，鋼琴家
Our jazz band needs a pianist.

3) **hardship** [`hɑrdʃɪp] (n.) 困苦，艱難
Many families are facing financial hardship.

4) **graduation** [ˌɡrædʒu`eʃən] (n.) 畢業
Are your parents coming to the graduation ceremony?

5) **stage** [stedʒ] (v.) 上演，把…搬上舞台
The drama club stages two plays each year.

6) **meantime** [`minˌtaɪm] (adv.) 同時
Kelly wants to be a reporter, but in the meantime she's working as an editor.

進階字彙

7) **screenwriter** [`skrinˌraɪtɚ] (n.) 劇本作家，編劇家
Who was the screenwriter for that movie?

8) **stardom** [`stɑrdəm] (n.) 明星地位
The young actor seems destined for stardom.

朗讀 MP3 91 單字 MP3 92 英文文章導讀 MP3 93

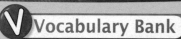

1) **Famed** actor, 7) **screenwriter**, director and produce Orson Welles was born into a creative family in Kenosh Wisconsin on May 6, 1915. His father, Richard, was a wealth inventor and his mother, Beatrice, was a talented conce 2) **pianist**. As a child, Welles showed a gift for music an art. Despite this, his childhood was filled with man 3) **hardships**. His father became an alcoholic, and his parent separated soon after. Welles' mother died when he was onl eight years old, and his father died when he was fifteen In his teens, Welles attended the Todd School for Boys i Illinois, where he became interested in drama. Before lon he was starring in—and even directing—school plays Though Welles was awarded a scholarship to Harvard afte 4) **graduation**, he turned it down to go traveling. On a trip t

Ireland in 1931, he made his professional stage debut at the Gate Theater in Dublin.

Afterwards, Welles returned to America to pursue a career in the theater. In New York, he played two roles in *Romeo and Juliet*, and directed an all-black production of *Macbeth*. He even returned to the Todd School to 5)**stage** his own drama festival, which turned out to be a huge success. In the 6)**meantime**, Welles also worked as a radio actor to earn extra money. He quickly became recognized for his rich, deep voice. In 1937, Welles got together with producer John Houseman and a number of fellow theater and radio actors to found the Mercury Theater in Manhattan. This theater company would **1 pave his way to** international 8)**stardom**.

Mini Quiz 閱讀測驗

❶ **What is one of the hardships Welles experienced in his youth?**
(A) His father passed away when he was in his teens.
(B) His mother died when he was in his teenage years.
(C) He lost his scholarship to attend Harvard University.
(D) He showed a gift for music and art as a child.

❷ **Where did Welles first appear on the stage?**
(A) At the Gate Theater in Dublin
(B) At a theater in New York
(C) At the Todd School for Boys
(D) In an all-black production of Macbeth

中 Translation

知名的演員、編劇、導演兼製作人奧森威爾斯在一九一五年五月六日生於威斯康辛州肯諾莎市一個極富創意的家庭。他的父親理查是個富裕的發明家，母親碧翠絲是才華洋溢的鋼琴演奏家。威爾斯從小就展現出音樂和藝術的天分。儘管如此，他的童年卻備嘗艱辛。他的父親變成酒鬼，沒多久雙親便離婚了。威爾斯的母親在他年僅八歲時過世，接著父親也在他十五歲時與世長辭。青少年時期，威爾斯就讀伊利諾州的托德男校，在那裡培養出對戲劇的興趣，不久，他便開始主演——甚至執導——學校的話劇。畢業後，威爾斯雖然獲得哈佛大學獎學金，但他婉拒入學，選擇到各地旅行。一九三一年到愛爾蘭旅行時，他在都伯林的蓋特劇院登台演出他以戲劇為業的處女秀。

之後，威爾斯回到美國發展戲劇生涯。在紐約，他於《羅密歐與茱莉葉》劇中分飾兩角，並執導全由黑人演出的《馬克白》。他甚至回到托德學校籌畫他自己的戲劇節，結果大獲成功。在此同時，威爾斯也兼任電台演員，好多賺一點錢，他很快便以低沉渾厚的聲音出名。一九三七年，威爾斯和製作人約翰郝斯曼及多位戲劇、電台演員同僚一起在曼哈頓成立水星劇團，該劇團為他日後的國際巨星之路奠定基礎。

Tongue-tied No More

1 pave the way for 替……鋪路

這句話意思是為了目標做準備，因為路鋪好了，走得才會更順利，目標也就更容易達成囉！所以要形容為了某個目的而做了事先準備就用 pave the way for 後加名詞，若是 pave the way to 就加動詞原形。

A: I don't really like Nirvana's first album.
我不是很喜歡超脫樂團的第一張專輯。

B: Me neither, but at least it paved the way for their success.
我也是，但至少它為他們的成功鋪了條路。

Language Guide

Macbeth 莎士比亞悲劇《馬克白》

《馬克白》與《哈姆雷特》*Hamlet*《奧賽羅》*Othello*、《李爾王》*King Lear* 並列莎士比亞四大悲劇，《馬克白》是其中最短、也是最後完成的一齣。故事講述蘇格蘭大將馬克白因戰功彪炳深受國王鄧肯賞賜，卻因女巫的預言燃起篡位野心，加上馬克白夫人從旁慫恿，他殺死鄧肯而後稱王。為了鞏固政權，馬克白夫婦展開一連串殺戮，後來馬克白夫人受不了良心譴責發瘋自殺，馬克白也因眾叛親離死於仇敵之手。歐森威爾斯因為演員全部是黑人，遂將《馬克白》場景改為海地，女巫變成巫毒教巫醫，因此這個版本被稱為「巫毒馬克白」Voodoo *Macbeth*。

解答 ❶ (A) ❷ (C)

Vocabulary Bank

1) **executive** [ɪgˋzɛkjətɪv] (a./n.) 執行的，主管級的；高階主管
Roberta works as an executive secretary.

2) **adapt** [əˋdæpt] (v.) 改編，改寫
(n.) adaption [ˌædæpˋteʃən]
Several of the author's novels have been adapted for film.

3) **bulletin** [ˋbʊlɪtɪn] (n.) 新聞快報，公報
The TV program was interrupted for a news bulletin.

4) **invasion** [ɪnˋveʒən] (n.) 入侵，侵略
Do you think the invasion of Iraq was justified?

5) **spaceship** [ˋspesˌʃɪp] (n.) 太空船，或稱 spacecraft
In the future, people will travel to other planets by spaceship.

6) **speculate** [ˋspɛkjəˌlet] (v.) 推測，揣測
The media is speculating on the cause of the crash.

7) **alien** [ˋeliən] (a./n.) 外星人（的）
Do you believe in aliens?

8) **furious** [ˋfjʊriəs] (a.) 狂怒的，狂暴的，兇猛的，猛烈的
My parents were furious when they saw my report card.

進階字彙

9) **prank** [præŋk] (n.) 惡作劇
Billie likes playing pranks on his friends.

10) **stir** [stɝ] (n.) 騷動，轟動
The politician's affair caused a big stir.

11) **hoax** [hoks] (n.) 騙局，惡作劇
It turned out that the bomb threat was just a hoax.

朗讀 MP3 94 單字 MP3 95 英文文章導讀 MP3 96

As [1)]**executive** producer of the Mercury Theater, Welles acted, directed, and produced plays. Nevertheless, his focus soon shifted to radio. He [2)]**adapted** *Les Misérables* into a radio series, and then played the role of Lamont Cranston in the popular radio show, *The Shadow*. In 1938, CBS hired his theater company to create a series of radio shows based on classic novels. On October 30, Welles directed and narrated a show based on *The War of the Worlds*, the famous science fiction novel by H.G. Wells. The broadcast, which was meant to be a Halloween [9)]**prank**, ended up causing more of a [10)]**stir** than anyone could have imagined.

The broadcast consisted of a series of news [3)]**bulletins** about a Martian [4)]**invasion** of Earth. One bulletin claims that a [5)]**spaceship** has landed in a small New Jersey town and killed a crowd of people with a ray gun. A later bulletin describes Martian weapons destroying power stations, bridges and railroads. Welles had voice actors play scientists who [6)]**speculate** about [7)]**alien** technology. Other actors played government officials advising people about the crisis. *The War of the Worlds* ran without commercial breaks, which made it seem even more real. Although the broadcast was meant as a joke, thousands of listeners believed it to be true. Many people panicked and fled their homes. Some listeners were [8)]**furious** when they found out

that the whole thing was a [11]**hoax**. Even so, *The War of the Worlds* broadcast made Welles a superstar. Soon after, job offers from Hollywood began flooding in.

Mini Quiz 閱讀測驗

❶ **Which of the following did Welles NOT do as a member of the Mercury Theater?**

(A) Play the role of Lamont Cranston in The Shadow
(B) Adapt Les Misérables into a series of radio shows
(C) Direct a show based on The War of the Worlds, by H.G. Wells
(D) Play a character in the broadcast of The War of the Worlds

❷ **According to the article, how did some listeners react to *The War of the Worlds* broadcast?**

(A) They panicked and ran into their homes.
(B) They were angry when they found out it was fake.
(C) They followed the instructions provided in the bulletins.
(D) They thought it was meant as a joke

中 Translation

身為水星劇團的執行製作人，威爾斯身兼戲劇的演、導、製作數職。不過，他的重心很快轉移到廣播。他將《悲慘世界》改編成廣播連續劇，並在頗受歡迎的廣播劇《影子奇俠》扮演拉蒙克蘭斯頓。一九三八年，哥倫比亞廣播公司聘請他的劇團以經典小說為藍本製作一系列廣播劇。十月三十日，威爾斯執導一齣改編自 H. G. 威爾斯著名科幻小說《世界大戰》的廣播劇，並擔任旁白。這個原本只是萬聖節惡作劇的廣播節目，最後卻引發始料未及的騷動。

該節目包含一連串新聞快報，報導火星人入侵地球。其中一則報導聲稱一艘太空船已降落在紐澤西一個小鎮，並用雷射槍殺死一群民眾。稍後一則又描述火星人的武器摧毀了發電廠、橋樑和鐵路。威爾斯要一些聲音演員扮演科學家，推測外星人的科技，其他演員則扮演政府官員，告知民眾如何面對危機。《世界大戰》節目沒有穿插廣告，因此更顯真實。雖然本意是純屬玩笑，卻有數千名聽眾信以為真。很多人恐慌地逃離家園，有些聽眾在發現這整件事是個惡作劇之後，簡直怒不可遏。儘管如此，《世界大戰》廣播節目已使威爾斯成為超級巨星，不久，好萊塢的工作邀約開始如潮水般湧來。

Language Guide

The War of the Worlds
科幻小說《世界大戰》

出版於一八九八年的《世界大戰》是英國作家赫伯特喬治威爾斯（Herbert George Wells，常簡稱為 H.G. Wells）的成名代表作。小說內容旨在描述十九世紀末期火星人來到地球後對英國發動戰爭的故事，作者以目擊者的角度描述人類與火星人的抗爭。因書中清楚記載外星人特徵及其與地球人之間可能引發的文明衝突，成了日後相關科幻小說的參考範本，一九三八年還被美國 CBS 廣播公司改編成廣播劇，只是登陸地點換成美國，當時身兼節目製作人和主持人的奧森威爾斯 因成功營造出外星人入侵地球的氛圍，引起地方恐慌，因而聲名大噪。該小說於一九五三年被改編拍成電影，但較為人所知的是二〇〇五年由史蒂芬史匹柏 (Steven Spielberg) 執導的同名版本，另外一部於一九九六年上映的《ID4 星際終結者》*Independence Day* 據說靈感也源自這本小說。

解答 ❶ (D) ❷ (B)

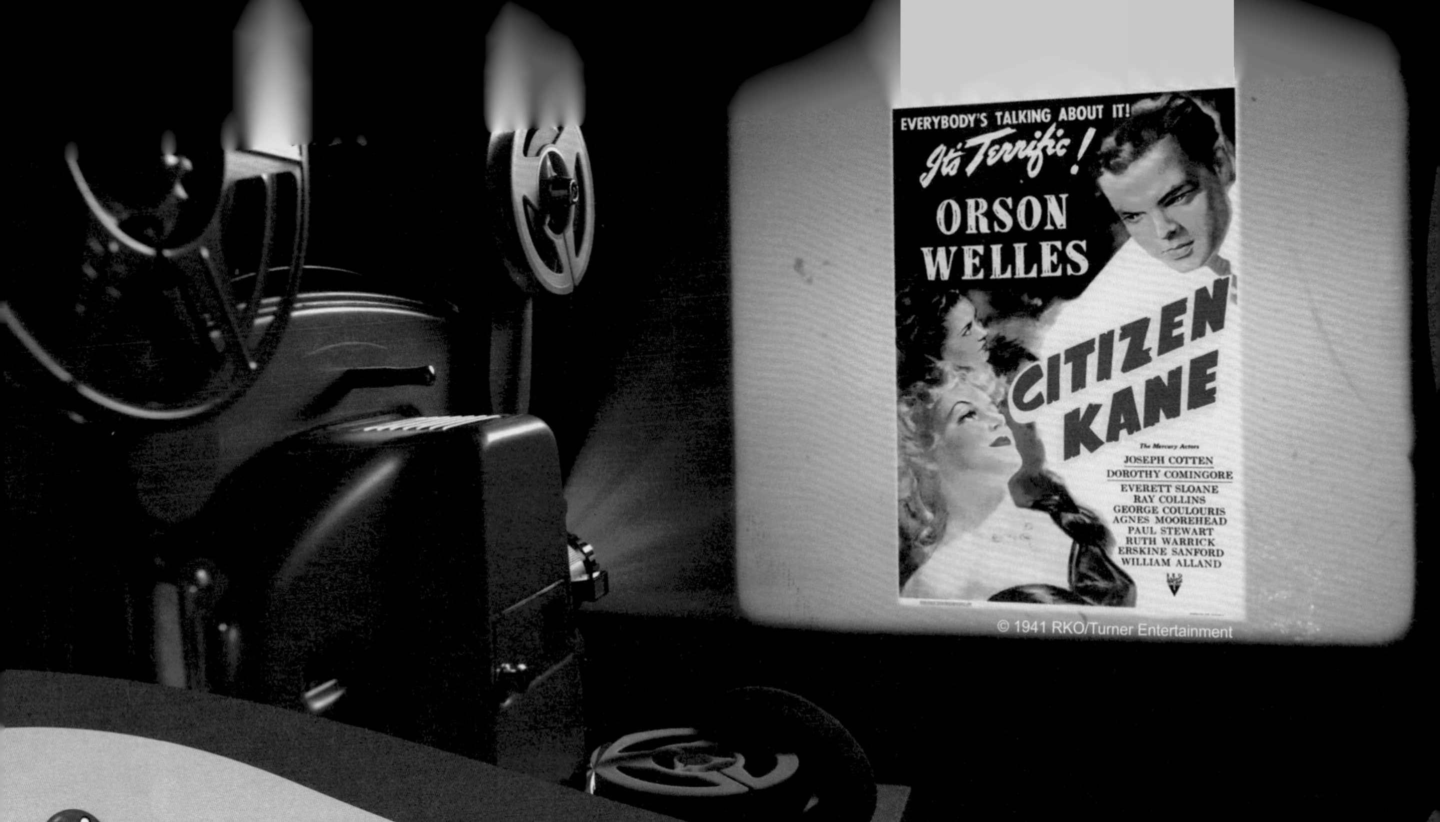

V Vocabulary Bank

1) **loosely** [ˋlusli] (adv.) 大致地，不嚴謹地
The poem is loosely translated from the Russian original.

2) **innovative** [ˋɪnə͵vetɪv] (a.) 創新的
Apple is famous for its innovative products.

3) **accomplish** [əˋkɑmplɪʃ] (v.) 完成，實現，達到
I feel like I didn't accomplish anything today.

4) **steadily** [ˋstɛdəli] (adv.) 持續地，穩定地
Prices have risen steadily over the past year.

5) **recognition** [͵rɛkəgˋnɪʃən] (n.) 賞識，知名度
The author never received the recognition he should have.

6) **institute** [ˋɪnstɪ͵tut] (n.) 學會，協會，研究機構
Bradley works as a researcher at a scientific institute.

7) **pass away** [pæs əˋwe] (phr.) 過世
Stephen's father passed away last year.

進階字彙

8) **magnate** [ˋmægnet] (n.) 巨頭，權貴
The oil magnate left his entire fortune to charity.

9) **screenplay** [ˋskrin͵ple] (n.) 電影劇本
Each actor was given a copy of the screenplay to study.

10) **guild** [gɪld] (n.)（互助性的）團體，協會，聯合會
Several famous authors are members of the writers' guild.

朗讀 MP3 97 單字 MP3 98 英文文章導讀 MP3 99

In 1941, Welles co-wrote, produced, directed and starred in what many people consider the greatest movie ever made. *Citizen Kane*, which is [1]**loosely** based on the life of William Randolph Hearst, tells the story of the rise and fall of a newspaper [8]**magnate**. While the movie wasn't a success at the box office, it was well received by critics and won an Oscar for Best Original [9]**Screenplay**. Welles use of dramatic lighting, low camera angles and heart stopping music was bold and [2]**innovative**. In Welles own words, "A film is never really good unless the camer is an eye in the head of a poet." One could say that h [3]**accomplished** this with *Citizen Kane*. Welles went on t make more films, but they were also commercial failures Frustrated, Welles escaped to Europe, where his films wer more popular. He eventually returned to Hollywood, wher he found more work as an actor than as a director.

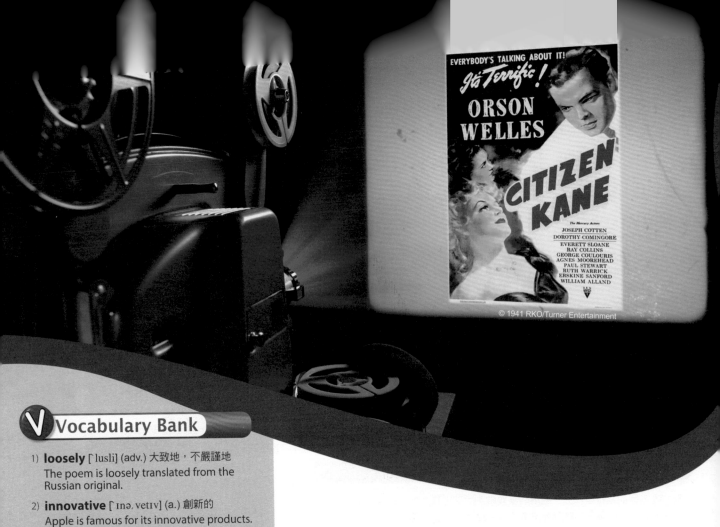

Welles continued working [4]**steadily** throughout his life, putting most of the money he made as an actor and narrator into film projects he believed in. He paid a price in his personal life, though. The first two of Welles' three marriages ended in divorce. When asked about their divorce, his second wife, famous Hollywood actress Rita Hayworth, said "I can't take his genius anymore." Welles put filmmaking above everything else in his life. In his later years, he finally began receiving the [5]**recognition** he deserved. In 1975, he won the American Film [6]**Institute's** Lifetime Achievement Award. In 1984, the Director's [10]**Guild** of America awarded him its highest honor. Although Orson Welles [7]**passed away** in 1985, his influence on filmmaking continues to this day.

Mini Quiz 閱讀測驗

1. **Which of the following is true about *Citizen Kane*?**
   (A) It was a financial success.
   (B) It won several Oscars.
   (C) It stars Orson Welles.
   (D) Critics didn't appreciate it.

2. **How many times did Welles get divorced?**
   (A) One time
   (B) Two times
   (C) Three times
   (D) Four times

中 Translation

一九四一年，威爾斯合寫、製作、執導、主演一部被許多人喻為史上最偉大電影的作品。大致改編自威廉藍道夫赫斯特生平的《大國民》，描述一位報業鉅子的起落。儘管票房不怎麼樣，本片卻大獲影評讚賞，並贏得奧斯卡最佳原創劇本獎。威爾斯大膽、創新地運用了變化多端的燈光、低攝影角度及驚心動魄的音樂。套一句威爾斯自己的話：「攝影機要像通往詩人內心的眼睛，電影才能真的拍得好。」我們可以說，他用《大國民》做到了這點。威爾斯繼續拍攝更多電影，但依然不賣座。備感挫折的威爾斯避走歐洲，他的電影在歐洲較受歡迎。最後他又重回好萊塢，只不過演員的工作比導演來得多。

威爾斯終其一生都不斷在工作，將他擔任演員及旁白賺到的錢投入他看重的一些拍片計畫，但他在私生活方面付出了代價。威爾斯三段婚姻中的前兩段皆以離婚收場。他的第二任妻子，好萊塢知名女演員莉塔海沃斯在被問及兩人為何離婚時表示：「我再也無法忍受他的才華。」威爾斯把拍電影看得比什麼都重要。晚年，他終於開始獲得他應得的肯定。一九七五年，他贏得美國電影學會頒發的終身成就獎。一九八四年，美國導演工會把最高榮譽頒給他。儘管奧森威爾斯在一九八五年逝世，但他對電影製作的影響至今不滅。

若有疑問請來信：eztalkQ@gmail.com

Language Guide

Citizen Kane **影史經典名片《大國民》**

拍攝於一九四一年的《大國民》是年僅二十五歲的奧森威爾斯自導自演之成名代表作，被評選為美國百大經典電影的榜首。《大國民》是一部傳記式電影，講述美國報業大亨查爾斯福斯特凱恩 (Charles Foster Kane) 不平凡的一生。身為導演兼任男主角的威爾斯以側面的敘事手法，從不同角度剖析及探討劇中人物。電影一開始先以一則新聞短片簡述凱恩的生平，接著鏡頭拉到凱恩臨終前的遺言——玫瑰花蕾 (rosebud)，於是全劇便以玫瑰花蕾為主軸慢慢展開，並利用五個曾經跟凱恩共事或生活的人來勾勒出這個傳奇人物的真實一生，這些如同拼圖般片斷、不連續的資訊，也挑起觀眾們想一探究竟的好奇心，但該片因被指控影射當時的報業大亨威廉赫斯特，險些無法上映。總體來說，威爾斯的《大國民》無論在敘事結構、主題、掌鏡、燈光、剪接和場景調度等方面都有別於當時的好萊塢片，徹底影響了日後的電影發展。

解答 1 (C) 2 (B)

Vocabulary Bank

1) **sneak** [snik] (v.) 偷偷地走，溜
The boys snuck into the movie theater without paying.

2) **enthusiastic** [ɪn͵θuziˋæstɪk] (a.) 熱中的，熱情的
Jack is an enthusiastic baseball fan.

3) **lot** [lɑt] (n.) 電影製片廠
Most of the movie was filmed on a studio lot.

4) **promising** [ˋprɑmɪsɪŋ] (a.) 有前途的，大有可為的
The young athlete has a promising career ahead of him.

進階字彙

5) **screen** [skrin] (v.) 放映，播放
The director's new film will be screened at the film festival.

6) **internship** [ˋɪntɝn͵ʃɪp] (n.) 工作實習
An internship will look good on your college application.

Tongue-tied No More

1 take a liking to sb./sth.
喜歡上某人 / 某事

liking 是名詞，為喜歡、愛好的意思。take a liking to sb./sth. 形容對某人 / 某事感到喜愛或有好感。

A: Was your roommate mad at you for getting a dog?
你室友對你養狗的事有發脾氣嗎？

B: She was at first, but she's taken a liking to him.
一開始有，但現在她很喜歡牠。

© Featureflash/shutterstock.com

Steven Spielberg
Bringing Dreams to Life on the Silver Screen
史蒂芬史匹柏 大銀幕上的美夢成真

朗讀 MP3 100 單字 MP3 101 英文文章導讀 MP3 102

Imagine the following scene: it's the mid-1960s, and teenager is visiting Universal Studios in Hollywood. During th tour, he 1)**sneaks** away from the group and encounters a film editor busy at work. The editor **1 takes an immediate likin to** the boy and shows him a few **2 tricks of the trade**. Th 2)**enthusiastic** teen returns to the 3)**lot** the following day t learn more, and this routine continues for the whole summe Fast forward a decade or so, and he's well on his way t becoming one of the most influential figures in the moder movie industry. Who could this [4]**promising** young filmmaker be? Why, it's none other than Steven Spielberg, the director who would go on to make *E.T., Jurassic Park, Schindler's List* and a great many other memorable movies.

Steven was born to parents Arnold and Leah Spielberg in Cincinnati, Ohio on December 18, 1946. The family had to move often due to Arnold's job as a computer engineer, but movies were always a big part of young Steven's life. As a boy, he made short films that he showed to his family, and in high school he directed *Firelight*, a sci-fi feature that made a one-dollar profit when it was [5]**screened** at a Phoenix theater. After his parents divorced, Steven moved with his father to California, where he entered California State University, Long Beach. Being so close to Hollywood, however, the allure of the movies proved too strong, and he dropped out of college to pursue an [6]**internship** at Universal Studios.

Mini Quiz 閱讀測驗

❶ **When did Steven Spielberg make his first full-length film?**
(A) In the mid-1960s
(B) In his early childhood
(C) In high school
(D) In college

❷ **According to the article, which of the following is true about Spielberg?**
(A) He attended high school in California.
(B) He was well on his way to becoming famous in the 1960s.
(C) He made a large profit on his first sci-fi feature.
(D) He spent a summer on a movie lot in his teens.

中 Translation

想像一下以下的場景：時值一九六〇年代中期，一名青少年造訪好萊塢環球製片廠，他在參觀過程中偷偷脫隊，巧遇一位忙著工作的電影剪輯師。剪輯師立刻對這男孩產生好感，並告訴他這一行的一些秘訣。隔天，這位充滿熱忱的青少年又來到製片廠學習更多事情，而且這個慣例持續了整個夏天。時間快轉至大約十年後，他步上坦途，逐步成為現代電影業最具影響力的人物之一。這位前途似錦的年輕電影人是誰呢？除了史蒂芬史匹柏還會有誰？當然就是這位日後拍攝出《E.T. 外星人》、《侏儸紀公園》、《辛德勒的名單》等許多令人懷念電影的導演。

史蒂芬在一九四六年十二月十八日生於俄亥俄州辛辛那提，雙親是阿諾和莉雅・史匹柏。一家人常因阿諾電腦工程師的工作而必須搬遷，但電影一直是小史蒂芬生活中的重要部分。小時候，他便製作了多部短片播放給家人看，念高中時，他執導了科幻劇情長片《火光》，在鳳凰城一家戲院上映後賺了一美元的利潤。雙親離婚後，史蒂芬與父親搬到加州，就讀加州州立大學長堤分校。但由於距好萊塢很近，電影的誘惑實在太過強大，他選擇休學，進環球片廠實習。

Tongue-tied No More

2 trick of the trade 伎倆，祕訣

這句話用來形容做各種事情的不同竅門，也可以指每行業不同的潛規則或處事方式，或是做某件事情要注意的「眉角」。抓住這些祕訣，做起事來即可順手許多。

A: Could you teach me how to take better pictures?
你可以教我怎麼把照片拍好嗎？

B: Sure. I'd be happy to show you a few tricks of the trade.
沒問題。我很樂意教你一些祕訣。

Language Guide

史蒂芬史匹柏經典電影

一九八二年的電影《E.T. 外星人》是史蒂芬史匹柏執導的經典科幻鉅作。片名 E.T. 為 the Extra-Terrestrial 的縮寫，就是外星人。故事主軸圍繞在小男孩和外星人之間的誠摯友情，為了順利將外星人送回家，他們展開了一連串的冒險之旅。

一九九三年的電影《侏儸紀公園》是改編自麥可克萊頓 (Michael Crichton) 一九九〇年的同名小說，被視為是大量使用電腦繪圖（CGI，即為 computer-generated imagery）的先鋒之一。《侏儸紀公園》是史匹柏執導作品當中票房最高者，目前為影史排名第十八名。

電影《辛德勒名單》描述一位由連恩尼遜 (Liam Neeson) 所飾演的德國商人奧斯卡辛德勒 (Oskar Schindler) 從納粹手中拯救受迫害的猶太人。這部紀錄片風格的黑白電影改編自湯瑪斯肯納利 (Thomas Keneally) 的小說《辛德勒方舟》(*Schindler's Ark*)，一舉奪下第六十六屆奧斯卡最佳影片、最佳導演、最佳改編劇本等大獎。

解答 ❶ (C) ❷ (D)

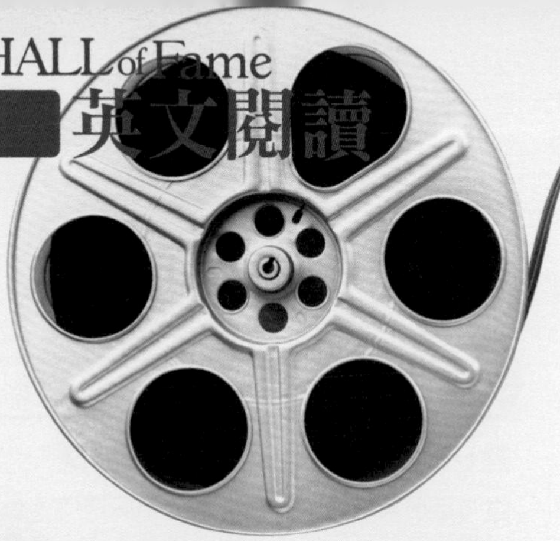

朗讀 MP3 103 單字 MP3 104 英文文章導讀 MP3 105

At Universal, Spielberg cut his teeth directing TV shows, and quickly graduated to a made-for-TV movie called *Duel* (1971), a [1]**thriller** in which a [2]**motorist** is chased by a large [3]**tanker** down a desert highway. By the mid-'70s, he was making full-length [4]**theatrical** [5]**releases** and *Jaws* (1975), with its great white shark and scary music, announced Spielberg's arrival as a major director. In addition to winning three Oscars, the movie [6]**grossed** over $100 million, making it the world's first summer blockbuster. Next, the sci-fi classic *Close Encounters of the Third Kind* (1977) [7]**cemented** Spielberg's status and continued a successful [8]**run** of movies that would [9]**extend** into the 1980s with *Raiders of the Lost Ark* (1981) and *E.T. the Extra-Terrestrial* (1982).

Among all of Spielberg's hits, *E.T.* is [15]**arguably** his most [10]**beloved** film. In some ways, the film is [11]**autobiographical**, as Spielberg based the title character on an imaginary friend he had as a child following his parents' divorce. In addition to the advanced special effects, like the memorable scene in which Elliot and his friends 1 **take to the air** on their bicycles, *E.T.* was among the first movies to use product placement, now a [12]**staple** in filmmaking. By now an [13]**accomplished** director, Spielberg decided to try his hand at producing. His early credits in this area include *Poltergeist* (1982), *Gremlins* (1984) and *Back to the Future* (1985). In 1994, Spielberg got together with entertainment moguls Jeffrey Katzenberg and David Geffen to found movie studio DreamWorks, which went on to produce and [14]**distribute** dozens of box-office hits.

Vocabulary Bank

1) **thriller** [ˋθrɪlɚ] (n.) 驚悚片、小說
Jenny likes to read thrillers and mystery novels.

2) **motorist** [ˋmotərɪst] (n.) 開車的人
Starting next year, motorists will be fined for using cell phones while driving.

3) **tanker** [ˋtæŋkɚ] (n.) 油槽車，油船
The tanker flipped over, spilling oil on the highway.

4) **theatrical** [θiˋætrɪkəl] (a.) 戲劇的
The film will make its theatrical debut next week.

5) **release** [rɪˋlis] (n.) 發行的電影、專輯、書等
The band's new release is getting good reviews.

6) **gross** [gros] (v.) 獲得…總收入
The movie grossed 20 million but didn't make a profit.

7) **cement** [səˋmɛnt] (v.) 加強、鞏固（地位、關係等）
The couple decided to have children to cement their relationship.

8) **run** [rʌn] (n.) 連續的事，一連串
After a long run of cloudy days, the sun finally came out.

9) **extend** [ɪkˋstɛnd] (v.) 延伸，伸展
The forest extends from the coast to the mountains.

10) **beloved** [bɪˋlʌvɪd / bɪˋlʌvd] (a.) 深受喜愛的
Terry's beloved aunt passed away recently.

11) **autobiographical** [ˌɔtəˌbaɪəˋgræfɪkəl] (a.) 自傳的，自傳體的
(n.) autobiography [ˌɔtəbaɪˋɑgrəfi]
The author's first novel was autobiographical.

12) **staple** [ˋstepəl] (n.) 主要成分，要素
Reality shows are a prime-time staple.

13) **accomplished** [əˋkɑmplɪʃt] (a.) 熟練的，有造詣的
Professor Adams is an accomplished scholar.

14) **distribute** [dɪˋstrɪbjut] (v.) 發行，經銷
The company markets and distributes its products to retail stores.

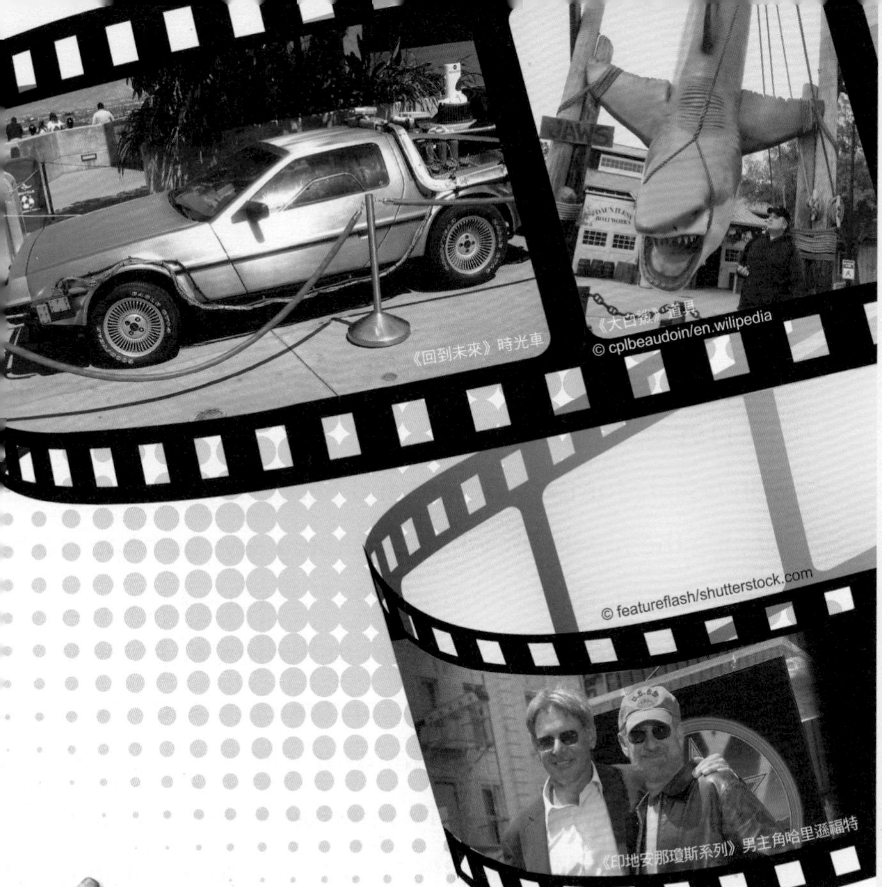
《回到未來》時光車
《大白鯊》道具
© cplbeaudoin/en.wilipedia
© featureflash/shutterstock.com
《印地安那瓊斯系列》男主角哈里遜福特

進階字彙

15) **arguably** [ˋɑrguəblɪ] (adv.) 可說是⋯
That restaurant has arguably the best sushi in town.

Tongue-tied No More

1 take to the air 起飛

air 這裡是「天空」的意思，此句話與片語 take off 為同義詞。

例 The flock of birds took to the air.
鳥群向空中飛去。

Language Guide

blockbuster 賣座電影

block 是指四周都有街道的街區，buster 則可指「剋星」或具有巨大破壞力的東西。blockbuster 這個字源自二次世界大戰，指的是一種威力強大，能將敵方陣營摧毀的巨型炸彈，後來引申為「賣座電影」，不但廣受歡迎、風靡一時、且叫好又叫座。目前全世界最賣座的前五名電影依序是《阿凡達》(*Avatar*)、《鐵達尼號》(*Titanic*)、《哈利波特：死神的聖物 2》(*Harry Potter and the Deathly Hallows: Part 2*)、《變形金剛 3》(*Transformers: Dark of the Moon*)、《魔戒三部曲：王者再臨》(*The Lord of the Rings: The Return of the King*)。

product placement 置入性行銷

product placement 字面上是「產品置入」的意思，也可稱為 embedded advertising，即為「置入性行銷」。置入性行銷為一種常見的廣告手法，將行銷的商品、服務或理念藉由電視節目、電影、音樂錄影帶等媒介達到曝光目的，如：劇中演員的使用，來增加產品知名度及達到廣告效果。而這種方式有時不易被觀眾察覺為廣告，所以也稱為「隱性廣告」。

Mini Quiz 閱讀測驗

1 **Which of the following films was not shown at theaters?**
(A) *Raiders of the Lost Ark*
(B) *E.T. the Extra-Terrestrial*
(C) *Duel*
(D) *Jaws*

2 **Which of the following is true about *E.T.*?**
(A) It was the first film to use product placement.
(B) It is partially about Spielberg's own life.
(C) Everyone agrees that it's Spielberg's best film.
(D) The title character is based on Spielberg.

中 Translation

在環球片廠，史匹柏以執導電視節目開始，並很快取得資格執導名為《飛輪喋血》（一九七一年）的電視電影，這是一部描述一位汽車駕駛被大型油槽車司機沿沙漠公路追趕的驚悚片。七〇年代中期，他已經在拍劇情長片，一九七五年的《大白鯊》以那頭大白鯊和恐怖音樂宣告史匹柏躋身大導演之林。除了贏得三座奧斯卡獎，這部電影席捲了超過一億美元的票房，成為全球第一部暑期賣座鉅片。接下來，科幻經典《第三類接觸》（一九七七年）鞏固了史匹柏的地位，並持續以一連串成功電影進入一九八〇年代，包括《法櫃奇兵》（一九八一年）和《E.T. 外星人》（一九八二年）。

在史匹柏所有暢銷鉅片中，《E.T.》可說是最受喜愛的一部電影。這部片某種程度算是自傳，因為史匹柏是根據他童年時在雙親離異後幻想結交的一個朋友，來塑造 E.T.的角色。除了先進的特效，例如那個雋永的場景：艾略特和友人踩腳踏車騰空往天空飛去，《ET》也是第一批運用產品置入的電影之一，如今產品置入已成為電影拍攝的必須品。如今成為造詣深厚的導演之後，史匹柏決定嘗試製片。他在該領域的早期榮耀包括《鬼哭神號》（一九八二年）、《小精靈》（一九八四年）和《回到未來》（一九八五年）。一九九四年，史匹柏和娛樂鉅子傑佛瑞凱森柏格和大衛葛芬合作成立「夢工場」製片公司，接連製作及配銷數十部賣座強片。

解答 1 (C) 2 (B)

Vocabulary Bank

1) **consciousness** [ˋkɑnʃəsnɪs] (n.) 意識，知覺
Meditation can be used to reach a higher state of consciousness.

2) **issue** [ˋɪʃu] (n.) 議題，問題
We have several issues to discuss at today's meeting.

3) **gripping** [ˋgrɪpɪŋ] (a.) 引人入勝的
The novel was so gripping that I couldn't put it down.

4) **tackle** [ˋtækəl] (v.) 著手處理，對付
The government has promised to tackle inflation.

5) **colonial** [kəˋloniəl] (a.) 殖民地的，殖民的
The city is known for its colonial architecture.

6) **sacrifice** [ˋsækrə͵faɪs] (n./v.) 犧牲
The couple made many sacrifices to send their children to college.

7) **generation** [͵dʒɛnəˋreʃən] (n.) 代，世代
We should all do our part to preserve the planet for future generations.

8) **brutal** [ˋbrutəl] (a.) 殘忍的，粗暴的
The small country is ruled by a brutal dictator.

9) **terrorist** [ˋtɛrəɪst] (n.) 恐怖份子，恐怖主義
The terrorists responsible for the bombing were never caught.

10) **consistent** [kənˋsɪstənt] (a.) 始終如一的
(adv.) consistently [kənˋsɪstəntli]
The student's grades have shown consistent improvement.

11) **estimate** [ˋɛstə͵met] (v.) 估計
I estimate that the project will be completed by Tuesday.

12) **visual** [ˋvɪʒuəl] (a.) 視覺的
Did you use visual materials in your presentation?

13) **house** [hauz] (v.) 收藏，提供空間、住處給…
The prison houses over 2,000 prisoners.

朗讀 MP3 106 單字 MP3 107 英文文章導讀 MP3 108

While Spielberg may be best known for his summe blockbusters, he has also made dramas that aim to raise [1]**consciousness** about important social [2]**issues**. *Schindler's List* (1993), a [3]**gripping** story of the Jews during WWII won Oscars for Best Picture and Best Director. Along with *E.T.*, it's the movie for which Spielberg says he hopes to be remembered. Next, *Amistad* (1997) [4]**tackled** the complex issues of slavery and freedom in [5]**colonial** America. He then went on to explore the contributions and [6]**sacrifices** of America's "Greatest [7]**Generation**" in the WWII epic *Saving Private Ryan* and TV mini-series *Band of Brothers*. More recently, *Munich* (2005) told the story of the Israel government's response to the [8]**brutal** murders of eleven o its Olympic athletes by Palestinian [9]**terrorists** in 1972.

The [10]**consistent** success of Spielberg's movies at the box office has led to a second career for him in philanthropy. One [14]**beneficiary** of his wealth, which *Forbes*

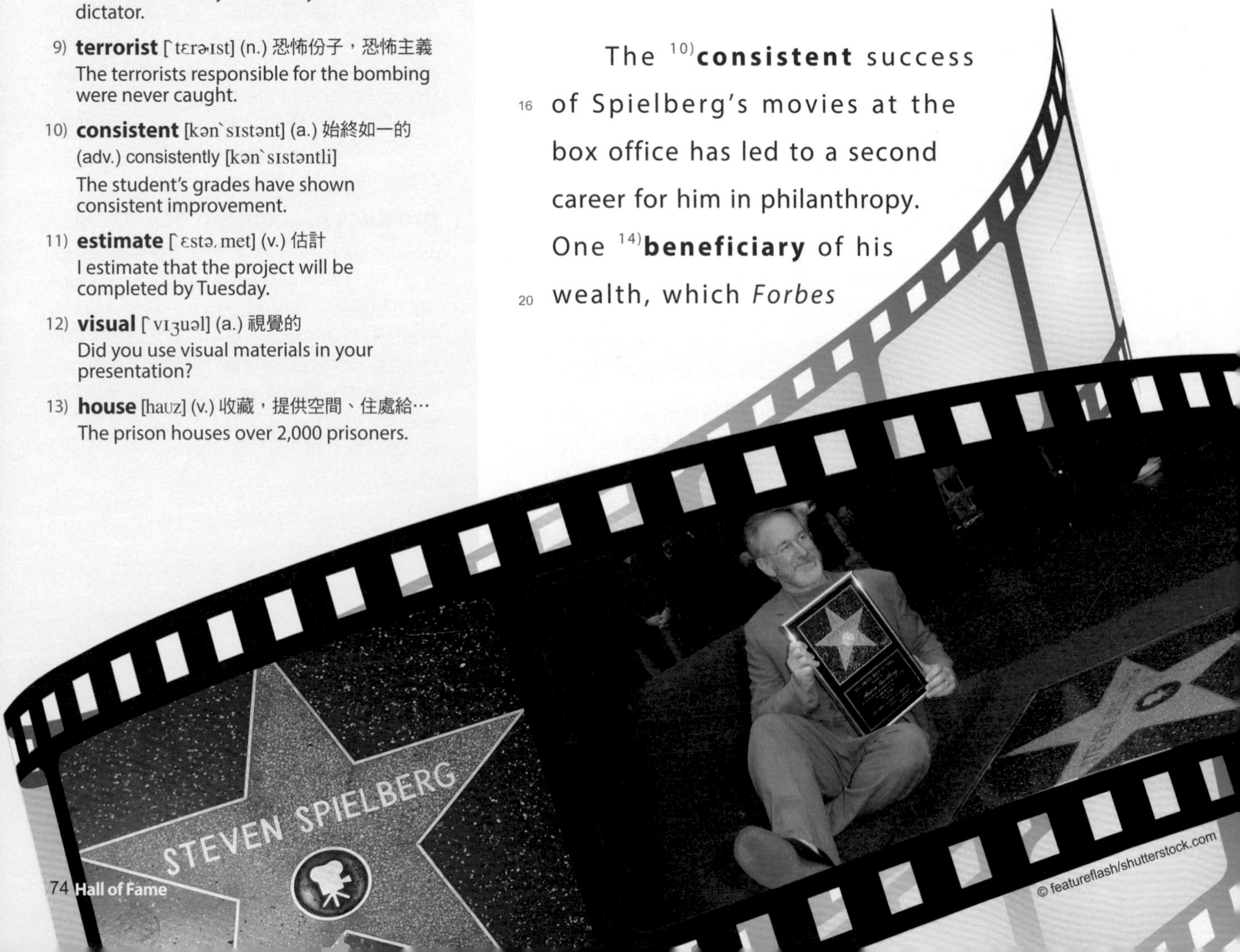

© featureflash/shutterstock.com

[11]**estimates** at US$3 billion, is the Shoah Foundation Institute for Visual History and Education. This group collects the accounts of Holocaust survivors, some 50,000 of which are stored in the [12]**Visual** History Archive. [13]**Housed** at USC, the video [15]**archive** is the largest collection of its kind in the world. Whether as a philanthropist, producer or movie director, Spielberg shows no signs of slowing down. "I have no plans to quit," he said while promoting his most recent movie, *War Horse*. So moviegoers can look forward to being entertained and informed for many years to come.

Mini Quiz 閱讀測驗

❶ **Which of the following films is set furthest back in time?**
(A) *Schindler's List*
(B) *Amistad*
(C) *Saving Private Ryan*
(D) *Munich*

❷ **How much is Spielberg worth?**
(A) Exactly US$3 billion
(B) Less than US$3 billion
(C) Around US$3 billion
(D) More than US$3 billion

中 Translation

雖然史匹柏最著名的是他的暑期賣座強檔，但他也製作一些意圖喚醒民眾對重要社會議題的意識的劇情片。《辛德勒的名單》（一九九三年），一部引人入勝、描述二次世界大戰期間猶太人的事件，贏得奧斯卡最佳影片和最佳導演獎。這部片和《E.T.》都是是史匹柏說他希望能被世人記住的電影。接下來，《勇者無懼》（一九九七年）處理了美國殖民時代奴隸與自由的複雜議題。接著他繼續以二次世界大戰史詩片《搶救雷恩大兵》及電視迷你影集《諾曼第大空降》探索美國「最偉大世代」的貢獻與犧牲。較近期的《慕尼黑》（二〇〇五年）則描述一九七二年以色列政府對該國十一名奧運選手遭巴勒斯坦恐怖份子殘殺的反應。

史匹柏在電影票房上一路長紅的成就，造就了他的第二事業：慈善。《富比世》雜誌估計他的財產高達三十億美元，而他財產的受益人之一，是「浩劫視覺歷史與教育基金會」。這個團體蒐集了納粹大屠殺生還者的紀錄，有大約五萬份存檔在視覺歷史檔案館。這座位於南加大的影像檔案館，收藏冠於世界同類型資料庫。無論身為慈善家、製片或電影導演，史匹柏的腳步都沒有慢下來的跡象。「我沒有退休的計畫，」他在宣傳他的最新電影《戰馬》時這麼說道。所以影迷可以期待，未來許多年仍能繼續享受娛樂、充實知識。

若有疑問請來信：eztalkQ@gmail.com

進階字彙

10) **beneficiary** [ˌbɛnəˋfɪʃiˌɛri] (n.) 受益人，受惠者
Our company was the main beneficiary of the deal.

15) **archive** [ˋɑrkaɪv] (n.) 檔案（館、庫），紀錄
Many old movies are stored in the film archive.

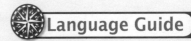

Language Guide

Forbes《富比世》雜誌

《富比世》雜誌於一九一七年創刊，是美國紐約的富比世傳播媒體及出版公司所發行的商業雙週刊。《富比世》以各種富豪、權威人士等名人榜聞名。如 The Forbes 400 是美國的富豪排行榜，最新的排行仍是由比爾蓋茲 (Bill Gates) 繼續蟬聯。以過去一年名人的收入、網路點擊率和媒體曝光度等來計算的 The Celebrity 100 百大名人權力榜，二〇一一年則由女神卡卡 (Lady Gaga) 奪下榜首，小賈斯汀 (Justin Bieber) 也首次進榜便奪下第三名。The World's Billionaires 全球億萬富翁排行榜則是由墨西哥電信業大亨卡洛斯史林家族 (Carlos Slim Helu & family) 居冠。

the Holocaust 猶太人大屠殺

一九三〇年代起，德國納粹展開一連串反猶太人活動。猶太人被集中管理或強迫隔離，一九四一年起，納粹開始出動部隊大規模殺害猶太人，為了實行「最終解決方案」(Final Solution)，猶太人被送至滅絕營 (extermination camp)，以毒氣室 (gas chamber) 毒死。據估計，約有六百萬名猶太人在二次大戰期間遭到屠殺。

解答 ❶ (B) ❷ (C)

©Featureflash / Shutterstock.com

©Featureflash / Shutterstock.com

Ang Lee 李安

Bridging East and West through Film

用電影連結中西文化的橋樑

朗讀 MP3 109 單字 MP3 110 英文文章導讀 MP3 111

Ang Lee was born on October 23, 1954 in a small town in Pingtung County, a rural area in southern Taiwan. His father, a scholar who had fled to Taiwan from Jiangxi after the Chinese Civil War, placed a strong 1)**emphasis** on education, encouraging him to 2)**excel** at school, and teaching him calligraphy and the Chinese classics during summer vacations. Although Lee attended the 3)**prestigious** Tainan First Senior High School, where his father was principal, he was an average student whose only escape from the intense 4)**academic** pressure was watching movies at the local theater. After twice failing the national university entrance exam, he entered the Theater and Film program at the National Taiwan 5)**Academy** of Arts, a three-year 6)**vocational** school.

This was a great disappointment to Lee's father, who allowed him to attend on the condition that he would further his studies in the U.S. And so, after graduating from the Academy—where he enjoyed acting and making short films—and completing his military service, he entered the University of Illinois as a theater major. Finding that he had a greater interest in directing than acting, Lee went on to complete a master's in film 7)**production** at NYU. In graduate school, he made a number of short films, one

Vocabulary Bank

1) **emphasis** [ˋɛmfəsɪs] (n.) 重點，強調
(v.) emphasize [ˋɛmfə͵saɪz]
Schools should put more emphasis on math and science.

2) **excel** [ɪkˋsɛl] (v.) 擅長於，表現優異
Lisa excels in English and history.

3) **prestigious** [prɛsˋtɪdʒəs] (a.) 著名的，有名望的
The author has won many prestigious awards.

4) **academic** [͵ækəˋdɛmɪk] (a.) 學術的
Shelly has a good academic record.

5) **academy** [əˋkædəmi] (n.) 學院，藝術院
Pauline is studying at an art academy in France.

6) **vocational** [voˋkeʃənəl] (a.) 職業（訓練）的，就業指導的
Tom is taking vocational courses at the local junior college.

7) **production** [prəˋdʌkʃən] (n.) 製作，（電影等）攝製
Michael has a job in television production.

8) **annual** [ˋænjuəl] (a.) 全年的，一年一次的
Does that credit card have an annual fee?

進階字彙

9) **thesis** [ˋθisɪs] (n.) 論文，畢業論文、製作
How long did it take to write your master's thesis?

©Phil Stafford / Shutterstock.com

of which—*Shades of the Lake*—won Best Short Film at Taiwan's Golden Harvest Film Festival. Lee also worked as a cameraman on classmate Spike Lee's [9]**thesis** film, and his own thesis work, *Fine Line*, won Best Film and Best Director at NYU's [8]**annual** film festival.

Mini Quiz 閱讀測驗

❶ **When did Ang Lee probably become interested in movies?**

(A) In primary school
(B) In high school
(C) In university
(D) In graduate school

❷ **According to the article, why was Lee's father disappointed?**

(A) Because he wanted to further his studies in the United States
(B) Because he wasn't accepted to a good arts academy
(C) Because he entered a vocational school instead of a university
(D) Because he was an average student in high school

中 Translation

李安於一九五四年十月二十三日出生在南台灣農村地區屏東縣的小鎮。他的父親是在國共內戰後從江西逃到台灣，非常重視教育，除了鼓勵他在校努力向學，也利用暑假期間教他書法和中國古籍。雖然李安高中就讀父親擔任校長的名校台南一中，但他只是成績普通的學生，而平常逃離繁重課業壓力的唯一消遣就是去當地的戲院看電影。兩度在大學聯考中落榜之後，他進入三年制的國立台灣藝專，念戲劇電影科。

這令李安的父親大失所望，他允許李安就讀，但條件是畢業後要赴美深造。因此，從台灣藝專畢業——他在那裡很喜歡演戲、拍短片——並服完兵役後，他進入伊利諾大學主修戲劇。李安發現自己對導戲的興趣大於演戲，於是到紐約大學完成電影製作碩士學位。念研究所時，他拍了多部短片，其中一部——《蔭涼湖畔》——贏得台灣金穗獎最佳劇情短片獎。李安也擔任同學史派克李畢業作品的攝影師，而他自己的畢業作品《分界線》贏得紐約大學年度電影節的最佳影片及最佳導演獎。

Language Guide

Golden Harvest Film Festival 金穗獎

金穗獎自一九七八年開始舉辦，為提升電影作品的素質及內涵，並鼓勵國內電影工作人拍攝非商業性的創作影片而設立。參賽者不侷限身分，影片不限制類型 (genre)。只要影片規格符合規定，劇情片 (feature film)、紀錄片 (documentary)、實驗電影 (experimental film) 或是動畫 (animation) 都可以參加徵選。金穗獎將國內電影的創作實力都激發出來，不僅培育出許多傑出的電影人才，更可說是指標性的影片競賽，現今許多著名的導演，像是蔡明亮、魏德聖、柯一正還有本文介紹的李安……等等，都是從金穗獎的淬煉而來，相信金穗獎未來還能栽培出更多優秀的國片工作者。

© [Mooi] / filickr.com

Spike Lee 史派克・李

有「黑人教父」之稱的史派克・李，本名為 Shelton Jackson Lee。在就讀紐約大學時，與李安結識。他的電影製作公司——四十英畝及一頭騾 (40 Acres & A Mule Filmworks) 製作的電影常將政治社會問題反映出來，尤以黑人議題為首要。美夢成箴 (*She's Gotta Have It*)、為所應為 (*Do the Right Thing*)、叢林熱 (*Jungle Fever*) 還有黑潮：麥爾坎 X (*Malcolm X*) 都是他早期有名的作品。

© nicogenin / flickr.com

解答 ❶ (B) ❷ (C)

朗讀 MP3 112 單字 MP3 113 英文文章導讀 MP3 114

Even more importantly, *Fine Line* attracted the attention of William Morris, the world's largest talent [1]**agency**. Lee had been planning to return to Taiwan, but a call from the agency convinced him to stay in New York. Yet even with William Morris as his agent, his poor English made it difficult to find producers for his film projects. So Lee spent the next six years as a stay-at-home dad while his wife Jane, a [9]**microbiologist** he met at university, worked to support the family. Lee never gave up on his filmmaking dreams, however, and his opportunity finally came when two of his screenplays won first and second place in a [2]**contest** sponsored by Taiwan's Government Information Office.

Vocabulary Bank

1) **agency** [ˋedʒənsi] (n.) 代理商
(n.) agent [ˋedʒənt] 代理人
Which travel agency did you book your tour with?

2) **contest** [ˋkɑntɛst] (n.) 競賽，競爭
Danny won second place in the speech contest.

3) **retire** [rɪˋtaɪr] (v.) 退休
We plan on moving to Florida after we retire.

4) **explore** [ɪkˋsplor] (v.) 探索，探究，瞭解
You should explore your options before you choose a major.

5) **theme** [θim] (n.) 主題，議題
What is the theme of your essay?

6) **nomination** [͵nɑməˋneʃən] (n.) 提名
The actress has received many Oscar nominations.

7) **momentum** [moˋmɛntəm] (n.) 氣勢，動力
The politician's campaign is gaining momentum.

8) **break into** [brek ˋɪntu] (phr.) 進入（演藝圈等難進入的行業）
Many young actors hope to break into the movies.

進階字彙

9) **microbiologist** [͵maɪkrobaɪˋɑlədʒɪst] (n.) 微生物學家
(n.) microbiology [͵maɪkkrobaɪˋɑlədʒɪ]
A group of microbiologists has discovered a new type of virus.

10) **hit** [hɪt] (n.) 成功、受歡迎的事物
The clown was a big hit at Timmy's birthday party

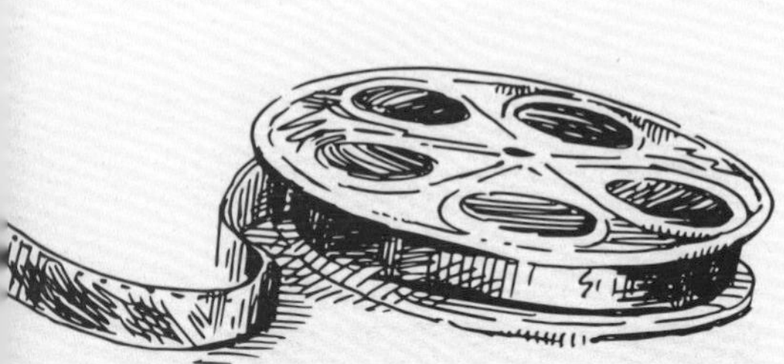

I call for a Decade of Action
for Road Safety 2010-2020
Together we can save millions of lives. It is time for action.
MAKE ROADS SAFE
The Campaign for Global Road Safety

With the support of Taiwan's largest movie studio, Lee was able to turn both screenplays into feature motion pictures: *Pushing Hands* (1992) and *The Wedding Banquet* (1993). Both films—the first about a tai chi master who [3]**retires** to New York to live with his son and American daughter-in-law, the second about a gay Taiwanese-American who marries a Chinese woman to please his parents—[4]**explore** the conflicts that occur when different cultures and generations clash. While *Pushing Hands* was a big [10]**hit** in Taiwan, *The Wedding Banquet* was an international success, winning a Golden Bear at the Berlin Film Festival. Lee's next movie, *Eat Drink Man Woman* (1994), a story about a retired Taipei chef and his three daughters that further explores the [5]**themes** of his first two films, was an even greater success. The film won Best Foreign Language Film [6]**nominations** for both the Golden Globe and Academy Awards, giving him the [7]**momentum** he needed to [8]**break into** Hollywood.

Mini Quiz 閱讀測驗

❶ **Why did Lee become a stay-at-home dad?**
(A) Because he was better with children than his wife
(B) Because it gave him time to write screenplays
(C) Because he couldn't find work as a filmmaker
(D) Because he gave up on his filmmaking dreams

❷ **Which of the following films was most successful?**
(A) The Wedding Banquet
(B) Fine Line
(C) Eat Drink Man Woman
(D) Pushing Hands

Translation

更重要的是，《分界線》引起全球最大明星經紀公司威廉莫里斯的關注。李安原本計畫回台灣，但該公司一通電話說服了他留在紐約。但就算有威廉莫里斯這個經紀公司，李安蹩腳的英文還是讓他很難為拍片企畫找到製片。所以李安接下來六年，都在家當家庭主夫，由他在大學認識的妻子，微生物學家林惠嘉工作養家。但李安從來沒有放棄拍電影的夢想，而在他的兩部電影劇本於台灣政府新聞局主辦的一項比賽包辦第一、二名之後，他的機會終於來臨。

在台灣最大電影製片公司的支持下，李安得以將這兩個劇本拍成電影：《推手》（一九九二年）和《囍宴》（一九九三年）。兩部電影——第一部描述一位太極大師退休後到紐約與兒子和美國媳婦同住，第二部則是一位台裔美籍男同性戀娶了中國妻子取悅父母的故事——皆探討了不同文化與世代碰撞時所發生的衝突。《推手》在台灣相當賣座，《囍宴》則在國際大放異彩，贏得柏林影展金熊獎。李安的下一部電影《飲食男女》（一九九四年）——一名退休的台北廚師和他三個女兒的故事，進一步探討前兩部片的主題——獲得更大的成就。這部電影同時獲得金球獎和奧斯卡金像獎最佳外語片提名，給了他所需的動能打進好萊塢。

Language Guide

父親三部曲

李安早期的華語電影：《推手》、《喜宴》和《飲食男女》，也被稱作「家庭三部曲」，皆以世代親子間的思想衝突為主題。在新時代中，傳統被瓦解之後在重組，在這個過程中，家庭關係該如何取得平衡，李安的這三部電影綻露無疑。

© cvbercherry / fickr.com

《推手》的劇本在一九九九年編寫完成後，便獲得中華民國新聞局優良劇本。徐立功 (Hsu Li Kong) 的慧眼獨具，讓李安擁有首次執導的機會，隔年便順利搬上大銀幕。養兒防老不僅是父母對兒女的期待，也是子女應盡的義務。太極大師朱父退休後搬去美國與兒子一家同住，不料，傳統的生活習慣卻與西式的洋媳婦格格不入。中西文化背景的差異再加上語言的隔閡，家變成衝突發生的地點。傳統的倫理關係，在日新月異的時代文化交流下，該如何維持下去？

© hto2008 / flickr.com

《推手》的評價甚高，李安順勢拍攝第二 三部並上映「不孝有三，無後為大」，李安在《喜宴》大膽挑戰傳統婚姻關係及傳宗接代的價值。劇中的偉同受到傳統的壓力，無法勇敢地向父母表白自己的性向；高父也因傳統的束縛，無法承認兒子的真實性向。李安用同性戀 (homosexual) 題材來說明一個想做自己的人，在面對自我與符合傳統中相互拔河。

不同於前面兩部角色設定在華裔美國人，《飲食男女》抽離文化衝擊和父子關係，開始著墨於父女情感。餐桌是父女間唯一說話的場合，這意味著父女之間出現代溝 (generation gap)，所有事情都在飯桌上宣布，衝突也在餐桌上爆發。三個女兒都想離開家中，擁有真正的自我。最後，女兒開始一個個離去，老朱也跨出了傳統的界限，開始自己的新人生。李安曾說：「片中的食物和飯桌只是比喻，象徵家庭的解構，天下無不散的筵席，但解構的目的是為了再結構。」

解答 ❶ (C) ❷ (C)

朗讀 MP3 115 單字 MP3 116 英文文章導讀 MP3 117

Lee's first Hollywood feature, *Sense and Sensibility* (1995), was a skillful adaptation of the Jane Austen novel starring Emma Thompson and Hugh Grant. The film was a critical and commercial success, paving the way for two more Hollywood films: *The Ice Storm* (1997), a 1970s family drama starring Sigourney Weaver and Kevin Kline, and *Ride with the Devil* (1999), a Western movie set during the Civil War. While these two films were well received by critics, they failed at the box office, a [1]**setback** that [2]**prompted** Lee to return to his roots. *Crouching Tiger, Hidden Dragon* (2000), a Chinese-language [3]**martial** arts epic made for Western audiences, finally brought Lee the recognition he deserved. Shot on a small budget with a cast and crew from Taiwan, Hong Kong and China, the film won four Academy Awards, including Best Foreign Language Film, and became the highest-grossing foreign film in U.S. history.

Now more popular than ever, Lee was chosen to direct *Hulk* (2003), a big-budget comic book adaptation starring Eric Banna and Jennifer Connelly. Unfortunately, the movie was such a critical and commercial failure that he considered retiring early. With encouragement from his father, though, Lee returned to the director's chair for *Brokeback Mountain* (2005), a low-budget independent film about the relationship between two [4]**gay** ranch hands in 1960s Wyoming. This sensitive story about [5]**forbidden** love became a box office hit and cultural [6]**phenomenon**. It also received 71 awards, including an Oscar for Best Director. Since this career high, Lee has continued exploring new [7]**genres** with films like *Lust, Caution* (2007), a spy thriller set in 1940s Shanghai and *Taking Woodstock* (2009), a light comedy about the famous 1969 music festival.

Vocabulary Bank

1) **setback** [ˋsɛt͵bæk] (n.) 挫折，失敗，阻礙
The project was delayed due to setbacks.

2) **prompt** [prɑmpt] (v.) 引發，促使
What prompted Sarah to change her mind?

3) **martial** [ˋmɑrʃəl] (a.) 好戰的，尚武的，martial art 即「武術」
Tae kwon do is the most popular martial art in the world.

4) **gay** [ɡe] (a./n.) 同性戀的；同性戀
Do you have any gay friends?

5) **forbidden** [fɚˋbɪdən] (a.) 禁止的，禁忌的
(v.) forbid [fɝˋbɪd]
Smoking is forbidden in all areas of the building.

6) **phenomenon** [fəˋnɑmə͵nɑn] (n.) 意想不到、非凡的人事物，現象
Jeremy Lin became a basketball phenomenon almost overnight.

進階字彙

7) **genre** [ˋʒɑnrə] (n.)（藝文作品的）類型
What's your favorite genre of literature?

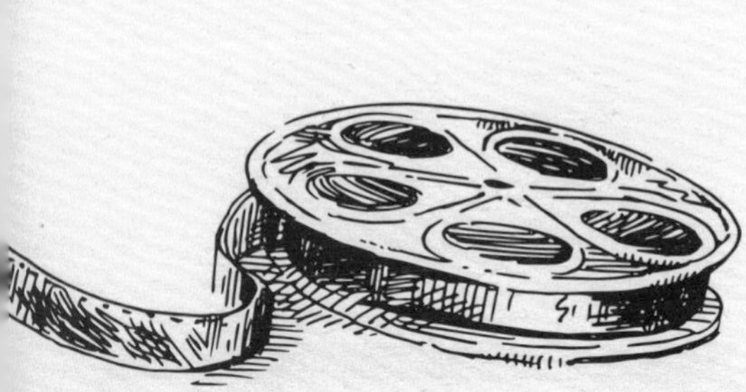

Mini Quiz 閱讀測驗

❶ **According to the article, which of the following films was based on a book?**
(A) Ride with the Devil
(B) Sense and Sensibility
(C) Crouching Tiger, Hidden Dragon
(D) Ice Storm

❷ **Which of the following is true about Brokeback Mountain?**
(A) It won nearly 70 awards.
(B) It won an Oscar for Best Picture.
(C) It was relatively cheap to film.
(D) It is about a gay marriage.

中 Translation

李安的第一部好萊塢長片《理性與感性》（一九九五年）巧妙地改編了珍奧斯汀的名著小說，由艾瑪湯普森和休葛蘭領銜主演。這部片叫好又叫座，為他獲得執導接下來兩部好萊塢電影的機會：《冰風暴》（一九九七年），雪歌妮薇佛和凱文克萊主演的一九七〇年代家庭生活劇，以及《與魔鬼共騎》（一九九九年），以南北戰爭為背景的西部片。這兩部電影雖然都廣受好評，這次挫敗促使李安決定回到他的創意源頭。《臥虎藏龍》（二〇〇〇年），是為西方觀眾拍攝的華語武俠史詩，終於讓李安贏得他應得的肯定。這部小成本電影，採用台灣、香港和中國的演員及工作人員，贏得四座奧斯卡獎包括最佳外語片在內，還成為美國史上最賣座的外語片。

當下人氣更勝以往的李安獲選執導《綠巨人浩克》（二〇〇三年），一部大成本的漫畫改編電影，由艾瑞克班納和珍妮佛康納莉主演。可惜這部片的影評及票房皆慘遭滑鐵盧，使他考慮提早退休。但在父親的鼓勵下，李安重回導演椅，於二〇〇五年交出《斷背山》，一部小成本獨立影片，描述一九六〇年代懷俄明州兩位同性戀牧場工人的戀情。這篇細述禁忌之愛的感人故事除了席捲票房，更成為文化現象。此外還贏得七十一個獎，包括奧斯卡最佳導演。在此事業顛峰之後，李安繼續探索新電影類型，推出《色，戒》（二〇〇七年）和《胡士托風波》（二〇〇九年），前者是以一九四〇年代上海為背景的間諜驚悚片，後者則是描述一九六九年那場著名音樂節的輕喜劇。

若有疑問請來信：eztalkQ@gmail.com

© Featureflash / Shutterstock.com

© human_species / ficker.com

Language Guide

李安經典電影

一九九九年在徐立功的邀約下，隔年便發表改編自王度廬的武俠小說《臥虎藏龍》為依據的同名電影作品。首部將傳統武俠傳說的魅力發揚光大，並在國際市場大放異彩的中國武俠電影。以原音搭配英文字幕的《臥虎藏龍》締造美國有史以來最賣座的華語電影，並榮得奧斯卡最佳外語片 (Best Foreign Language Film) 的殊榮（是唯一也是第一部獲得最佳外語片的華語電影）。

劇情以安妮．普露 (Annie Proulx) 所著小說《近鄉情怯：懷俄明故事集》(*Close Range: Wyoming Stories*) 中的短篇故事《斷背山》改編。《斷背山》描述出六〇年代兩個男人之間複雜的情感關係。在保守的懷俄明州，對外維持大家眼中正常的生活，心裡卻不斷壓抑情感，在二〇〇五年上映時，此部電影除了大獲好評之外，對於從未拿出檯面討論的同性議題也引起很大的迴響力與討論，「斷背山」後來甚至成為同性戀的代名詞。李安也因為此片榮獲奧斯卡最佳導演獎 (Academy Award for Best Director)。

© K 嘛 / flickr.com

二〇〇七年李安把觀眾又帶回了中國，電影《色，戒》改編自張愛玲的同名短篇小說。故事發生在第二次世界大戰日本大舉入侵中國之時，汪精衛成立偽政府對抗國民政府。正值多事之秋的中國，救國情感高漲的青年們對於一眾漢奸更是看不起，故事男主角易先生是在汪政府底下工作的特務頭目，於是謀殺易先生的行動祕密地展開了。精彩的劇情鋪陳讓此片在台灣金馬獎 (Golden Horse Awards) 上抱回最佳劇情片 (Best Feature Film) 和最佳導演 (Best Director) 兩項大獎。

© eliot. / flicker.com

解答 ❶ (B) ❷ (C)

1992	推手 Pushing Hands
1993	喜宴 The Wedding Banquet
1994	飲食男女 Eat Drink Man Woman
1995	理性與感性 Sense and Sensibility
1997	冰風暴 The Ice Storm
1999	與魔鬼共騎 Ride with the Devil
2000	臥虎藏龍 Crouching Tiger, Hidden Dragon
2002	（B MW 廣告短片）The Hire
2003	綠巨人浩客 Hulk
2005	斷背山 Brokeback Mountain
2007	色，戒 Lust, Caution
2009	胡士托風波 Taking Woodstock
2012	少年 Pi 的奇幻旅程 Life of Pi

Life of Pi 小說、電影大不同

李安的話題作品，少年 Pi 的奇幻漂流（*Life of Pi*）是加拿大作家楊馬泰爾（Yann Martel）的同名暢銷小說改編（adaptation）。原小說是一本奇幻怪誕，又天真寫實的奇幻文學作品，因此翻拍電影難度很高，為了拍攝需要，李安巧思重新改寫成電影劇本，其中有幾個有趣的不同處：

1 **Pi is old enough in the film to be interested in girls.**

電影裡，Pi 太著迷於舞蹈課遇到的女孩，無心發現他爸爸正在為了動物園經營傷透腦筋。因為這樣，Pi 之後在海上的漂流旅程才特別辛苦，也讓他成長最多。

2 **In the movie, Pi learns about religion from his mother, who is far more religious than in the book.**

電影中的 Pi 透過母親信了教，比小說中的他對宗教更為著迷。電影版本中的母親在 Pi 心中有特別的位置，也深深影響了他對宗教的看法。他們親密的關係，讓電影最後，Pi 自己述說的第二段故事更耐人尋味。

3 **Unlike in the book, Pi is never able to tame Richard Parker.**

和小說不同的，電影中的 Pi 從來沒有馴服 Richard Parker。小說中的 Pi 使用他對動物行為和馬戲團訓練的瞭解來訓練和控制 Richard Parker，但電影中，Pi 和 Richard Parker 維持一種危險的恐怖平衡。Pi 從來沒有能夠完全控制老虎，但是李安用這個危險的關係來解釋，為什麼 Pi 可以在荒海上漂流卻維持求生意志。

4 **There is more beauty and less suffering in Ang Lee's version of the story.**

李安的版本中，Pi 的旅程雖然驚心動魄，也充滿了美麗的時刻，讓人感覺不虛此行，比如藍鯨從海中破海而出的壯觀。

5 **Pi and the tiger only spend a day on the meerkat island**

在小說中，Pi 和 Richard Parker 在島上花了不少時間逗留。電影中為了片長的限制，李安安排他們倆只在島上停留一天。不過小說裡，Pi 在植物中發現人類牙齒的懸疑成份依然被保留在電影裡面，增加故事的可看性。

Vocabulary Bank

1) **sentence** [ˋsɛntəs] (v.) 判刑
The judge sentenced the thief to a year in prison.

2) **repay** [rɪˋpe] (v.) 償還，清償
I have six months to repay my loan.

3) **material** [məˋtɪriəl] (n.) 素材，資料
Tracy went to the library to gather material for her report.

4) **troubled** [ˋtrʌbəld] (a.) 困難重重的，困頓的
Peace has finally come to the troubled region.

5) **awesome** [ˋɔsəm] (a.) 令人欽佩的，驚人的
The Panama Canal is an awesome achievement.

6) **realistic** [ˌriəˋlɪstɪk] (a.) 寫實的，逼真的
The animation is so realistic that you can't tell it from the real thing.

7) **mean** [min] (a.) 鄙陋的，（地位）卑賤的
Jason grew up in a mean neighborhood.

8) **orphaned** [ˋɔrfənd] (a.) 失去父母的，孤兒的
There are many orphaned children living on the streets.

9) **miser** [ˋmaɪzɚ] (n.) 吝嗇鬼，守財奴
The old miser left all her money to her cat.

10) **murderer** [ˋmɝdərɚ] (n.) 謀殺犯
The murderer was sentenced to life in prison.

11) **funeral** [ˋfjunərəl] (n.) 葬禮
The star's funeral was attended by thousands of fans.

12) **mourner** [mɔrnɚ] (n.) 哀悼者
(v.) mourn [mɔrn] 哀悼，憂傷
The mourners were all dressed in black.

進階字彙

13) **empathy** [ˋɛmpəθi] (n.) 共鳴，同理心
The man's empathy for the poor led him to start a charity.

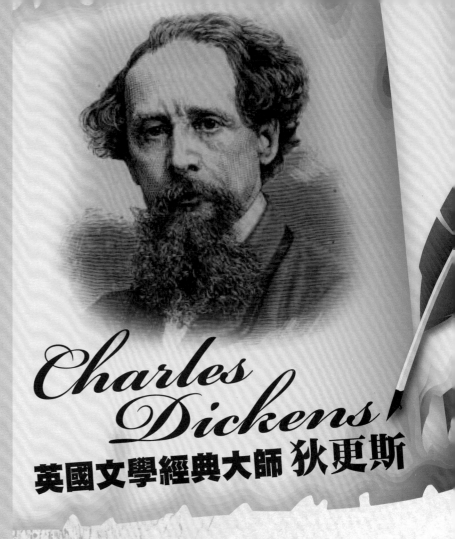

Charles Dickens
英國文學經典大師 狄更斯

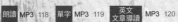

朗讀 MP3 118 單字 MP3 119 英文文章導讀 MP3 120

Charles Dickens was born in England on February 7, 1812, the son of a clerk working for the British Navy. Although Dickens was later one of England's most successful authors, he didn't have an easy childhood. In 1824 his father was [1]**sentenced** to the Marshalsea Prison for failing to [2]**repay** his debts, a harsh environment where many prisoners died. This meant Dickens' family didn't have the money to pay for his education anymore. At the age of twelve, he started working in a boring factory to help support his family, a job that he especially hated. But the experience gave him plenty of real-life [3]**material** for his later novels, including *David Copperfield*. It was Dickens' [4]**troubled** childhood and his [13]**empathy** for the poor, plus his experience as a reporter as well as his [5]**awesome** talent that helped him write fifteen novels that were [6]**realistic** Ⓖyet magical.

Having lived in London's [7]**mean** streets, Dickens filled his stories with [8]**orphaned** and starving children, [9]**misers**, [10]**murderers**, abusive schoolteachers and other characters from real life. He brings the best and the worst of 19th-century London to life on every page. One of his most famous novels is *A Christmas Carol*, which was originally written to show the widening gap between the rich and the poor during the Industrial Revolution. However, the novel's popularity also helped make Christmas into the important holiday it is today. By the time Dickens died, he was world-famous. He hadn't wanted a fancy [11]**funeral** but because he was so popular, he was buried in Poet's Corner, Westminster Abbey, surrounded by flowers from thousands of [12]**mourners**.

中 Translation

查爾斯狄更斯一八一二年二月七日生於英國，父親是一名英國海軍職員。儘管狄更斯後來成為英國最有成就的文豪之一，他的童年並不好過。一八二四年他的父親因無法償還債務而被判入馬夏爾西監獄，那裡的環境惡劣，許多服刑者在牢裡死去。這意味著狄更斯的家人再也沒錢支付他的教育。十二歲時，狄更斯開始在一家枯燥無趣的工廠工作，協助維持家計，他特別痛恨這份工作。但這段經歷為他後來的小說，包括《塊肉餘生記》，提供了豐富的真實題材。正是狄更斯困頓的童年、對窮人的同理心、擔任記者的經歷，以及驚人的天分，讓他得以寫出十五部寫實又令人讚嘆的小說。

住過倫敦鄙陋街頭的狄更斯，故事裡盡是孤苦挨餓的孩童、守財奴、謀殺者、施暴的教師和其他現實生活的角色。他把十九世紀倫敦最好與最壞的一面都重現在書中每一頁。他最負盛名的小說之一是《小氣財神》，原本是為呈現工業革命時期日益擴大的貧富差距而寫，但這部小說蔚為流行，也使得聖誕節成為今日重要的節日。狄更斯去世時已是舉世皆知的人物。他並沒有要求奢華的葬禮，不過他實在太受歡迎，因此被葬在西敏寺的詩人隅，被成千上萬悼祭者致獻的鮮花所圍繞。

Language Guide

Industrial Revolution 工業革命

十八世紀中葉，人類歷史因機械革新而有重大轉變，原以人力為主的生產模式被機械所取代，生產力瞬間大增，工廠制度興起，運輸及交通也日趨便利。工業革命促使經濟自由體系建立，社會上產生新的階層：資本家及勞工，因此工業革命後的社會被認為是資本主義社會的雛形。這樣的驟變在當時提供許多人工作機會，普遍提高人民生活品質，但也衍生出極大的問題，例如人口都市化與貧富差距，如何在這當中取得平衡，至今仍是令社會及經濟學者傷腦筋的難題。

Westminster Abbey 西敏寺小檔案

位於英國倫敦，已有千年歷史的西敏寺，是一座大型的哥德式教堂，自一〇六六年初興建以來，一直是英國各代君主舉辦加冕典禮之處。西元一二四五年，亨利三世改建此處成為現今的西敏寺，共有十七位君主長眠於此地，除此之外，許多偉大的貴族、將軍、詩人、科學家也在此安葬。第一位葬於西敏寺的詩人是喬叟 (Geoffrey Chaucer)（著有 *The Canterbury Tales*《坎特伯利故事集》等），之後許多英國出色文人也陸陸續續埋葬在喬叟的墓周圍，於是西敏寺便多了一處詩人隅，或稱詩人之角 (Poet's Corner)，能在西敏寺安葬或豎立紀念碑逐漸成為一種榮耀。西敏寺現為英國皇室的名勝古蹟，被列為世界文化遺產之一。

Grammar Master

yet 的用法

1. yet 作為連接詞，用以連接兩個單字、片語或子句，表示「然而」。

例 ● The weather is cold, **yet** bright and sunny.
天氣很冷，不過仍是陽光普照。

2. yet 作為副詞，表示某事到目前為止尚未發生。yet 常出現在否定或疑問句，中文意思是「還沒……」。

例 ● I am surprised that you **haven't** told him anything **yet**.
真沒想到，你居然什麼事都還沒告訴他。

● Have you had your lunch **yet**?
吃過午餐了嗎？

A CHRISTMAS CAROL
小氣財神

朗讀 MP3 121 單字 MP3 122 英文文章導讀 MP3 123

Charles Dickens' novel *A Christmas* [1]***Carol*** is the story of how a mean [2]**accounting** firm owner, Ebenezer Scrooge, sees the error of his ways on Christmas night. The story begins by showing an angry Scrooge who [3]**resents** the happiness of those around him on Christmas Eve. He's [4]**determined** to [7]**stamp out** all happiness, [5]**particularly** that of his clerk, Bob Cratchit. On his way home, Scrooge is stopped and asked to donate money to the poor. He replies that there should be more than enough work camps or prisons to house them. Although he has [8]**grudgingly** allowed Cratchit the next day off to celebrate Christmas, he doesn't plan to celebrate the holiday himself. He goes home to eat thin [9]**porridge** in front of a tiny fire, even though he's very wealthy.

Vocabulary Bank

1) **carol** [ˋkærəl] (n.) 頌歌
We always sing Christmas carols on Christmas Eve.

2) **accounting** [əˋkaʊntɪŋ] (n.) 會計
(n.) account [əˋkaʊnt] 帳目
Carol wants to study accounting in college and become an accountant.

3) **resent** [rɪˋzɛnt] (v.) 怨恨，嫉妒
Kevin resents his brother for his success.

4) **determined** [dɪˋtɝmɪnd] (a.) 有決心的
I'm determined to finish writing this report before I go home.

5) **particularly** [pɚˋtɪkjələli] (adv.) 特別，尤其
Alice is particularly good at tennis.

6) **in store (for sb.)** [ɪn stor] (phr.) 某事即將發生（在某人身上）
I have a surprise in store for you when you get home.

進階字彙

7) **stamp out** [stæmp aʊt] (phr.) 撲滅，消滅
The new mayor promised to stamp out crime.

8) **grudgingly** [ˋgrʌdʒɪŋli] (adv.) 勉強地，不情願地
Michael grudgingly admitted that he was wrong.

9) **porridge** [ˋpɔrɪdʒ] (n.) 粥，稀飯
We often have porridge for breakfast on cold mornings.

That night Scrooge is visited by the ghost of his former partner, Jacob Marley. The ghost carries heavy chains and explains that he can never enjoy peace. He warns Scrooge that a similar fate is [6)]**in store** for him too unless he becomes a better person. Marley's ghost says it's too late for himself and tells Scrooge that three ghosts will visit him over the next three nights. They will take him on a journey through the past, present and future. After Marley's ghost leaves, Scrooge looks out the window and is shocked to see hundreds of ghosts in chains wandering down the street. [G]Scared half to death, Scrooge hides behind his bed curtains.

中 Translation

狄更斯的《小氣財神》描述一位刻薄的會計事務所老闆史艾柏納澤史古基如何在聖誕夜發現自己的行為過失。故事一開始，憤怒的史古基在聖誕夜對身邊眾人的歡樂感到怨忿，他決定撲滅一切歡樂，特別是對他的職員鮑伯克拉契特。回家途中，史古基被攔住，要他捐錢給窮人。他回答說，勞動營或監獄應該夠多讓窮人去住。雖然他勉為其難地讓克拉契特隔天休假去慶祝耶誕，他自己卻不打算慶祝。他回到家中，在微弱的爐火前吃很稀的稀飯，即便他其實非常富有。

當晚，前合夥人雅各馬利的鬼魂找上史古基。鬼魂身繫沉重鐵鍊，說他始終不得安寧。他警告史古基，這樣的命運也在等著他，除非他能成為比較好的人。馬利的鬼魂說自己為時已晚，並告訴史古基，接下來三個晚上會有三個鬼魂來找他，他們將帶他走一趟過去、現在和未來之旅。馬利的鬼魂離開後，史古基往窗外一望，驚訝地看到數百個身繫鎖鍊的鬼魂在街上遊蕩。史古基嚇得半死，趕緊躲到床帷後面。

G Grammar Master

to death 的兩種用法

1. V+ to death →表示「……（到）死」

例 ● These villagers will **starve to death** unless they receive help soon.
再不快點獲得援助，這些村民就會餓死。

2. be 動詞 + 形容詞 + to death →描述「……得要命／得要死」

例 ● The talk went on for hours, we were all **bored to death**.
這場演講已經持續好幾個鐘頭，我們都要無聊死了！

to death 在文法上稱為補語，常與動詞連用，作為補充說明動詞的現行狀態，或是用以誇飾個人情緒，語意上通常具有負面的涵義。

What's New?

經典文學《小氣財神》（或譯《聖誕頌歌》）(*A Christmas Carol*) 是狄更斯最廣為流傳的聖誕節系列故事之一。一開始狄更斯只是為了解決債務上的燃眉之急而撰寫這部道德劇，以惹人厭的史古基 (Scrooge) 來傳達聖誕節精神的故事卻極具戲劇張力，讓此作品兩世紀以來不斷被改編成各種語言的舞台劇、卡通、電視劇以及電影。這個歷久彌新的好故事今年又被搬上大銀幕，由喜劇泰斗金凱瑞扮演死要錢的守財奴，將會為這部經典名著帶來什麼新意？好奇的讀者在讀完 EZ TALK 介紹的原著故事後，不妨去瞧瞧這部片，看看是否真如導演所說：「狄更斯當初這個故事若是寫來拍電影的，那部電影就會是《聖誕夜怪譚》(*Disney's A Christmas Carol*)。」

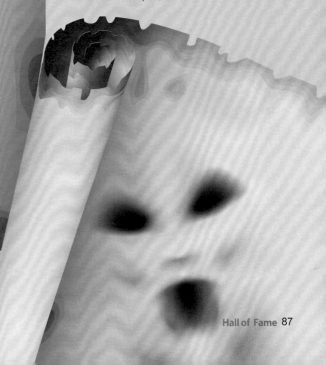

Vocabulary Bank

1) **cripple** [ˋkrɪpəl] (n./v.) 瘸子；使跛，使殘廢
The boy became a cripple after stepping on a mine.

2) **horrify** [ˋhɔrəfaɪ] (v.) 使驚嚇
We were horrified to hear of the airplane crash.

3) **comment** [ˋkɑmɛnt] (n./v.) 意見，評論；發表意見
If you have any comments, please raise your hand.

4) **valuable** [ˋvæljəbəl] (n.)（固定用複數）貴重物品
You should never leave any valuables in your car.

5) **grave** [grev] (n.) 墓穴，埋葬處
Thousands of people visit Mozart's grave each year.

6) **shed a tear** [ʃɛd ə tir] (phr.) 流淚，傷心難過
He shed a tear when he heard that his old pet dog had died.

7) **butcher** [ˋbutʃɚ] (n.) 肉販，屠夫
We buy all our meat from the butcher on the corner.

8) **festivity** [fɛˋstɪvəti] (n.)（常用複數）慶祝活動，慶典
The small town is famous for its Christmas festivities.

進階字彙

9) **urchin** [ˋɝtʃɪn] (n.) 流浪兒
The streets of Calcutta are full of urchins.

10) **scratch out** [skrætʃ aʊt] (phr.) 艱苦度日
The man scratched out a living by collecting cans and bottles.

11) **undertaker** [ˋʌndɚ͵tekɚ] (n.) 殯葬員
The undertaker lowered the coffin into the ground.

朗讀 MP3 124 單字 MP3 125 英文文章導讀 MP3 126

The Ghost of Christmas Past arrives and shows Scrooge how he used to be happy until a failed love affair made him ©love money instead of people. The Ghost of Christmas Present introduces him to Bob Cratchit's happy but poor home and to his sweet child, Tiny Tim, a [1]**cripple** who walks with a crutch. The ghost then shows Scrooge how two street [9]**urchins** [10]**scratch out** a living. Scrooge is [2]**horrified**, but the ghost mocks Scrooge's earlier [3]**comment** that work houses and prisons should be good enough for the poor. Finally, the Ghost of Christmas Yet to Come reveals the unhappiest scenes of all. Tiny Tim has passed away because the Cratchits don't have enough money for a good doctor. At Scrooge's funeral, the [11]**undertaker** and housekeeper steal his clothes and [4]**valuables**. Scrooge's [5]**grave** is deserted and nobody [6]**sheds a tear** over his death.

When Scrooge wakes up, he realizes that the ghosts have completed all their visits. He goes to his bedroom window and asks a boy down below what day it is. When he finds out that it is Christmas morning, he tells the boy to buy the prize-winning turkey down at the [7]**butcher** shop and send it to the Crachit family. He puts on his best clothes and attends a Christmas party at the home of his nephew. When Bob Cratchit, tired from the [8]**festivities**, is late for work the next day, Scrooge smiles and gives him some warm punch and promises him a raise. From that day on, Scrooge is like a father to Tiny Tim. He has **1 turned over a new leaf** and celebrates Christmas and life itself with more generosity than any other man.

中 Translation

往日聖誕的鬼魂找上門，讓史古基看到他過去是多麼快樂，直到一場失敗的戀情讓他開始愛財不愛人。今日聖誕的鬼魂則帶他去看鮑伯克拉契特快樂但貧窮的家庭，還有他可愛的孩子小提姆，一個得拄拐杖行走的跛子。這個鬼魂還讓史古基看到兩名街頭流浪兒如何艱苦度日。史古基嚇壞了，但鬼魂接著奚落史古基先前所說，勞動營和監獄對窮人應該綽綽有餘了。最後，未來聖誕的鬼魂揭露了最不快樂的畫面。小提姆因為克拉契特沒有足夠的錢找好醫生而去世；在史古基的葬禮上，殯葬業者和管家偷走他的衣物和貴重物品，史古基的墳墓荒蕪，沒有人為他的死掉一滴淚。

當史古基一覺醒來，他知道鬼魂已經來找過他了。他走到臥室窗邊，問窗下一個男孩今天是什麼日子，得知是聖誕節早晨之後，他請男孩幫他到肉店買最好的火雞肉，送去克拉契特家中。他穿上他最體面的衣服，參加姪兒家中的聖誕派對。隔天鮑伯克拉契因慶祝得太累而上班遲到，史古基微笑以對，溫暖地捶了他幾下，承諾給他加薪。從那天開始，史古基把小提姆當成親生兒子。他改頭換面，比任何人都大肆地頌揚聖誕以及人生。

若有疑問請來信：eztalkQ@gmail.com

Tongue-tied No More

1 turn over a new leaf
改頭換面，改過自新

有句話說「翻開新的一頁」，形容除舊迎新，重新開始，英文也有一模一樣的說法，連形容的方式都很像，就叫做 turn over a new leaf，但要注意的是 leaf 在這裡是指 page，也就是「書頁」，可不是「樹葉」喔！

A: I heard Jerry has turned over a new leaf.
我聽說傑瑞洗心革面了。

B: Yeah. He's stopped drinking and gambling, and now he spends all his time with his family.
是啊，他不再喝酒賭博了，現在他把時間都花在家人身上。

Grammar Master

instead of + N/Ving
而不是……，以（前者）取代（後者）

欲表達兩樣東西，後者應該被前者替代，或前者才是應該做的事情而不是後者時，我們可以用 instead of 插入在這兩者之中，使用句型如下：

- A instead of B → 要 A 而不是 B，應該做 A 而不是 B

例 Could I have tuna fish **instead of** chicken?
我能要鮪魚（口味）而不是雞肉的嗎？
We should do something **instead of** just talking about it.
我們應該做點什麼，而不是空談而已。

Mini Quiz

1. According to the article, who did NOT pay a visit to Mr. Scrooge on night?
(A) Bob Cratchit
(B) Jacob Marley
(C) The Ghost of Christmas Present
(D) The ghost of Christmas Yet to Come

2. On Christmas night, Scrooge decides to go home and eat thin porridge in front of a tiny fire ____________ celebrating the holiday.
(A) rather
(B) instead
(C) instead of
(D) and not

3. True or False
At the very end of the story, Mr. Scrooge hasn't changed. He becomes even meaner than before.

解答 1 (A) 2 (C) 3 (False)

Vocabulary Bank

1) **lecturer** [ˋlɛktʃərɚ] (n.) 講師
Donna is being promoted from lecturer to assistant professor.

2) **stammer** [ˋstæmɚ] (n.) 口吃，結巴
The boy stammers when he gets nervous.

3) **on top of** [ɑn tɑp əv] (phr.) 除此之外
On top of being beautiful, Priscilla is also sweet.

4) **sequel** [ˋsikwəl] (n.) 續集
I think the sequel's even better than the original.

5) **logic** [ˋlɑdʒɪk] (n.) 邏輯
I fail to see the logic of your argument.

6) **pneumonia** [nuˋmonjə] (n.) 肺炎
Pneumonia can sometimes be fatal.

進階字彙

7) **pseudonym** [ˋsudə͵nɪm] (n.) 筆名，雅號
The author writes under a pseudonym.

8) **deacon** [ˋdikən] (n.)（英國國教教會等的）執事
The deacon's job is to assist the minister.

Lewis Carroll
路易斯卡羅

朗讀 MP3 127 單字 MP3 128 英文文章導讀 MP3 129

Author Charles Lutwidge Dodgson, better known by his [7]**pseudonym** Lewis Carroll, was born on January 27th, 1832 in Daresbury, England. Homeschooled until he was 14, Dodgson was an excellent student in mathematics and was under great pressure to follow in the footsteps of his father, who was an Anglican priest and former mathematics [1]**lecturer** at Oxford. After attending Oxford himself, Dodgson was also offered a position as a mathematics lecturer there. Yet while he became an Anglican [8]**deacon**, he never did become a priest. Some people believe that this was because he suffered from a [2]**stammer** and did not believe in his ability to preach.

[3]**On top of** his mathematical talents, Dodgson showed promise as a writer of poetry and short stories. Ⓖ But he didn't become internationally known until he published *Alice's Adventures in Wonderland* in 1865 under the pen name Lewis Carroll. The book was an instant success, enjoyed by both children and adults alike. Famous fans of the story included Queen Victoria and Oscar Wilde. Carroll went on to publish a [4]**sequel**, *Through the Looking Glass and What Alice Found There*, in 1871, and wrote books on mathematics and [5]**logic** as well.

Caroll was also known as a photographer and an inventor of games and puzzles. Although it has been reported that Charles was unhappy and bored with his mathematics teaching at Oxford, he stayed there until his death from [6]**pneumonia** in 1898.

中 Translation

作家查爾斯路特維奇道奇森，以他的筆名路易斯卡羅較為人知，一八三二年一月二十七日出生於英格蘭的戴斯伯理。道奇森十四歲之前都是在家自學，是位數學資優生，身負繼承父親衣缽的強大壓力，他的父親是英國國教的牧師，也曾任牛津大學數學講師。在他自己就讀牛津之後，道奇森也受邀在此擔任數學講師的職位。雖然後來他成為英國國教教會的執事，但終究沒有成為牧師。有人認為這是因為他深受口吃之苦，不相信自己有能力講道。

除了數學天分，道奇森還展現出成為詩人和短篇小說作家的潛力。但是直到一八六五年他以路易斯卡羅這個筆名出版《愛麗絲夢遊奇境》，他才揚名國際。這本書一推出就大獲成功，小孩和大人同樣都喜歡。這個故事的知名粉絲包括維多利亞女王和作家奧斯卡王爾德。一八七一年，卡羅繼續出版續集《愛麗絲鏡中奇緣》，也撰寫關於數學和邏輯的書。

Oxford University

卡羅也是知名的攝影家以及遊戲和猜謎的發明家。儘管查爾斯據說在牛津教數學並不快樂，而且感到厭倦，但他直到一八九八年死於肺炎之前都待在牛津。

Language Guide

愛麗絲夢遊仙境內的文字遊戲

卡羅在瘋狂茶會上玩了許多文字遊戲，顛倒文字順序，雖然是雞同鴨講的對話，但是也非常有學習價值。例如：

三月兔要求愛麗絲「想什麼就說什麼」：

You should **say what you mean.**

愛麗絲認為她「至少我說的就是我想的」：

At least **I mean what I say** -- that's the same thing, you know.

意思真的一樣嗎？大家不妨想一想。

另外瘋帽匠說的「我看到我所吃的」I **see what I eat** 和「我吃我所看到的」I **eat what I see** 一樣令人玩味。

再舉諧音的例子，在睡鼠說故事的時候：「我的故事 (tale) 又長又悲傷！」。愛麗絲卻低頭疑惑地看著老鼠的尾巴說：「它的確是條長尾巴 (tail)，但你為何說它悲傷呢？」（tail「尾巴」和 tale「故事」同音）

同樣的例子也發生在愛麗絲與瘋帽匠的對話，愛麗絲跟瘋帽匠說：「不該把時間 (time) 浪費在說沒有謎底的謎語上。」瘋帽商說：「假如你和我一樣認識時間的話」，妳就不會說浪費它 (waste it) 了。應該說他 (waste him)」。接著又說：「我敢說妳甚至從來沒和時間說過話。」愛麗絲答說：「或許沒有吧，但我知道學音樂要打拍子 (beat time)。」瘋帽匠恍然大悟說：「啊！原因就在此，他受不了打擊的。」

從時間 (time) 雞同鴨講地說到打拍子 (beat time)，又說他（時間）受不了打擊。書中這類諧音的文字趣味在在都是，有興趣的讀者不妨再讀一遍這個故事，看您是否可以了解箇中趣味。

Grammar Master

not…until… 直到……才……

until 本身就含有「直到……前」的意思，後面可接名詞當介系詞用（如文中第 31 行的情況），也可接一個完整子句當連接詞用。中文表達「直到……之後才……」英文則是反過來說 not…until…「在……之前都沒有……」。

例
- 我到最後一分鐘才寫完考卷。
  I **didn't** finish the test **until** the last minute.
  （英文要說：在最後一分鐘前我都沒寫完考卷。）
- 她做完工作才會去睡覺。
  She **won't** go to bed **until** she finishes her work.
  （英文要說：在她做完工作前她不會去睡覺。）

Vocabulary Bank

1) **refer (to)** [rɪ`fɝ] (v.) 指的是，提及
(n.) reference [`rɛfrəns] 提及，暗示
Which study are you referring to?

2) **boredom** [`bɔrdəm] (n.) 無聊
They relieved their boredom by playing video games.

3) **offense** [ə`fɛns] (n.) 冒犯，得罪
The man's remarks caused great offense.

4) **concept** [`kɑnsɛpt] (n.) 觀念，概念
Risk is a difficult concept to understand.

5) **substitution** [ˌsʌbstə`tuʃən] (n.) 代替，代換
The substitution of milk for cream made the recipe more healthy.

6) **variable** [`vɛriəbəl] (n.) 變數，可變因素
The success of the plan depends on many variables.

進階字彙

7) **tantalize** [`tæntəˌlaɪz] (v.) 強烈吸引，使著迷
The magician tantalized the audience with amazing tricks.

8) **behead** [bɪ`hɛd] (v.) 砍頭，斬首
The spy was beheaded for treason.

9) **inverse** [ɪn`vɝs] (a.) 反向的，倒轉的
There is an inverse relationship between pressure and volume.

10) **semantic** [sə`mæntɪk] (a.) 語義的，語義學的
Our teacher told us to do a semantic analysis of the sentence.

Tongue-tied No More

1 mad as a hatter 瘋瘋癲癲

hatter「帽匠」是指縫製帽子的人，據說在十九世紀的歐洲，帽匠在製帽過程中須將毛皮放入硝酸汞的溶劑中，因吸入過多化學物質而導致行為舉止怪異，所以才有此一說，以 mad as a hatter 來形容某人「瘋瘋癲癲」。

A: Why is that guy walking down the street with no pants on?
為什麼那名男子沒穿褲子在逛大街？

B: Because he's mad as a hatter.
因為他是個瘋子。

© 達志 / UPI PHOTO

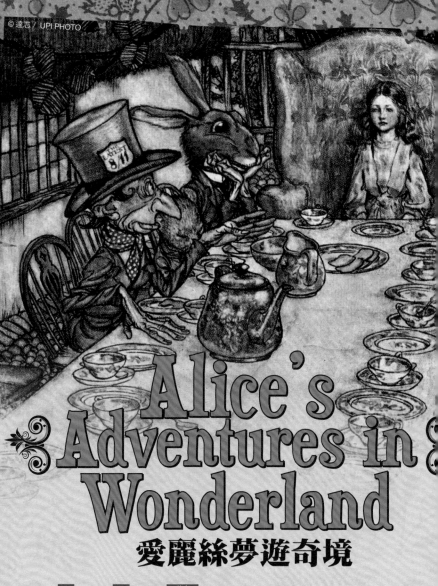

Alice's Adventures in Wonderland
愛麗絲夢遊奇境

朗讀 MP3 130 單字 MP3 131 英文文章導讀 MP3 132

It was well over a century ago that *Alice's Adventure in Wonderland* (often [1]**referred** to by its shortened form *Alice in Wonderland*) was published and quickly became one of the most beloved stories of all time. A product o the complex mind of Lewis Carroll, the tale of Alice and her journey through Wonderland is far from a simple children's story. Ⓖ The magical tale, with its use of literary nonsense and references to mathematics and history [7]**tantalizes** readers both young and old and continue to influence popular culture around the world.

The story begins when Alice's [2]**boredom** send her overactive imagination on a trip down a rabbi hole and into Wonderland, where she has a number o encounters with its strange residents. There is Ⓖa white rabbit with a watch who is always late; a smoking caterpillar on a magical mushroom; Ⓖthe Cheshire Cat, with his mysterious grin; the Mad Hatter, who is **1** **mad as a hatter**; and the Queen of Hearts, who cries "Off with their heads!" at the slightest [3)]**offense**. The tale ends with Alice avoiding a [8)]**beheading** ordered by the Queen when her sister wakes her up for tea and she discovers that it was all just a dream.

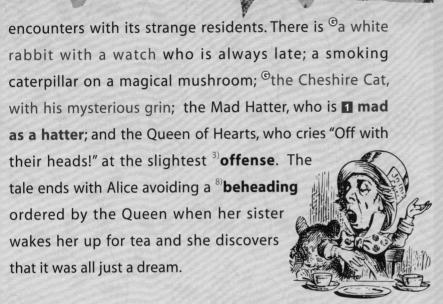

Written into the magical tale of Alice's adventures are many mathematical [4)]**concepts**, which are included in the most unlikely of places. The concept of limits is hinted at when Alice changes sizes after eating and drinking different items; [9)]**inverse** relationships are suggested during the discussion of the [10)]**semantic** values of sentences at the Mad Tea Party; and the [5)]**substitution** of [6)]**variables** is referred to when a pigeon says that little girls are like snakes because they both eat eggs. Very strange indeed!

中 Translation

《愛麗絲夢遊奇境》（經常簡稱為 *Alice in Wonderland*）遠在一個多世紀之前出版，而且很快就成為有史以來最受喜愛的故事之一。愛麗絲的故事以及她遊歷奇境的旅程是路易斯卡羅複雜腦袋的產物，完全超乎單純的兒童故事。這個魔幻故事運用咬文嚼字的扯淡（編註：即玩弄文字和邏輯的無厘頭寫作方式）也涉及了數學和歷史方面，緊緊扣住老少讀者的心弦，至今持續影響整個世界的流行文化。

故事開始於愛麗絲因太無聊，她過於活躍的想像力便將她帶往上一段旅程，從墜入兔子洞而進入奇境的她在這裡遇到許多奇怪的居民。有隨身帶著一只錶卻老是遲到的白兔、在魔法蘑菇上抽菸的毛毛蟲、帶著神祕微笑的柴郡貓、非常瘋狂的瘋帽匠，還有只要稍微遭到冒犯就會大喊「把他們的頭砍下來！」的紅心皇后。故事的結局是，她姊姊叫醒她來喝茶，剛好讓愛麗絲躲過皇后下的砍頭令，她也才發現原來一切只是一場夢。

愛麗絲歷險的魔幻故事寫進了許多數學概念，這些概念隱藏在最意想不到的地方。愛麗絲吃喝各種不同東西後會變大變小，暗示「極限」的概念；瘋狂茶會上討論句子的語義價值時，則是提到了「反比關係」；當鴿子說小女孩就跟蛇一樣，因為他們都會吃蛋時，則是意指「變數代換」。確實非常奇怪！

Language Guide

limit 極限概念
數學的「極限」(limit) 概念為何？舉例來說 f(x)=1/x，當 x 值趨近無限大時，f(x) 會趨近於零，但不等於零。愛麗絲在縮小的過程中冷靜地思考自己會縮小到什麼程度，「可能會像蠟燭燒到最後熄滅（就停止縮小）」(for it might end in going out altogether, like a candle)，就是運用到極限概念。

inverse relationship 反比關係
反比關係在語義學上是指「調換句中字詞順序時，句意就會隨之改變」譬如在第七章瘋狂茶會 (Mad Tea Party) 上，愛麗絲和兔子及瘋帽匠對於句子說法的討論：我看到我吃的東 (I see what I eat) 和我吃我看到的東西 (I eat what I see) 各位讀者也可以自己想想這兩句話有什麼不一樣。

substitution of variables 變數代換
這是簡單的邏輯概念，若 A = B，B = C，則 A = C。在第五章毛毛蟲的忠告 (Advice from a Caterpillar) 中，鴿子說小女孩吃蛋，蛇 (serpent) 也吃蛋，所以小女孩跟蛇一樣邪惡，即書中應用變數代換的一例，但等式就真的這麼成立了嗎？這就是卡羅要讀者思考的問題。

Grammar Master

with 的不同用法
介系詞 with 在句子中通常表示兩種不同的意思：

- with 表伴隨的情況或原因，作「因為」或「隨著」解釋。
  句型： with＋名詞（片語）, S＋V
  with 可放在句首或句中。

例 We need to make a lot of changes in our lives (S＋V 子句) **with** the arrival of our baby daughter. (名詞片語)
=**With** the arrival of our baby daughter, we need to make a lot of changes in our lives.
隨著女兒的誕生，我們必須在生活上做許多改變。

或像文中第 8 行的 **with** its use of literary nonsense and…, (the magical tale) tantalizes readers….

- with 表「附帶狀況」解釋。
  句型：with＋受詞＋受詞補語
  句型中的受詞補語可以是現在分詞、過去分詞、形容詞或介系詞片語。
  例如文中第 14 行的 a white rabbit **with** a watch…、第 16 行的 the Cheshire Cat, **with** his mysterious grin…

Vocabulary Bank

1) **badge** [bædʒ] (n.) 徽章，標誌
The policeman was ordered to hand in his badge.

2) **rival** [ˋraɪvəl] (n.) 對手，競爭對手
Some companies succeed by making better products than their rivals.

3) **impact** [ˋɪmpækt] (n.) 影響，衝擊
The book had a huge impact on my thinking.

4) **erect** [ɪˋrɛkt] (v.) 豎立，建設
The building was erected in 1862.

5) **numerous** [ˋnumərəs] (a.) 為數眾多的
The snowstorm caused numerous traffic accidents.

6) **version** [ˋvɜʒən] (n.) 版本
Which version of Windows do you have on your computer?

7) **translate** [ˋtrænslet] (v.) 翻譯
Can you translate this document into English for me?

8) **out of print** [aut əv prɪnt] (phr.) 絕版，銷售一空
The book has been out of print for decades.

9) **destined** [ˋdɛstɪnd] (a.) 命中注定的
The young singer is destined for greatness.

10) **cherished** [ˋtʃɛrɪʃd] (a.) 受到珍愛的，珍視的
What is your most cherished childhood memory?

進階字彙

11) **loathe** [loð] (v.) 極討厭，厭惡
Phil loathes country music.

12) **slate** [slet] (v.) 排定，預定（通常用被動式）
The rocket is slated for launch in June.

13) **ongoing** [ˋɑn͵goɪŋ] (a.) 進行中的，持續的
Many have lost their jobs in the ongoing financial crisis.

Tongue-tied No More

1 pick up on 發現，察覺

A: Did you notice that Haley was in a bad mood?
你有發現海莉心情不好嗎？

B: No. I didn't pick up on that at all.
沒有，我完全沒察覺。

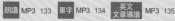

朗讀 MP3 133 單字 MP3 134 英文文章導讀 MP3 135

Carroll also included many historical references i his tale. Perhaps the most obvious reference is to th War of the Roses. When Alice finds herself in the garde of the Queen of Hearts, she learns that the queen like red roses and [11]**loathes** white roses. While not apparen to most children reading the story, adults can easil **1 pick up on** this reference to the [1]**badges** of th English House of Lancaster (a red rose) and their [2]**rivals** the House of York (a white rose).

In the nearly 150 years since its debut, *Alice i Wonderland* Ⓖhas had a significant [3]**impact** on popula culture. Spanish artist Salvador Dali Ⓖproduced severa paintings based on the tale. Statues of Alice, the Whit Rabbit and the Mad Hatter were [4]**erected** in Centra Park in New York City. The story has also been turne into theatrical productions in many countries aroun the world. And musicians fron the Beatles to Gwen Stefan have received inspiratio for song lyrics from Alice' curious adventures [5]**Numerous** film [6]**version** of the story have also bee produced, including th newest adaptation by Tin Burton, [12]**slated** to hi theaters in 2010.

Alice in Wonderland has been [7]**translated** into 125 languages and has never been [8]**out of print**. With over a hundred editions of the book, its popularity among people of all ages and [13]**ongoing** cultural influence, Carroll's magical tale is [9]**destined** to be a [10]**cherished** classic for many years to come!

中 Translation

卡羅在他的故事裡也加入了許多歷史暗示。最明顯的或許就是玫瑰戰爭。當愛麗絲發現自己置身於紅心皇后的花園，她得知皇后喜歡紅玫瑰、厭惡白玫瑰。雖然對大多數讀這個故事的小孩來說並不明顯，但大人可以輕易察覺這指的是英國蘭開斯特王朝的國徽（紅玫瑰），以及他們的死對頭約克王朝的國徽（白玫瑰）。

自從首度問世以來，《愛麗絲夢遊奇境》在這將近一百五十年當中對流行文化有重大影響。西班牙藝術家薩爾瓦多達利根據這個故事創作了幾個畫作；紐約市中央公園裡佇立著愛麗絲、白兔和瘋帽匠的雕像；這個故事也在世界各國改編成許多劇場版本；還有從披頭四到關史蒂芬妮等音樂人，也從愛麗絲的奇遇歷險獲得歌詞靈感。這個故事也拍成許多電影版本，包括提姆波頓的最新改編版本，預計於二〇一〇年上映。

《愛麗絲夢遊奇境》被翻譯成一百二十五種語言，從未絕版。這本書有一百多個版本、受到各年齡層的歡迎、文化影響力也持續不墜，卡羅的魔幻故事在未來好多年注定仍是受到珍藏的經典作品！

若有疑問請來信：eztalkQ@gmail.com

Language Guide

Wars of Roses 玫瑰戰爭

玫瑰戰爭是英國內戰 (civil war)，發生於一四五五年，歷時三十年。英格蘭的兩大家族：蘭開斯特家族 (House of Lancaster) 和約克家族 (House of York) 為了爭奪王位而發生內戰。「玫瑰戰爭」一詞是在十六世紀，莎士比亞在《亨利六世》中以兩朵玫瑰為戰爭標誌後才成為普遍用語。此名稱源於兩個家族所選的家徽，蘭開斯特的紅玫瑰和約克的白玫瑰。玫瑰戰爭最後因為亨利七世 (Henry VII) 與約克家族的伊莉莎白 (Elizabeth of York) 通婚而結束。

Grammar Master

易混淆時態：過去簡單式和現在完成式

文中第 10 行 ...*Alice in Wonderland* **has had** a significant impact on...，使用了現在完成式，但是第第 12 行 ...Salvador Dali **produced** several paintings... 又是用過去簡單式，才上下兩句之隔，怎麼就有兩種不同時態呢？

In the nearly 150 years since its debut...，這句話要表達從一百五十前首度發行「一直以來都……」，所以應該用形容「從過去持續到現在的動作或事情」的**現在完成式**。而第二句話句意要表達的是「某人在過去做了某事」，並沒有要強調動作的「延續」或是「進行」，所以用**過去簡單式**即可。

在選擇時態時我們要有一個觀念：除了簡單式外，其他時態往往不只是時間和句型上的變化而已，而是一種「語意」的傳達。尤其在完成式和進行式的使用上，常常不僅是在描述「發生動作時間」而已，還有「強調」某事持續不斷或是正在運行的暗示。多把這樣的邏輯放在腦裡，時態就不容易搞混囉！

Mini Quiz

❶ Which of the following is true about the author of *Alice in Wonderland*?
(A) His real name was Lewis Carroll.
(B) He liked teaching math at Oxford.
(C) He served as an Anglican priest.
(D) He was educated at home as a boy.

❷ In recent years, China ________ into an economic powerhouse.
(A) transformed
(B) has transformed
(C) transforms
(D) is transforming

❸ We're looking for people ________ at least three years of related experience.
(A) with (B) from
(C) have (D) for

解答 ❶ (D) ❷ (B) ❸ (A)

© 達志 / UPI PHOTO

Sir Arthur Conan Doyle 柯南道爾

Vocabulary Bank

1) **fiction** [ˋfɪkʃən] (n.) 小說
(a.) fictional [ˋfɪkʃənəl] 虛構的，小說的
Who is your favorite science fiction author?

2) **publish** [ˋpʌblɪʃ] (v.) 出版，發行
What company is this magazine published by?

3) **observation** [ˏɑbzɝˋveʃən] (n.) 觀察，瞭望
The patient was kept at the hospital for observation.

4) **feature** [ˋfitʃɚ] (v./n.) 以…為特色，以…為號召；特色
The dinner menu features seafood and pasta dishes.

進階字彙

5) **breathtaking** [ˋbrɛθˏtekɪŋ] (a.) 令人驚嘆的，驚人的
The scenery in Yosemite is breathtaking.

6) **sprout** [spraʊt] (v.) 萌芽，生長
It took two weeks for the seeds to sprout.

7) **deduction** [dɪˋdʌkʃən] (n.) 推論，推理
(v.) deduce [dɪˋdus]
The police detective used deduction to solve the murder.

8) **fanatical** [fəˋnætɪkəl] (a.) 狂熱的，入迷的
Kenneth is a fanatical coffee drinker.

9) **supernatural** [ˏsupɚˋnætʃərəl] (n./a.) 超自然的，靈異的。the supernatural 即「靈異現象」
Do you believe in the supernatural?

口語補充

10) **tyke** [taɪk] (n.) 小男孩，小孩
The McDonalds was full of screaming tykes.

朗讀 MP3 136 單字 MP3 137 英文文章導讀 MP3 138

Arthur Conan Doyle, creator of literature's most famous detective, was born in Edinburgh, Scotland on May 22, 1859. ©While his father was a good-for-nothing alcoholic, his mother was a master storyteller with a passion for books. According to Doyle, the stories she told him as a [10]**tyke** were so [5]**breathtaking** that they replaced many memories of his real childhood. Indeed, it was his mother who planted the literary seed that [6]**sprouted** in grade school, where his storytelling talent made him popular with his classmates. While later studying medicine at the University of Edinburgh, Doyle

began writing short [1]**fiction** for fun, and had his first story [2]**published** when he was just 20. After graduating in 1882, he opened a medical practice, but business was slow at first. So, while waiting for customers, he began writing and publishing short stories again.

Doyle's first novel, *A Study in Scarlet*, was published in 1887. In it, he introduced detective Sherlock Holmes, who was modeled on Dr. Joseph Bell, an actual teacher of his who was a master at [3]**observation**, logic and [7]**deduction**. Unfortunately, it didn't sell well. He tried again in 1889 with *The Sign of Four*, his second novel [4]**featuring** Holmes. While it was a modest success, Doyle really **1 hit his stride** in 1891 when he began writing his Sherlock Holmes short stories. These stories gained such a [8]**fanatical** following that he ended up publishing 56 of them. While Sherlock Holmes won Doyle fame and fortune, he eventually became bored with the character. His interest turned to the [9]**supernatural**, and he spent most of his later years trying to prove that ghosts and fairies were real.

中 Translation

亞瑟柯南道爾，一手創造出文學作品中最有名的偵探，一八五九年五月二十二日在蘇格蘭愛丁堡出生。雖然他的父親是個一無是處的酒鬼，但母親是個說故事大師，對書本充滿熱忱。根據道爾的說法，小時候母親說給他聽的故事非常精彩，取代了他真實童年的許多記憶。的確就是他母親種下的這顆文學種籽，在他小學時期萌芽，讓他有說故事的天分，在同學間大受歡迎。後來在愛丁堡大學攻讀醫學時，道爾開始以玩票性質撰寫短篇小說，才二十歲就出版他第一篇故事。一八八二年畢業後，他開始執業行醫，但一開始生意門可羅雀，因此他利用等待客人上門的空檔，再次開始撰寫、出版短篇小說。

道爾的第一本小說《血字的研究》於一八八七年出版，在這本小說中，夏洛克福爾摩斯首次出現，這個角色是以他現實生活中的老師喬瑟夫貝爾醫生為藍本，這位老師擁有卓越的觀察力、邏輯和推理能力。可惜這本小說賣得不好。一八八九年，他再次嘗試以福爾摩斯為主角，推出第二本小說《四簽名》。這次小有成就，但直到一八九一年開始以夏洛克福爾摩斯推出短篇小說，道爾才真正步上軌道。這些故事贏得一群狂熱書迷追隨，最後總共出版了五十六本。儘管夏洛克福爾摩斯為道爾贏得名聲和財富，他最後還是對這個角色感到厭倦。他的興趣開始轉向靈異現象，晚年幾乎都致力於證明鬼魂和精靈是真的存在。

Tongue-tied No More

1 hit one's stride 進入狀況

stride 是指人走路跨出的一大步，有「發展、進展」的意思。hit one's stride 則用來形容某人開始慢慢在某件事情上展現實力、發揮水準。

A: How come the quarterback keeps fumbling the ball?
那個四分衛怎麼一直掉球啊？

B: He usually doesn't hit his stride till the second quarter.
他通常要等到第二節才會進入狀況。

Language Guide

《血字的研究》*A Study in Scarlet*

《血字的研究》是第一本以福爾摩斯為主角的作品。書名是根據小說中一段對話，福爾摩斯描述這起案件為「血字的研究」，並對華森醫生說 There's the scarlet thread of murder running through the colourless skein of life, and our duty is to unravel it, and isolate it, and expose every inch of it.「謀殺案就像是摻雜在毫無色彩生活中的紅絲線，我們的任務就是要把它拆開，分離出來，把每一吋都暴露出來。」整個故事起始於一件兇殺案現場，案發現場牆上塗著血字「RACHE」（德語「復仇」之意），福爾摩斯猶如現代 CSI 一樣，根據血字留下的各種線索，推測出犯人的大致特徵。福爾摩斯和華森醫生 (Dr. John H. Watson) 也是在這部小說中相遇而成摯友，進而有福爾摩斯系列小說產生。

Grammar Master

while 子句的兩種用法

1. 作副詞子句，用於直接對應，表示「前者」正好是「後者」的相反。

例 ● Mason and Jason are twin brothers. Mason is an extrovert, **while** Jason is an introvert.
馬森與傑森是雙胞胎兄弟。馬森活潑外向，而傑森則害羞內向。

例 ● That region has plenty of natural resources, **while** this one has none.
那個地區天然資源豐富，這個地區卻什麼也沒有。

2. 作時間子句，用以表示「在那段時間內」。

例 ● **While** I was taking a shower, the phone rang.
我在洗澡的時候，電話響了。

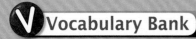

Vocabulary Bank

1) **piercing** [ˋpɪrsɪŋ] (a.) 銳利的，有觀察力的
The policeman's piercing gaze made the suspect nervous.

2) **private eye** [ˋpraɪvɪt aɪ] (n.) 私家偵探
How much does it cost to hire a private eye?

3) **homebody** [ˋhom͵bɑdi] (n.) 足不出戶的人，宅男（女）
Roger is more of a homebody now that he's married.

4) **put up with** [put ʌp wɪθ] (phr.) 忍受
I used to live downtown, but I couldn't put up with the noise.

5) **tough** [tʌf] (a.) 艱難的，高難度的
The questions on the exam were really tough.

6) **whereupon** [͵wɛrəˋpɑn] (adv.) 於是，隨之
I told Sally I was leaving her, whereupon she started crying.

7) **apparently** [əˋpærəntli] (adv.) 似乎，據說，看樣子
The forest fire was apparently caused by lightning.

8) **eccentric** [ɪkˋsɛntrɪk] (n./a.) 怪胎；古怪的，奇特的
My uncle Harry is a bit of an eccentric.

9) **lookout** [ˋlʊk͵aʊt] (n.) 監視者，把風
The robbers placed a lookout by the bank entrance.

10) **unfold** [͵ʌnˋfold] (v.) 發展，呈現
As the story unfolds, we learn that the main character is not who he seems.

11) **skim** [skɪm] (v.) 略過，瀏覽
Arthur skimmed the book and decided not to buy it.

進階字彙

12) **sleuth** [sluθ] (n.) 偵探
(n.) sleuthing [ˋsluθɪŋ] 偵查
Unfortunately, the sleuth's investigation didn't turn up any clues.

13) **unmistakable** [͵ʌnmɪˋstekəbəl] (a.) 不會認錯的，明顯的
The smell of stinky tofu is unmistakable.

14) **outwit** [͵aʊtˋwɪt] (v.) 智勝，騙過
The chess master had no trouble outwitting his opponent.

口語補充

15) **sidekick** [ˋsaɪd͵kɪk] (n.) 跟班，伙伴
Robin is Batman's sidekick.

Sherlock Holme[s] [12]Master Sleuth
偵探界的典範 夏洛克福爾摩斯

朗讀 MP3 139 單字 MP3 140 英文文章導讀 MP3 141

Sherlock Holmes, that most well-known of fictiona detectives, was born on January 6th, 1854 and lives i the foggy never-never land of 19th-century London. Hi look is [13]**unmistakable**: the hawk-like face and [1]**piercin** eyes, the dressing gown and pipe, the hunting cap an magnifying glass. He's the world's top [2]**private eye** with unique gift for observation and reasoning. But he's also [3]**homebody** who only [4]**puts up with** people if they brin him a [5]**tough** case to solve, [6]**whereupon** he become so involved in sleuthing that he often forgets to eat. An when a case is solved, he amuses himself by taking drug and playing the violin. [7]**Apparently** he has nothin better to do. So he's a genius, but an [8]**eccentric** too.

Holmes has only one friend in the world, Dr. Watson, who shares his apartment. Watson helps out with cases, serving as Holmes' [15]**sidekick**, [9]**lookout** and messenger. He also writes down case details and tells us how they [10]**unfold**. Naturally, Watson greatly admires Holmes just like we do. But Holmes often treats him coldly and criticizes him for writing stories that just [11]**skim** the surface of his scientific [G]approach to solving cases. Strangely, Holmes has no female companions. As a matter of fact, he tends to avoid women because he finds them impossible to understand. The only one he seems to pay any attention to is Irene Adler, and that is probably because she once [14]**outwitted** him in a criminal case.

中 Translation

夏洛克福爾摩斯，最廣為人知的虛構偵探人物，一八五四年一月六日出生，住在想像中十九世紀的霧都倫敦。他的外表絕對不會讓人認錯：鷹臉、銳利的雙眼、睡袍外加菸斗、狩獵帽和放大鏡（編註：放大鏡的英文為 magnifying glass)。他是擁有獨一無二觀察與推理天分的世界頂尖私家偵探，但他也是個宅男，只有帶著難解案子上門的人他才勉強忍受，一旦接下案子，他就十分投入查案，甚至常常忘了吃飯。等到破案之後，他就會以嗑藥和拉小提琴來自娛。他似乎沒有其他更好的事可以做。所以他是個天才，也是個怪胎。

福爾摩斯在這世上只有一個朋友，就是和他共住一間公寓的華森醫生。華森醫生協助辦案，是福爾摩斯的跟班、把風的和信差。他也負責記錄案情細節並告訴我們案情的發展。理所當然，華森跟我們一樣非常仰慕福爾摩斯，但是福爾摩斯卻常對華森冷漠以待，而且批評華森寫的故事只有輕略帶過他破案科學方法的表面。奇怪的是，福爾摩斯沒有什麼女伴。事實上，他往往會迴避女人，因為他認為女人無法令人理解。唯一看似引起他注意的女性是艾琳艾德勒，大概是因為她曾經在某件刑案中機智勝過福爾摩斯。

Language Guide

19th-century London 霧都倫敦

十九世紀倫敦的特色之一即大霧瀰漫，這是因為當時大部分的人都使用煤作為家用燃料而產生大量煙霧。這些煙霧再加上當地潮濕的氣候，造成了「倫敦霧」(London fog)，倫敦也因此被稱作「大煙」(The Smoke) 或「霧都」。而文中提到 never-never land 的說法則是來自《小飛俠彼得潘》(*Peter Pan*)，故事中的小孩在小飛俠的帶領下，一同飛向所謂的「永不長大之地」(never-never land)，故這個字後來就被引申為「想像中的（國度）」或「虛構的（理想境地）」。

What's New?

《福爾摩斯》*Sherlock Holmes*

去年以《鋼鐵人》(*Iron Man*) 和《開麥拉驚魂》(*Tropic Thunder*) 兩部片重返影壇的小勞勃道尼 (Robert Downey Jr.) 今年與裘德洛 (Jude Law) 共同攜手演出電影《福爾摩斯》(*Sherlock Holmes*)。本片以一九八九年，英國國力最強盛的維多利亞時代的倫敦為背景，主角福爾摩斯（小勞勃道尼飾）與助手華森醫生（裘德洛飾）聯手阻止邪教破壞英國的陰謀，同時幫助警方逮捕了作惡多端的邪教教主。新一代的《福爾摩斯》電影對這兩大主角有新的詮釋，福爾摩斯不再只是個文質彬彬、拿著放大鏡四處尋找犯罪線索的名偵探，小勞勃道尼所飾演的福爾摩斯除了破解敵人留下的種種線索外，槍戰、肉搏都難不倒他，成為一個能文能武的角色，與小說中的形象頗有出入；而原本意見很少的助手華森醫生也變得比較「有個性」，雖然跟著福爾摩斯一起出生入死，但會對福爾摩斯發牢騷碎碎念。想要一睹新世代福爾摩斯與華森的風采，別忘了進電影院一探究竟。

圖片提供：華納兄弟電影公司

Grammar Master

介系詞 to 當所有格表示

英文裡有一類名詞的所有格，既不是加 of，也不是加 's，而是以介系詞 to 來表示。

例 ❶ the key to the door 開這個門的鑰匙
❷ the secretary to the managing director 總經理的秘書
❸ a right to the throne 王位的繼承權
❹ a solution to a problem 解決問題的方法
❺ an approach to solving cases 破案的方法

在上面的例子裡，介系詞 to 所連接的兩個名詞之間有一種「屬於」的含意（如例 ❶、❷）。另一方面，以 to 連接的兩個名詞也可以用來表示「與……有關」（如例 ❸～❺）。值得注意的是，例 ❺ 中的介系詞 to 後，如果接動詞時，應改為動名詞的形式，即 solving。

Vocabulary Bank

1) **clumsy** [ˋklʌmzi] (a.) 笨拙的，不靈巧的
Roger is so clumsy—he's always breaking things.

2) **elementary** [͵ɛləˋmɛntəri] (a.) 基本的，初級的，基礎的
Free elementary education is a basic right.

3) **sole** [sol] (n.) 腳底，鞋底
I have a hole in the sole of my shoe.

4) **scrape** [skrep] (v.) 刮，挖
The teacher made the student scrape his gum off the desk.

5) **keen** [kin] (a.) 敏銳的，靈敏的
Owls have keen eyesight.

6) **psychology** [saɪˋkɑlədʒi] (n.) 心理學，心理特質
It's important for coaches to have an understanding of sports psychology.

7) **portray** [porˋtre] (v.) 扮演，表現
Leonardo DiCaprio portrays Howard Hughes in The Aviator.

進階字彙

8) **once-over** [ˋwʌns͵ovɚ] (n.) 看一眼，檢查一下
The doctor gave Evan the once-over and told him it was just a cold.

9) **encyclopedic** [ɪn͵saɪkləˋpidɪk] (a.) 知識廣博的
(n.) encyclopedia [ɪn͵saɪkləˋpidiə] 百科全書
The professor has an encyclopedic knowledge of international law.

10) **residue** [ˋrɛzɪ͵du] (n.) 殘餘，殘渣
Vinegar can be used to remove soap residue from bathtubs.

11) **upwards of** [ˋʌpwɚdz ʌv] (phr.) 多於，以上
Upwards of thirty million tourists visit Ireland each year.

Tongue-tied No More

1 have something up one's sleeve 身懷絕技

從這個片語字面上的意思「袖子裡藏著某東西」，可以知道除了看得到的方法外，暗地還藏了一手，以備不時之需。這片語的類似用法還有 have a card up one's sleeve「在袖子裡藏了一張王牌」，意指如果牌都出完了，最後留下的這一手（一張牌）就能派上用場，轉敗為勝。

A: Isn't that pitcher getting kind of old?
那位投手不會有點老嗎？

B: Yeah, but he still has a few tricks up his sleeve.
對啊，但是他依舊身懷絕技。

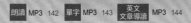

朗讀 MP3 142 單字 MP3 143 英文文章導讀 MP3 144

A good example of Holmes' powers of deduction is th time he gives Watson the [8]**once-over** and tells him he' been out in the rain and has a [1]**clumsy** housekeepe When Watson asks him how he knows this, Holme replies: "It's [2]**elementary**!" He points to Watson' left shoe, noting six new cuts on the insid [3]**sole**, and correctly deducing that they wer caused by someone carelessly [4]**scraping** mu off his shoes. Holmes also **1 has many othe skills up his sleeve**, like his [9]**encyclopedi** memory for shoe prints, bullet types, gunpowde [10]**residue** and cigarette brands. And he has a [5]**kee** understanding of human [6]**psychology** as well. Like th time he fakes a fire to get Irene Adler to run for a prize photo she is hiding in her house.

Although most of the Sherlock Holmes stories wer written over 100 years ago, the master sleuth has had lasting impact on popular culture. The earliest know film about the detective is *Sherlock Holmes Baffled*, one-minute short made by the Edison Company i 1900. Since then, over 70 actors have played Sherloc Holmes, and *The Guinness Book of World Records* list Sherlock Holmes as the "most [7]**portrayed** movi character." There have also bee [11]**upwards of** 750 radio adaptation ©such as *The New Adventures o Sherlock Holmes* series, which ra throughout the 1940s. On th small screen, Holmes has bee

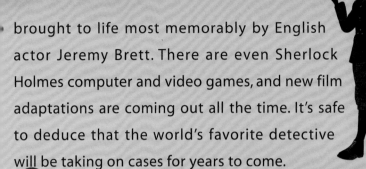

brought to life most memorably by English actor Jeremy Brett. There are even Sherlock Holmes computer and video games, and new film adaptations are coming out all the time. It's safe to deduce that the world's favorite detective will be taking on cases for years to come.

中 Translation

見證福爾摩斯的推理能力其中一個好例子是，有一次他只看一眼華森就可以告訴他，他剛剛在外面淋雨，而且有個笨手本腳的管家。華森問說他怎麼知道，福爾摩斯回答：「這是最基本的！」他指著華森左腳穿的鞋子，指出鞋底內側有六道新的刮痕，正確推論出這些刮痕是因為被人草率刮掉鞋上泥巴時造成的。福爾摩斯還擁有許多其他絕技，譬如他對鞋印、子彈種類、火藥殘渣和香菸品牌都有百科全書般的記憶。而且他十分能洞悉人類心理，像是有一次他假造一場火災，迫使艾琳衝回家拿她藏在家裡的一張珍貴的相片。

儘管夏洛克福爾摩斯的故事大多撰寫於一百多年前，這位大師級偵探對流行文化的影響卻延續至今。目前已知最早的福爾摩斯電影是《福爾摩斯的困惑》，愛迪生公司在一九〇〇年製作的一分鐘短片。從那時候開始，至今已有超過七十位演員扮演過福爾摩斯，《金氏世界紀錄》將福爾摩斯列為「搬上大銀幕次數最多的角色」。還有超過七百五十個廣播劇改編版本，例如在整個一九四〇年代播放的《福爾摩斯新歷險》系列。至於在小螢幕上，英國演員傑洛米巴特所扮演的福爾摩斯最令人難忘。現在甚至有福爾摩斯的電腦和電視遊戲，而且隨時都有新的電影版本推出。這樣的推論肯定錯不了：這位全世界最喜愛的偵探未來都還會繼續辦案。 若有疑問請來信：eztalkQ@gmail.com

Language Guide

Holmes on drugs 福爾摩斯是個毒蟲

熟悉福爾摩斯小說的粉絲應該都知道，福爾摩斯雖然是鼎鼎有名的偵探，卻有一個罕為人知的嗜好，那就是吸毒。根據小說中福爾摩斯自己的說法以及華森的描述，福爾摩斯閒來無事經常喜歡給自己來一針毒品！沒錯，福爾摩斯是偵探英雄，但也是個不折不扣的毒蟲！而且，以現今的標準來看，他慣用的毒品是今日列管為一級毒品的古柯鹼 (cocaine) 與嗎啡 (morphine)。根據華森的描述，福爾摩斯吸毒的習慣已經有段時日，他不但會熟練地自行施打毒品，手臂上還「布滿了數不清的針孔」。柯南道爾在第二本小說《四簽名》(*The Sign of Four*) 中的開場，就透過華森仔細描繪福爾摩斯使用毒品的過程，這段詳盡的描述相當駭人聽聞，對於習慣接受福爾摩斯英勇正面形象的讀者來說，可能極具震撼。

Grammar Master

such as + 名詞：例如、像是……

例 Brad enjoys team sports **such as** basketball, football, and volleyball.
布萊德喜歡團隊運動，像是籃球、美式足球以及排球。

此外，也可以用大家熟悉的 for example 來表示。不過，要注意的是，for example 後面要接一個完整的句子，而不能只接名詞。

例 Brad enjoys team sports. **For example**, he likes basketball, football, and volleyball.

Mini Quiz

1. According to the article, which of the following is NOT true about Sherlock Holmes?
   (A) He was born in the 19th century.
   (B) He always works alone.
   (C) He has a very distinctive look.
   (D) He understands human psychology.

2. Why did Arthur Conan Doyle turn his interest to ghosts and fairies?
   (A) Because his novels featuring Holmes didn't sell well.
   (B) Because he hit a speed bump.
   (C) Because he lost interest in Holmes .
   (D) Because he was too clever.

3. While some parts of the world get plenty of rain, others ______________.
   (A) get little or none
   (B) get a lot
   (C) are hot and humid
   (D) are cold and wet

解答 1 (B) 2 (C) 3 (A)

Vocabulary Bank

1) **wreck** [rɛk] (n.)（車、船等）撞毀，事故
(phr.) train wreck 出軌、追撞……等火車事故。常用來比喻失控、混亂的人、事、物
Allen's life was a train wreck after he started drinking.

2) **foster** [ˋfɑstɚ] (a.) 收養的
The boy lived in a foster home after his parents died.

3) **suffer** [ˋsʌfɚ] (v.) 遭受，受苦
The man suffered many setbacks before achieving success.

4) **physical** [ˋfɪzɪkḷ] (a.) 身體的，肉體的
Stress can affect your physical and metal health.

5) **abuse** [əˋbjus] (n.) 虐待，濫用（藥物，職權等）
(v.) abuse [əˋbjuz]
The parents were accused of child abuse.

6) **emerge** [ɪˋmɝdʒ] (v.) 從…出來，出現，浮現
The country is waiting for a new leader to emerge.

7) **observe** [əbˋzɝv] (v.) 奉行，遵守
Students are expected to observe school rules.

8) **lengthy** [ˋlɛŋθi] (a.) 長期的，冗長的
The treaty was finally signed after lengthy negotiations.

進階字彙

9) **Cinderella** [͵sɪndəˋrɛlə] (n.) 灰姑娘
Cinderella story 即「麻雀變鳳凰的故事」
Susan Boyle's rise to fame is a classic Cinderella story.

10) **munition** [mjuˋnɪʃən] (n.) 軍需品，軍火（固定用複數）
Several soldiers were injured during the munitions tests.

11) **screen test** [skrin tɛst] (n.) 試鏡
(v.) screen-test
The studio invited the actress to come in for a screen test.

Grammar Master

與過去事實相反的假設句型

If + 過去完成式子句, ...would / could have p.p.
子句 1 子句 2
＊前後兩個子句可顛倒

例
- If I had bought a lottery ticket with those numbers, I would have won ten million dollars!
  要是我有用那些號碼買樂透彩券，我就中一千萬了！（事實上沒有買）
- He wouldn't have succeeded if he hadn't had his wife's support.
  要是沒有他太太的支持，他不會成功。（事實上他太太有支持他）

Marilyn Monroe

瑪麗蓮夢露

朗讀 MP3 145 單字 MP3 146 英文文章導讀 MP3 147

Marilyn Monroe was born in 1926, and by the tim she died in 1962, she was the most famous actress i the world. But while her public life was a Hollywoo 9)**Cinderella** story, her private life was a tragic trai 1)**wreck** of broken relationships. Because her mother wa mentally and financially unstable, Monroe was put in 2)**foste** care at an early age. Her mother took her back when she wa seven, but soon 3)**suffered** a mental breakdown and wa

committed to a mental hospital. Monroe was sent to an orphanage, and then lived in a series of foster homes, where she suffered [4]**physical** and sexual [5]**abuse**. In 1942, she married a neighbor just to stay out of yet another foster home.

While working in a [10]**munitions** factory during WWII, she was discovered by an Army photographer. Because models with lighter hair got more work, she began dying her hair blond, and quickly [6]**emerged** as a successful model. In 1946, a [11]**screen test** was arranged, and she became a contract employee at 20th Century Fox. Now that she was **1 going places**, she abandoned her husband. As she **2 put it**, "[G]If I'd [7]**observed** all the rules, I'd never have got anywhere." Her first few movies were unsuccessful, but in 1948 she was hired by Columbia Pictures and received [8]**lengthy** training from the studio's drama coach. By the time she appeared in the Marx Brothers film *Love Happy* in 1949, her performances were catching the eye of studio executives.

中 Translation

瑪麗蓮夢露生於一九二六年，而當她於一九六二年過世時，已經是世上最知名的女演員。然而，雖然她的公眾生活宛如好萊塢版的灰姑娘故事，她的私生活卻是由一段段破碎關係串連成的悲劇。由於母親的精神和財務狀況皆不穩定，夢露很小就被送往寄養家庭。母親在她七歲時接她回家，但不久便精神崩潰而被送入精神療養院。夢露先是被送往孤兒院，之後一連住過數個寄養家庭，屢遭肢體暴力及性侵害。一九四二年，她嫁給鄰居，只為了避免再被送入另一個寄養家庭。

第二次世界大戰期間，她在一間軍火工廠工作時被一位陸軍攝影師發掘。因為淺色頭髮的模特兒工作機會較多，於是她開始把頭髮染成金色，很快便成為成功的模特兒。一九四六年，她在參加一場試鏡後成為二十世紀福斯公司的約聘人員。現在她前程似錦了，便離棄丈夫。她這麼說：「如果遵守所有規矩，我就永遠不會成功了。」她的前幾部電影並不賣座，但一九四八年她受僱於哥倫比亞影業，接受該電影公司的戲劇老師長期的訓練。等到一九四九年她出現在馬克斯兄弟的《快樂愛情》電影中，她的演出立刻吸引公司高層的目光。

Language Guide

Marx Brothers 馬克斯兄弟

Marx Brothers 是一個雜耍歌舞團家族，在 1900 年代到 1950 年代紅極一時。這個喜劇團體以五兄弟中最年長的三位哥哥為核心人物，在百老匯及電影中大搞無厘頭。大哥 Chico 非常會彈鋼琴，但英文其破無比，還故意裝濃濃的義大利腔引人發噱（他們家是猶太移民）；三哥 Groucho 非常會唱歌、彈吉他，外加講話超快又爆笑；二哥 Harpo 鋼琴和吉他都彈得超爛，但很會彈豎琴（harp，他的藝名即因此而來），特色是表演時從來不講話，但很會用嘴模仿各種聲音（口技），而且雜耍玩得很棒。Marx Brothers 的老四 Gummo 從未參加電影演出，老么 Zeppo 只參與初期幾部電影的演出，年紀最小的這兩位後來都離開演藝圈另謀發展。

Marx Brothers 演出的 13 部電影有 5 部獲選為美國影藝學院 (American Film Institute) 百大電影，其中《輕而易舉》*Duck Soup* 和《歌劇之夜》*A Night at the Opera* 更名列前十二大。

Tongue-tied No More

1 go places 功成名就

go places 字面上是「前往許多地方」，其實是「縱橫天下」，也就代表「極為成功」。文中接下來引述瑪麗蓮夢露的話，其中的片語 get anywhere 也是「成功」的意思，常用於否定句。

A: Do you remember Patrick? He's the head of a law firm now.
你還記得派崔克嗎？他現在是一家律師事務所的老闆。

B: I always knew he'd go places.
我早就知道他會出人頭地。

2 put it 表達

put 在這邊是「說」的意思，總是與 it 連用。

A: So what does Kevin's new girlfriend look like?
凱文的新女友長相如何？

B: Let me put it this way—he's gone out with better looking girls.
我就這麼說吧——他跟更漂亮的女孩交往過。

Vocabulary Bank

1) **launch** [lɔntʃ] (v.) 展開，發起
The police have launched an investigation into the murder.

2) **elevate** [ˋɛlə͵vet] (v.) 提升（位階、地位等）
Kris Allen's American Idol win elevated him to national fame.

3) **glamorous** [ˋglæmərəs] (a.) 具有魅力的，迷人的
The young millionaire is dating a glamorous model.

4) **severe** [səˋvɪr] (a.) 嚴重的，劇烈的
The accident victim was in severe pain.

5) **feature** [ˋfitʃɚ] (n.)（報章雜誌）特別報導
Did you read the Time feature on Las Vegas?

6) **navel** [ˋnevəl] (n.) 肚臍
Catherine never wears clothes that show her navel.

7) **vulgar** [ˋvʌlgɚ] (a.) 粗俗的，下流的
Vulgar language isn't allowed on this forum.

進階字彙

8) **naiveté** [nɑ͵ivəˋte] (n.) 天真（的模樣、行為）
Richard laughed at the naiveté of his younger days.

9) **vulnerability** [͵vʌlnərəˋbɪləti] (n.) 柔弱，容易受傷害
Engineers are testing the operating system's vulnerability to viruses.

10) **accessibility** [æk͵sɛsəˋbɪləti] (n.) 容易親近
Mr. Roberts is a popular teacher because of his accessibility.

11) **defuse** [dɪˋfjuz] (v.) 消弭（危險性、緊張、敵意等），拆除（炸彈的）雷管
Diplomats were successful in defusing the international crisis.

12) **sultry** [ˋsʌltri] (a.) 撩人的，悶熱的
The woman gave the man a sultry look as she left the room.

口語補充

13) **sexpot** [ˋsɛks͵pɑt] (n.) 性感的女人
The politician was caught having an affair with a young sexpot.

14) **moan** [mon] (v.) 悲歎，發牢騷
Rick is always moaning about his job.

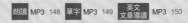

朗讀 MP3 148 單字 MP3 149 英文文章導讀 MP3 150

Then Monroe appeared in *The Asphalt Jungle*, the movie that truly [1]**launched** her career. Next, she displayed her comedic ability and sex appeal in *Gentlemen Prefer Blondes*, *How to Marry a Millionaire* and *The Seven Year Itch*, which [2]**elevated** her to superstar status. Yet despite her [3]**glamorous**, [13]**sexpot** image, fellow star Jane Russell described her as shy and sweet and "far more intelligent than people **1 gave her credit for**." Monroe had to work very hard to achieve her screen look, and always suffered from [4]**severe** stage fright. She later [14]**moaned** that "dreaming about being an actress is more exciting than being one." But what audiences saw was a [8]**naiveté**, [9]**vulnerability** and [10]**accessibility** that men found sexy and women found touching.

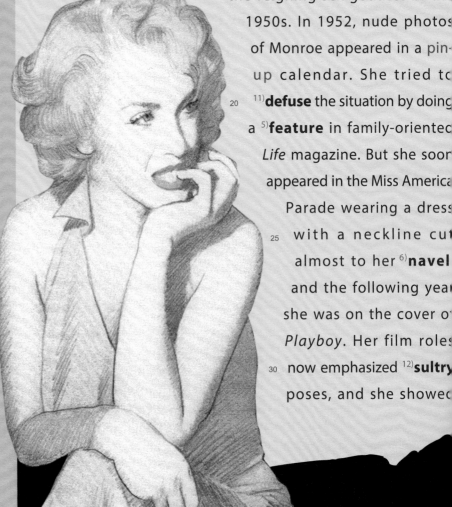

Marilyn Monroe's lasting fame is due to her status as the reigning sex goddess of the 1950s. In 1952, nude photos of Monroe appeared in a pin-up calendar. She tried to [11]**defuse** the situation by doing a [5]**feature** in family-oriented *Life* magazine. But she soon appeared in the Miss America Parade wearing a dress with a neckline cut almost to her [6]**navel** and the following year she was on the cover of *Playboy*. Her film roles now emphasized [12]**sultry** poses, and she showed

up at the *Photoplay* Awards dinner in a skintight gold dress. Fellow star Joan Crawford called her [7]**vulgar**, but male fans loved it. Eventually, however, Monroe began to regret her sexy image, explaining, "A sex symbol becomes a thing. I just hate to be a thing."

中 Translation

接著夢露在《夜闌人未靜》中演出，這部電影真正開啟了她的星途。接下來，她在《紳士愛美人》、《願嫁金龜婿》和《七年之癢》中展現她的喜劇能力與性感魅力，這幾部片也將她提升至超級巨星的地位。不過，儘管她的形象迷人又性感，同為影星的珍妮羅素卻形容她害羞、甜美、「遠比他人想像聰明」。夢露必須非常努力才能塑造她銀幕上的模樣，而且始終飽受嚴重舞台恐懼症所苦。她後來感嘆說：「夢想當演員比實際當個演員令人興奮。」但觀眾看到的卻是一個天真、脆弱又平易近人的女子，令男人覺得性感，女人動容。

瑪麗蓮夢露能有這般不朽名聲，當歸功於她在五〇年代無人能及的性感女神地位。一九五二年，夢露的裸照出現在美女月曆上。她試圖透過在家庭取向的《生活》雜誌刊登特寫報導來扭轉局面，但她不久後在美國小姐遊行現身，穿著領口幾乎開到肚臍的洋裝，次年更成為《花花公子》的封面人物。現在她的電影角色開始強調撩人的姿態，她也以一襲緊身金色洋裝出席 *Photoplay* 雜誌的頒獎晚宴。同為影星裘的恩克萊佛說她低俗，但男性粉絲就愛這味。然而最後，夢露開始為她的性感形象懊悔，她說：「性感象徵會變成物品。我討厭變成物品。」

Language Guide

blonde 還是 blond？

有的字典上寫說：blonde [blɑnd] (n./a.) 金髮女（的），blond [blɑnd] (n./a.) 金髮男（的），但現在形容詞都直接用 blond，blonde 單指「金髮女性」。解釋多說無益，直接看例句：

blonde (n.) 金髮女

Is it true that blondes have more fun?

金髮女生真的過得比較開心嗎？

blond (n.) 金髮男

Linda said she only dates blonds.

琳達說她只願意跟金髮男性約會。

blond (a.) 金髮的

It's a myth that most Swedes are blond.

說大多數瑞典人都是金髮，是個迷思。

pin-up 性感寫真

pin-up [ˋpɪnˏʌp] 也拼作 pinup，這是口語的用法，表示全裸或半裸的性感照片或圖畫。pin up 這個動詞片語是「用大頭針釘在牆上」的意思，pin-up 寫真照片就是因為總被人釘在牆上（或阿兵哥的置物櫃門內側……）而得名。拍攝這種照片的藝人就是 pin-up girl（寫真女星）、pin-up model（寫真模特兒）。

The walls of Mike's bedroom are covered with pin-ups.

麥克的臥室四面牆上貼滿性感寫真照。

Tongue-tied No More

1 give sb. credit (for sth.)（為某事）誇獎某人

credit 是「讚譽，功勞」的意思。

A: I can't believe that guy tried to pick you up. You're so out of his league.
真不敢相信那個男的竟然想把妳，他完全配不上妳。

B: Well, you gotta give him credit for trying.
呃，還是得誇獎他勇於嘗試。

Grammar Master

much / far / way / a lot + 比較級形容詞或副詞表示「……得多」

例
- Gina is **much** taller than her older sister.（taller：比較級形容詞）
  吉娜比她姐姐高得多。
- Kenny drives **far** more carefully than Hank.（more carefully：比較級副詞）
  肯尼開車比漢克小心多了。
- I'm **way** better than my brother at tennis.（better：比較級形容詞）
  我的網球打得比我哥哥好多了。
- Nathan is **a lot** smarter than he looks.（smarter：比較級形容詞）
  南森比外表看起來聰明多了。

Vocabulary Bank

1) **pay off** [pe ɔf] (phr.) 得到好結果，取得成功
I hope all our hard work pays off.

2) **hail** [hel] (v.) 為…喝采，稱讚
Michael Phelps has been hailed as the greatest Olympic athlete of all times.

3) **eternally** [ɪˋtɝnəli] (adv.) 永恆地，永久地，無休止地
I'll be eternally grateful for everything you've done for me.

4) **curl up (with)** [kɝl ʌp] (phr.) 與（某人或寵物）緊緊窩在一起，也常與書連用，表示「舒服坐臥著讀書」
Elaine likes to curl up with a good book when it rains.

5) **cruelty** [ˋkruəlti] (n.) 殘酷的行為，刻薄傷人的言語
The charity is dedicated to the prevention of cruelty to animals.

6) **convert** [kənˋvɝt] (v.) 皈依，改變信仰 (n.) convert [ˋkɑnvɝt] 皈依者
Sean was raised as a Catholic but later converted to Islam.

7) **deteriorate** [dɪˋtɪrɪə͵ret] (v.) 退化，惡化
Rainy weather causes roads to deteriorate rapidly.

進階字彙

8) **typecast** [ˋtaɪp͵kæst] (n.)（演員）定型，一再扮演同類型角色
The actor was tired of being typecast as villains.

9) **leech** [litʃ] (n.) 血蛭，常用於比喻「詐取他人金錢者、寄生蟲」
I don't know why she doesn't divorce that leech.

10) **incurably** [ɪnˋkjʊrəbli] (adv.) 無可救藥地
Alison's boyfriend is incurably romantic.

11) **rocky** [ˋrɑki] (n.) 困難重重的，搖晃的
The couple's rocky marriage ended in divorce.

12) **solace** [ˋsɑlɪs] (n.) 慰藉
The woman sought solace in religion after her husband's death.

13) **fast** [fæst] (a.) 放蕩的，fast crowd 即「豬朋狗友」
Matt blew all his money on fast women and fast cars.

14) **overdose** [ˋovɚ͵dos] (n./v.)（藥物等）過量
Many famous musicians have died of drug overdoses.

15) **intentional** [ɪnˋtɛnʃənəl] (a.) 故意的
Do you think the insult was intentional?

朗讀 MP3 151 單字 MP3 152 英文文章導讀 MP3 153

To overcome being [8]**typecast** as a dumb blonde, Monroe studied at the Actors Studio and also formed Marilyn Monroe Productions to gain more control over her roles. She told the *New York Times*, "I want to grow and develop and play serious dramatic parts. My dramatic coach tells everybody that I have a great soul, but so far nobody's interested in it. "Nevertheless, the hard work [1]**paid off** when her dramatic performances were [2]**hailed** by critics, and she won a Gol den Globe and several European awards for her performance in *The Prince and the Showgirl*. ⒼThough she still suffered from stage fright, and her costars worried that her drama coaches were just [9]**leeches**, everything seemed to be going well for Marilyn.

Yet Marilyn Monroe's childhood made her [3]**eternally**, perhaps [10]**incurably**, lonely. "A career is wonderful, but you can't [4]**curl up** with it on a cold night," she complained. But she was never able to find the right man. Her second marriage was in 1954 to baseball player Joe DiMaggio, who became annoyed that his fans were more interested in her. She soon filed for divorce

1 **on grounds of** mental 5)**cruelty**. In 1956, she married playwright Arthur Miller and 6)**converted** to Judaism to make him happy. But their relationship became 11)**rocky** and she turned to drugs for 12)**solace**. By the time she divorced him in 1961, she was hanging out with a 13)**fast** crowd and her health was 7)**deteriorating**. In 1962, she died from an 14)**overdose** of barbiturates, probably 15)**intentional**.

中 Translation

為了克服被定型為「無腦金髮女」，夢露去演員工作室學習，並成立瑪麗蓮夢露製作公司來掌控自己的角色。她告訴《紐約時報》：「我想要成長、進步，演出嚴肅的戲劇角色。我的戲劇老師告訴大家我有很棒的內在，但目前為止沒人對此感興趣。」不過，她的努力有了回報，她的戲劇表演贏得影評讚賞，在《遊龍戲鳳》中的演出也為她贏得金球獎及數座歐洲電影獎。雖然她仍為舞台恐懼症所苦，與她同台的影星也擔心她的戲劇老師只是吸血蟲，但瑪麗蓮似乎一切順遂。

可是，瑪麗蓮夢露的童年讓她永遠——也許是無可救藥的——孤獨。「演藝事業固然好，但你無法在冰冷的夜晚與事業纏綿」，她埋怨道。她始終無法找到真命天子。她於一九五四年再婚，嫁給職棒球員狄馬喬，由於球迷對夢露更感興趣，使狄馬喬惱羞成怒，沒多久她即以精神虐待為由申請離婚。一九五六年，她嫁給劇作家亞瑟米勒，並皈依猶太教來取悅他，但這段婚姻困難重重，她開始尋求藥物的慰藉。等到兩人在一九六一年離婚時，她正與一群放浪形骸的人鬼混，身體每況愈下。一九六二年，她因過量服用巴比妥鹽過世，應該是故意如此。

若有疑問請來信：eztalkQ@gmail.com

Language Guide

barbiturate 巴比妥酸鹽

barbiturate [͵bɑrˋbɪtʃurɪt] 巴比妥酸鹽是一種中樞神經系統 (central nervous system) 鎮定劑，早年常做為安眠藥物，但因為容易造成病人藥癮，過量使用還有造成呼吸停止的危險，現在多以其他藥物取代。

Tongue-tied No More

1 on grounds of... 以……為由

ground 在這裡是指「做一件事的基本條件、原因」，在這個定義下常用複數形式。on grounds of... 表示「以……為由」或「設定……的條件」。

A: I didn't get the job. They said I was too old for the position.
我沒得到那份工作。他們說我去做那個職位嫌太老了。

B: Hey, they can't do that! Discrimination on grounds of age is against the law.
嘿，他們不可以那樣！年齡歧視是違法的。

Grammar Master

表示「雖然……」的句型變化

「雖然、縱使、儘管……」英文就用 although、despite、in spite of 來表達，其中 despite 和 in spite of 是屬於「介系詞」，而 although 屬於「連接詞」，所以雖然三者意思相同，用法卻不太一樣，正確的句型如下：

- Although / Even though / Though + 子句
- Despite / In spite of + 名詞或名詞片語
- Despite / In spite of the fact that + 子句

例 ● **Although** he is rich, he is not happy.
= **Despite** his wealth, he is not happy.
= **In spite of** the fact that he is rich, he is not happy.
雖然他很富有，但並不快樂。

Vocabulary Bank

1) **stutter** [ˋstʌtə] (v./n.) 說話結結巴巴；結巴
Ryan stutters whenever he gets nervous.

2) **rifle** [ˋraɪfəl] (n.) 步槍，來福槍
The man accidentally shot himself while cleaning his rifle.

3) **rebel** [rɪˋbɛl] (v.) 叛逆，反抗
(a.) rebellious [rɪˋbɛljəs]
It's normal for teenagers to rebel against their parents.

4) **blend** [blɛnd] (n./v.) 混合（物）
This coffee is a blend of Indonesian and Brazilian beans.

5) **clown (around)** [klaʊn] (v.) 開玩笑，扮小丑裝傻
Stop clowning around and get to work!

進階字彙

6) **spineless** [ˋspaɪnlɪs] (a.) 沒骨氣的，懦弱的
The new mayor is just another spineless politician.

7) **rock** [rɑk] (n.) 像岩石一樣堅實穩固、可以信賴的人事物。文中戲稱貓王的父親是 jellybean[ˋdʒɛl͵bin]（豆子形狀的軟糖，也拼作 jelly bean），相較於 rock，是軟弱的象徵
The Lord is my rock.

8) **flashy** [ˋflæʃi] (a.) 俗豔的，炫耀的
Veronica likes to wear flashy jewelry.

9) **sideburn** [ˋsaɪd͵bɜn] (n.) 鬢角
Sideburns are back in style again.

10) **minstrel** [ˋmɪnstrəl] (n.)（中世紀的）吟遊詩人；歌手，樂手，詩人
Traveling minstrels were common in the middle ages.

口語補充

11) **muff** [mʌf] (v.) 搞砸，表現笨拙
The actor kept muffing his line.

12) **mama** [ˋmɑmə] (n.) 性感、有韻味的女人，妻子
I met a pretty little mama at the dance.

Grammar Master

動詞後接形容詞修飾主詞的用法

一般來說，動詞（片語）後面應放副詞來修飾該動詞（片語）。不過，若是要指主詞在做該動作時的一種狀態，可以在動詞（片語）後接形容詞來修飾主詞。

例 ● She sat there speechless.
主詞 動詞片語 形容詞
她坐在那兒，一句話也說不出來。

● I woke up tired this morning.
主詞 動詞片語 形容詞
我今天早上醒來時覺得很累。

ELVIS PRESLEY
貓王傳奇

©達志 / UPI PHOTO

朗讀 MP3 154 單字 MP3 155 英文文章導讀 MP3 156

Elvis Presley was born in 1935 in a two-room shotgun shack in Tupelo, Mississippi. He [G]grew up poor because his father was a "jellybean," someone weak, [6]**spineless** and lazy. The family moved around a lot because his father was frequently getting in trouble, and at school kids threw rotten fruit at Elvis because he [1]**stuttered** and was shy. His mother, however, was a [7]**rock**, and Elvis was very close to her. In 1946, Elvis received his first guitar. He had wanted a [2]**rifle**, but his parents couldn't afford one. Over the next year, he received guitar lessons from his uncle Vester. When Elvis started high school after the family moved to Memphis, Tennessee, he [3]**rebelled** by wearing [8]**flashy** clothes and growing [9]**sideburns**. But he also went on to win his school's 1952 "Annual [10]**Minstrel** Show."

Elvis was discovered by accident. He went to Sun Records to record a song for his mother right when the studio was looking for somebody who could deliver a [4]**blend** of black blues and boogie-woogie music to white audiences. When studio boss Sam Phillips heard Elvis's recording, he knew it was just what they were looking for. Elvis was invited back to record with several studio musicians, but he was so nervous that he [11]**muffed** it. It was only during a break, when he was [5]**clowning** around with a song, that his potential was revealed. He recorded several songs in early 1954, the first being "That's All Right, [12]**Mama**," which was an instant success.

中 Translation

艾維斯普瑞斯里於一九三五年出生在密西西比州杜佩洛一棟狹長型、只有兩個房間的簡陋小屋裡（編註：請見 p. 110 完整介紹）。由於父親是個「吃軟飯的奶油小生」，軟弱、沒有骨氣又懶惰，所以艾維斯在貧窮中成長。一家人因父親常惹事生非而到處搬家；在學校，同學常拿爛水果丟艾維斯，因為他講話結巴又生性害羞。不過他的母親堅如磐石，艾維斯與她非常親近。一九四六年，艾維斯獲得生平第一把吉他，他原本想要的是把來福槍，但父母買不起。隔年，叔叔韋斯特幫他上吉他課。全家人搬到田納西州的曼菲斯後，艾維斯開始念高中，他以衣著俗豔又留鬢角來表現反叛，但也贏得學校一九五二年的「年度黑人歌曲演唱獎」。

艾維斯會被發掘純屬偶然。他去太陽唱片公司為母親錄製一首歌曲時，該公司正在尋找能將黑人藍調及布基烏基融合，唱給白人聽眾聽的人。唱片公司老闆山姆菲立普一聽到艾維斯的錄音，就知道這是他們要找的聲音。艾維斯獲邀回唱片公司，和多位錄音室樂手一起錄音，但他太緊張卻反而搞砸了。直到他在休息時間搞笑唱一首歌，他的潛力才顯露出來。他在一九五四年年初灌錄了數首歌曲，第一首〈沒關係，小妞〉立刻造成轟動。

Language Guide

從 shotgun shack 到 Graceland 的 貓王傳奇

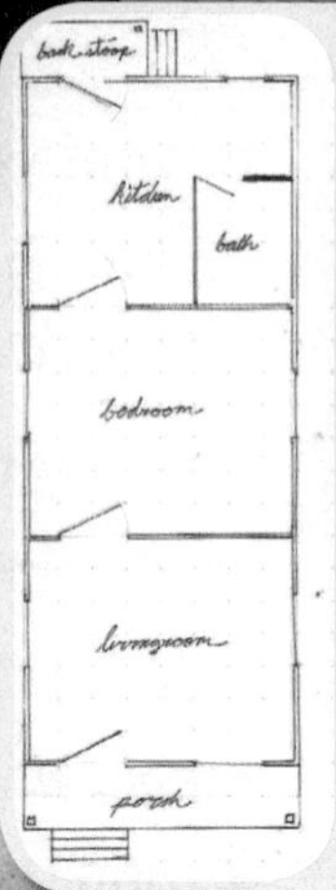

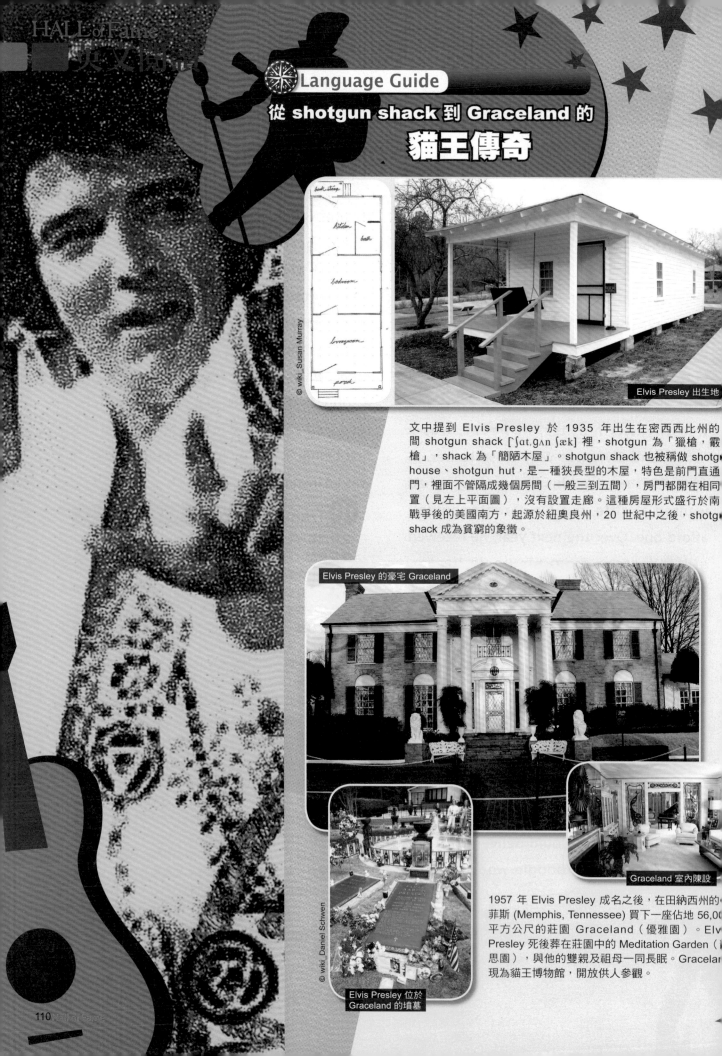

© wiki_Susan Murray

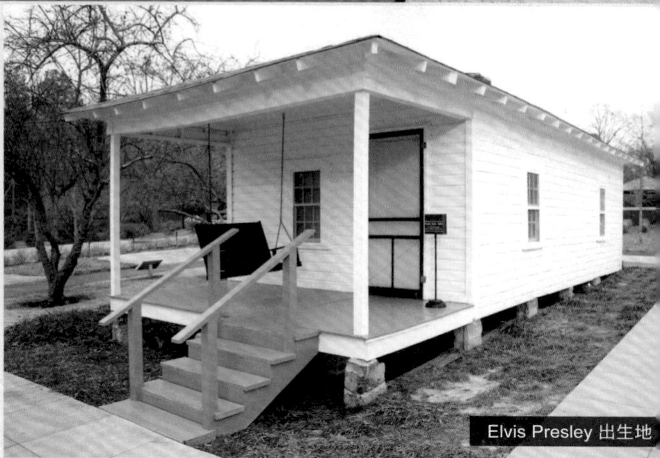

Elvis Presley 出生地

文中提到 Elvis Presley 於 1935 年出生在密西西比州的
間 shotgun shack [ˋʃɑt,gʌn ʃæk] 裡，shotgun 為「獵槍，霰
槍」，shack 為「簡陋木屋」。shotgun shack 也被稱做 shotg
house、shotgun hut，是一種狹長型的木屋，特色是前門直通
門，裡面不管隔成幾個房間（一般三到五間），房門都開在相同
置（見左上平面圖），沒有設置走廊。這種房屋形式盛行於南
戰爭後的美國南方，起源於紐奧良州，20 世紀中之後，shotg
shack 成為貧窮的象徵。

Elvis Presley 的豪宅 Graceland

© wiki_Daniel Schwen

Elvis Presley 位於 Graceland 的墳墓

Graceland 室內陳設

1957 年 Elvis Presley 成名之後，在田納西州的
菲斯 (Memphis, Tennessee) 買下一座佔地 56,0
平方公尺的莊園 Graceland（優雅園）。Elv
Presley 死後葬在莊園中的 Meditation Garden（
思園），與他的雙親及祖母一同長眠。Gracelar
現為貓王博物館，開放供人參觀。

影響 Elvis Presley 的
黑人音樂形式

boogie woogie
布基烏基

boogie woogie 是一種以鋼琴彈奏的藍調音樂，左手不斷重複和弦，右手即興表演，曲調非常輕快。這種音樂盛行於 1930-1940 年代初期，電影中常見到鄉下小酒館裡彈奏 boogie woogie 讓客人跳舞的場景，而 boogie woogie 的起源，的確就是 20 年代四處巡迴，替舞會伴奏的黑人樂隊所演奏的音樂。

gospel music
福音音樂

gospel music 是一種表現個人或團體對上帝的感謝，及宗教生活喜樂的基督教音樂，主要是由人聲演唱，並大量使用和聲 (harmony [ˋhɑrmənɪ])。相較於傳統的基督教聖歌 (hymn [hɪm])，gospel music 的特色在於演唱風格突出（歌詞不斷重複、演唱者彼此呼應）、節奏強烈（大量使用切分音，即重音落在弱拍），這都是受到黑人基督教會靈歌 (spiritual) 的影響。

我們可以說 gospel music 算是一種宗教式的藍調音樂，本身不但發展成多種現代形式，如葛萊美獎公布的類別就有搖滾或饒舌福音 (Rock or Rap Gospel)、當代流行福音 (Pop/Contemporary Gospel)、南方、鄉村或藍草福音 (Southern, Country, or Bluegrass Gospel)、傳統福音 (Traditional Gospel)、當代節奏藍調福音 (Contemporary R&B Gospel)，gospel music 脫離宗教色彩之後，也成為爵士樂及搖滾樂的濫觴。

rhythm & blues
節奏藍調

rhythm & blues 也常拼寫為 R&B、R'n'B 或 RnB。1940 至 50 年代初期剛出現這個名詞時，是用來泛指當時的黑人流行音樂——節奏強烈、帶點搖滾及爵士色彩的都會音樂。

待 60 年代受 R&B 啟發的搖滾樂 (rock and roll) 獨立成為一種音樂類型之後，R&B 被視為融合了電子藍調音樂 (electric blues)、福音音樂及靈魂樂 (soul) 等黑人音樂。到了 70 年代，R&B 是靈魂樂及放客音樂 (funk) 的統稱。90 年代之後的當代節奏藍調 (Contemporary R&B) 演變為一種帶有靈魂樂及放客音樂色彩的流行音樂。

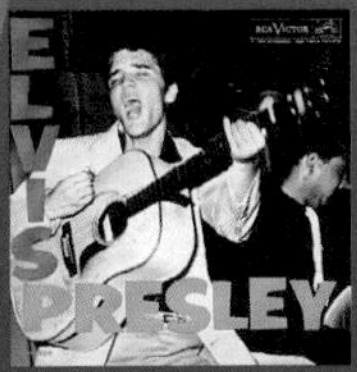

Elvis Presley
被稱做「貓王」的原因

美國鄉村音樂 (country music) 是在 1920 年代發源於美國南方及阿帕拉契山脈 (Appalachian Mountains)，融合了傳統民謠及福音音樂。剛開始這種音樂被稱為 hillbilly music，hillbilly 是指「阿帕拉契山區居民」，但後來演變為「鄉巴佬」的貶抑意味，於是到了1940 年代開始改以country music 稱呼。

言歸正傳，Elvis Presley 剛出道時，被廣播電台主持人取了個 Hillbilly Cat 的綽號，中文的「貓王」即由此而來。而 Elvis Presley 也不負此稱號，他的確是鄉村音樂史上銷售量數一數二的藝人。

Vocabulary Bank

1) **assume** [ə`sum] (v.) 以為，認為
I assumed you wouldn't be coming to the meeting.

2) **reception** [rɪ`sɛpʃən] (n.) 接受，反應，接待
Critics gave the album a cool reception.

3) **accusation** [ˌækjə`zeʃən] (n.) 指控，罪名
The terrorist denied accusations that he was involved in the bombing.

4) **pervert** [`pɚvɝt] (n.) 性變態的人，色狼
You have to watch out for perverts in public restrooms.

5) **intensity** [ɪn`tɛnsəti] (n.)（情感、表現的）強度，強烈
The class was moved by the intensity of the poem.

6) **vocal** [`vokəl] (a./n.) 聲音的，歌唱的；（歌曲中）歌唱部份，聲音部份（常用複數）
It takes years of vocal training to become an opera singer.

7) **label** [`lebəl] (n.) 唱片公司
The singer is thinking of switching labels.

8) **dismiss** [dɪs`mɪs] (v.) 排拒，屏棄
The boss dismissed my idea as impractical.

9) **defend** [dɪ`fɛnd] (v.) 辯護，辯解
(n.) defense [dɪ`fɛns]
Why are you always defending his bad behavior?

進階字彙

10) **captivating** [`kæptəˌvetɪŋ] (a.) 令人著迷的，迷人的
The candidate gave a captivating speech.

11) **win over** [wɪn`ovɚ] (phr.) 贏得支持、贊同
Helen Mirren won over critics with her performance in The Queen.

12) **obscene** [əb`sin] (a.) 淫穢的，猥褻的
The student was suspended for using obscene language.

口語補充

13) **pan** [pæn] (v.) 嚴厲批評
Critics panned the author's second novel.

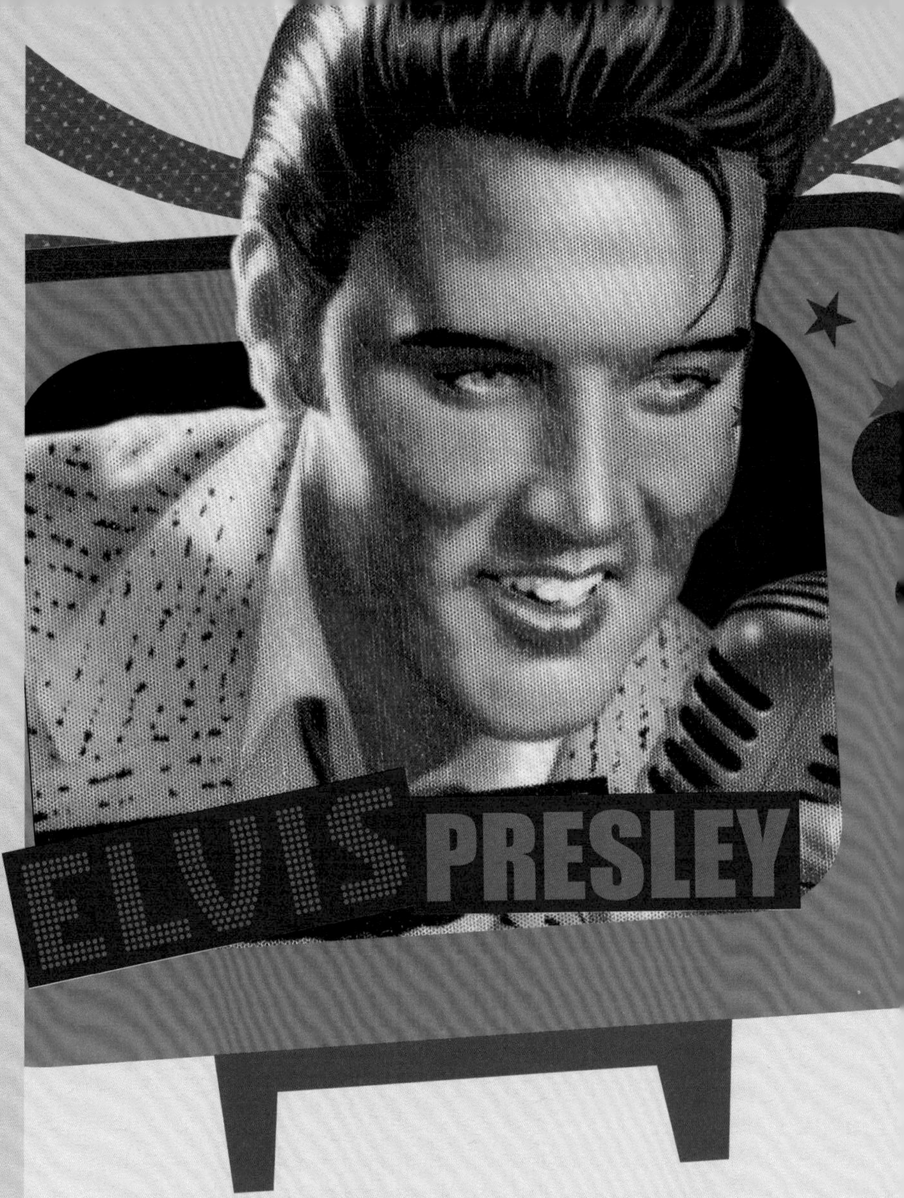

朗讀 MP3 157 單字 MP3 158 英文文章導讀 MP3 159

Because his style was a blend of gospel, rhythm & blues, and country music, most listeners [1]**assumed** Elvis was black when they heard him on the radio. When he showed up in person and people saw that he was white, he wasn't always given a friendly [2]**reception**. And though shaking his legs and swinging his hips made for [10]**captivating** performances and drove female fans crazy, it also led to [3]**accusations** that he was a sexual [4]**pervert**. But Elvis responded that he hadn't really noticed that his "body was movin'. It was a natural thing to me." Though Elvis started out shy on stage, the [5]**intensity** of his performances, his unique body language, impressive [6]**vocal range**, and great looks [11]**won** audiences **over**.

Elvis signed with a major [7]**label**, RCA, in November, 1955, and put out his self-titled debut album the following March. *Elvis Presley* topped the charts for 10 weeks, and became the label's first million-dollar record. Elvis launched his acting career in April, 1956, signing a seven-year contract with Paramount Pictures. His first picture, *Love Me Tender*, which was released that November, was [13]**panned** by critics but popular with audiences. He also began appearing on TV shows like *The Milton Berle Show*, though some critics [8]**dismissed** him as "vulgar" and "[12]**obscene**." Elvis [9]**defended** himself, saying, "I have to move around. I can't stand still. I've tried it, and I can't do it." By the end of the year, Elvis had more songs in the top 100 than [G]any other artist in history.

中 Translation

由於艾維斯的演唱風格融合了福音、節奏藍調和鄉村音樂，多數聽眾從廣播聽到他的聲音時，都以為他是黑人。等他本人現身，人們看到他是白人時，他並非每次都獲得友善的歡迎。抖腿和擺臀固然構成了迷人的表演，令女性粉絲瘋狂不已，但也引來指責，說他是性變態。不過艾維斯的回應是，他其實並沒注意到自己「身體有在動，那對我而言是自然而然的事」。雖然艾維斯初上舞台時相當羞澀，但他演出時散發的熱力、他獨一無二的肢體語言、令人佩服的音域以及出色的外表，已贏得觀眾的心。

艾維斯在一九五五年十一月和大型唱片公司 RCA 簽約，次年三月發行同名首張專輯。《艾維斯普瑞斯里》在排行榜稱霸十個星期之久，成為該唱片公司第一張百萬美元專輯。艾維斯在一九五六年四月展開戲劇生涯，和派拉蒙影業簽下七年合約。他的首部電影《溫柔地愛我》在同年十一月推出，被影評批評得一文不值，卻大受觀眾歡迎。他也開始上《米爾頓貝利秀》等電視節目，不過一些影評斥責他「下流」又「淫穢」。艾維斯替自己辯護說：「我必須四處走動，我沒辦法乖乖站在那裡。我試過，但沒辦法。」到同年年底，艾維斯登上排行榜前一百名的單曲比史上任何藝人都多。

Language Guide

音樂巨擘談貓王

Elvis is the greatest cultural force in the twentieth century. He introduced the beat to everything, music, language, clothes, it's a whole new social revolution... the 60's comes from it.

貓王是二十世紀最重要的文化推手。他將動感引進每個層面，不論是音樂、語言還是服飾，這是一場全新的社會革命……六〇年代就是由此而生。

——古典音樂指揮家、作曲家伯恩斯坦 (Leonard Bernstein)

Nothing really affected me until I heard Elvis. If there hadn't been an Elvis, there wouldn't have been a Beatles.

聽到貓王的音樂之前，沒有音樂真能打動我。要是沒有貓王，就不會有披頭四。

——披頭四成員約翰藍儂 (John Lennon)

Elvis was the King. No doubt about it. People like myself, Mick Jagger and all the others only followed in his footsteps.

貓王是搖滾之王。這點毫無疑問。像我、米克傑格（滾石合唱團主唱）及其他一干人等，只不過是跟隨他的腳步。

——搖滾歌手洛史都華 (Rod Stewart)

When I first heard Elvis' voice I just knew that I wasn't going to work for anybody; and nobody was going to be my boss. Hearing him for the first time was like busting out of jail.

第一次聽到貓王的歌聲之後，我就知道我不會效力任何人了，沒有人能讓我稱臣。第一次聽他的歌就好像衝破鐵牢。

——美國音樂詩人鮑伯狄倫 (Bob Dylan)

Grammar Master

any other + 單數名詞
任何一個其他的……

表示「任何一個其他的……」，除了用「any other + 單數名詞」以外，也可以用「all the other + 複數名詞」。

例 ● He is better than **any other student** in this class.
= He is better than **all the other students** in this class.
他比班上其他學生都要優秀。

Vocabulary Bank

1) **draft** [dræft] (v.)（美）徵（兵）；徵兵（制）
Allen left the country to avoid getting drafted.

2) **triumph** [ˋtraɪəmf] (n./v.) 成功，勝利
Michael Phelps is famous for his olympic swimming triumphs.

3) **concentrate** [ˋkɑnsən͵tret] (v.) 全神貫注，集中
How can you concentrate with all that noise?

4) **ridicule** [ˋrɪdɪ͵kjul] (v./n.) 嘲笑，奚落
Overweight children often get ridiculed at school.

5) **cape** [kep] (n.) 斗篷，披肩
Batman always wears a mask and cape.

6) **orchestra** [ˋɔrkəstrə] (n.) 管弦樂團
Matt plays cello in the school orchestra.

7) **backup** [ˋbæk͵ʌp] (n.) 伴唱，伴奏
Marc Anthony used to be a backup singer for Menudo.

8) **coma** [ˋkomə] (n.) 昏迷，不省人事
The man has been in a coma since the accident.

9) **mumble** [ˋmʌmbəl] (v.) 含糊說話，咕噥
Don't mumble when you talk.

朗讀 MP3 160 單字 MP3 161 英文文章導讀 MP3 162

Elvis was [1)]**drafted** in 1958 and spent most of his military service in Germany, where he met his wife-to-be, Priscilla. When he returned to America, there were concerns that he might have lost his magic. But his 1960 album, *Elvis is Back*!, was a [2)]**triumph** on every level. Nevertheless, he stopped giving live performances to [3)]**concentrate** on his movie career. His films, [G]of which there were dozens in the 1960s, were mostly [10)]**fluffy** romantic comedies. While critics [4)]**ridiculed** them, fans loved them, and they made money consistently, as did their [11)]**soundtracks**. After completing his movie contract, Elvis was nervous about reappearing on stage, but he insisted on making what was later dubbed the '68 Comeback Special. This Christmas TV special was a huge success, and [1] **breathed new life into** his [12)]**flagging** career.

When Elvis returned to the concert stage in 1969, he wore a [13]**jumpsuit** and [5]**cape** and played with an [6]**orchestra** and [7]**backup** singers. Although he was back on top and putting out hit singles again, some criticized his song choices and said he was out of touch with musical trends. After divorcing his wife in 1973, Elvis began gaining weight and abusing prescription drugs, spending three days in a [8]**coma** that year from an overdose of barbiturates. By 1976, he was [9]**mumbling** onstage, forgetting his lyrics, and firing members of his [14]**entourage**. When he died of a sudden heart attack the following year, he was just 42 years old. It happened so fast that some fans claim he's just gone into hiding. They still can't believe he's really gone.

中 Translation

艾維斯在一九五八年被徵召入伍，軍旅生涯大半時間在德國，並在那邂逅了他未來的妻子普莉西拉。返回美國之後，有人擔心他可能已經失去魔力。但他一九六〇年的專輯《艾維斯回來了！》仍所向披靡。儘管如此，他停止現場演出，全心發展電影事業。他在一九六〇年代拍攝的數十部電影大多是空洞的愛情喜劇，雖屢遭影評奚落，卻大得粉絲芳心，而且都能賺錢——原聲帶也是如此。在履行完電影合約後，艾維斯對於重回舞台感到緊張，但他堅持進行後來被稱為「一九六八復出特輯」的耶誕特別節目，該節目大獲成功，為他漸趨衰落的演藝生涯注入一劑強心針。

一九六九年，當艾維斯回到演唱會舞台時，他穿著連身衣褲、披著斗篷，和管弦樂隊及和聲歌手一起演出。雖然他重回頂峰，接連推出多首暢銷單曲，但有些人批評他的選歌，說他跟音樂潮流脫節。一九七三年與妻子離異後，艾維斯開始發胖並濫用處方藥物，那一年曾因服用巴比妥酸鹽（編註：一種中樞神經鎮定劑，容易造成藥癮）過量而昏迷三天。到一九七六年，他在舞台上發出囈語，忘記歌詞，解雇隨行人員。次年他因突發性心臟病過世時才四十二歲。這件事發生得太過突然，使得有些粉絲聲稱他只是躲起來罷了，他們仍不相信他真的已離開人世。

若有疑問請來信：
eztalkQ@gmail.com

進階字彙

10) **fluffy** [ˋflʌfi] (a.) 空洞的，沒有內容的
Tiffany listens to fluffy pop music.

11) **soundtrack** [ˋsaʊd͵træk] (a.) 電影原聲帶（電影中使用的歌曲）
Have you heard the soundtrack to Dreamgirls?

12) **flagging** [ˋflægɪŋ] (a.) 欲振乏力的，衰退的
The company is trying to boost its flagging sales.

13) **jumpsuit** [ˋdʒʌmp͵sut] (n.) 連身衣褲，空軍穿的跳傘裝
The members of the band wore matching jumpsuits.

14) **entourage** [ˋɑntʊ͵rɑʒ] (n.) 隨行人員
The rap star always travels with his entourage.

Tongue-tied No More

1 breathe (new) life into... 為⋯⋯注入新鮮感、活力

breathe 是「吹氣」，這裡的吹氣的人、事、物可是吐氣如蘭，被吹到的人都如沐春風般振作起來呢。

A: The new CEO says he's going to breathe new life into the organization.
新上任的執行長說他要為組織注入新活力。

B: Yeah, sure. That's what the last one said.
最好是啦。上一任執行長也是這樣說。

Grammar Master

關係代名詞當受詞時的用法

關係代名詞代替的先行詞可為主詞也可為受詞，若代替主詞用 who、which、that，代替受詞則用 whom、which、that。在正式的英語寫作中，接受介系詞片語的受詞轉為關係代名詞時，要把介系詞置於關係代名詞之前，且只能用 whom 及 which，不能用 that。

例　先行詞為受詞　關代，是 listen to 的受詞

- The music (which/that) we **listened to** last night was from Louis Armstrong's first album.
（一般寫法：關代為受詞時可被省略）
= The music **to which** we listened last night was from Louis Armstrong's first album.
（正式寫法：把 listened to 的介系詞放到關係代名詞受格 which 之前）
我們昨晚聽的音樂出自路易斯阿姆斯壯的第一張專輯。

Michae
—A Life in th
麥可傑克森——聚光燈下的一

朗讀 MP3 163 單字 MP3 164 英文文章導讀 MP3 165

Michael Joseph Jackson was born on August 29, 195 in Gary, Indiana, an industrial suburb of Chicago. The son c Joseph, a steel worker, and Katherine, a 6)**devout** Jehovah Witness, he was the seventh of nine children. His fathe originally 1)**aspired** to be a professional R&B guitar playe but was forced to give up his dreams when his band faile to get a recording deal. He then turned his attention to h children, who all showed musical talent from a young age In 1962, he formed a musical group, The Jackson Brother around his three oldest sons, Jackie, Tito and Jermaine Michael was considered too young at the time, but wa allowed to join the following year after he **1 brough down the house** singing in a school talent show.

With the addition of Michael and his brother Marlor the Jackson Brothers became the Jackson 5. Michael starte out singing backup, but with his 2)**soulful**, 7)**precociou** vocals and 3)**funky** dance moves, he soon emerged as th lead singer. With their father as manager, the brother began performing on the Chitlin' 8)**Circuit**, opening for suc famous 4)**acts** as The Temptations, Jackie Wilson and th O'Jays. Their growing 5)**popularity** brought them to th attention of Berry Gordy, founder of Motown Records, wh

Vocabulary Bank

1) **aspire** [ə`spaɪr] (v.) 渴望，立志要
The film student aspires to become a famous director.

2) **soulful** [`solfəl] (a.) 充滿感情的，扣人心弦的
The singer gave a soulful performance.

3) **funky** [`fʌŋki] (a.) 節奏強烈的
Kim likes to dance to funky music.

4) **act** [ækt] (n.) 表演團體、節目
Led Zeppelin was one of the most popular acts in rock history.

5) **popularity** [͵pɑpjə`lærəti] (n.) 普及，流行，廣受歡迎
The popularity of video games continues to grow.

進階字彙

6) **devout** [dɪ`vaʊt] (a.) 篤信宗教的，虔誠的
Maria comes from a family of devout Catholics.

7) **precocious** [prɪ`koʃəs] (a.) 早熟的，超齡的
Hollywood is full of precocious child actors.

8) **circuit** [`sɝkɪt] (n.) 巡迴（表演或比賽的）路線
The champion is planning to retire from the Formula One circuit.

9) **mentor** [`mɛntɔr ə`mɛntə] (n.) 良師益友，精神導師
You should find a mentor to advise you on your career.

Tongue-tied No More

1 bring down the house
贏得滿堂彩

這個用法是形容表演非常精彩，全場歡聲雷動，好像房頂都要被掀翻一樣。

A: How was the Coldplay concert?
酷玩樂團的演唱會如何？

B: It was great. They really brought down the house.
很棒，全場都為他們喝彩。

Jackson
Spotlight

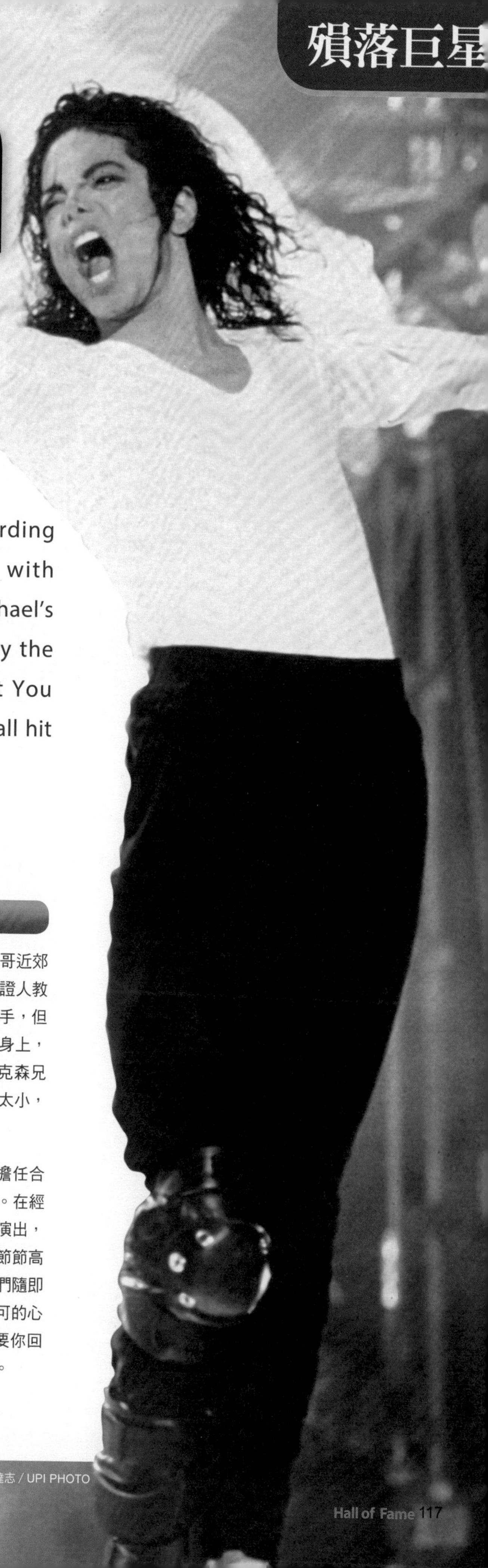

signed them to the label in 1969. They began recording immediately, and frequently performed together with fellow label mate Diana Ross, who would become Michael's [9]**mentor** and lifelong friend. The band made history the following year when their first four singles, "I Want You Back," "ABC," "The Love You Save," and "I'll Be There" all hit No. 1 on the charts.

中 Translation

麥可約瑟夫傑克森一九五八年八月二十九日生於印地安那州蓋瑞市，芝加哥近郊一個工業區。他的父親約瑟夫是鋼鐵工人，母親凱瑟琳是虔誠的耶和華見證人教徒，他在九個小孩中排行第七。他的父親原本渴望成為專業節奏藍調吉他手，但他的樂團未能獲得唱片合約，他被迫放棄夢想。接著他將注意力轉到孩子身上，他們全都從小就嶄露音樂天分。一九六二年，他組了一支音樂團體：傑克森兄弟，團員是最年長的三個兒子，傑基、提托和傑曼。當時麥可被認為年紀太小，但他次年在學校才藝表演博得滿堂彩之後，也獲准加入團體。

麥可和哥哥馬倫加入後，傑克森兄弟遂成為傑克森五人組。麥可一開始擔任合聲，但他的歌聲扣人心弦又早熟，舞步深富節奏感，很快便竄起當上主唱。在經紀人父親的牽線下，傑克森兄弟開始在各黑人娛樂劇場 (Chitlin' Circuit) 演出，替誘惑合唱團、賈奇威爾森和歐傑斯合唱團等知名表演暖場。他們的人氣節節高升，引起摩城唱片創辦人貝瑞戈帝的注意，他在一九六九年簽下他們。他們隨即開始灌錄唱片，並常與同公司歌手戴安娜羅斯同台演出，戴安娜也成了麥可的心靈導師和終身摯友。這支樂團在隔年寫下歷史：他們的頭四首單曲〈我要你回來〉、〈ABC〉、〈你拯救的愛〉和〈我會在那裡〉全都拿下排行榜冠軍。

Language Guide

chael Jackson 歷年個人錄音室專輯

Got to Be There
1972

Ben
1972

Music & Me
1973

Forever, Michael
1975

Off the Wall
1979

Thriller
1982

Bad
1987

Dangerous
1991

HIStory
1995

Blood on the Dance Floor
1997

Invincible
2001

Michael Jackson 的非凡成就

銷售成就 Sales Achievements

Worldwide best-selling album of all time
Thriller 是全球史上最暢銷音樂專輯，破紀錄售出 1.4 億張。

Third best-selling musical artist in history
史上最暢銷歌手第三名，前兩名為披頭四合唱團 (The Beatles) 和貓王 (Elvis Presley)。

U.S. top selling album in two continuous years
Thriller 是美國史上唯一連續兩年奪得年度銷售冠軍的專輯。

Highest-grossing tour in history
1987-1989 年間的 Bad World Tour 演唱會打破演唱會總收入紀錄，成為進帳最多、最成功的演唱會。這個紀錄被他自己1992-1993 年的 Dangerous World Tour 打破，接下來1996-1997 年間 HIStory World Tour 又再度打破自己的演唱會銷售紀錄。

Highest international attendance for world tour
HIStory World Tour 是國際間參加人次最多的演唱會，美國以外就有四百四十萬人參加。

Fastest selling concert tickets in history
Michael Jackson 生前預訂在 2009 年進行的 This Is It 系列演唱會（據稱結束後將不再公開表演），70 萬張門票在四個小時內便瘋狂銷售一空，為史上門票銷售最快速的演唱會。

告示牌排行榜成就 Billboard Chart Achievements

Album in the Top 10 over a year
Thriller 蟬聯 *Billboard Top 200 前十
80 週之久，是第一張停留榜上 top 10 超
年以上的專輯。目前只有艾拉妮絲莫莉
(Alanis Morissette) 的《小碎藥丸》*Jag
Little Pill* 還有席琳狄翁 (Celine Dion) 的
愛》*Falling Into You* 有同樣紀錄。

Four Top 10 singles from one album
Off the Wall 是第一張有四首 top 10 單曲的專

Seven Top 10 singles from or album
Thriller 是第一張有七首 top 10 單曲的專

Simultaneous No. 1 album & single
Michael Jackson 是第一位在 Billboard
Charts 和 Billboard Black Charts 同時拿
輯和單曲冠軍的藝人。

Five No. 1 singles from one album
Bad 是史上唯一擁有五支冠軍單曲的專
分別為 "Bad"、"The Way You Make
Feel"、"Man In the Mirror"、"I Just C
Stop Loving You"、"Dirty Diana"。

Most No. 1 singles in the 1980s
1980-1990 年間 Michael Jackson 共有
冠軍單曲，無人能及。

First single to debut at No. 1
HIStory 專輯中的 "You Are Not Alone"
一首發行首週便登上 *Billboard Hot 100
的單曲。

音樂錄影帶成就
Music Video Achievements

est-selling VHS music deos

on Walker《月球漫步》和 *The Making Michael Jackson's Thriller*《戰慄製作錄帶》為兩支最暢銷的 VHS 音樂錄影帶。

argest MV viewership ever

91 年 11 月 14 日全球 25 個國家同步播 "Black or White" 音樂錄影帶，估計約有億人同時收看這支 MV，創下史上 MV 高收視率的紀錄。

ost expensive MV in history

妹妹 Janet Jackson 合唱的歌曲 cream" 是史上製作費用最高的 MV。

音樂獎項成就
Music Award Achievements

Most music awards in a single year

Michael Jackson 在 1984 年同時贏得 8 項葛萊美獎 (Grammy Awards) 和 8 項美國音樂獎 (American Music Awards)，並在 1996 年獲得 5 項全球音樂獎 (World Music Awards)，創下單一年度贏得最多音樂獎項藝人之紀錄。

Most music awards in history

Michael Jackson 是史上贏得最多音樂獎項的藝人，共計有 197 座獎。

Inducted into the Rock and Roll Hall of Fame twice

「搖滾名人堂」，坐落於美國俄亥俄州的博物館，用來表揚最受歡迎及最有影響力的音樂人，Michael Jackson 分別在 1997 以及 2001 年被迎入此音樂聖殿，是極少數被列名兩次的音樂家。

其他個人成就
Other Individual Achievements

Presidential Humanitarian Award

1984 年美國總統雷根頒與「人道主義總統獎」。

Artist of the Decade

1990 年美國總統布希頒與「十年最佳藝人獎」。

Most money donated to charity by a celebrity

Michael Jackson 為最支持慈善活動的歌手，長年捐款和參加慈善活動，是《金氏世界紀錄》當中慈善捐款最多（總計超過 3 億美元）的藝人。

編註：

*Billboard Top 200 是美國告示牌暢銷專輯的排行榜，依據每週專輯的銷售數字來排名。

*Billboard Hot 100 是美國告示牌人氣單曲的排行榜，依據每週各單曲的電台播放率以及銷售量來排名。

©達志 / UPI PHOTO

Vocabulary Bank

1) **solo** [ˋsolo] (a./adv.) 單獨的，單獨表演的；單獨地
The explorer made a solo trip to the South Pole.

2) **alongside** [əˋlɔŋˋsaɪd] (prep./adv.) 在…旁邊，並排的
The dog ran alongside its owner.

3) **composer** [kəmˋpozɚ] (n.) 作曲家，作者
(v.) compose [kəmˋpoz]
Mozart is my favorite classical composer.

4) **infectious** [ɪnˋfɛkʃəs] (a.) 有感染力的
Michelle has an infectious smile.

5) **team up** [tim ʌp] (phr.) 與…合作，組成團隊
The two companies teamed up to develop a new video game.

6) **yield** [jild] (v.) 產生，出產
The research has yielded some valuable results.

7) **credit (with)** [ˋkrɛdɪt] (v.) 把…歸功於
Thomas Edison is often credited with inventing the light bulb.

8) **revive** [rɪˋvaɪv] (v.)（使）復甦，（使）復醒
All attempts to revive the economy have failed.

9) **slump** [slʌmp] (n.)（經濟）衰退，不景氣
The slump in the auto industry lasted for two years.

10) **air** [ɛr] (v.) 播送，播放
The classical music show airs every evening at 8 p.m.

進階字彙

11) **unprecedented** [ʌnˋprɛsə͵dɛntɪd] (a.) 前所未有的，空前的
The small country is experiencing unprecedented economic growth.

12) **groundbreaking** [ˋgraʊnd͵brekɪŋ] (a.) 開創性的
The groundbreaking novel won several prestigious awards.

朗讀 MP3 166 單字 MP3 167 英文文章導讀 MP3 168

In 1972, Michael launched his [1]**solo** career, although he continued to perform with the Jackson 5. He put out a number of hits over the next several years, including "Got to Be There," "Rockin' Robin" and his first solo No. 1 single "Ben," the title song from a children's movie about a boy and his pet rat. In 1977, Michael won a starring role [2]**alongside** Diana Ross in *The Wiz*, an all-black musical film based on *The Wizard of Oz*. It was on the set that he met [3]**composer** Quincy Jones, who agreed to produce his next album. 1979's *Off the Wall*, an [4]**infectious** blend of pop, disco and funk, produced four Top 10 singles ("Don't Stop 'til You Get Enough" and "Rock with You" reached No. 1) and won Michael a Grammy for Best Male R&B Vocal Performance.

Amazingly, Michael wasn't satisfied. He thought he could do better, and he was right. He and Jones [5]**teamed up** again on 1982's *Thriller*, which [6]**yielded** an [11]**unprecedented** seven Top 10 singles, won eight Grammys (including Album of the Year), and went on to become the best [G]selling album of all time. Indeed, the album was so successful that it is

often [7]**crediting** with [8]**reviving** the music industry, which had entered a [9]**slump** in the early 80s. *Thriller* was also supported by [12]**groundbreaking** music videos—the video for "Billie Jean" became one of the first by a black artist to be [10]**aired** on MTV, and the 14-minute "Thriller" video, which features Michael leading a dance troupe of rotting zombies, holds a Guinness World Record for the most successful music video.

中 Translation

一九七二年，麥可展開他的單飛生涯，不過仍持續和傑克森五人組同台演出。接下來幾年，他推出好幾首暢銷單曲，包括〈一定會去〉、〈搖滾羅賓〉和他的首支個人冠軍單曲〈班〉——一部描寫一個男孩和他的寵物老鼠的兒童電影主題曲。一九七七年，麥可贏得一個主角角色，和戴安娜羅絲共同演出黑人音樂電影《新綠野仙蹤》（改編自《綠野仙蹤》）。麥可就是在該片片廠遇到作曲家昆西瓊斯，他答應替麥可製作下一張專輯。一九七九年的《牆外》極具感染力地融合了流行、迪斯可和放克等元素，造就出四首十大單曲（〈不夠不要停〉和〈跟你一起搖滾〉雙雙拿下冠軍），也為麥可贏得葛萊美最佳節奏藍調男演唱人獎。

令人驚訝的是，麥可不以此為滿足。他認為自己可以做得更好，而他是對的。他和瓊斯再次聯手打造一九八二年的《顫慄》，這張專輯前所未有的產出七首十大單曲，贏得八項葛萊美獎（包括年度專輯），還成為史上最暢銷專輯。的確，這張專輯非常成功，甚至常被歸功振興了音樂產業（該產業在在八〇年代初期曾陷入衰退）。《顫慄》也有開創性的音樂錄影帶為後盾——〈比莉珍〉的錄影帶成為第一支在 MTV 台播出的黑人歌手單曲之一，而長達十四分鐘的〈顫慄〉錄影帶，主打麥可帶領一群腐爛殭屍跳舞的畫面，目前仍是金氏世界紀錄中最成功的音樂錄影帶。

Language Guide

為何被稱作 King of Pop？

Michael Jackson 除了在音樂創作上首開許多先河，造就了空前絕後的紀錄，與貓王和披頭四齊名為流行音樂史上最偉大的歌手之外，他也是偉大的舞者，舞台上滑行流暢的「月球漫步」moonwalk以及反地心引力、不可思議的「45度傾斜」anti-gravity [ˋgrævəti] lean 都是 Michael Jackson 知名的原創舞步。不僅如此，他同時也傾力創辦、贊助許多慈善機構，促進黑白人種和諧，並獲多位西方大國領袖召見，對於八〇和九〇年代的流行文化有巨大影響力，好友伊麗莎白泰勒稱讚他為 King of Pop，此名也因他在音樂史上堅不可摧的地位而廣為流傳。

Grammar Master

物品 + sell 的主動語態

一般在學 sell 這個單字時，它的意思是「賣」，容易讓人誤以為它的主詞一定要用人。事實上在英文裡， sell 這個字是可以用物品當主詞的，用主動語態而非被動。

例
- The writer's new book is selling very well.
  這位作家的新書賣得很好。
- That album sold over one million copies.
  那張專輯賣了一百多萬張。

Vocabulary Bank

1) **pyrotechnics** [͵paɪrə`tɛknɪks] (n.) 煙火，煙火表演
Did you watch the New Year pyrotechnics on TV?

2) **operation** [͵ɑpə`reʃən] (n.) 手術，開刀
The operation was performed by an experienced surgeon.

3) **drastically** [`dræstɪkəli] (adv.) 徹底地，猛烈地
Tommy's life changed drastically when his parents died in the car crash.

4) **rumor** [`rumɚ] (n.) 謠傳
There are many rumors surrounding Whitney Houston's death.

5) **circulate** [`sɝkjə͵let] (v.) 散播，流傳
News of the star's suicide circulated quickly.

6) **chamber** [`tʃembɚ] (n.) 室，房間（尤指寢室）
The human heart consists of four chambers.

7) **exotic** [ɪg`zɑtɪk] (a.) 非本土的，異國風味的
That shop sells exotic plants.

8) **subsequent** [`sʌbsɪkwənt] (a.) 隨後的，後續的
We'll keep you informed about subsequent developments.

9) **fodder** [`fɑdɚ] (n.) 題材，原意為「飼料」
The Hollywood couple's relationship is providing fodder for the gossip columns.

進階字彙

10) **tabloid** [`tæblɔɪd] (n.) 小報，八卦報
Don't believe everything you read in the tabloids.

11) **falsetto** [fɔl`sɛto] (n.)（歌唱）假音
The Bee Gees sang many of their songs in falsetto.

12) **wacko** [`wæko] (a./n.) 古怪的，瘋瘋癲癲的；怪人，瘋子
Morgan's wife is totally wacko!

13) **eclipse** [ɪ`klɪps] (v.)（使）黯然失色，（使）蒙上陰影
Traditional cell phones have been eclipsed by smartphones.

14) **molest** [mə`lɛst] (v.) 猥褻（孩童），調戲（女性）
(n.) molestation [molɛs`teʃən] 性騷擾
The man was arrested for molesting his daughter.

朗讀 MP3 169 單字 MP3 170 英文文章導讀 MP3 171

Yet just as Michael was reaching the peak of his fame, things began to go wrong. While filming a Pepsi commercial in 1984, he suffered burns to his face and scalp after [1]**pyrotechnics** accidently set his hair on fire, requiring several [2]**operations**. His appearance began to change [3]**drastically**—©his skin grew paler, and his nose smaller—prompting [4]**rumors** of multiple plastic surgeries. Rumors also began to [5]**circulate** about Michael's eccentric behavior, and the [10]**tabloids** were full of stories about him sleeping in an oxygen [6]**chamber**, taking female hormones to maintain his [11]**falsetto**, and buying the bones of the Elephant Man. He didn't actually buy the bones, but he did buy a large ranch in California, name it Neverland and fill it with amusement park rides and [7]**exotic** animals. No wonder the press started calling him "[12]**Wacko** Jacko."

While Michael's [8]**subsequent** albums did well (Bad, Dangerous and HIStory all produced No. 1 hits), his musical career was increasingly [13]**eclipsed** by his personal life, which provided endless [9]**fodder** for the tabloids. In 1993, he was accused of [14]**molesting** a 13-year-old boy, and although charges were never brought, he ended up paying a huge settlement anyway. Next came two brief marriages, first to Elvis Presley's daughter Lisa Marie, and then to nurse Debbie Rowe, who bore him two children. A third child followed, this time through artificial insemination with a surrogate mother. Michael was again accused of child molestation in 2003, and after being acquitted in 2005, he moved to Bahrain and disappeared from the public eye. Tragically, he passed away on June 29, 2009 due to cardiac arrest, just weeks before he was scheduled to perform a series of comeback concerts in London.

©達志 / UPI PHOTO

Translation

但正當麥可的聲勢如日中天之際，事情開始出差錯。一九八四年他在拍攝一支百事可樂廣告時，煙火特效意外使他的頭髮著火，燒傷了他的臉和頭皮，需要動好幾項手術。此後他的面貌開始大幅改變——皮膚愈來愈白，鼻子愈來愈小——引發他做過多次整型手術的傳言。也有謠言開始散布麥可光怪陸離的行徑，小報充斥著他睡在氧氣槽裡、服用女性荷爾蒙來維持假音、購買象人骨骸的報導。他其實沒有買象人的骨骸，但確實在加州買下一座大農場，取名為「夢幻莊園」，置入許許多多遊樂設施和珍禽異獸。怪不得媒體開始稱他為「瘋子傑克」。

雖然麥可後續的專輯皆創下佳績（《飆》、《危險之旅》和《他的歷史》都出了冠軍單曲），他的音樂事業卻逐漸因他的私生活而黯然失色，也為小報提供了源源不絕的題材。一九九三年，他被指控猥褻一名十三歲男童，雖然對方始終未提出控告，他最後還是付出鉅額和解金。接下來是他兩段短暫婚姻，第一任妻子是（貓王）艾維斯普瑞斯萊之女麗莎瑪莉，第二任是替他生了兩個孩子的護士黛比羅伊。之後他又有了第三個孩子，這一次是透過和代理孕母人工受精。二〇〇三年，麥可再次被指控猥褻兒童，二〇〇五年獲判無罪後，他搬到巴林，從公眾眼前消失。令人傷感的是，他於二〇〇九年六月二十九日因心跳停止過世，離他預定於倫敦舉行一系列復出演唱會的日子僅數個星期。

若有疑問請來信：eztalkQ@gmail.com

Language Guide

Michael Jackson 和他的 Neverland 莊園

Neverland 是蘇格蘭作家 J.M. Barrie 之作品《彼得潘》*Peter Pan* 中，彼得潘、小精靈 (Tinker Bell)、迷途男孩 (Lost Boys) 等人居住的地方。住在 Neverland 的人永遠可以保持孩子的模樣，所以常被人用來象徵永恆的童年 (eternal childhood)、童稚 (childishness)、不朽 (immortality) 及逃避現實 (escapism)。雖然 Neverland 是個虛構的國度，但 Michael Jackson 打造的 Neverland 就如同將故事中充滿歡樂和冒險的島嶼搬到現實般，充滿了各類動物、遊樂設施和愉快玩樂的孩子。Michael Jackson 曾在訪問中表達自己的內心就跟 Peter Pan 一樣，所以把自己的家命名為Neverland。

附帶一提，1983 年心理學家丹凱利 (Dan Kiley) 之著作《彼得潘症候群：不曾長大的男人》中首度發表「彼得潘症候群」Peter Pan Syndrome 這個現代流行心理學名詞，專指無法獨立、拒絕成熟而變成社會化不成熟的成人。此症候群雖非正式精神醫學診斷，但普遍存在於諮商個案中，許多人認為 Michael Jackson 的人格存在著多種彼得潘症候群的特徵。

Michael Jackson 新聞相關「醫學」用字

plastic surgery 整型手術

skin graft 皮膚移植

skin whitening 皮膚漂白手術

nose job/rhinoplasty 鼻整型手術

vitiligo 白斑

lupus 狼瘡

artificial insemination 人工受孕

surrogate mother 代理孕母

cardiac arrest 心臟停跳

Grammar Master

對稱句型結構中省略重複動詞

像第六句中 ...his skin grew paler, and his nose smaller 這樣的句子，本來後面那句也應該是 his nose grew smaller，但因為兩句結構對稱，動詞也一樣是 grew，所以後面那句的動詞就被省略了。這樣的寫法可避免句子太累贅。要注意的是，只有用連接詞 and 連接，或以分號隔開的兩個對稱句才能這樣寫。

例
- I bought the white T-shirt, and he (bought) the blue one.
  我買了白色的 T 恤，他買了藍色的。
- To err is human; to forgive (is) divine.
  犯錯為人之常情，寬恕為聖人之舉。

Vocabulary Bank

1) **dominate** [ˋdɑmə͵net] (v.) 佔主要地位，佔優勢
The Arab Spring dominated the headlines last year.

2) **synonymous** [sɪˋnɑnəməs] (a.) 同義的
Picasso's name is synonymous with modern art.

3) **reputation** [͵rɛpjəˋteʃən] (n.) 名譽，名聲
The scandal destroyed the senator's reputation.

4) **charge** [tʃɑrdʒ] (v./n.) 衝鋒
The army charged the enemy at dawn.

5) **waterfront** [ˋwɔtɚ͵frʌnt] (n.)（城市的）濱水區
There are many seafood restaurants on the waterfront.

6) **reform** [rɪˋfɔrm] (n./v.) 改過，自新，reform school 即專收行為偏差少年的「少年感化院」
The government has recognized the need for educational reform.

進階字彙

7) **stand** [stænd] (v.) 維持不變，仍然有效
As far as I know, the agreement still stands.

8) **infancy** [ˋɪnfənsi] (n.) 嬰兒時期
The singer's love of music began in her infancy.

9) **saloon** [səˋlun] (n.)（美）酒吧，酒館，為舊式用法，現在通稱 bar
On payday, all the cowboys rode into town to drink at the saloon.

10) **fend for oneself** [fɛnd fɔr wʌnˋsɛlf] (phr.) 自立更生，照顧自己
The boy had to fend for himself after his parents died.

Grammar Master

little？a little？還是 a few？

a little 和 a few 都是「有一些⋯⋯」的意思，不過 a little 後面接不可數名詞，而 a few 後面接複數的可數名詞。little 和 few 則是「很少；幾乎沒有」的意思，所以在閱讀時要看清楚，才不會完全誤會文意囉！

- He has little knowledge of Chinese culture.
  他對中國文化幾乎一無所知。
- He has a little knowledge of Chinese culture.
  他懂一點中國文化。

BABE RUTH
棒球名人中的名人 貝比魯斯

朗讀 MP3 172 單字 MP3 173 英文文章導讀 MP3 174

When many young people hear the name Babe Ruth they're more likely to think of a tasty candy bar than sports hero, but to baseball fans Babe Ruth is one of th greatest baseball players in history. He [1]**dominated** th sport while playing for the New York Yankees in the 1920 and 1930s, and many of the records he set during hi long career [7]**stand** to this day. His fame was so great tha his name has become [2]**synonymous** with excellence i sports—even Michael Jordan has been called "the Bab Ruth of basketball." And his [3]**reputation** isn't limited t the land of his birth. When Japanese soldiers [4]**charge** American troops in World War II, they didn't cry "To hel with Roosevelt!" or "To hell with MacArthur!" but rather "T hell with Babe Ruth!"

George Herman Ruth, Jr. was born to German American parents in a poor neighborhood in Baltimore Maryland in 1895. Although Ruth was one of eight childrer he and his sister Mamie were the only ones to surviv past [8]**infancy**. Ruth's parents, who owned and ran a loca [9]**saloon**, had Ⓖlittle time for their children. Left to [10]**fen for himself** on the rough streets of Baltimore's [5]**waterfront**

©達志 / UPI PHOTO

Ruth was constantly getting into trouble. When he was seven years old, his father sent him to live at St. Mary's Industrial School for Boys, a Catholic [6]**reform** school and orphanage. It was there that Ruth met Brother Matthias, a strict but kind priest who not only taught him to read and write, but also introduced him to the game of baseball.

中 Translation

許多年輕人聽到貝比魯斯這個名字的時候，很可能會想到一種好吃的巧克力棒，而不是想到一位運動英雄，但對棒球迷而言，貝比魯斯是史上最偉大的棒球選手之一。他在二○、三○年代效力於紐約洋基隊時，在棒球界呼風喚雨，而他在漫長職業生涯所創下的許多紀錄至今仍然屹立不搖。他的名氣如此之大，就連他的名字也成為運動優異表現的同義詞——甚至連麥可喬丹都被稱為「籃球界的貝比魯斯」。而且他的名聲並不只侷限在他的出生地。日本士兵在第二次世界大戰進攻美軍時，他們不是大喊「羅斯福去死吧！」或「麥克阿瑟去死吧！」，而是喊「貝比魯斯去死吧！」

喬治赫爾曼魯斯二世的父母是德裔美國人，他於 1895 年在美國馬里蘭州巴爾的摩市一個貧窮社區出生。雖然魯斯是八個孩子之一，但只有他和他妹妹美咪度過嬰兒期，存活下來。魯斯的父母擁有並經營一間當地酒吧，很少有時間陪孩子，讓他在巴爾的摩濱水區的街頭上自生自滅，魯斯不斷惹麻煩。七歲時，他的父親把他送到聖瑪麗工業男校寄宿，那是一所天主教感化院兼孤兒院。就在那裡，魯斯遇到了馬蒂亞斯修士，他是一位嚴格但仁慈的神父，不僅教他讀書寫字，還介紹他認識棒球運動。

Language Guide

Baby Ruth candy bar

candy bar 絕大多數都是花生乾果、餅乾、焦糖醬夾心，外裹巧克力的巧克力棒。文中說美國年輕人聽到 Babe Ruth 會想到巧克力棒，指的就是 Baby Ruth 這種巧克力棒（裡面包的是焦糖、花生、牛軋糖）。這個品牌於 1921 年首次推出，發售 Baby Ruth 巧克力棒的公司宣稱產品名稱源於美國總統 Grover Cleveland（任期 1893~1897）的女兒 Ruth Cleveland。但當時 Babe Ruth 聲勢如日中天，而 Ruth Cleveland 卻已經去世 15 年！因此許多人相信，這只是廠商規避鉅額明星代言費的取巧作法罷了。

看棒球一定要會唱！

如果要幫美國職棒選出一首代表歌曲，那一定非 Take Me Out to the Ball Game（帶我去看棒球賽）莫屬了！美國職棒比賽每到第七局上半結束時，會有一段讓觀眾活動筋骨、到處走動的休息時間，稱為 seventh-inning stretch，此時球場廣播總會響起這首歌（全曲很長，現在都只唱副歌）：

Take Me Out to the Ball Game
詞 Jack Norworth，曲 Albert Von Tilzer

Take me out to the ball game,
Take me out with the crowd;
Buy me some peanuts and Cracker Jack,
I don't care if I never get back.
Let me root, root, root for the home team,
If they don't win, it's a shame.
For it's one, two, three strikes, you're out,
At the old ball game.

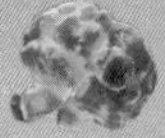

歌曲中的 Cracker Jack 是一種點心的牌子，是裹焦糖漿的爆米花和花生。而 2001 年 911 攻擊事件之後，一些球賽在 seventh-inning stretch 時也會播放 God Bless America（天祐美國）這首歌，有時甚至會將 Take Me Out to the Ball Game 完全取代。

Vocabulary Bank

1) **take to** [tek tu] (phr.) 喜歡上，成為興趣或習慣
The man took to drinking after he lost his job.

2) **minor** [ˋmaɪnɚ] (n.) 未成年者
The bar was fined for selling alcohol to minors.

3) **ballpark** [ˋbɔl͵pɑrk] (n.)（美）棒球場
Let's go down to the ballpark and hit some balls.

4) **catch on** [kætʃ ɑn] (phr.) 受到歡迎，成為流行
The new diet is starting to catch on.

5) **last** [læst] (v.) 持久，維持
How long will these batteries last?

進階字彙

6) **varsity** [ˋvɑrsəti] (n./a.)（美）學校代表（隊）
Kevin played varsity football in college.

7) **option** [ˋɑpʃən] (v.)（棒球）大聯盟球員換至小聯盟備選，在一段期間內可隨時被召回大聯盟
Several of the team's players have been optioned to the minors.

8) **prowess** [ˋpraʊɪs] (n.) 傑出的能力
President Obama is known for his prowess as a public speaker.

9) **play...as...** [ple æz] (phr.) 讓（某球員）擔任…
The coach decided to play Steve as a pitcher in the championship game.

Tongue-tied No More

bring sb./sth. to the attention of 使某人注意某人事物

形容某人被注意及關注，受到矚目。

A: Thanks for bringing the error to my attention.
謝謝你讓我注意到這個錯誤。

B: Not at all.
不客氣。

Ruth [1]**took to** the game immediately, and was soon playing both catcher and pitcher for St. Mary's [6]**varsity** team. At the age of 19, he was **1 brought to the attention of** Jack Dunn, owner and manager of the minor-league Baltimore Orioles. Impressed by his pitching skills, Dunn signed Ruth to pitch for his club in February, 1914. Because Ruth was still a [2]**minor** at the time, Dunn also had to become his legal guardian. When the young Ruth showed up at the [3]**ballpark**, one of the team's coaches said, "Well, here's Jack's newest babe." The name [4]**caught on**, and he was known as Babe Ruth from then on. After only five months with the Orioles, however, Ruth was sold to the major-league Boston Red Sox.

Ruth's first taste of the majors didn't [5]**last** long—the Red Sox were already so crowded with star players that they [7]**optioned** him to the minor-league Providence Grays so he could play every day and gain experience. [G]It was at that time that he met and married Helen Woodward, a 17-year-old waitress at a Boston coffee shop. He was called back to the Red Sox later that season, and became a regular pitcher the following year. Led by Ruth, the Red Sox won the World Series in 1915, 1916, and 1918. Despite his [8]**prowess** as a pitcher, he was beginning to develop an even greater reputation as a slugger. The team began [9]**playing** Ruth **as** an outfielder to take advantage of his hitting skills, and he led the American League in home runs in both 1918 and 1919.

中 Translation

魯斯立即愛上棒球，不久便替聖瑪麗學校代表隊擔任捕手和投手。19 歲時，有人向傑克鄧恩提到魯斯，他是巴爾的摩金鶯隊這支小聯盟球隊的老闆兼總教練。鄧恩對他的投球技巧相當欣賞，於是在 1914 年 2 月簽下魯斯替他的球隊投球。由於魯斯在當時尚未成年，因此鄧恩也必須成為他的法定監護人。當年輕的魯斯出現在球場，球隊一位教練說：「傑克的新寶貝來了。」這個名字傳了開來，從此他就被稱為貝比（寶貝）魯斯。然而，在金鶯隊只待了 5 個月之後，魯斯就被交易到大聯盟的波士頓紅襪隊。

魯斯的大聯盟初體驗並沒有持續很久——紅襪隊已經滿是明星球員，因此他們將他下放到小聯盟的普羅登斯灰人隊，讓他可以每天上場、吸取經驗。就是在那個時期，他認識了海倫伍德沃，波士頓一家咖啡店的 17 歲女服務生，並與她結婚。他在那個球季後半被召回紅襪隊，並在隔一年成為正規投手。在魯斯領軍之下，紅襪在 1915、1916 和 1918 年奪得世界大賽冠軍。儘管他是個傑出的投手，但他已開始以強打者的身分建立更大的聲譽。紅襪隊開始讓魯斯擔任外野手，善加利用他的打擊技巧，他在 1918 和 1919 年的全壘打數都在美國聯盟居冠。

G Grammar Master

It is / was… that… 強調句型

當想要強調某個人、事、物、時間或地點時，我們就可以把原本直述句型分裂為兩個部分：
「由 It is/was 帶出欲強調之物」，以及「用 that 後面的子句來界定和修飾此物」。
以文中句子為例：

直述句： He met and married Helen Woodward at that time.
他在那時遇見海倫伍德沃，並與她結婚。

強調句型：**It was <u>at that time</u> that <u>he met and married Helen Woodward.</u>**
（at that time：強調重點；he met and married Helen Woodward：修飾說明重點）
就是在那個時候，他遇見海倫伍德沃，並與她結婚。

Language Guide

認識美國職棒

美國職棒大聯盟 (MLB, Major League Baseball) 成立於 1869 年，分為「美國聯盟」及「國家聯盟」，包含美國（29隊）及加拿大（1隊）的棒球隊伍，每個球隊所屬球團 (club) 旗下還有小聯盟 (Minor League Baseball) 球隊。

美聯及國聯球賽的打法及規則大致相同，唯一的差別是美聯採指定打擊制 (Designated Hitter Rule)，即投手不必上場打擊，由指定打擊者上場。

American League (AL) 美國聯盟

各區隊伍及其主場

West Division 西區	1 Los Angeles Angels of Anaheim (LAA)	洛杉磯天使隊	◆ Angel Stadium
	2 Oakland A's (OAK)	奧克蘭運動家隊	◆ Oakland-Alameda County Coliseum
	3 Seattle Mariners (SEA)	西雅圖水手隊	◆ Safeco Field
	4 Texas Rangers (TEX)	德州游騎兵隊	◆ Rangers Ballpark
Central Division 中區	5 Chicago White Sox (CWS)	芝加哥白襪隊	◆ U.S. Cellular Field
	6 Cleveland Indians (CLE)	克里夫蘭印地安人隊	◆ Progressive Field
	7 Detroit Tigers (DET)	底特律老虎隊	◆ Comerica Park
	8 Kansas City Royals (KC)	堪薩斯皇家隊	◆ Kauffman Stadium
	9 Minnesota Twins (MIN)	明尼蘇達雙城隊	◆ Hubert H. Humphrey Metrodome
East Division 東區	10 Baltimore Orioles (BAL)	巴爾的摩金鶯隊	◆ Oriole Park
	11 Boston Red Sox (BOS)	波士頓紅襪隊	◆ Fenway Park
	12 New York Yankees (NYY)	紐約洋基隊	◆ Yankee Stadium
	13 Tampa Bay Rays (TB)	坦帕灣光芒隊	◆ Tropicana Field
	14 Toronto Blue Jays (TOR)	多倫多藍鳥隊	◆ Rogers Centre

National League (NL) 國家聯盟

各區隊伍及其主場

West Division 西區	15 Arizona Diamondbacks (ARI)	亞利桑那響尾蛇隊	◆ Chase Field
	16 Colorado Rockies (COL)	科羅拉多落磯隊	◆ Coors Field
	17 Los Angeles Dodgers (LAD)	落杉機道奇隊	◆ Dodger Stadium
	18 San Diego Padres (SD)	聖地牙哥教士隊	◆ Petco Park
	19 San Francisco Giants (SF)	舊金山巨人隊	◆ AT&T Park
Central Division 中區	20 Chicago Cubs (CHC)	芝加哥小熊隊	◆ Wrigley Field
	21 Cincinnati Reds (CIN)	辛辛那提紅人隊	◆ Great American Ball Park
	22 Houston Astros (HOU)	休士頓太空人隊	◆ Minute Maid Park
	23 Milwaukee Brewers (MIL)	密爾瓦基釀酒人隊	◆ Miller Park
	24 Pittsburgh Pirates (PIT)	匹茲堡海盜隊	◆ PNC Park
	25 St. Louis Cardinals (STL)	聖路易紅雀隊	◆ Busch Stadium
East Division 東區	26 Atlanta Braves (ATL)	亞特蘭大勇士隊	◆ Turner Field
	27 Florida Marlins (FLA)	佛羅里達馬林魚隊	◆ Dolphin Stadium
	28 New York Mets (NYM)	紐約大都會隊	◆ Citi Field
	29 Philadelphia Phillies (PHI)	費城費城人隊	◆ Citizens Bank Park
	30 Washington Nationals (WAS)	華盛頓國民隊	◆ Nationals Park

美國各州職棒球隊分佈

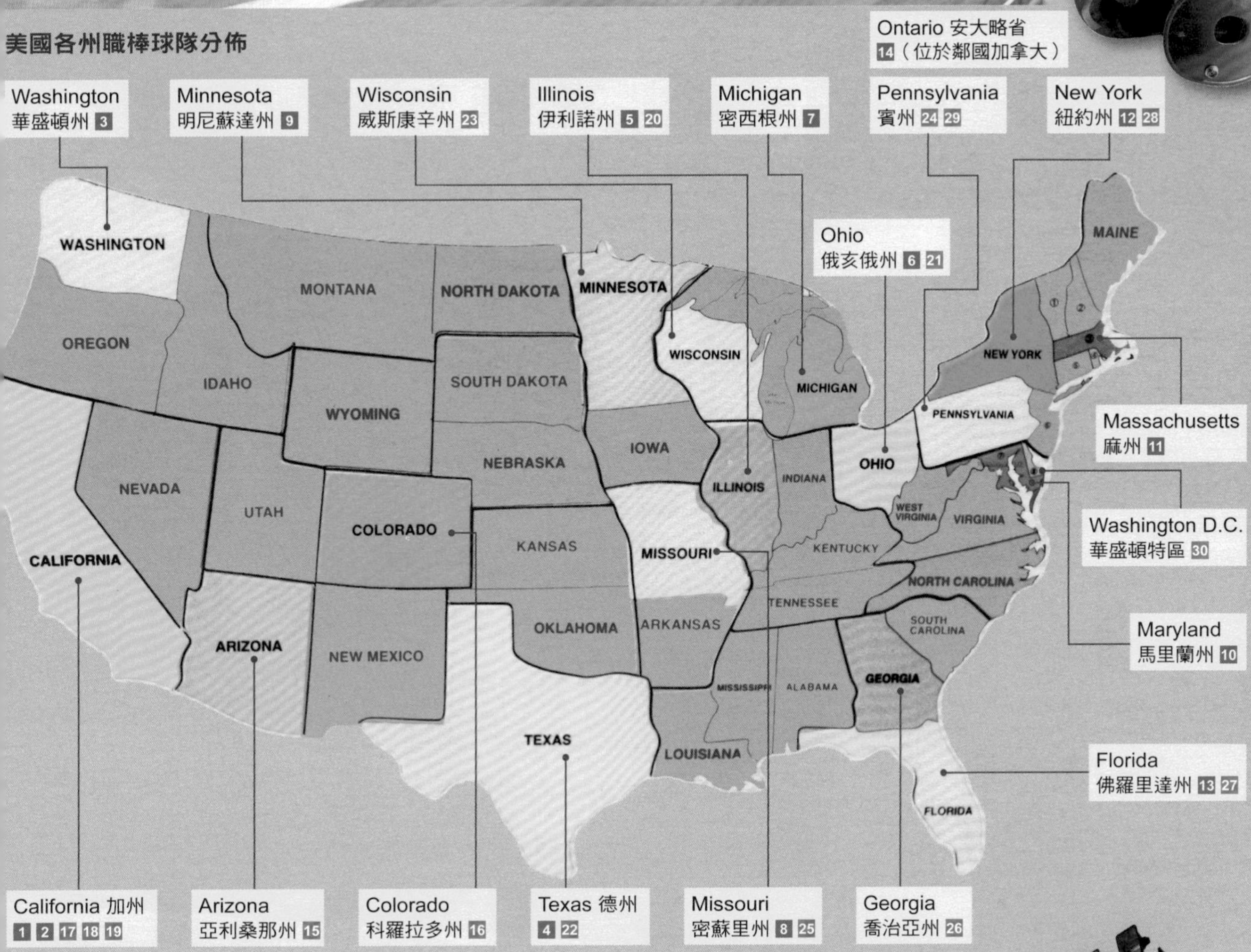
Ontario 安大略省
14（位於鄰國加拿大）
Washington
華盛頓州 3
Minnesota
明尼蘇達州 9
Wisconsin
威斯康辛州 23
Illinois
伊利諾州 5 20
Michigan
密西根州 7
Pennsylvania
賓州 24 29
New York
紐約州 12 28
Ohio
俄亥俄州 6 21
Massachusetts
麻州 11
Washington D.C.
華盛頓特區 30
Maryland
馬里蘭州 10
Florida
佛羅里達州 13 27
California 加州
1 2 17 18 19
Arizona
亞利桑那州 15
Colorado
科羅拉多州 16
Texas 德州
4 22
Missouri
密蘇里州 8 25
Georgia
喬治亞州 26
WASHINGTON
MONTANA
NORTH DAKOTA
MINNESOTA
MAINE
OREGON
IDAHO
SOUTH DAKOTA
WISCONSIN
MICHIGAN
NEW YORK
WYOMING
PENNSYLVANIA
IOWA
NEBRASKA
OHIO
ILLINOIS
INDIANA
NEVADA
UTAH
COLORADO
WEST VIRGINIA
VIRGINIA
KANSAS
MISSOURI
KENTUCKY
CALIFORNIA
NORTH CAROLINA
TENNESSEE
OKLAHOMA
ARKANSAS
SOUTH CAROLINA
ARIZONA
NEW MEXICO
MISSISSIPPI
ALABAMA
GEORGIA
TEXAS
LOUISIANA
FLORIDA

棒球球員及裁判位置

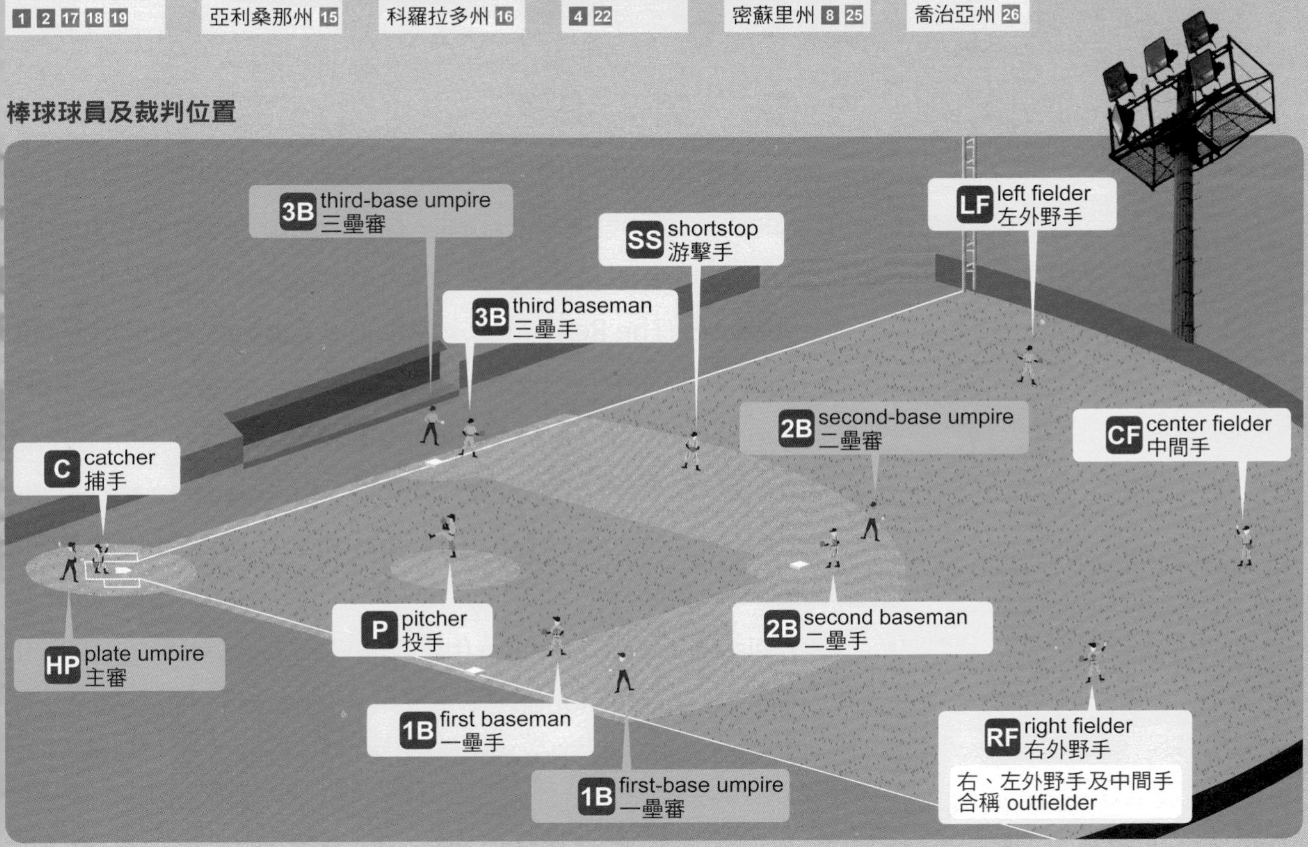
3B third-base umpire
三壘審
SS shortstop
游擊手
LF left fielder
左外野手
3B third baseman
三壘手
2B second-base umpire
二壘審
CF center fielder
中間手
C catcher
捕手
P pitcher
投手
2B second baseman
二壘手
HP plate umpire
主審
1B first baseman
一壘手
RF right fielder
右外野手
右、左外野手及中間手
合稱 outfielder
1B first-base umpire
一壘審

©達志 / UPI

Vocabulary Bank

1) **flock** [flɑk] (v./n.) 成群結隊前往；群眾
Millions of Muslims flock to Mecca each year.

2) **lineup** [ˋlaɪn͵ʌp] (n.) 表演者名單，（球賽）選手陣容。也可做 line-up。
Our team has a strong lineup this season.

3) **title** [ˋtaɪtəl] (n.)（體育）冠軍頭銜
The boxer has a good chance of winning the heavyweight title.

4) **era** [ˋɛrə] (n.) 時代，年代，紀元
The president has promised a new era of peace.

5) **decline** [dɪˋklaɪn] (v./n.) 下跌，衰退
Wages have declined over the past several years.

進階字彙

6) **pennant** [ˋpɛnənt] (n.) 聯盟冠軍
The Red Sox have won a total of 12 pennants.

口語補充

7) **homer** [ˋhomɚ] (n.) 全壘打，為 home run 的簡稱
The player hit a two-run homer to win the game.

Language Guide

World Series 世界大賽

美國職棒大聯盟每隊每年要打 162 場例行賽 (regular season)，整個球季從四月第一個星期天一路打到十月第一個星期天（或九月最後一個星期天），待例行賽結束後即進行季後賽 (post-season playoff)，由國聯、美聯各分區（東、西、中三區）冠軍及各區第二名之中紀錄最佳球隊（即「外卡」wild card）參加，因此加起來共有八隊。

季後賽分為三輪，均採淘汰制，三輪季後賽的名稱分別為：分區系列賽（American /National League Division Series，採五戰三勝 (best-of-five) 制）、聯盟冠軍賽（American /National League Champion Series，採七戰四勝 (best-of-seven)）和世界大賽（World Series，採七戰四勝），由一支國聯和一支美聯勝出的球隊爭冠軍。

朗讀 MP3 178 單字 MP3 179 英文文章導讀 MP3 180

Although Ruth was hugely popular with Boston fans Red Sox owner Harry Frazee decided to sell him to the New York Yankees in 1920 to cover his losses in other business ventures. The Red Sox' loss was the Yankees' gain. In his first year as a Yankee, Ruth nearly doubled his previous [7]**home run** record, and fans began [1]**flocking** to Ⓖsee him hit ball out of the park. With Ruth on their [2]**lineup**, the Yankees won their first [6]**pennant** in 1921, another in 1922, and their first World Series in 1923. By that time, the team could afford to build their own stadium (they previously shared one with the Giants), and although it was named the Yankee Stadium, fans began calling it "The House That Ruth Built."

In his 15 years as a Yankee, Ruth won 10 home run [3]**titles** and participated in seven World Series, leading his team to victory in four. He reached his home run peak in 1927, hitting an amazing 60 [7]**homers**, a record that stood until 1969, when Roger Maris hit 61. By 1930, Ruth was earning $80,000 a year, a huge figure in that [4]**era**. When asked by a reporter why he should make more than President Hoover, who earned $75,000, he replied, "Why not. I had a better year than he did." Ruth's performance began to [5]**decline** in the mid-30s, however, and he retired from the Yankees after the 1934 season. His career total of 714 home runs stood as a major league record until Hank Aaron topped it in 1974.

中 Translation

雖然魯斯深受波士頓球迷喜愛，紅襪隊老闆哈利弗雷齊還是決定在 1920 年將他賣到紐約洋基隊，以支應他在其他生意投資的虧損。紅襪的損失是洋基的收穫。在他成為洋基人的第一年，魯斯幾乎將以前的全壘打紀錄翻一倍，球迷開始群集去看他將球打出球場。有了魯斯加入陣容，洋基隊在 1921 年贏得第一次聯盟冠軍，1922 年又贏得一次，1923 年贏得他們首次世界大賽冠軍。到了那時，洋基隊已經有財力興建自己的球場（他們以前與巨人隊共用），雖然球場命名為洋基球場，但球迷開始稱之為「魯斯興建的家。」

在 15 年的洋基生涯，魯斯贏得 10 次全壘打王頭銜，參加 7 次世界大賽，帶領球隊拿下 4 次冠軍。他的全壘打在 1927 年達到巔峰，擊出驚人的 60 支全壘打，這項紀錄維持到 1969 年，當時羅傑馬力斯擊出 61 支。到了 1930 年，魯斯一年賺 8 萬美金，在那個年代是一筆龐大的數字。當記者問他為什麼可以賺得比胡佛總統的 7.5 萬美金還多，他回答說：「為什麼不行，我這一年的表現比他更出色。」不過，魯斯的表現在 30 年代中期開始下滑，他在 1934 年球季之後從洋基退休。他的職業生涯總共 714 支全壘打，一直是大聯盟的紀錄，直到漢克阿倫在 1974 年超越。

Grammar Master

感官動詞 see、hear、smell、feel + 受詞 + 原形動詞 或 Ving 的區別

在學文法時，會說感官動詞後接原形動詞或 Ving 都可以，事實上只能說兩者都正確，但其實意思是不同的。感官動詞 see、hear、smell、feel 接原形動詞時只是單純描述看到的景象，或聽到的聲音，通常是常態性的；但 Ving 則有強調受詞當時「正在⋯⋯」的意味。

表示常態

- I see people litter all the time.
  我老是看到有人亂丟垃圾。

表示正在發生

- I see someone littering.
  我看到有人在亂丟垃圾。

Mini Quiz

1. According to the article, how many World Series did Babe Ruth play in?
   (A) 7 (B) 8 (C) 10 (D) 11

2. Why was the Yankee Stadium called "The House that Ruth Built"?
   (A) Because it was built by Babe Ruth
   (B) Because Ruth's popularity allowed the team to afford building it
   (C) Because Ruth won the World Series there
   (D) Because the stadium was named after Babe Ruth

3. Kevin is so busy with school and work that he has _________ time to relax.
   (A) few (B) none (C) a little (D) little

4. I think I smell something _________ in the kitchen.
   (A) burns (B) burn
   (C) burning (D) burned

解答：1 (C) 2 (B) 3 (D) 4 (C)

Vocabulary Bank

1) **span** [spæn] (v.) 持續，橫跨（時空）
The author's career spanned half a century.

2) **awkward** [ˋɔkwɚd] (a.) 笨拙的，彆扭的
Brian is awkward and bad at sports.

進階字彙

3) **stilt** [stɪlt] (n.) 高蹺
Walking on stilts is very difficult.

4) **feat** [fit] (n.) 豐功偉業，事蹟
Winning four gold medals was an impressive feat for the athlete.

5) **all-time** [ˋɔl͵taɪm] (a.) 空前的，破紀錄的
Gas prices are at an all-time high

6) **self-conscious** [ˋsɛlfˋkɑnʃəs] (a.) 害羞扭捏的，不自在的
Michael is very self-conscious about his braces.

7) **root (for)** [rut] (v.) 為…加油，打氣
Which team are you rooting for?

8) **dexterity** [dɛkˋstɛrɪtɪ] (n.) 身手敏捷
Flying a helicopter requires great dexterity.

9) **stand out** [stænd aʊt] (phr.) 脫穎而出，引人注目
Lots of people applied for the job, but one stood out from the rest.

Language Guide

聖經故事中的 Goliath

Goliath [gəˋlaɪəθ] 哥利亞是聖經故事中身高三公尺的巨人，他是以色列敵邦腓力斯(Philistine)的戰士。以色列人畏於哥利亞的驍勇魁梧，只能任由他在陣前叫囂 40 天，沒人敢與他對戰，最後是一位牧羊少年大衛 (David) 秉著對上帝的信仰，認為以色列不可能會輸，只帶著 5 顆石頭和一個投石器 (sling) 就去應戰。最後大衛投出第一個石頭就擊穿哥利亞的頭骨，還將他的首級割下。

因此在英文裡，Goliath 與 David 的故事就象徵著「以小博大」。

- *The Insider* tells the David and Goliath story of one man's fight against the tobacco industry.
《驚報內幕》這部電影講述一個人以小博大對抗香菸產業的故事。

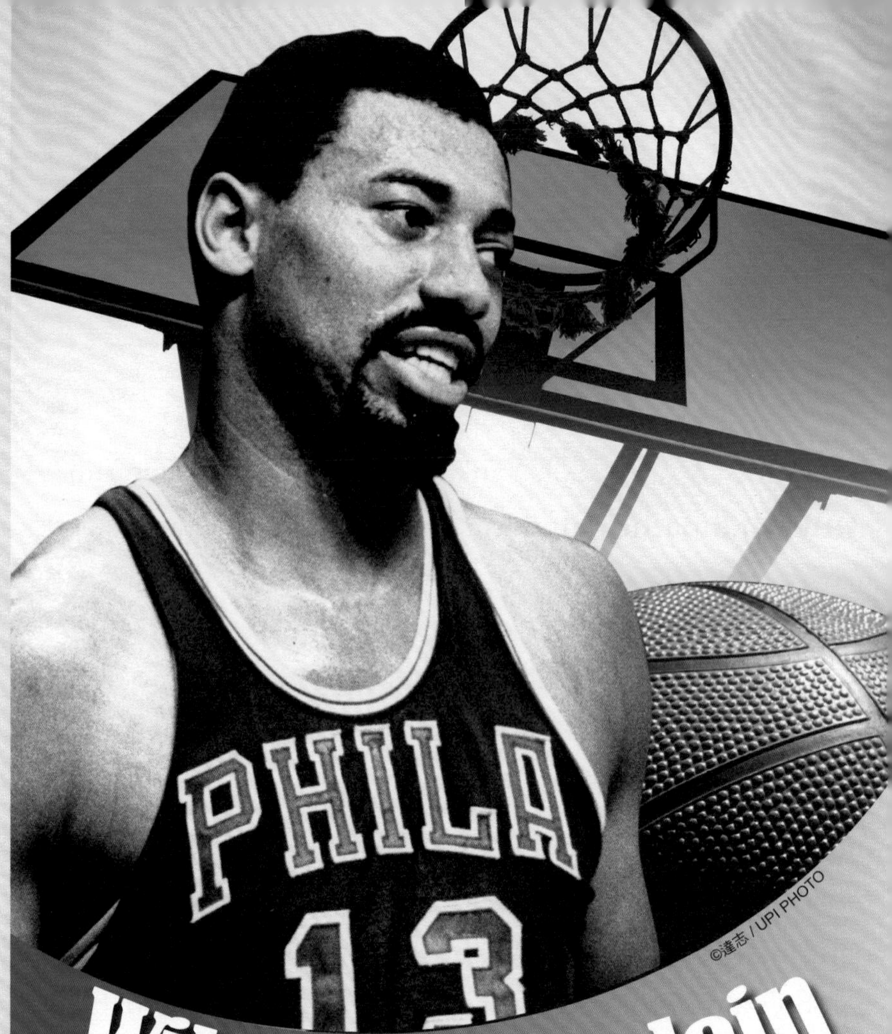

©達志 / UPI PHOTO

Wilt Chamberlain
籃球巨人中的巨人 張伯倫

朗讀 MP3 181 單字 MP3 182 英文文章導讀 MP3 183

Wilton Norman Chamberlain, a.k.a. Wilt "The [3]**Stilt,** was an American professional basketball player well know for his [4]**feats** both on the court and off. Standing tall a seven-foot-one (216 cm.), Wilt was one of the NBA's [5]**all-time** best centers, and in a career that [1]**spanned** 15 year and four professional teams, Wilt broke many records— some of which, like scoring 100 points in a single game, sti stand today.

Born in 1936 to a middle-class family in Philadelphia, Wi was one of eleven children. He was an [2]**awkward** child, an was very [6]**self-conscious** about his height. Wilt remaine sensitive about his height even during his professiona basketball career, and became famous for saying "Nobody [7]**roots** for Goliath." This is a reference to the fact that back in the early days of basketball, a tall player's height was seen as something of an unfair advantage.

And yet it was Wilt's height and [8]**dexterity** that helped him [9]**stand** out from the crowd. Universities across the nation began to notice him while he was playing for his high school team in Philly. He had his choice of schools, and in the end he chose to play for the University of Kansas under famed coach Phog Allen. Ⓖ This was the first big step in what would become one of basketball's most celebrated careers.

Translation

威爾頓諾曼張伯倫，又名威爾特「高腳仔」，是美國職業籃球選手，球場上與球場外的事蹟同樣家喻戶曉。身高七呎一吋（216 公分）的威爾特，是 NBA 有史以來最厲害的中鋒之一，在他曾經效力於四支職業球隊、橫跨十五年的職業生涯裡，打破了許多紀錄——其中某些紀錄至今仍屹立不搖，像是在單場比賽拿下 100 分。

威爾特於 1936 年出生在費城一個中產階級家庭，家中共有十一個小孩。他是個彆扭的孩子，對於自己的身高感到很不自在。即使當了職業籃球選手，威爾特仍舊對自己的身高很敏感，而且因為說了這句話而出名：「沒有人會幫巨人哥利亞加油。」這句話的由來是因為在籃球運動早期，高個子選手的身高被視為是一種不公平的優勢。

然而，幫助威爾特從人群中脫穎而出的，正是他的身高和敏捷。他在費城為自己的高中打球比賽時，美國的各大學就開始注意到他。有眾多學校等著他挑，最後他選擇替堪薩斯大學打球，接受名教練福格艾倫的調教，這是他邁向籃球界最著名職業生涯之一的第一大步。

Grammar Master

關係代名詞 what 的用法

子句中的關係代名詞到底該用 that 還是 what 常令人困惑。但請抓住下列兩個重點：

- that用來代指句子裡一個明確的名詞（先行詞）或子句。

  例 I didn't like the movie that he recommended.

  先行詞　形容詞（從屬）子句

  （that 代替先行詞 the movie，後接 he recommended 以補充說明 the movie，that 當受詞用，可以省略）

- what 代表的是 the thing(s) which...、all that...，已經等於是「先行詞＋關係代名詞」，或稱做「複合關係代名詞」，所以 what 前面不應該再有先行詞出現。用途是引導在句子中當主詞或受詞的「名詞子句」。

  例 ● I will never forget what my father told me that day.
  = I will never forget the things which my father told me that day.
  （what 引導出子句 my father told me that day，當受詞用，動詞 forget 並非先行詞。what 指的是不明確的說話內容。）

  ● What she said scared me.
  = The things which she said scared me.
  （what 引導子句 she said，當主詞用）

Language Guide

籃球位置

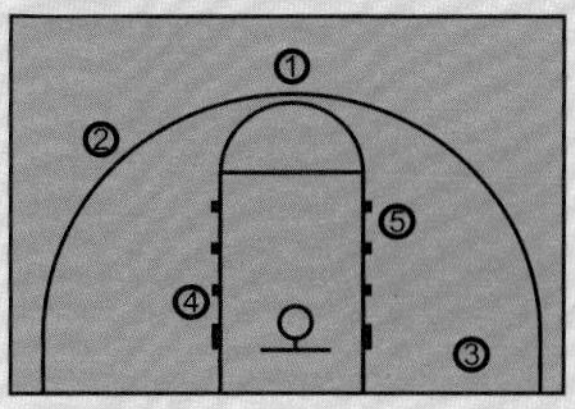

Small Forward (SF) 小前鋒
籃球播報時稱為「三號位置」。小前鋒最重要的工作就是得分，而且是較遠距離的得分。皮朋 (Scottie Pippen)、拉瑞博德 (Larry Bird) 是代表人物。

Power Forward (PF) 大前鋒
亦稱做 Forward，籃球播報時稱為「四號位置」。大前鋒的工作在於搶籃板、防守、卡位，而非得分。羅德曼 (Dennis Rodman) 是代表人物。

Center (C) 中鋒
籃球播報時稱為「五號位置」。中鋒除了能引導隊友在籃下得分，自己也有得分能力；除了阻擋對方進攻，還能支援隊友防守上的漏洞，因此中鋒無論在進攻或防守上，都是球隊的中樞。張伯倫、賈霸 (Kareem Abdul-Jabbar)、羅素 (Bill Russell)、歐拉朱旺 (Hakeem Olajuwon) 是代表人物。

Shooting Guard (SG) 得分後衛
籃球播報時稱為「二號位置」。得分後衛以得分為主要任務，是場上僅次於小前鋒的得分手。要擔任這個位置的條件是外線準、出手速度快、命中率高。麥可喬丹 (Michael Jordan) 是代表人物。

Point Guard (PG) 控球後衛
籃球播報時稱為「一號位置」。控球後衛是球場主要持球者，負責將球從後場帶到前場，再傳給其他隊友，因此運球、傳球能力極為重要，還要組織攻勢，讓進攻更為流暢。約翰史托克頓 (John Stockton) 是代表人物。

Vocabulary Bank

1) **hail (from)** [hel] (v.) 來自
Where do you hail from?

2) **integrated** [ˋɪntə͵gretɪd] (a.) 融合不同種族、民族、宗教的
Troy's grandfather was the first in his family to attend an integrated school.

3) **harmony** [ˋhɑrməni] (n.) 和諧，融合
The Indian tribe lives in harmony with nature.

4) **patron** [ˋpetrən] (n.) 客人，老顧客
The neighborhood bar has many regular patrons.

5) **indifferent** [ɪnˋdɪf(ə)rənt] (a.) 平庸的，漠不關心的
Fans were angered by the team's indifferent performance.

6) **tournament** [ˋtɝnəmənt] (n.) 錦標賽，聯賽
The chess player has won many tournaments.

7) **subject (to)** [səbˋdʒɛkt] (v.) 使蒙受，使遭遇
Many of the prisoners were subjected to torture.

進階字彙

8) **concurrent** [kənˋkɝənt] (a.) 同時發生的
The prison is serving two concurrent life sentences.

9) **biographer** [baɪˋɑgrəfɚ] (n.) 傳記作家
The singer's biography was written by a famous biographer.

10) **measure** [ˋmɛʒɚ] (n.) 一些，些許
The actor's first film brought him a measure of success.

11) **pelt** [pɛlt] (v.)（連續）投擲、攻擊
The crowd pelted the politician with eggs.

12) **debris** [dəˋbri] (n.) 瓦礫，垃圾
Many earthquake victims were hit by falling debris.

13) **vile** [vaɪl] (a.) 污穢的，惡劣的
Samantha has a vile temper.

14) **epithet** [ˋɛpɪ͵θɛt] (n.) 稱號，罵人的話
The policeman was accused of using a racial epithet.

15) **overtime** [ˋovɚ͵taɪm] (n.) 超過時間，（球賽）延長時間
The Rams beat the Jets in overtime play.

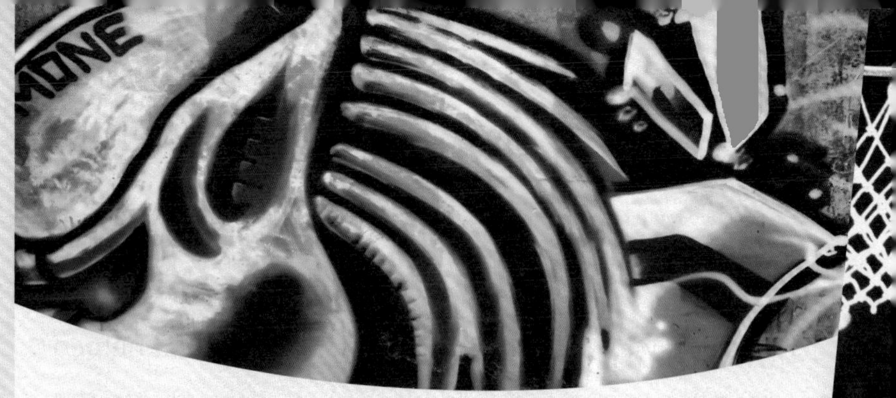

朗讀 MP3 184 單字 MP3 185 英文文章導讀 MP3 186

Wilt's career in basketball was [8]**concurrent** with two major changes in the game, and Wilt played an important role in both of them. The first had to do with racial segregation. [1]**Hailing** from the [2]**integrated** North, Wilt experienced serious culture shock when he (G)arrived in Lawrence, Kansas, a Midwestern city that was still segregated. According to Chamberlain's [9]**biographer** Robert Cherry, Wilt helped bring a [10]**measure** of racial [3]**harmony** to the small city. He ignored signs directing blacks to use separate entrances to restaurants, theaters and jazz clubs, and found that the white [4]**patrons** were largely [5]**indifferent**. Cherry explained that Wilt helped pave the way for others to follow.

On the court, however, racism was still a serious issue. In a 1957 [6]**tournament** in Dallas, Texas, the Kansas team faced the all-white Southern Methodist team. In the words of John Parker, one of Wilt's teammates, "Their crowd was brutal. We were spat upon, [11]**pelted** with [12]**debris**, and [7]**subjected** to the [13]**vilest** racial [14]**epithets** imaginable. The officials did little to maintain order. There were so many uncalled fouls, each more outrageous than the last, that Maurice and Wilt risked serious injury simply by staying in the game, and, incredibly, they responded with some of the best basketball of their lives. We escaped with a 73-65 [15]**overtime** win."

©達志 / UPI PHOTO

Language Guide

fouls and violations 犯規與違例

簡單來說，籃球犯規分為 personal foul（個人犯規，碰觸對手身體的阻擋拉扯行為）、technical foul（技術犯規，違反運動精神的非碰觸犯規）、及 flagrant foul（惡意犯規，違反運動精神的碰觸犯規，常被判立即離場）。犯規的次數是有上限的，超過就要被判「罰球」free throws，美國 NBA 職籃規定，球員於一場比賽中犯規六次要「犯滿離場」foul out。

charging 帶球撞人

blocking 阻擋

pushing 推擠

holding 拉扯

hand-checking 以手推擋進攻者

違例」violation 則是違反籃球運動的相關規範，次數不受限制，只計入團體失誤當中。

traveling 走步（或稱 walking 或 walk）

double dribble 兩次運球

carrying the ball
翻球（運球時手掌朝上持球）

shot clock violation
24秒未投籃或碰觸籃框（此為 NBA 規則）

eight-second violation
8秒未將球運過中場（此為 NBA 規則）

three-second violation 籃下3秒

goaltending
空中截球（當籃球向籃框落下或在籃框上面或籃網內時，守方球員觸球或改變球運動的方向）

Grammar Master

arrive + 介系詞 + 地點

中文裡的「抵達」後面會直接接地點，以至於許多人在用 arrive 這個字時也如法炮製。要注意：英文的 arrive 這個字後面加地點時，一定要在中間放適當的介系詞。

例
- He arrived Taipei yesterday. (x)
- He arrived in Taipei yesterday. (o)
- The police just arrived on the third floor. (o)

中 Translation

威爾特的籃球生涯同時伴隨著籃球比賽兩項重大改變，他也在兩者中扮演了重要角色。第一項改變與種族隔離有關。威爾特出身種族融合的北方，來到堪薩斯州勞倫斯這個仍然有種族隔離的中西部城市，體驗到嚴重的文化衝擊。根據張伯倫的傳記作者羅勃切瑞表示，威爾特替這個小城帶來了些許種族和諧。他對餐廳、戲院、爵士俱樂部中用來指引黑人使用不同入口的標示視而不見，也發現白種客人大多不在意。切瑞說，威爾特幫忙鋪路，讓其他人跟進。

然而，在球場上，種族歧視仍舊是嚴重的問題。1957 年，在一項德州達拉斯舉辦的錦標賽當中，堪薩斯大學隊遇上了全都是白人的南方衛理公會大學隊。根據威爾特隊友約翰帕克的說法：「他們的觀眾真是野蠻，我們被吐口水，被丟擲垃圾，被你想像得到最難聽的種族歧視字眼羞辱。主辦單位並沒有想要維持秩序，有許多犯規都沒有被裁判吹哨，犯規一次比一次粗暴，莫瑞斯和威爾特光是繼續比賽就等於冒著受重傷的危險了，不過難以置信的是，他們卻以堪稱個人生涯最精彩的表現來回應。後來我們在延場賽中以 73 比 65 獲勝。」

Vocabulary Bank

1) **witness** [ˋwɪtnɪs] (v./n.) 目擊，證明；目擊者，證人
Dozens of people witnessed the accident.

2) **compensation** [͵kɑmpənˋseʃən] (n.) 報酬，薪資
The workers are demanding better compensation.

3) **norm** [nɔrm] (n.) 常態，常規
These days, smaller families have become the norm.

4) **routine** [ruˋtin] (n.) 表演橋段
We need to practice our routine for the dance contest.

5) **autobiography** [͵ɔtəbaɪˋɑgrəfi] (n.) 自傳
Have you read Benjamin Franklin's autobiography?

進階字彙

6) **playboy** [ˋple͵bɔɪ] (n.) 花花公子
Bill Clinton is known as a playboy.

7) **ritzy** [ˋrɪtsi] (a.) 豪華的，最高級的
The beach is lined with ritzy hotels.

8) **womanizing** [ˋwʊmə͵naɪzɪŋ] (n./a.) 沈溺女色（的）
The woman divorced her husband because of his womanizing.

9) **far cry** [fɑr kraɪ] (phr.) 相差甚遠
Today's cell phones are a far cry from the huge phones of the 1980s.

10) **icon** [ˋaɪkɑn] (n.) 偶像
Mickey Mantle is a baseball icon.

朗讀 MP3 187 單字 MP3 188 英文文章導讀 MP3 189

The second major change that Wilt [1]**witnessed** Ⓖhad to do with [2]**compensation**. Wilt began his career long before multi-million dollar contracts were the [3]**norm**. In fact, Wilt left the University of Kansas after his junior year in order to make more money playing for the Harlem Globetrotters, an exhibition team known for its comic [4]**routines**. After a year with the Globetrotters, Chamberlain signed with the Philadelphia Warriors for a record $30,000 a year. He later became the first player to earn more than $100,000 a year.

With the big bucks he earned later in his career playing for the Philadelphia 76ers and the Los Angeles Lakers, Wilt lived the life of a [6]**playboy**. He built a large mansion in L.A.'s [7]**ritzy** Bel Air neighborhood, collected exotic cars and became known for his [8]**womanizing**. A [9]**far cry** from his self-conscious teenage years, the middle-aged Wilt earned a reputation for promiscuity, even claiming in his [5]**autobiography** to have slept with 20,000 women.

But since his death in 1999, Wilt's extravagant lifestyle has faded from people's memories. He is now remembered by friends, fellow players and coaches as one of the major [10]**icons** of basketball, as a man who loved basketball more than anything else and whose many contributions to the sport will never be forgotten.

中 Translation

威爾特所經歷的第二個重大改變和薪水有關。早在數百萬美元的合約
為常態之前，威爾特的職業生涯就開始了。事實上，威爾特念完大
三之後就離開堪薩斯大學，以便能效力哈林花式籃球隊——一個以搞
笑花招著名的表演隊伍——賺取更多的薪水。在哈林花式籃球隊待了
一年之後，張伯倫和費城勇士隊簽下破紀錄的年薪三萬美元合約，後
來他成為第一位年薪十萬美元以上的球員。

他在往後的職業生涯中，陸續效力過費城七六人隊與洛杉磯湖人隊，
賺進大把鈔票，開始過著花花公子的生活。他在洛杉磯的高級貝萊爾
社區蓋了一棟大豪宅，收集異國名車，沉迷女色的花名遠播。步入中
年的威爾特被貼了淫亂的標籤，甚至在自傳中宣稱與兩萬名女性睡過
覺，這與他害羞的青少年時代真是天壤之別。

不過，自從他 1999 年過世之後，威爾特放縱的生活方式也從人們的
記憶中褪去，如今在朋友、球員與教練的心中，他是籃球界主要代表
人物之一，是一個熱愛籃球勝過一切的人，而且他對籃球的諸多貢獻
將名留青史。

G Grammar Master

have **a lot / everything / something / nothing** **to do with...**

和……有（很大的／完全的／一點／沒有）關係

have to do with... 這個片語基本上是「和……有關係」的意思，
可以在 have 後面加上 a lot、something、nothing 等字來表達關
係的程度。

例
- The decision has a lot to do with our financial situation
- The accident had little to do with the icy road.
- His headache has nothing to do with stress.

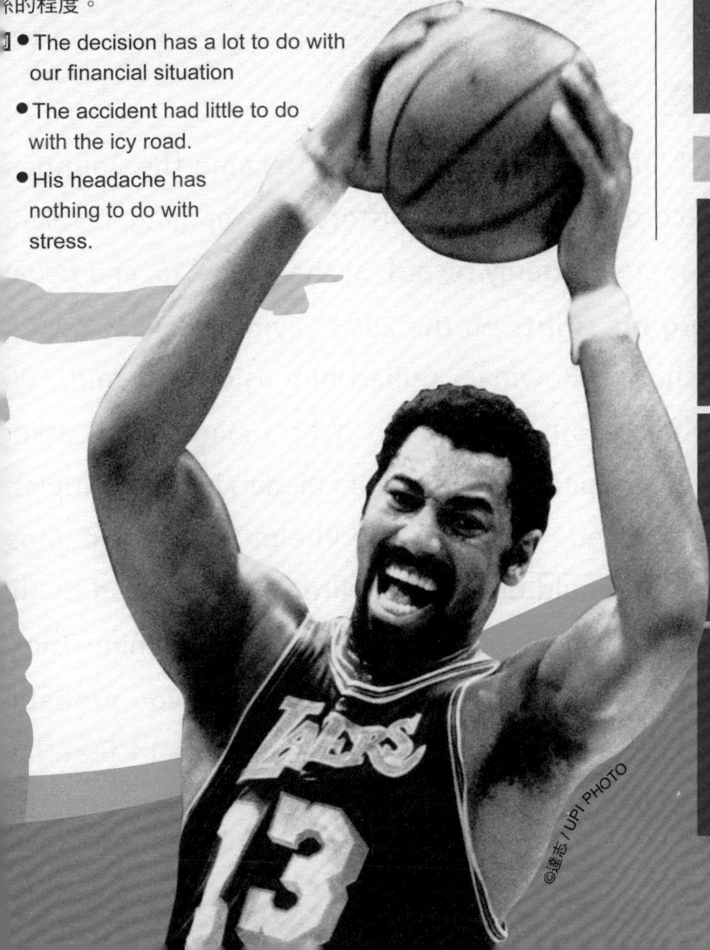
©達志 / UPI PHOTO

Language Guide

Harlem Globetrotters 哈林籃球隊

Harlem Globetrotters [ˋhɑrləm ˋglob͵trɑtɚz] 是美國非裔籃球員組成的職業籃球隊，1926 年於芝加哥成軍。這支球隊以球技精湛及一邊打球一邊搞笑著稱，受邀全球巡迴演出超過半個世紀。

美國職業籃球

美國職籃 NBA（National Basketball Association，國家籃球聯盟）分為西區聯盟 (Western Conference) 和東區聯盟 (Eastern Conference)，二聯盟各十五隊，均分為三區 (division)。

Western Conference 西區聯盟

Northwest 西北區	1 Denver Nuggets	丹佛金塊隊
	2 Minnesota Timberwolves	明尼蘇達灰狼隊
	3 Oklahoma City Thunder	奧克拉荷馬雷霆隊
	4 Portland Trail Blazers	波特蘭拓荒者隊
	5 Utah Jazz	猶他爵士隊
Pacific 太平洋區	1 Golden State Warriors	金州勇士隊 文中 Philadelphia Warriors 搬到加州仍用原名
	2 Los Angeles Clippers	洛杉磯快艇隊
	3 Los Angeles Lakers	洛杉磯湖人隊
	4 Phoenix Suns	鳳凰城太陽隊
	5 Sacramento Kings	沙加緬度國王隊
Southwest 西南區	1 Dallas Mavericks	達拉斯小牛隊
	2 Houston Rockets	休士頓火箭隊
	3 Memphis Grizzlies	曼斐斯灰熊隊
	4 New Orleans Hornets	紐奧良黃蜂隊
	5 San Antonio Spurs	聖安東尼奧馬刺隊

Eastern Conference 東區聯盟

Atlantic 大西洋區	1 Boston Celtics	波士頓塞爾蒂克隊
	2 New Jersey Nets	紐澤西籃網隊
	3 New York Knicks	紐約尼克隊
	4 Philadelphia 76ers	費城七六人隊
	5 Toronto Raptors	多倫多暴龍隊
Central 中央區	1 Chicago Bulls	芝加哥公牛隊
	2 Cleveland Cavaliers	克里夫蘭騎士隊
	3 Detroit Pistons	底特律活塞隊
	4 Indiana Pacers	印第安那溜馬隊
	5 Milwaukee Bucks	密爾瓦基公鹿隊
Southeast 東南區	1 Atlanta Hawks	亞特蘭大老鷹隊
	2 Charlotte Bobcats	夏洛特山貓隊
	1 Miami Heat	邁阿密熱火隊
	4 Orlando Magic	奧蘭多魔術隊
	5 Washington Wizards	華盛頓巫師隊

Vocabulary Bank

1) **holder** [ˋholdɚ] (n.)（紀錄）保持者，（獎項、冠軍）得主
Who is the current holder of the world heavyweight title?

2) **shrug** [ʃrʌg] (v.) 聳肩（表示不知道、不屑、無所謂等）
The man shrugged when I asked him what time it was.

3) **intimidate** [ɪnˋtɪmə͵det] (v.) 使敬畏、害怕，威嚇
The candidate hired thugs to intimidate voters.

4) **stormy** [ˋstɔrmi] (a.)（關係）充滿爭吵、不穩定
The couple had a stormy marriage.

5) **refuge** [ˋrɛfjudʒ] (n.) 避難（處）
The hikers took refuge from the storm under a large tree.

6) **diagnose** [ˋdaɪəg͵nos] (v.) 診斷
More and more children are being diagnosed with diabetes.

7) **outlet** [ˋaʊtlɛt] (n.) 發洩精力、感情的途徑，發揮創意的管道
Painting provided Maria with a creative outlet.

8) **excess** [ˋɛksɛs] (a.) 過量的
Passengers will be charged for excess baggage.

9) **competitively** [kənˋpɛtətɪvli] (adv.) 參加比賽地，有競爭力地
Arnold Palmer no longer plays golf competitively.

進階字彙

10) **trooper** [ˋtrupɚ] (n.) 騎警，state trooper 即「（美國）州警察」
Troy was pulled over by a trooper for speeding.

11) **hyperactive** [͵haɪpɚˋæktɪv] (a.)（過度）好動的，（醫）過動的
My kids always get hyperactive when they eat too much junk food.

12) **ADHD** (Attention Deficit Hyperactivity Disorder)（醫）注意力缺陷過動症，即「過動症」
Children with ADHD often do poorly in school.

13) **aquatic** [əˋkwætɪk] (a.) 水上的，水中的，水生的
The government is building a new aquatic sports center.

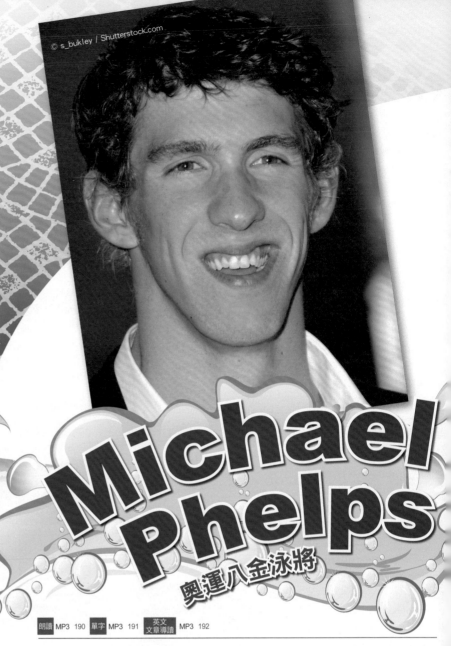

© s_bukley / Shutterstock.com

Michael Phelps
奧運八金泳將

朗讀 MP3 190　單字 MP3 191　英文文章導讀 MP3 192

Back in 2001, Michael Phelps became the youngest world record [1)]**holder** in the history of swimming, breaking the 200-meter butterfly record at the age of 15, and began **1 setting his sights** on the 2004 Olympics. That's when his coach, Bob Bowman, pulled him aside and said, "We need to talk about Mark Spitz." "Who's Mark Spitz?" asked Phelps. "Mark Spitz won seven gold medals in one Olympics," Bowman replied. "Pretty good," Phelps [2)]**shrugged**. Most 15-year-olds would be at least a little [3)]**intimidated** by the greatest achievement in Olympic history, but not him. Those are some pretty big **2 shoes to fill**, but as you probably already know by now, Phelps, with his size-14 feet, has succeeded in doing just that.

Phelps was born in Baltimore, Maryland in 1985 to Fred, a state [10]**trooper**, and Debbie, a middle school teacher. His parents had a [4]**stormy** relationship, and his two older sisters found [5]**refuge** swimming at the local pool. Phelps was a [11]**hyperactive** child (he was later [6]**diagnosed** with [12]**ADHD**), and when he followed his sisters into the pool at the age of seven, swimming proved to be a great [7]**outlet** for his [8]**excess** energy. Although he was afraid to even put his face in the water at first, it wasn't long before Phelps was swimming [9]**competitively**. Realizing his potential, his parents took him to see Bob Bowman, senior coach at the North Baltimore [13]**Aquatic** Club, when he was 11. Bowman recognized Phelps' talent immediately and agreed to take over his training.

© Geoff Nelson / Shutterstock.com

中 Translation

打破兩百公尺蝶式紀錄，並且開始放眼二〇〇四年奧運。當時，他的教練巴伯包曼將他拉到一旁說：「我們得好好聊聊馬克史皮滋。」「馬克史皮滋是誰啊？」菲爾普斯問起。「馬克史皮滋在一屆奧運上贏得七面金牌。」包曼回答他。「還不錯啊，」菲爾普斯聳聳肩說。大多數十五歲年輕人至少會稍微被奧運史上最輝煌的成績給嚇到，但他沒有。那是難以望其項背的成就，不過你大概已經知道，菲爾普斯用他的 14 號大腳輕易達成了。

菲爾普斯於一九八五年出生在馬里蘭州的巴爾的摩，父親佛瑞德是一位州警，母親黛比是中學老師。他的雙親感情並不融洽，兩位姊姊在當地游泳池找到了避風港。菲爾普斯是個極為好動的孩子（後來被診斷出患有注意力缺陷過動症），七歲那年跟隨兩位姊姊到游泳池，游泳就成了他過剩精力的絕佳出口。儘管他一開始甚至不敢把頭埋入水中，但不久之後，他就開始參加游泳比賽。他的雙親發現了他的潛能，於是帶他去見北巴爾的摩水上運動俱樂部的資深教練巴伯包曼，當時他才十一歲。包曼立刻看出菲爾普斯的天賦，於是同意接手訓練他。

Tongue-tied No More

1 set one's sights on...
將…視為目標

sight是「眼光;抱負」的意思，這片語直翻就是「把某人的眼光放在某物上」，所以就是把那視為目標的意思。

A : Do you know what Jeremy plans to do after he graduates?
你知道傑若米畢業之後計畫要做什麼？

B: I hear he's set his sights on law school.
我聽說他把法學院當作目標。

2 fill sb. shoes
取代某人的工作 / 地位

這句話是「取代並勝任某人工作」的意思。文中用這句話開雙關語的玩笑，因為 fill someone's shoes 字面上的意思是「填滿某人的鞋子」，因此筆者說以 Michael Phelps 出了名的大腳丫（美國男鞋 14 號相當於腳長 32 公分！），應該能輕易填滿前輩留下的大鞋子（即難以突破的紀錄）。

A : I can't believe Rich is leaving the company.
真不敢相信里奇要離開這間公司了。

B : Yeah, it's gonna be hard to find someone who can fill his shoes.
對啊，要找到人接手他的工作會很困難。

Language Guide

Michael Phelps 奧運八金紀錄

項　　目	分：秒
400 m individual medley 四百公尺個人四式混合	4:03.84 破世界記錄
4 x 100 m freestyle relay 四乘一百公尺自由式接力	3:08.24 破世界記錄
200 m freestyle 兩百公尺自由式	1:42.96 破世界記錄
200 m butterfly 兩百公尺蝶式	1:52.03 破世界記錄
4 x 200 m freestyle relay 四乘兩百公尺自由式接力	6:58.56 破世界記錄
200 m individual medley 兩百公尺個人四式混合	1:54.23 破世界記錄
100 m butterfly 一百公尺蝶式	0:50.58 破奧運記錄
4 x 100 m medley relay 四乘一百公尺四式混合接力	3:29.34 破世界記錄

© Geoff Nelson / Shutterstock.com

朗讀 MP3 193 單字 MP3 194 英文文章導讀 MP3 195

Under Bowman's strict training 6)**regimen**, Phelps made rapid progress and soon began setting age group records. Although he made it to the U.S. National 1)**Championships** in 1999, he © finished last place in the 200-meter butterfly. Phelps 2)**bounced** back the following year with a third place finish, however, and then became a surprise 3)**qualifier** for the 2000 Olympics in Sydney. When he arrived with the rest of the U.S. swim team, he was the youngest American male swimmer to participate in the Olympics since 1932. Yet despite his age and lack of international experience, he made it to the finals and finished fifth in the 200-meter butterfly. Just five months later, Phelps became the youngest world record holder in the sport's history when he set a new record in the same event at the World Championships.

Although still in high school, Phelps began setting records in every event he entered. In the 2002 National Championships, he set U.S. records in the 100-meter butterfly and 200-meter individual 7)**medley**, and a world record in the 400-meter medley. The media began comparing Phelps to Ian Thorpe, the Aussie swimmer who won three golds in the 2000

Vocabulary Bank

1) **championship** [ˋtʃæmpiən͵ʃɪp] (n.) 錦標賽，冠軍頭銜
The team won a surprise victory in the championship.

2) **bounce** [baʊns] (v.) 彈回，彈跳，bounce back 即「受挫折後恢復原狀」
Everyone was amazed how quickly Sam bounced back after his surgery.

3) **qualifier** [ˋkwɑlə͵faɪɚ] (n.) 取得資格者 (v.) qualify [ˋkwɑlə͵faɪ]
Eight qualifiers will be moving on to the next stage of the competition.

4) **astonishing** [əˋstɑnɪʃɪŋ] (a.) 令人驚嘆的
The magician performed astonishing tricks.

5) **sensation** [sɛnˋseʃən] (n.) 轟動（的人事物）
The president's speech caused a sensation.

進階字彙

6) **regimen** [ˋrɛdʒəmən] (n.) 養生法，（體能等）嚴謹的訓練
My doctor has me on a diet and exercise regimen.

7) **medley** [ˋmɛdli] (n.) 混合泳，混合曲
Michael Phelps holds the world record in the 400 m individual medley.

8) **run-up** [ˋrʌn͵ʌp] (n.) 重要活動的前夕
Tensions increased during the run-up to the election.

9) **hype** [ˋhaɪp] (v./n.) 大肆宣傳
The studio is hyping its latest movie.

口語補充

10) **best** [bɛst] (v.) 打敗，勝過
The fighter from Japan easily bested the other contestants.

Sydney Games, but the comparisons ended when he [10]**bested** Thorpe in nearly every contest at the 2003 World Championships in Barcelona, winning five medals and setting an [4]**astonishing** five world records. It was during the [8]**run-up** to the 2004 Athens Olympics, however, that Phelps became a media [5]**sensation**, as he was heavily [9]**hyped** to beat Mark Spitz's seven gold-medal wins at the 1972 Munich Olympics.

© Sergei Bachlakov / Shutterstock.com

Translation

在包曼嚴格的訓練計畫之下，菲爾普斯進步神速，不久後就開始打破他那個年齡分組的紀錄。儘管一九九九年時，他游進美國國家錦標賽，但在兩百公尺蝶式項目敬陪末座。然而，隔年菲爾普斯捲土重來，拿下第三名，並跌破眾人眼鏡，獲得參加二〇〇〇年雪梨奧運的資格。他和美國游泳隊其他隊員抵達當地時，成為一九三二年以來美國最年輕的男子游泳奧運選手。不過，雖然他年紀輕，又缺乏國際賽經驗，他仍游進了兩百公尺蝶式決賽，獲得第五名。僅僅五個月後，菲爾普斯就在世界錦標賽打破兩百公尺蝶式的紀錄，成為游泳運動史上最年輕的世界紀錄保持人。

雖然還在念高中，菲爾普斯開始每次參加比賽都打破紀錄。二〇〇二年的美國國家錦標賽中，他在一百公尺蝶式與兩百公尺個人混合式項目中，打破了全國紀錄，還打破四百公尺混合式的世界紀錄。媒體開始將他和澳洲游泳選手伊恩索普相提並論，索普在二〇〇〇年雪梨奧運獲得三面金牌，不過當他在二〇〇三年巴塞隆納所舉行的世界錦標賽中，幾乎每一次遭遇都打敗索普，贏得五面金牌，驚人地打破五項世界紀錄之後，兩人的比較就此終結。不過，菲爾普斯是在二〇〇四年雅典奧運前夕才成為媒體焦點，媒體極力吹捧他能打破馬克史皮滋在一九七二年慕尼黑奧運的七金紀錄。

Language Guide

各種游泳姿勢

front crawl 捷式
極速 5.34 mph（哩 / 每小時）
也稱為 forward crawl，與仰式 (backstroke) 同為 long axis stroke（長軸划水）姿勢，即從指尖到腳尖呈一直線，雙手沿著一條長軸在水中划水前進。捷式不是正式游泳比賽規定的姿勢，但因為速度最快，在自由式 (freestyle) 項目中廣為採用，因此常被稱為自由式。

backstroke 仰式
極速 4.57 mph
也稱為 back crawl，基本上是上下顛倒的捷式動作。是游泳比賽中唯一在水中出發的項目。

breaststroke 蛙式
極速 4.11 mph
蛙式動作將臉沒入水中的時間較少，因此廣受游泳初學者歡迎。但在追求速度的比賽場合，蛙式選手所採的動作與平常不同，對於耐力及下肢力量非常要求，還要避免出現蝶式的下半身動作，因此儘管蛙式速度最慢，卻被認為是四式比賽中最困難的一個項目。

butterfly 蝶式
極速 4.87 mph
簡稱 fly。對初學者來說，蝶式是最難學的泳姿，雙手、肩部及胸部上半須整個抬出水面、下半身搭配 butterfly kick（或稱 dolphin kick）的協調動作，只要有一點閃失就游不起來，因此唯有泳技高超的人才能勝任。蝶式與蛙式同為雙手划水，但因下身運動方式不同，比蛙式省力、快速許多。

dog paddle 狗爬式
或稱 doggy paddle，頭抬出水面、四肢在水下交互划動，與狗等動物游水的姿勢相同，是人類最早採用的泳姿，也是一般小孩的玩水姿勢。

sidestroke 測泳
以單手划水，雙腿剪水前進，目的是要空出一隻手運送物品。這是救生員救難時常採用的姿勢。

Grammar Master

「獲得第……名」的說法

雖然一般在用序數 first、second、third……及 last 等字時，前面都要放定冠詞 the，但表示「獲得第……名」時卻不加 the，直接用 win first / second place，或 finish first / second / last。

例 ● She won first place in the writing contest. 她贏得寫作比賽第一名。

● Who finished last in the race?
是誰賽跑最後一名？

朗讀 MP3 196 單字 MP3 197 英文文章導讀 MP3 198

Vocabulary Bank

1) **fashion** [ˋfæʃən] (n.) 模樣，方式
Please exit the building in an orderly fashion.

2) **dash** [dæʃ] (v.) 擊碎，使（希望等）破滅
The bad weather dashed their hopes for a picnic.

3) **relay** [ˋrile] (n.) 接力賽
Which team won the relay race?

4) **take on** [tek ɑn] (phr.) 接受、承擔（挑戰、責任、任務等）
We're looking for employees who are willing to take on new challenges.

5) **stroke** [strok] (n.)（游泳）划水法
The butterfly is a difficult stroke to learn.

6) **maximum** [ˋmæksəməm] (a./n.) 最大的，對多的；最大量、數等
The maximum sentence for murder is life in prison.

Phelps opened at Athens in impressive [1)]**fashion** winning gold in the 400-meter individual medley, an setting a new world record 1 **in the process**. His hope of beating Spitz's record were [2)]**dashed** several days late however, when he and his teammates finished behind Sout Africa and Australia in the 4x100 freestyle [3)]**relay**. Phelp nevertheless went on to win a total of eight medals (six gold and two bronzes), matching the previous record for the mos medals won at a single Olympics set by Aleksandr Dityati in 1980. After Athens, Phelps enrolled at the University o Michigan Ⓖso he could continue to train with Bob Bowma who had taken up the position of head coach for the school' varsity swimming team.

© s_bukley / Shutterstock.com

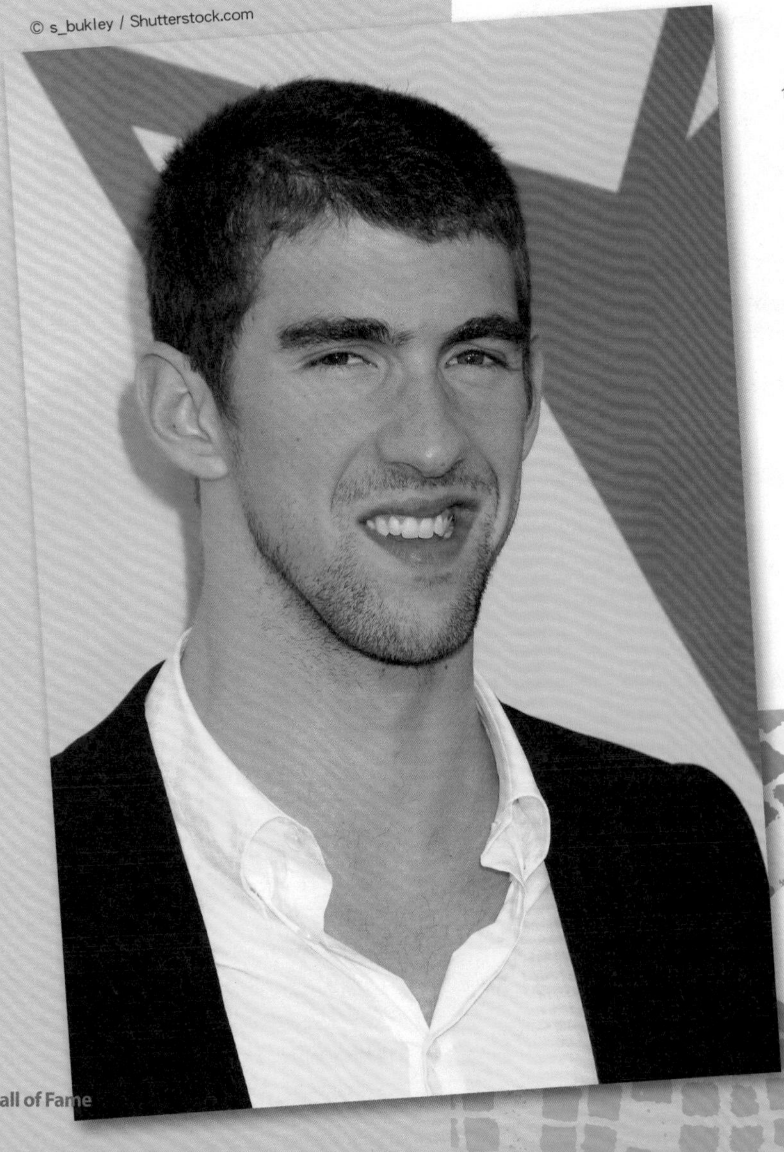

After breaking Ian Thorpe's previou record by winning seven gold medal at the 2007 World Championships i Melbourne, Australia, Phelps qualifie for eight events in the 2008 Beijin Olympics, giving him a secon chance to [4)]**take on** Spitz's record And this time he didn't disappoint Swimming in 17 races over nin days, Phelps won the gold meda in all eight events, setting worl records in seven and an Olympi record in the eighth. While Spitz' record stood for 36 years, Phelps

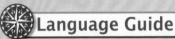

record may be even harder to beat. Back in 1972, Spitz only swam two [5]**strokes** (freestyle and butterfly) for a [6]**maximum** distance of 200 meters. Phelps, on the other hand, swam four strokes (freestyle, butterfly, breaststroke and backstroke) for a maximum distance of 400 meters. Maybe the only one who has a chance of beating Phelps is Phelps—look for him at the London Olympics in 2012!

中 Translation

菲爾普斯在雅典奧運一開場即令人驚豔，在四百公尺個人混合式贏得金牌，並刷新世界紀錄。不過，他打破史皮茲紀錄的希望在幾天後破滅，他和隊友在 4x100 公尺自由式接力賽中輸給南非和澳洲。儘管如此，菲爾普斯依舊帶回了總共八面獎牌（六金二銅），打平了阿列克桑德季佳京一九八〇年所創的單屆奧運最多獎牌紀錄。雅典奧運之後，菲爾普斯進入密西根大學就讀，以便繼續讓巴伯包曼訓練他，包曼當時已經是密西根大學游泳代表隊的總教練。

菲爾普斯在二〇〇七年澳洲墨爾本的世界錦標賽中，以七面金牌打破伊恩索普先前的紀錄之後，合格參加二〇〇八年北京奧運的八項競賽，再度有機會挑戰史皮滋的紀錄。這回他沒有讓大家失望。在九天的十七項競賽中，菲爾普斯在八項競賽中都拿下金牌，其中七項打破世界紀錄，另一項打破奧運紀錄。雖然史皮滋的紀錄屹立不搖三十六年，菲爾普斯的紀錄可能更難被打破。一九七二年，史皮滋只使用兩種泳式（自由式與蝶式），最遠游兩百公尺，而菲爾普斯用了四種泳式（自由式、蝶式、蛙式和仰式），最遠游四百公尺。或許唯一有機會擊敗菲爾普斯的人，就是菲爾普斯——等著看他二〇一二年倫敦奧運的表現吧！

若有疑問請來信：eztalkQ@gmail.com

Tongue-tied No More

1 in the process 過程中

in the process 字面意思是「在過程中」，但有時因句子本身的語意也可解釋為 because of the process，表示因為在過程中產生了結果。

A：How come you decided to take up yoga?
你為什麼決定學瑜伽？

B：It's supposed to be a great way to stay healthy, and hopefully I can lose weight in the process.
聽說是保持健康的好方法，而且我也希望我可以在過程中瘦下來。

Language Guide

individual medley 個人四式混合

單一游泳選手以四種不同泳姿完成比賽，四式游泳距離均等。四式順序為：蝶式 → 仰式 → 蛙式 → 自由式。

嚴格來說，自由式是指前三種泳姿以外的任何姿勢，但因為游泳比賽是在競速，絕大多數選手會選擇速度最快的捷式，久而久之，捷式就被認為是所謂的自由式了。

medley relay 四式混合接力

四位游泳選手各以一種泳姿完成接力比賽。四式順序為：仰式 → 蛙式 → 蝶式 → 自由式。

同樣的，自由式經常採用捷式。游泳接力是在前一位選手的手碰到池緣時，下一位選手跳入水中，而仰式是唯一在水中出發的泳姿，因此被排在第一棒，才不會干擾前一棒選手回到池邊。至於第二至四棒是依照速度排列，蛙式最慢排第二棒，自由式（捷式）最快，適合衝刺，排在最後一棒。

▲仰式預備出發動作

▲其他三式出發動作

Grammar Master

到底是 so？還是 so (that)…？

so 這個字有很多意思，當連接詞時，若是指「所以……」，必須放在兩個句子中間，且前面要有逗點。若是指「如此一來就……」，也是放在兩個句子中間，但前面不加逗點，後面帶出子句用的 that 可以省略。

例
- I didn't have enough cash, so I paid with my credit card.
  我的現金不夠，所以用信用卡付錢。
- You should pay attention so (that) you won't miss anything important.
  你應該專心聽，如此一來就不會錯過任何重點。

Benjamin Franklin

朗讀 MP3 190 單字 MP3 191 英文文章導讀 MP3 192

Benjamin Franklin was arguably the most importar of America's Founding Fathers. Born in Boston on Janua 17, 1706, he was the 15th child and youngest son of a soa maker. While Ben's father [1]**intended** for him to enter th clergy, his future turned out very different.

His interest in writing began with the establishment b his older brother James of the first [2]**genuine** newspaper i Boston. Forbidden by James from writing for the paper, Be wrote letters under the name of a fictional [3]**widow**, Silenc Dogood. The letters were filled with advice and were ver critical of how women were treated. They were [4]**immensel** popular with readers.

Vocabulary Bank

1) **intend** [ɪn`tɛnd] (v.) 想要，打算
How long do you intend to stay in the U.S.?

2) **genuine** [`dʒɛnjuɪn] (a.) 真的，名符其實
Our shop only sells genuine antiques.

3) **widow** [`wɪdo] (n.) 寡婦
The widow never married again after her husband died.

4) **immensely** [ɪ`mɛnsli] (adv.) 非常，極為
Whitney Houston was an immensely talented singer.

5) **subscription** [səb`skrɪpʃən] (n.) 訂閱，會員費
Would you like to renew your subscription?

6) **insurance** [ɪn`ʃʊrəns] (n.) 保險
Do you have fire insurance on your home?

7) **involve (in)** [ɪn`vɑlv] (v.) 致力於，涉入
My parents got involved in charity work after they retired.

8) **delegate** [`dɛləgɪt] (n.) 會議代表，代表團員
How many delegates is your company sending to the convention?

進階字彙

9) **champion** [`tʃæmpiən] (v.) 擁護，支持
The lawyer has championed women's rights for years.

10) **treatise** [`tritɪs] (n.) 論文，專題著作
The professor wrote a treatise on modern art.

Language Guide

subscription library 是什麼？

「會員圖書館」subscription library 就像是一種讀書「互助會」，加入會員必須繳費，所繳的費用會用於採購館藏圖書，參加的人越多，每個人能讀到的書種就越多。

In 1729, Ben bought and edited the *Pennsylvania Gazette*, which became the most widely read newspaper in the colonies. With this success, Franklin established the country's first [5]**subscription** library, Philadelphia's first hospital, and a fire [6]**insurance** company. He also famously investigated the nature of electricity.

Franklin became [7]**involved** in politics in the 1750s and started [9]**championing** the cause of independence in the 1770s. He was elected to the Second Continental Congress and helped draft the Declaration of Independence. Though most of the writing is Thomas Jefferson's, many of the ideas are Franklin's.

In the late 1770s, Franklin served as a [8]**delegate** to the Constitutional Convention and signed the Constitution. One of his last public acts was writing an anti-slavery [10]**treatise** in 1789. Franklin died on April 17, 1790 at the age of 84.

中 Translation

班傑明富蘭克林

班傑明富蘭克林可說是美國最重要的開國元老。他於一七〇六年一月十七日出生於波士頓，是家中第十五個孩子，也是最小的兒子，父親是肥皂製造商。班傑明的父親原本打算培養他從事神職工作，但他後來的發展卻非常不同。

他對寫作的興趣始於哥哥詹姆士創辦波士頓首份真正的報紙。詹姆士不准他為報紙寫稿，班傑明於是以一位虛構寡婦為名 —— 賽倫斯杜谷德（Silence Dogood，默默行善）投書。這些書信充滿建言，對女性所受待遇也多所批評，廣受讀者歡迎。

一七二九年，班傑明買下《賓夕維尼亞公報》，並參與編輯工作，成為殖民地最廣為傳閱的報紙。富蘭克林乘勝創辦了美國第一所付費會員圖書館、費城第一家醫院，以及一家火災保險公司。他也以研究電力這種自然現象聞名。

富蘭克林於一七五〇年代跨入政壇，在一七七〇年代開始鼓吹獨立理念。他獲選參加第二屆大陸會議，並協助起草《獨立宣言》，雖然大多出自湯瑪士傑佛遜之筆，但許多想法是來自富蘭克林。

到了一七七〇年代富蘭克林晚年的時候，他擔任憲法會議委員，簽署憲法。他最後參與的公共事務之一，是於一七八九年寫了一篇反對奴隸制度的論文。富蘭克林於一七九〇年四月十七日過世，享年八十四歲。

Language Guide

美國殖民時期小字典

以下是本文與美國殖民時期歷史有關的字彙：

- the colonies 是指美國獨立前被英國殖民的地區
- the Second Continental Congress [ˌkɑntəˋnɛntəl ˋkɑŋgrəs] 第二屆大陸會議（一七七五年），獨立宣言的決議文是在這次會議中通過（一七七六年七月二日）
- Declaration of Independence [ˌdɛkləˋreʃən əv ˌɪndɪˋpɛndəns] 獨立宣言，一七七六年七月四日通過，正式以 United States of America 為國號獨立
- Constitutional Convention [ˌkɑnstəˋtjuʃənəl kənˋvɛnʃən] 憲法會議，一七八七年五月於費城召開，因此也稱為 the Philadelphia Convention
- the Constitution [ˌkɑnstəˋtuʃən] 是指美國憲法 (the United States Constitution)，於一七八七年十二月十八日通過

這些字若要詳細解釋，EZ TALK 就變成美國歷史課本了，為了把篇幅留給其他資訊，在此建議對美國早期歷史有興趣的讀者造訪「美國國會圖書館」相關網頁。

美鈔名人錄

許多人對 Benjamin Franklin 的長相很熟悉，那是因為他被印在美鈔上。但你注意過印有 Benjamin Franklin 肖像美鈔的面額是多少嗎？其他面額美鈔上的人物，你都知道他們是誰嗎？

▶ George Washington
喬治華盛頓，美國第一任總統

▶ Thomas Jefferson
湯瑪士傑佛遜，美國第三任總統

▶ Abraham Lincoln
亞伯拉罕林肯，美國第十六任總統

▶ Alexander Hamilton
亞歷山大漢彌爾頓是美國第一任財政部長

▶ Andrew Jackson
安德魯傑克遜，美國第七任總統

▶ Ulysses S. Grant
尤里西斯格蘭特，美國第十八任總統

▶ Benjamin Franklin
班哲明富蘭克林

Franklin's Financial Wisdom 富蘭克林的理財智

朗讀 MP3 202 單字 MP3 203 英文文章導讀 MP3 204

In these troubled financial times, it's useful to take a look at the way we live our lives, and especially our approach to money and [1]**consumption**. We don't have to look far for a good mix of criticism and wisdom. In fact, we can turn to the works of Benjamin Franklin.

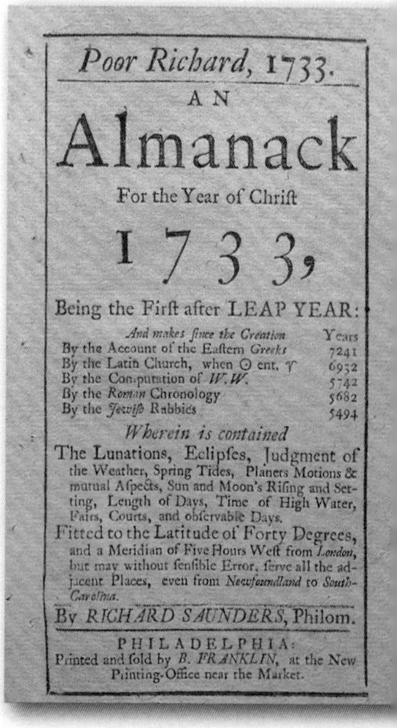
Poor Richard, 1733.
AN
Almanack
For the Year of Chriſt
1733,
Being the Firſt after LEAP YEAR:

And makes ſince the Creation	Years
By the Account of the Eaſtern *Greeks*	7241
By the Latin Church, when ☉ ent. ♈	6932
By the Computation of *W.W.*	5742
By the *Roman* Chronology	5682
By the *Jewiſh* Rabbies	5494

Wherein is contained
The Lunations, Eclipſes, Judgment of the Weather, Spring Tides, Planets Motions & mutual Aſpects, Sun and Moon's Riſing and Setting, Length of Days, Time of High Water, Fairs, Courts, and obſervable Days.
Fitted to the Latitude of Forty Degrees, and a Meridian of Five Hours Weſt from *London*, but may without ſenſible Error, ſerve all the adjacent Places, even from *Newfoundland* to *South-Carolina*.
By *RICHARD SAUNDERS*, Philom.
PHILADELPHIA:
Printed and ſold by *B. FRANKLIN*, at the New Printing-Office near the Market.

Benjamin Franklin penned *Poor Richard's* [9]***Almanac***, which contained a calendar, news and weathe reports, as well as [2]**proverbs** and [10]**aphorisms**, for 2 years under the pseudonym of Richard Saunders. In 175 the *Almanac's* final year of [3]**publication**, Franklin printe "The Way to Wealth." In this essay, one Father Abrahar [13]**dishes out** [14]**heaps** of sage financial advice in a [4]**sermo** [5]**summarizing** the wisdom [6]**set forth** in the *Almanac* ove the years.

Father Abraham begins by criticizing his audience. "W are taxed twice as much by our [7]**idleness**, three times a much by our pride, and four times as much by our [11]**folly** and from these taxes the [12]**commissioners** cannot ease o

Vocabulary Bank

1) **consumption** [kən`sʌmpʃən] (n.) 消費，消耗
Consumption is an important driver of economic growth.

2) **proverb** [`prɑvɝb] (n.) 諺語，俗語
My father has a proverb for every occasion.

3) **publication** [͵pʌblɪ`keʃən] (n.) 出版，出版物，刊物
The author became famous after the publication of his first novel.

4) **sermon** [`sɝmən] (n.) 佈道，說教
The priest gave a sermon on the importance of kindness.

5) **summarize** [`sʌmə͵ræɪz] (v.) 概述，總結
Can you summarize your findings for us?

6) **set forth** [sɛt forθ] (phr.) 提出
Plato set forth his philosophy in dialogues.

7) **idleness** [`aɪdəlnɪs] (n.) 怠惰，無所事事
(a.) idle [`aɪdəl]
Doctors warn that idleness can lead to many health problems.

8) **essential** [ɪ`sɛnʃəl] (a.) 基本的，必要的
Water is essential for all living things.

進階字彙

9) **almanac** [`ɔlmə͵næk] (n.) 年鑑，年曆
Frank gave his son a baseball almanac for his birthday.

10) **aphorism** [`æfə͵rɪzəm] (n.) 格言，箴言
One of Franklin's most famous aphorisms is "A penny saved is a penny earned."

11) **folly** [`fɑli] (n.) 愚蠢，愚行
It would be folly to date a married woman.

12) **commissioner** [kə`mɪʃənɚ] (n.) 官員，長官，委員
A new police commissioner will be appointed next month.

口語補充

13) **dish out** [dɪʃ aut] (phr.) 給與、提供（褒貶、賞罰等）
Our supervisor is always dishing out criticism.

14) **heap** [hip] (n.)（常為複數）一大堆，大量，許多
Our teacher always gives us heaps of homework.

deliver us." In other words, laziness prevents us from making as much money as we could. In addition, our pride and stupidity cause us to waste our earnings.

He also has much to say about leisure. Quoting Poor Richard, he says "…employ thy time well if thou meanest to gain leisure." Leisure is thus a time for doing useful things. What's more, if you're diligent and hardworking, you'll be able to create more leisure time later in life, while a lazy person will end up with less. The [8]**essential** message is that hard work will improve our lives, while being idle will not.

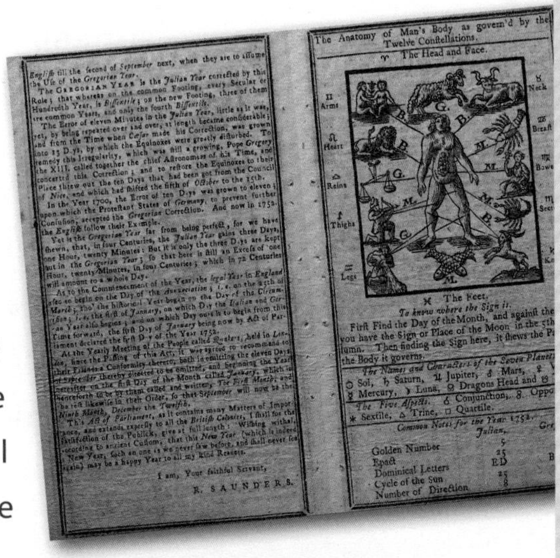

中 Translation

富蘭克林的理財智慧

值此財經困頓時期，審視一下我們的生活方式，尤其是對金錢與消費的看法，會有所幫助。我們不必費心尋找充滿智慧的評論，事實上，我們可以去讀一讀班傑明富蘭克林的著作。

班傑明富蘭克林所寫的《貧窮理查的年曆》包括了日曆、新聞及天氣預測，也有諺語和格言，二十五年來都以理查桑德斯這個筆名發表。一七五八年，《貧窮理查的年曆》出版的最後一年，富蘭克林發表了《致富之道》，在這篇文章中，一位亞伯拉罕神父在佈道中提出許多精闢的理財建議，把《貧窮理查的年曆》多年來提過的智慧摘要整理。

亞伯拉罕神父一開頭就批評聽眾：「懶散從我們身上課的稅，是我們繳稅金額的兩倍，驕傲課了三倍，愚蠢課了四倍，而且這些稅金是官員無法替我們減免的。」換句話說，懶惰讓我們無法賺到該賺的錢，此外，我們的驕傲和愚蠢導致我們虛擲所得。

他對於休閒也很有意見。他引述貧窮理查的話說：「如果你想要多一些休閒，就要好好利用時間。」（編註：thy、thou、meanest 皆為古字用法，意思分別為 your、you、mean）所謂休閒是用來做有意義的事的時間。再者，如果勤奮努力，你就能替下半輩子製造出更多休閒時光，而懶惰的人到最後休閒時間會比較少。基本上想傳達的就是，勤勞能改善我們的生活，懶散則不行。

Language Guide

Poor Richard's Almanac

一七三三年，富蘭克林用虛構人物理查桑德斯 (Richard Saunders) 的名義印行貧窮理查的年曆 (*Poor Richard's Almanac*) 這本年曆，窮理查所指的就是作者。在接下來的二十五年間，這本年曆一直是最暢銷的書籍（每年的發行量達一萬冊），不但被引進當時殖民美國的英國，還被翻譯成其他語言。亞伯拉罕神父一直到晚期才出現，也是富蘭克林杜撰來替自己發聲的人物。

富蘭克林在二十五年的年曆中，整理許多流傳於民間的諺語，也自行創作大量格言，成為後世重要的英文資產。以下是一些代表：

- God helps them that help themselves.
  天助自助者。
- Early to bed and early to rise, makes a man healthy, wealthy, and wise.
  早睡早起身體好、生活富裕又有智慧。
- Man's tongue is soft, and bone doth lack; yet a stroke therewith may break a man's back.
  人的舌頭柔軟無骨，卻能打斷人的脊椎骨。
- Don't throw stones at your neighbors, if your own windows are glass.
  如果你家的窗戶是玻璃做的，就別對鄰居扔石頭。
- Diligence is the mother of good luck.
  勤勉是幸運之母。
- One today is worth two tomorrows.
  一個今天勝過兩個明天。
  All things are easy to industry. All things are difficult to sloth.
  勤則萬事易，懶則萬事難。

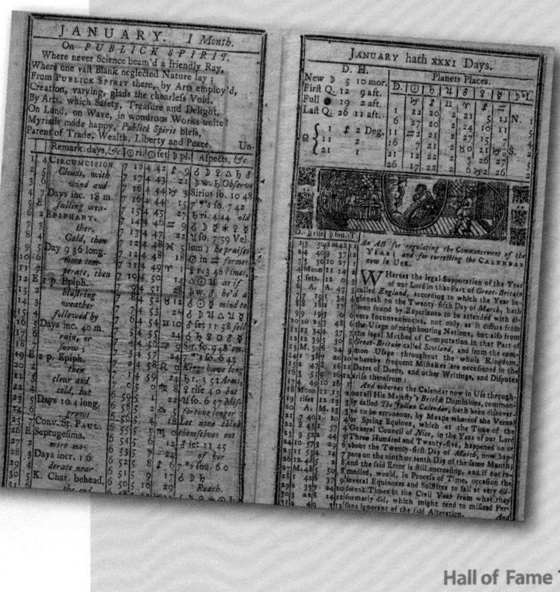

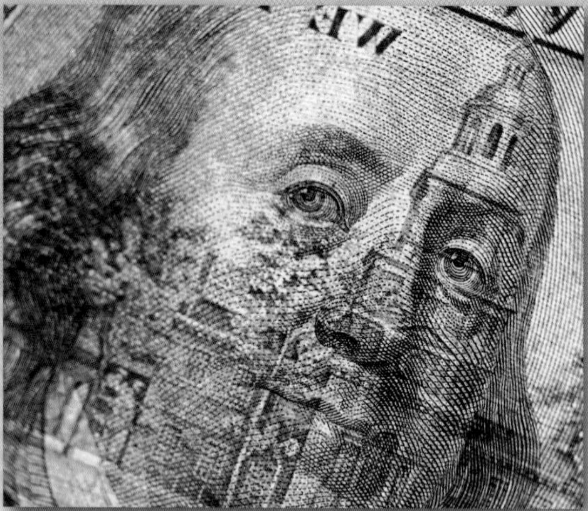

朗讀 MP3 205 單字 MP3 206 英文文章導讀 MP3 207

There is also excellent advice for [1]**prospectiv** managers and business owners. His main message Stay involved and do many things yourself. Frankli [2]**sums** these ideas **up** with two quotes: "...not to overse workmen is to leave them your purse open." In othe words, they will waste your money or even steal it. And ". if you would have a [3]**faithful** servant, and one that you lik serve yourself," which is [11]**self-explanatory**.

The final piece of advice is about frugality which means not overspending or wasting mone on unnecessary things. Father Abraham's advice "A man may, if he knows not how to save as he get **1** **keep his nose all his life to the grindstone** and die not worth a groat a last." So, no matter hov hardworking you are without saving yo will have to work ti you die. Frugality according

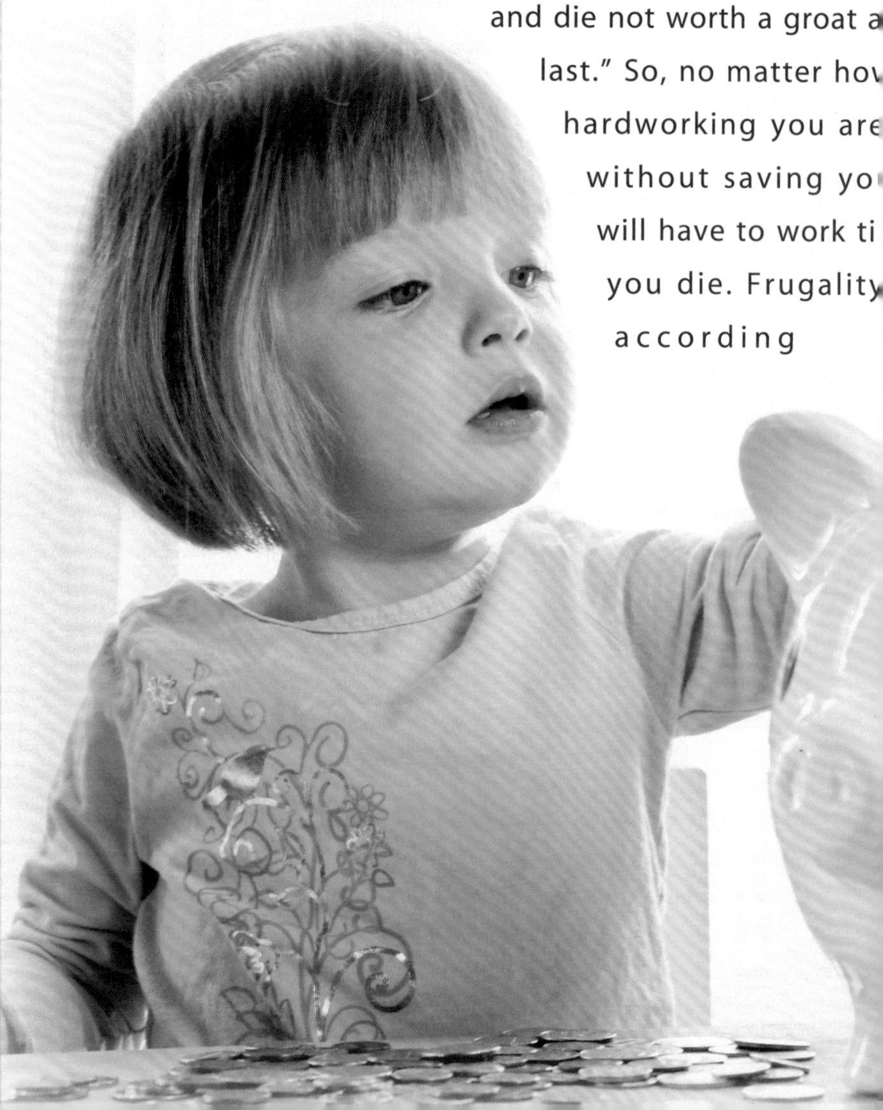

Vocabulary Bank

1) **prospective** [prə`spɛktɪv] (a.) 可能的，潛在的
Roger is meeting with a prospective client this afternoon.

2) **sum up** [sʌm ʌp] (phr.) 總結
The professor summed up his lecture by repeating the main points.

3) **faithful** [`feθfəl] (a.) 忠誠的，忠實的
Dogs make the most faithful pets.

4) **satin** [`sætɪn] (n./a.) 緞，緞子衣服；緞做的
This wedding dress is made of satin.

5) **scarlet** [`skɑrlɪt] (n./a.) 緋紅色（的），鮮紅色（的）
Elizabeth wore scarlet to the ball.

6) **velvet** [`vɛlvɪt] (n./a.) 天鵝絨（的），絲絨（的）
The singer was dressed in black velvet.

7) **means** [minz] (n.) 財力，收入
Credit cards make it easy to live beyond your means.

8) **consume** [kən`sum] (v.) 消費，消耗
The U.S. consumes more oil than any other country.

9) **removed (from)** [rɪ`muvd] (a.) 遠離的
They live in a suburb far removed from the city center.

10) **valid** [`vælɪd] (a.) 成立的，有效的
I hope you have a valid reason for your absence.

進階字彙

11) **self-explanatory** [͵sɛlfɪk`splænə͵tori] (a.) 不需加以說明的，容易懂的
Most of the charts in the text are self-explanatory.

12) **finery** [`faɪnəri] (n.) 華麗的服飾
The guests arrived at the wedding in their best finery.

to the Father, is also related to spending: "Many a one, for the sake of [12]**finery** on the back, have gone with a hungry belly, and half starved their families; silks and [4]**satins**, [5]**scarlet** and [6]**velvets**, as Poor Richard says, put out the kitchen fire." Simply put: live within your [7]**means**. Don't over-[8]**consume**. Save.

18th century America may seem far [9]**removed** from our modern world, but many of the lessons contained in "The Way to Wealth" are just as [10]**valid** today as they were back then. So if you need a little advice to help you on the path to wealth, don't forget the wise words of Benjamin Franklin.

中 Translation

文中也有給未來的管理階層與企業主的高明建議。他的主旨是什麼？持續參與工作並且要親力親為。富蘭克林借用兩句話來總結這些想法：「……不盯著員工，等於是把打開的錢包留給他們。」換句話說，他們會浪費掉你的錢，甚至偷走。還有「……如果你要一個忠誠的僕人，一個你很喜歡的僕人，那你就做自己的僕人吧。」道理不言自明。

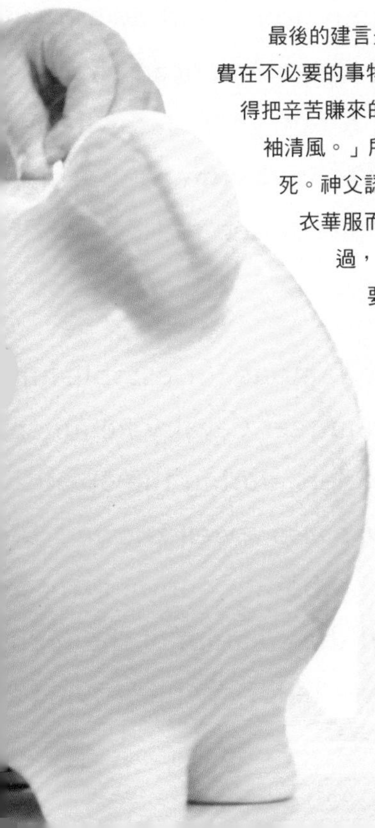

最後的建言是關於節儉，也就是不要過度消費，或把錢浪費在不必要的事物上。亞伯拉罕神父有什麼建議？「如果不懂得把辛苦賺來的錢存起來，就可能會終日勞碌，最後死時兩袖清風。」所以，不論你工作多麼努力，不儲蓄就得做到死。神父認為節儉也與花費息息相關：「多少人為了錦衣華服而挨餓，還連累家人填不飽肚子；貧窮理查說過，「綾羅綢緞會蓋熄廚房的爐火。」簡而言之：要量入為出，不要過度消費，要儲蓄。

十八世紀的美國似乎離我們現在的世界很遙遠，但《致富之道》裡的許多教誨在現在看來跟當初一樣有道理。如果你在致富的道路上需要一點建議，別忘了班傑明富蘭克林的金玉良言。

Tongue-tied No More

1 keep / put one's nose to the grindstone
終日辛苦奔波，日以繼夜工作

grindstone 是指「石磨，磨刀石，砂輪」，keep / put one's nose to the grindstone 這句話表示一個人整天都在工作，也可以用在學生用功的情況。

A: There's only a week left before finals.
只剩一個星期就期末考了。

B: Yeah, it's time to put our noses to the grindstone.
對啊，該是我們焚膏繼晷的時候了。

A: How long does it take to learn Spanish?
學會西班牙文要花多久時間啊？

B: If you keep your nose to the grindstone, you can become fluent in a year or two.
如果你非常用功，一兩年就能夠講得很流利。

Mini Quiz

1. When did *Poor Richard's Almanac* begin publication?
(A) 1735 (B) 1733
(C) 1758 (D) 1734

2. According to "The Way to Wealth," if you want a faithful servant you should ______.
(A) hire a servant that you like
(B) hire a faithful servant
(C) act as your own servant
(D) choose the servant yourself

3. Father Abraham says that if you don't save money ______.
(A) you will be poor when you die
(B) you will retire poor
(C) you will have to work hard
(D) you will have to put your nose to the grindstone

4. The scientist ______ his theory in a scientific paper.

5. I want to stay in a hotel ______ from the noisy city center.

解答 1 (B) 2 (C) 3 (A) 4 set forth 5 removed

Theodore Roosevelt

美國總統——老羅斯福

朗讀 MP3 208 單字 MP3 209 英文文章導讀 MP3 210

Theodore Roosevelt, born October 28, 1858 in Ne York City, was the 26th President of the United States c America. Although he was born into a wealthy famil he later developed a [1]**distrust** of wealthy businessme Roosevelt suffered from [2]**asthma** at an early ag but he was also a hyperactive and curious child wh excelled in [3]**biology**, geography, French and Germa He was mainly [11]**homeschooled**, and graduate from Harvard College in 1876. He married Alic Hathaway Lee in 1880, but she died tragicall shortly after giving birth to their daughter. Onl eleven hours earlier, his mother had died fror [12]**typhoid** fever in the same house. Following thi [4]**tragedy**, Roosevelt moved to the American [5]**frontie** where he owned a ranch. A few years later he los his [6]**herd**, and his $60,000 [7]**investment**, during winter storm, after which he returned to New York t [8]**resume** his political career.

Roosevelt first became famous for establishin and leading the 1st U.S. Volunteer Cavalry Regimen also known as the Rough Riders, during the Spanish American War of 1898. He was also a well-known [13]**bi game** hunter, and a cartoon about a hunting trip h made to Mississippi inspired the creation of the tedd bear (Roosevelt's nickname was Teddy). Ⓖ After serving a

Vocabulary Bank

1) **distrust** [dɪsˋtrʌst] (n.) 不信任，懷疑
The boy has a distrust of strangers.

2) **asthma** [ˋæzmə] (n.)（醫）氣喘病
My asthma usually gets worse in the spring and fall.

3) **biology** [baɪˋɑlədʒi] (n.) 生物學
Biology is the study of living things.

4) **tragedy** [ˋtrædʒədi] (n.) 悲劇，慘事，災難
It's a tragedy that so many people are out of work.

5) **frontier** [frʌnˋtɪr] (n.) 未開發的邊遠地區，邊疆
The family settled in a small town close to the frontier.

6) **herd** [hɝd] (n.) 牧群，獸群
Zebras always travel in herds.

7) **investment** [ɪnˋvɛstmənt] (n.) 投資（額、標的）
(v.) invest [ɪnˋvɛst]
Stocks can be good long term investments.

8) **resume** [rɪˋzum] (v.) 重新開始，繼續
The game resumed after a two-hour delay.

9) **monopoly** [məˋnɑpəli] (n.) 壟斷，獨佔
The United State has strict laws against monopolies.

10) **carve** [kɑrv] (v.) 雕刻，切
The statue was carved from a single block of marble.

進階字彙

11) **homeschool** [ˋhom͵skul] (v.) 自行在家教育小孩
The couple homeschooled both of their children.

12) **typhoid (fever)** [ˋtaɪfɔɪd] (n.) 傷寒
Thousands die from typhoid fever in Africa every year.

13) **big game** [bɪg gem] (n.) 大型獵物（野生動物、魚類）
Richard traveled to Africa to hunt big game.

© 達志 / UPI PHOTO

Governor of New York State and Vice President, he was President from 1901 to 1909. While in office, he helped break up 9)**monopolies** that were driving up oil and steel prices. He was also the first president to advocate national health care. Roosevelt is one of four presidents whose face is 10)**carved** on Mount Rushmore in South Dakota.

中 Translation

西奧多羅斯福在一八五八 年十月二十八 日出生於紐約市，為美國第二十六任總統。他雖然出身富裕家庭，後來卻不信任富商。羅斯福幼時罹患氣喘，但他也是個過動又好奇的小孩，並在生物、地理、法文和德文表現優異。他主要是在家中受教育，一八七六 年畢業於哈佛大學。一八八〇 年時他娶愛麗絲海瑟薇李為妻，但她卻在生下女兒不久後不幸過世。就在妻子死前十一個小時，羅斯福的母親才在同一個屋簷下因傷寒病逝。發生這樣的悲劇之後，羅斯福搬到自己位於美國邊境的牧場。數年後，一場冬季暴風雪讓他損失了畜群和六萬美金的投資，於是他回到紐約，重拾政治事業。

羅斯福開始出名是因為他在一八九八年美西戰爭期間成立並領導美國第一支自願騎兵隊（又稱為「莽騎兵」）。他熱中獵捕大型動物也眾所皆知，一則描述他到密西西比州打獵的漫畫還激發了「泰迪熊」的誕生（「泰迪」是羅斯福的小名）。擔任過紐約州長及副總統之後，他成為一九〇一到一九〇九年間的總統。 執政期間，他促成拆散哄抬石油和鋼鐵價格的壟斷企業。他也是第一位提倡全民健保的總統。南達科塔州的拉什莫爾山上所雕刻的四位總統面像，其中一位就是羅斯福。

Language Guide

the American frontier 美國邊境

美國領土擴張的順序，基本上是由東到西，因此一提到美國邊境，想到的就是「西部」the West，即歐洲移民未抵達定居之處。老羅斯福總統年輕時，就曾在位於達科塔地區 (Dakota Territory) 的自家牧場當了兩年西部牛仔。

the Spanish-American War 美西戰爭

美國於十九世紀末國力迅速壯大，發展出帝國主義，但苦於英、法等舊帝國勢力已根深蒂固盤據世界各地，沒有美國可以染指之處，因此當時國力衰退的西班牙，就成了美國帝國主義挑釁的對象。

一八九五年，古巴發生叛軍革命，欲脫離西班牙統治，接著美國軍艦緬因號 (USS Maine) 就在哈瓦那港「離奇」沈沒，美國因此於一八九八年向西班牙宣戰，展開「美西戰爭」Spanish-American War。美西戰爭開戰時，老羅斯福組織了一隊名為「莽騎兵」the Rough Riders 的自願騎兵（Volunteer Cavalry Regiment 即「馬背上的軍團」）。

美西戰爭的結果是，美國取得了菲律賓群島、波多黎各，以及夏威夷群島等地區的控制權。

泰迪熊的由來

老羅斯福（小名 Teddy）最令人稱道的傳奇之一，就是泰迪熊以他命名的故事。老羅斯福喜歡打獵眾所皆知，一九〇二年他到密西西比州打獵，部屬抓了一隻小黑熊要給他打，但遭到老羅斯福拒絕。

這個故事被著名漫畫家克利佛貝利門 (Clifford Berryman) 畫下來，刊登在《華盛頓郵報》上，引發玩具製造商的靈感，將絨毛玩具熊命名為 teddy bear，這段佳話也隨著玩具熊大受歡迎而流傳至今。

Grammar Master

後面省略主詞的用法

用 after、before、while 連接兩個子句時，若兩個子句的主詞一樣，可以省略 after、before、while 後面那個子句裡的主詞，接 Ving 或介系詞片語。不過要注意，若 after、before、while 後面的子句主詞為人名時，要把另一個子句中的代名詞用人名還原（上下文義清楚不在此限）。

- After Ted had breakfast, he went to work.
  = After having breakfast, Ted went to work.
- He was a bank manager before he was fired.
  = He was a bank manager before being fired.
- Sandy was too busy to answer the phone while she was at work.
  = Sandy was too busy to answer the phone while at work.

The Strenuous Life 奮起人生

V Vocabulary Bank

1) **entitle** [ɪnˋtaɪtəl] (v.) 替（書、作品）提名
Kurt Vonnegut's first novel was entitled Player Piano.

2) **undergo** [ˏʌndɚˋgo] (v.) 經歷，忍受
People underwent great hardship during the war.

3) **sickly** [ˋsɪkli] (a.) 多病的，不健壯的
The girl left school to take care of her sickly mother.

4) **prop** [prɑp] (v.) 支撐，頂住
I prop my head up with a pillow when I watch TV.

5) **take up** [tek ʌp] (phr.) 培養（興趣）
John plans to take up golf when he retires.

6) **prosper** [ˋprɑspɚ] (v.) 繁榮，成功
The company has continued to prosper under the new CEO.

7) **preach** [pritʃ] (v.) 鼓吹，宣揚，講道
Gandhi preached peace and nonviolence.

8) **doctrine** [ˋdɑkrɪn] (n.) 教條，信條
Do you believe in Church doctrine?

9) **toil** [tɔɪl] (n./v.) 辛勞，奮力工作
After years of toil, Martin saved enough to buy a house.

10) **shrink** [ʃrɪnk] (v.) 畏怯，退縮
David's parents taught him never to shrink from responsibility.

11) **splendid** [ˋsplɛndɪd] (a.) 輝煌的，壯麗的，出色的
The opera singer gave a splendid performance.

進階字彙

12) **strenuous** [ˋstrɛnjuəs] (a.) 費力的，奮發的
My doctor told me to avoid strenuous exercise for the next few weeks.

13) **adversity** [ədˋvɝsəti] (n.) 逆境，厄運
We all must learn to deal with adversity.

14) **ignoble** [ɪgˋnobəl] (a.) 不名譽的，可恥的
The man's ignoble behavior brought shame to his family.

15) **strife** [straɪf] (n.) 衝突，鬥爭，不和
After years of civil strife, the country is finally at peace.

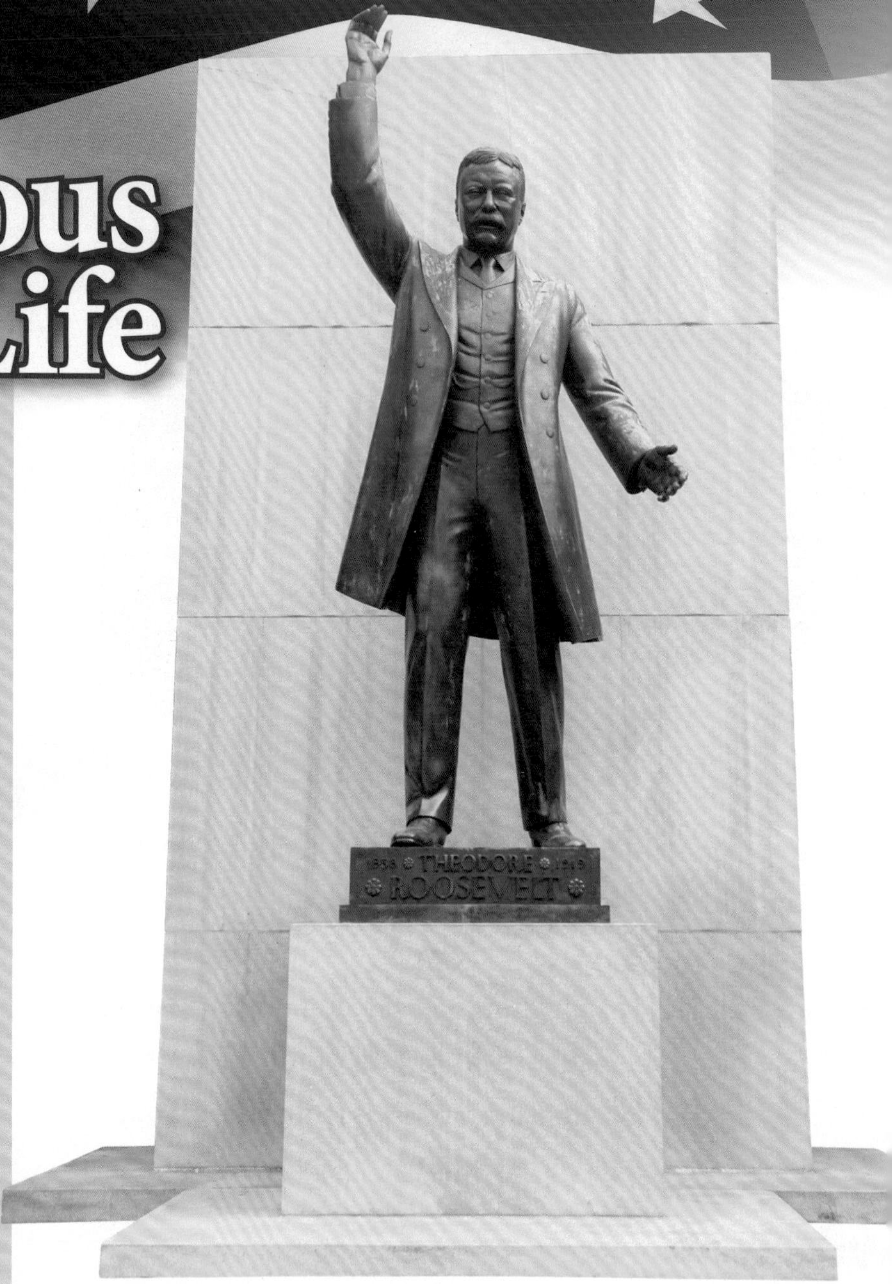

朗讀 MP3 211 單字 MP3 212 英文文章導讀 MP3 213

One of Teddy Roosevelt's most famous speeches i [1]**entitled** "The [12]**Strenuous** Life." The speech was largel shaped by the personal challenges that he [2]**underwen** despite his upper-class background. Roosevelt was [3]**sickly** child, and suffered from asthma so serious tha he had to sleep [4]**propped** up in his bed. In spite of hi poor health, his father encouraged him to [5]**take u** boxing as self-defense. When he was given a physical examination after graduating from Harvard, the doctor recommended he take a desk job and avoid strenuous activity due to his poor health. Roosevelt ignored the doctor's advice, however, and took up various sports, including tennis, hiking, rowing, polo and horseback riding. He also continued to box, even as President, until a blow to the head left him blind in his left eye.

Roosevelt had also experienced many hardships in his life, both personal and financial, and he used these experiences to make a point in his speech—that America, like himself, would [6]**prosper** by working hard and overcoming [13]**adversity**. In his own words: "[G]I wish to [7]**preach**, not the [8]**doctrine** of [14]**ignoble** ease, but the doctrine of the strenuous life, the life of [9]**toil** and effort, of labor and [15]**strife**; to preach that highest form of success which comes not to the man who desires mere easy peace, but to the man who does not [10]**shrink** from danger, from hardship, or from bitter toil, and who out of these wins the [11]**splendid** ultimate triumph."

中 Translation

羅斯福最著名的演講之一是一篇名為「奮起人生」的演說，演講內容主要是他雖然出身上流卻飽受挑戰的個人經歷。羅斯福是一個體弱多病的孩子，哮喘非常嚴重，因此他不得不斜靠著睡在床上。儘管他身體不好，他的父親鼓勵他培養拳擊運動作為自衛工具。在哈佛大學畢業後的一次身體檢查中，醫生建議他從事文書工作，避免費力的活動，因為他的健康狀況很差。然而，羅斯福不顧醫生的勸告，從事多種運動，包括網球、健行、划船、馬球和騎馬。即使當上了總統，他還是持續打拳擊，直到有一次被擊中頭部使他左眼瞎掉為止。

羅斯福一生中也經歷許多艱難困苦，包括個人方面和財務方面，他利用這些經驗，在演說中提出一個重點——美國，就像他自己一樣，可以透過辛勤工作和克服逆境而繁榮昌盛。套用他的話：「我想灌輸一個觀念，不是卑微低下的安逸，而是艱苦奮發的人生，也就是辛勞及努力、勞動及奮鬥的人生；我想鼓吹的是，成功的最高境界並不會降臨在只耽於安逸的人身上，而會降臨在不畏危險、困難或苦勞的人們身上，能夠一一克服這些的人才能贏得最終輝煌的勝利。」

Language Guide

美國人最景仰的總統之一

老羅斯福上任時年僅四十二歲，當時是美國歷史上最年輕的總統。他在美國人心中的地位非常崇高，美國南達科他州拉什莫爾山（Mount Rushmore，暱稱「總統山」）雕刻了四位總統的像，老羅斯福就是其中之一。他同時也是美國一毛錢銅板上的人像。

1. **George Washington** (1732~1799) 喬治華盛頓（美國開國元勛）
2. **Thomas Jefferson** (1743~1826) 湯瑪士傑佛遜（《獨立宣言》起草者）
3. **Theodore Roosevelt** (1858~1919) 西奧多羅斯福（奠定 20 世紀美國強大基礎）
4. **Abraham Lincoln** (1809~1865) 亞伯拉罕林肯（解放黑奴）

Grammar Master

閱讀長句的訣竅（一）

這種長句不是一般書寫或閱讀會碰到的，但在慷慨激昂的演說中倒是相當常見，本文就是摘錄老羅斯福的演講稿，才會出現這種句子。

閱讀長句的訣竅，就是要「去蕪存菁」！像這種一句裡面有很多逗點的句子，中間的插入語在第一次閱讀時可以先略過。方法是先找出句子裡重複的字組模式，像是 to preach、the doctrine of...、(life) of...、the man who...、(shrink) from...。再來，前面有 not... 的部分可以先不看，有重複模式的部分也可先不看（但若會影響意思的完整性，則取重複字組的第一或最後一部分）。

I wish to preach, ~~not the doctrine of ignoble ease, but~~ the doctrine of the strenuous life~~, the life of toil and effort, of labor and strife~~; to preach that highest form of success which comes ~~not to the man who desires mere easy peace, but~~ to the man who does not shrink from danger~~, from hardship, or from bitter toil, and who out of these wins the splendid ultimate triumph~~.

簡單地說，這麼長的句子重點只有：

I wish to preach the doctrine of the strenuous life; to preach that highest form of success which comes to the man who does not shrink from danger.

掌握重點後，若嫌句子有些「清淡」，再把省略掉的枝節慢慢還原，原文的輪廓就會更清晰囉！

Vocabulary Bank

1) **justify** [ˋdʒʌstə͵faɪ] (v.) 證明…是正當的，為…辨護
How can you justify killing another human being?

2) **isolated** [ˋaɪsə͵letɪd] (v.)（被）孤立的，（被）隔離的
The isolated village has little contact with the outside world.

3) **endeavor** [ɪnˋdɛvɚ] (n.) 努力，力圖
I hope you succeed in all your endeavors.

4) **reflection** [rɪˋflɛkʃən] (n.) 反映，反射
The clothes you wear are a reflection of your personality.

5) **expose (to)** [ɪkˋspoz] (v.) 使接觸到，使暴露於
The goal of the program is to expose students to art.

6) **live off** [lɪv ɔf] (phr.) 靠…過活，依賴…生活
I can't believe that Mike is still living off his parents.

7) **recreational** [͵rɛkriˋeʃənəl] (a.) 休閒的，消遣的，娛樂的
The summer camp offers a variety of recreational activities.

8) **athletics** [æθˋlɛtɪks] (n.) 運動，體育
The school board plans to cut the athletics budget next year.

9) **embrace** [ɪmˋbres] (v.) 全心採納，欣然接受，擁抱
It's difficult for old people to embrace new ideas.

10) **landmark** [ˋlænd͵mark] (a./n.) 劃世代的、意義重大的（事物）
In a landmark decision, women were given the right to vote.

進階字彙

11) **imperialism** [ɪmˋpɪriə͵lɪzəm] (n.) 帝國主義，擴張主義
The age of imperialism ended in the 20th century.

12) **feminization** [͵fɛmənəˋzeʃən] (n.) 女性化，雌性化
The feminization of men's fashion is a recent trend.

13) **masculinity** [͵mæskjəˋlɪnəti] (n.) 男性氣概
For some men, guns are a symbol of masculinity.

14) **patriotism** [ˋpetriətɪzəm] (n.) 愛國精神，愛國主義
No one can question the politician's patriotism.

15) **extol** [ɪkˋstol] (v.) 頌揚
The book extols the benefits of exercise and a healthy diet.

© 達志 / UPI PHOTO

朗讀 MP3 214 單字 MP3 215 英文文章導讀 MP3 216

Roosevelt believed that through hard work, peopl could achieve all of their goals. He called on American to continue working hard, not only for themselves, bu for America's future as well. He also used the speec to [1]**justify** American [11]**imperialism** at a time whe most Americans were content to remain [2]**isolate** from the rest of the world. The U.S. had just won th Spanish-American War, in which Roosevelt played a active role, thereby gaining control of the Philippines Cuba, Puerto Rico and Guam. He advocated a stron military and an American military presence beyond th national borders. Again from his speech: "ⒼAbove al let us shrink from no strife, moral or physical, within or without the nation, provided that we are certain that the strife is justified, for it is only through strife, through hard and dangerous [3]**endeavor**, that we shall ultimately win the goal of national greatness."

Roosevelt's speech was also a [4]**reflection** of American attitudes at the end of the 19th and beginning of the 20th century. As America industrialized and more and more people flocked to the cities, many were fearful that people would become weaker when no longer [5]**exposed** to the hardships of [6]**living off** the land. This led to the rise of college sports and [7]**recreational** [8]**athletics**. As women's movements began to grow in power, many also feared a [12]**feminization** of American culture. Society began to [9]**embrace** [13]**masculinity**, [14]**patriotism** and nationalism, all of which Roosevelt [15]**extolled** in his [10]**landmark** speech.

中 Translation

羅斯福相信，透過努力工作，人們可以實現自己所有的目標。他呼籲美國人繼續努力，不僅為自己，也是為了美國的未來。他也利用這場演講為美國帝國主義辯護，而當時正值大多數美國人滿足於與世隔絕的狀態。美國剛贏得美西戰爭——在此役中羅斯福扮演了積極的角色——因而得以控制菲律賓、古巴、波多黎各和關島。他主張要有強大的軍事力量，且美軍的勢力要超越國界。他在演講中還提到：「最重要的是，讓我們不畏衝突、無論是在道德或肉體上，無論在國境之內或之外，只要我們確信衝突是情有可原的，因為唯有透過衝突、透過辛勤和危險的努力，我們最終才會達成目標，成為偉大國家。」

羅斯福總統的演說也反映了美國在世紀末、世紀初的態度。隨著美國進入工業化，越來越多人湧入城市，許多人擔心當大家不再經歷靠土地維生的艱苦生活，將會變得衰弱。這造成了大學運動和娛樂性運動的崛起。隨著女性運動力量開始成長，許多人也擔心美國文化會女性化。社會開始擁抱男子氣概、愛國主義和國家主義，這些都是羅斯福在他劃時代的演講中所頌揚的。

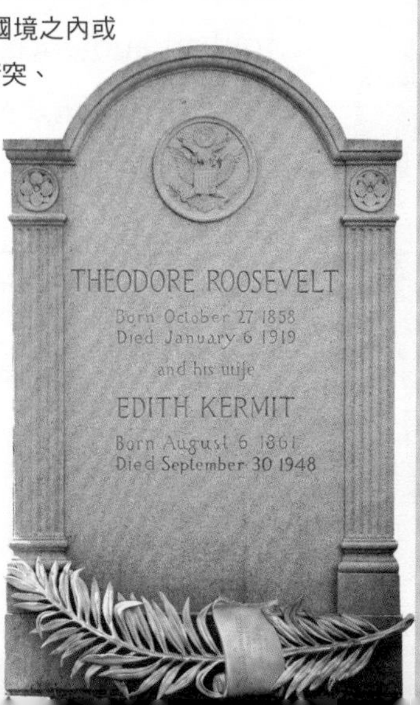

Language Guide

美國有兩位羅斯福總統

老羅斯福和第二次世界大戰時的美國總統富蘭克林羅斯福（Franklin Roosevelt，暱稱小羅斯福）是遠房親戚。

老羅斯福是美國第二十六任總統，於一九〇一～一九〇九年連續擔任兩屆美國總統，在他擔任總統期間，對內主張進步主義，積極推行改革，對外則致力於擴大美國勢力，對中國採門戶開放政策，對美洲其他國家則採壓力外交（又稱大棒外交）及金援外交，推動擴張主義與帝國主義，曾獲一九〇六年的諾貝爾和平獎。

小羅斯福是美國第三十二任總統，任期為一九三三～一九四五年，是美國史上唯一擔任超過兩屆的總統。他對內推行「新政」the New Deal，幫助勞動階層走出失業困境，度過三〇年代的「經濟大蕭條」the Great Depression。而他在第二次世界大戰時的政策，則成功引領美國走向世界舞台。

Grammar Master

閱讀長句的訣竅（二）

- 含有 no + 名詞的句子有時會令人困惑，不過事實上它就是一個否定句，比如 I have no money. 其實就是 I don't have (any) money.

let us not shrink from (any) strife

Above all, let us shrink from no strife~~, moral or physical, within or without the nation,~~ provided that we are certain that the strife is justified, for it is only through strife~~, through hard and dangerous endeavor,~~ that we shall ultimately win the goal of national greatness.

- provided that... 是用來補充條件的，意同 as long as...。
- 逗點後面的 for 通常是當作連接詞「因為」的意思，後面 through..., through... 是重複的模式，可以先取第一個就好。
- ...only...that... 的句型是「只有…才…」的意思。

掌握這些重點後，整句的意思就好懂多囉！（詳解請聽 MP3-74 中文講解）

Vocabulary Bank

1) **wardrobe** [ˋwɔrd͵rob] (n.)（整套）衣服、服裝
They each bought a new wardrobe for their European vacation.

2) **streak** [ˋstrik] (n.) 傾向
Jake is usually nice, but he also has a mean streak.

3) **condom** [ˋkɑndəm] (n.) 保險套
Many people are embarrassed to buy condoms.

4) **accessory** [ækˋsɛsəri] (n.) 配件，附件
The boutique sells women's clothing and accessories.

5) **bleach** [blitʃ] (v./n.) 漂白（使頭髮顏色變淺）；漂白水
She's not a natural blonde—she bleaches her hair.

6) **fitting** [ˋfɪtɪŋ] (a.) 適當的，合適的
The writer finally came up with a fitting ending to his novel.

7) **sketch** [skɛtʃ] (v./n.) 畫素描，寫生；素描
We sketched a nude model today in art class.

8) **sexuality** [͵sɛkʃuˋæləti] (n.) 性行為，性慾
The researchers conducted a study on human sexuality.

9) **forgetfully** [fəˋgɛtfəli] (adv.) 健忘地，粗心大意地
(a.) forgetful [fəˋgɛtfəl]
I forgetfully locked my keys in the car this morning.

10) **observer** [əbˋzɝvɚ] (n.) 觀察者，觀察家
Most political observers believe that Obama will win the election.

進階字彙

11) **sarong** [səˋrɔŋ] (n.) 紗籠（馬來西亞、印尼男女通用的一種裙子）
The waitresses at the Indonesian restaurant all wear sarongs.

12) **suggestive** [səgˋdʒɛstɪv] (a.) 引起聯想的，挑動性的
Marcy didn't approve of her coworker's suggestive remarks.

13) **pair** [pɛr] (v./n.) 搭配；一對，一雙
You'll look fabulous if you pair this silver top with a black skirt.

口語補充

14) **sport** [sport](v.)（炫耀地）穿戴、留（髮型）
Brad walked into the office sporting a new Armani suit.

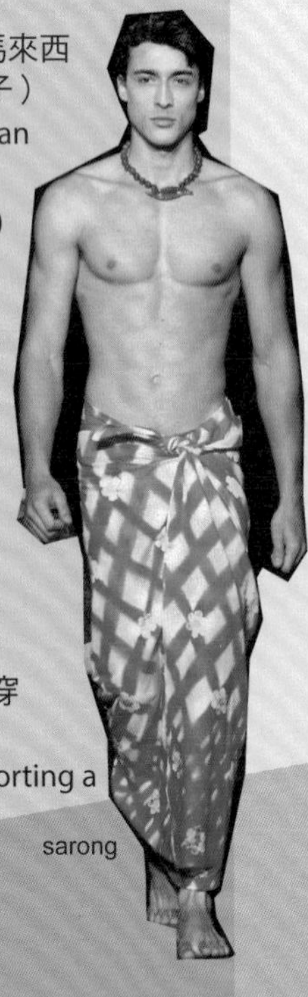

sarong

時尚頑童 高堤耶

Jean Paul Gaultier

朗讀 MP3 217 單字 MP3 218 英文文章導讀 MP3 219

French fashion designer Jean Paul Gaultier is **1 n** **stranger to** controversy. From the cone-shaped bra wor by Madonna on her Blonde Ambition tour in 1990 to th [11]**sarong** [14]**sported** by David Beckham at a nightclub i 1998, he's been behind some of the more outrageou [1]**wardrobe** choices in recent memory. Gaultier's fame naughty [2]**streak** was on display again in June, when h told an audience in New York that he wished he'd designe the [3]**condom**, calling it the "best [4]**accessory** in the world. Such [12]**suggestive** comments, [13]**paired** with his rebelliou and innovative designs, have led Gaultier to be nickname the *enfant terrible* of the fashion world. But just who is th French bad boy with the [5]**bleached** blond hair?

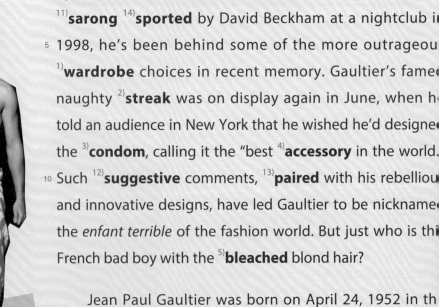

Jean Paul Gaultier was born on April 24, 1952 in th sleepy Paris suburb of Arcueil. He ©recalls not being

高堤耶（左）與蕭畢諾（右）早期合照
圖片提供：法國裝飾藝術博物館

normal boy or [6]**fitting** in much while growing up, and after designing a bra for his teddy bear at the age of eight, he knew he wanted to go into fashion. This was a bold choice for the son of an accountant and a secretary, but his grandmother encouraged him with his [7]**sketches**. Although his parents forbade it, she also let him watch lots of television, which introduced him to [8]**sexuality** at an early age. Gaultier once told a story about his grandmother [9]**forgetfully** leaving the house in nothing but her underwear and slip, prompting [10]**observers** to suggest that she was the original inspiration behind his "underwear as outerwear" look.

中 Translation

法國時裝設計師尚保羅高堤耶視爭議為家常便飯。從瑪丹娜在一九九〇年金髮雄心巡迴演唱會上穿的「木蘭飛彈」胸罩（編註：bra 為 brassiere [brəˋzɪr]）到一九九八年大衛貝克漢在一家夜店圍的紗籠裙，高堤耶一直是大家近期記憶裡一些最搞怪服裝背後的那雙手。高堤耶知名的玩世不恭作風再度於六月表露，當時他在紐約告訴觀眾，他真希望保險套是他設計的，並稱它作「世上最棒的配件」。諸如此類聳動的言論，加上他離經叛道又創新的設計，使高堤耶被稱為時尚世界的「頑童」。但這位染了金髮的法國壞男孩究竟是何方神聖？

尚保羅高堤耶在一九五二年四月二十四日生於巴黎近郊寂靜的的阿爾克伊。他記得他在成長時期就不是個正常或合群的男孩，八歲時，他替自己的泰迪熊設計了一件胸罩，此後便明白自己想進入時裝界發展。對於會計師及祕書之子而言，這是個大膽的選擇，但他的祖母卻對他的素描鼓勵有加。雖然父母禁止，但祖母也讓他看了很多電視節目，使他小小年紀就了解性事。高堤耶曾說過一個故事，他的祖母曾迷糊地僅穿內褲和襯裙就出門，觀察家認為祖母就是他「內衣外穿」的靈感來源。

Tongue-tied No More

1 no stranger to... 對……並不陌生

stranger 是「陌生人」，這個句子表示一個人常常聽說、處理某事物、有很多……的經驗，或常光顧某個地方。

A: Kevin built his own PC from scratch?
凱文從無到有組裝出自己的電腦？

B: Yeah. He's no stranger to computers.
是啊。他很懂電腦。

Grammar Master

recall 的用法

1. **主詞 + recall + N.** 回想、回憶起……

例 Chad couldn't **recall** the dates he'd memorized for the test.
查德想不起來那些為了考試而死背的日子。

2. **主詞 + recall + Ving** 回想起曾經做了……
（和 forget、remember 用法相同）

例 The witness **recalled** seeing the suspect at the scene of the crime.
目擊者回憶起在犯罪現場看到嫌犯。

也可以寫成：**主詞 + recall + that 子句**

例 Tom **recalled** that he'd been to the town before as a child.
湯姆回憶起他兒時曾經來過這個小鎮。

文中的 He recalls not being a normal boy or fitting in much while growing up, and after designing a bra... .

句子中 recall 後加 Ving，表示他是回想起以前「曾發生的事」。因此也可以寫成：

He recalls **that** he was (說明 1) not a normal boy and did not fit in (說明 2) much while growing up, and after designing a bra... .

說明 1：原句用 **being**，這裡為何改為 was ？
that 後要接子句，因為是過去的事，所以用 was。

說明 2：原句用 **fitting**，為何改為 did not fit in ？
that 後要接子句，因為是已經發生的事，再加上否定 not ，所以用 did not。

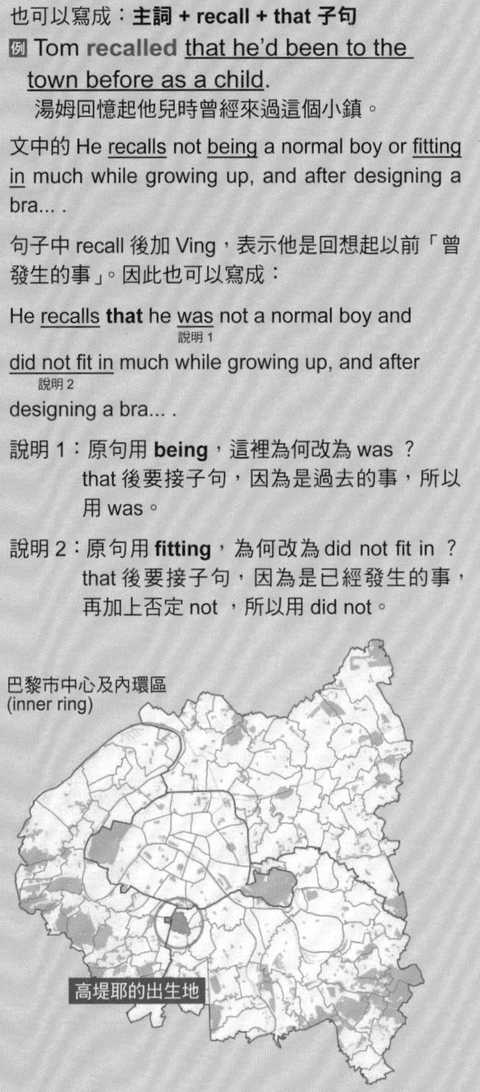

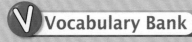

Vocabulary Bank

1) **consume** [kən`sum] (v.) 使全神貫注，使著迷，充滿…
The students were consumed with curiosity about their new classmate.

2) **visa** [`vizə] (n.) 簽證
You can't cross the border without a visa.

3) **cultivate** [`kʌltə͵vet] (v.) 培養
While living in France, Sue cultivated her interest in wine.

4) **distinct** [dɪ`stɪŋkt] (a.) 不同的，有區別的
Each spice has its own distinct flavor.

5) **liberally** [`lɪbərəli] (adv.) 大量地，大方地
(a.) liberal [`lɪbərəl]
Roger poured syrup liberally on his pancakes.

6) **aesthetic** [ɛs`θɛtɪk] (a.) 美觀的，美學的
Most of the town's buildings have little aesthetic value.

7) **ambiguity** [͵æmbɪ`gjuəti] (n.) 模稜兩可，含糊
(a.) ambiguous [͵æmbɪ`gjuəs]
There was no ambiguity in the president's speech.

8) **gender-bending** [`dʒɛndɚ͵bɛndɪŋ] (a.) 不男不女的
Lots of teenagers these days like to wear gender-bending clothes.

進階字彙

9) **couture** [ku`tʊr] (n.)（女性）時裝
haute couture [ot ku`tʊr] 即「高級時裝」
The designer is launching a new couture line.

10) **boutique** [bu`tik] (n.) 精品店，女裝店
That boutique sells beautiful jewelry.

11) **irreverent** [ɪ`rɛvərənt] (a.) 不敬的，諷刺的
The comedian is famous for his irreverent sense of humor.

12) **corset** [`kɔrsɪt] (n.) 馬甲，束腹
Women wear corsets to make their waists look smaller.

朗讀 MP3 220 單字 MP3 221 英文文章導讀 MP3 222

Despite lacking any formal training as a designe Gaultier began sending his sketches to the famou [9]**couture** houses of Paris in hopes of ❶ **catching a stylist eye**. His first break came in 1970, when Pierre Cardi recognized his talent and gave him an after-school jo as a design assistant. Gaultier's passion for the job s [1]**consumed** him that he recalls how he "failed brilliantly on his final exams at school. This was followed by brie stints with Jacques Esterel and Jean Patou, who taught hi the tools of the trade. Gaultier returned to Cardin in 197 Ⓖand was sent to manage the designer's [10]**boutique** i Manila. His designs were so popular there, he says, that th government denied him an exit [2]**visa** when it was time t leave. He was finally allowed to go home when he claime that his grandmother had passed away.

Back in Paris, Gaultier debuted his first individu collection in 1976, and would go on to [3]**cultivate** his ow [4]**distinct** style. His designs have always drawn [5]**liberall**

表演者穿著高堤耶設
的舞衣演出《聖喬治
©法國裝飾藝術博物
——時尚暨織品館，
宏、Tristan Valès 攝

from pop culture—from punk and the London street scene of the 1970s to the hip-hop [6]**aesthetic** of the 80s and 90s—which gives his creations a playful and even [11]**irreverent** air. Sex, or sexual [7]**ambiguity**, is another important theme in his collections, which have included such [8]**gender-bending** items as kilts and [12]**corsets** for men. And Gaultier's use of older and [13]**full-figured** models on the [14]**catwalk** has **2 raised many eyebrows**, to which he responds [15]**matter-of-factly**, "There is beauty in everything, not only in the very thin."

13) **full-figured** [ˋful.fɪgjəd] (a.) 豐滿的，肥胖的
That shop sells clothes for full-figured women.

14) **catwalk** [ˋkæt.wɔlk] (n.) 伸展台，runway [ˋrʌn.we] 亦是別稱
The model tripped and fell on the catwalk.

15) **matter-of-factly** [ˋmætəəv.fæktli] (adv.) 實事求是地，不帶感情地
The man talked matter-of-factly about his battle with cancer.

中 Translation

雖然沒受過正規的設計師訓練，高堤耶仍開始將設計圖寄給巴黎幾家著名的時裝設計公司，希望能獲得時裝設計師的青睞。他的第一次機會在一九七〇年到來，當時皮爾卡登賞識他的才華，給了他一份課後打工的設計助理工作。高堤耶對這份工作充滿熱情，幾乎花上全副心力，因此他「漂亮地當掉」學校期末考。接著他與賈克艾斯泰黑爾和尚巴度短暫共事，兩人傳授他這一行的技能。高堤耶在一九七四年回到卡登的公司，被派去管理這位設計師設於馬尼拉的流行服裝店。他說，他的設計在那裡大受歡迎，在他準備離開之際，菲律賓政府拒絕發給他出境簽證，直到他宣稱祖母過世才終於獲准返國。

回到巴黎後，高堤耶在一九七六年舉辦他的第一次個展，並繼續耕耘他獨特的個人風格。他的設計向來大量取材自流行文化——從龐克及一九七〇年代的倫敦街頭文化，到八〇及九〇年代的嘻哈美學——這賦予他的創作一種嬉鬧甚至不敬的氛圍。性，或者性別不明，是他作品中另一項重要主題，其中包括諸如蘇格蘭裙和男用馬甲等扭轉性別的單品。高堤耶用較年長和豐腴的模特兒走伸展台，也令許多人側目，對此他以平淡的口吻回應：「美存在於萬事萬物，不僅是瘦削之中。」

Tongue-tied No More

1 catch one's eye
吸引目光，引起興趣

不論是故意特立獨行，還是靜靜杵在那裡，只要能夠引人注意，都可以用這句描述。

A: Did you see anything you liked at the boutique?
你在那間精品店裡有看到喜歡的東西嗎？

B: Well, this cute blue dress did catch my eye.
這個嘛，有一件可愛的藍色洋裝讓我忍不住多看了幾眼。

2 raise eyebrows 引人側目

同樣是吸引目光，raise eyebrows 表示使人驚訝或反感。一般會說 raise a few eyebrows 或 raise some eyebrows。

A: Did you see what Sheila was wearing today?
你有看到席拉今天的打扮嗎？

B: Yeah, her miniskirt sure raised some eyebrows around the office.
有啊，她的迷你裙在辦公室裡真是引人側目。

punk 龐克

龐克源自一九七〇年代中期英美的青少年次文化 (subculture)，是對六〇年代嬉皮 (hippy) 文化和七〇年代流行樂的反動。典型龐克族會剃光頭（只留少數頭髮塑成尖刺狀）、穿釘滿鉚釘的黑皮衣、配掛象徵死亡的飾品並在身上穿孔、穿環，以粗暴的行為展現憤怒。龐克風格被設計師如 Vivienne Westwood、Jean Paul Gaultier 採用而商業化，成為八〇年代風行全球的時尚潮流。

Language Guide

hip-hop 嘻哈

嘻哈是源自七〇年代美國內陸城市的非裔青少年，及紐約市拉丁美洲裔青少年的次文化，透過音樂、舞蹈、服裝及塗鴉 (graffiti) 表現混跡街頭的生活形態。鮮豔的 tracksuit（薄尼龍製的田徑外套及長褲）、flight jacket（空軍飛行員的皮外套）、鞋帶過長的布鞋、超粗金項鍊、超大金耳環（即所謂 bling-bling 風格）、過大襯衫及過長褲子即典型的嘻哈風格。

V Vocabulary Bank

1) **disguise** [dɪs`gaɪz] (v./n.) 掩飾，偽裝
Claudia couldn't disguise her disappointment when she lost the beauty contest.

2) **retain** [rɪ`ten] (v.) 持有，保留
The owner was able to retain control of the company.

3) **signature** [`sɪgnətʃɚ] (a.) 代表的，招牌的
Fans always ask the band to play its signature song at concerts.

4) **fruitful** [`frutfəl] (a.) 收益好的，富有成效的
Christopher had a long and fruitful career as a writer.

5) **stellar** [`stɛlɚ] (a.) 極佳的，無與倫比的
The orchestra gave a stellar performance.

6) **solely** [`solli] (adv.) 完全，僅僅
Patrick is solely to blame for his divorce.

7) **fragrance** [`fregrəns] (n.) 香水，香味
What is that fragrance you're wearing?

8) **chic** [ʃik] (a.) 時髦的，別緻的
Have you seen Carla's chic new haircut?

9) **medium** [`midiəm] (n.)（藝術）媒介、材料、種類
Watercolor was the artist's favorite medium.

進階字彙

10) **laud** [lɔd] (v./n.) 讚美
The film was lauded by critics and fans alike.

11) **sophistication** [sə,fɪstɪ`keʃən] (n.) 高雅，文雅，老練
Shelly's taste in clothes reflects her sophistication.

12) **afield** [ə`fild] (adv.) 遠離著，偏離著
The hotel has guests from Canada, Europe and even further afield.

13) **torso** [`tɔrso] (n.) 人體軀幹
The man was stabbed in the torso and bled to death.

14) **collaborator** [kə`læbə,retɚ] (n.) 合作者，共同研究者
The scientist thanked all his collaborators when he received the award.

高堤耶於二〇〇四年舉辦的設計展，全部服裝均以麵包製成
© wiki_Daderot

朗讀 MP3 223 單字 MP3 224 英文文章導讀 MP3 225

While his playful looks may not take themselve too seriously, there's no [1]**disguising** the fact tha Gaultier remains a master tailor. His first haute coutur line, released in 1997, was [10]**lauded** as much for it [11]**sophistication** as it was for [2]**retaining** his [3]**signatur** style. The high fashion world **1** **sat up and took notic** and Hermès purchased 35% of the Jean Paul Gaultier labe in 1999, enabling the brand to expand further [12]**afiel** notably in East Asia. ©Continuing what Gaultier describe as "a dream marriage," Hermès hired him in 2004 t develop its women's wear line. This May, it was announce that after seven [4]**fruitful** years, Gaultier would be steppin down to devote more time to his own brand. His fina collection for Hermès, which is retaining its stake in th Jean Paul Gaultier company, will be shown in October.

Gaultier's [5]**stellar** career has not been built [6]**solely** o the runway. His credits include hosting the popular Britis

TV show *Eurotrash* and developing a successful [7]**fragrance** line, whose [13]**torso**-shaped bottles are themselves works of art. In addition to longtime fan and [14]**collaborator** Madonna, his clients include such diverse names as actress Nicole Kidman and rocker Marilyn Manson. Gaultier has also designed the wardrobes for many popular films, including French director Luc Besson's 1997 sci-fi hit *The Fifth Element*, and Gaultier's designs continue to appear on the big and small screen alike. So what ❷ **lies ahead** for fashion's *enfant terrible*? One thing's for sure, it'll be [8]**chic** and sexy whatever the [9]**medium**.

中 Translation

雖然他嬉鬧的設計作品感覺或許不太嚴肅，卻無法掩飾高堤耶仍是裁縫大師的事實。他在一九九七年發表他第一個高級時裝系列，既以高雅精緻博得好評，又以保有其招牌風格備受讚譽，立刻讓高級時尚圈刮目相看，愛馬仕在一九九九年買下尚保羅高堤耶商標百分之三十五的股份，使這個品牌得以進一步拓展版圖，特別是在東亞。延續高堤耶所謂的「夢幻結合」，愛馬仕在二〇〇四年聘請他研發該公司的女裝系列。今年五月，歷經成果豐碩的七年，高堤耶宣布將辭職投入更多時間發展他自己的品牌。他替愛馬仕——仍將繼續持有尚保羅高堤耶公司的股份——設計的最後一系列作品將在十月問世。

高堤耶如星光燦爛的事業不僅建立在伸展台之上，他的成績還包括主持知名的英國電視節目《歐洲廢物》及開發一系列成功的香水，其人體造型的瓶身本身就是藝術作品。除了他的長期粉絲及合作對象瑪丹娜之外，他的客戶尚包括女星妮可基嫚和搖滾歌手瑪麗蓮梅森等各界名人。高堤耶也替多部受歡迎的電影設計服裝，包括法國導演盧貝松一九九七年科幻賣座片《第五元素》，而且高堤耶的設計仍持續出現在大小螢幕。那麼前方還有什麼在等待這位時尚界的頑童？有一件事是確定的：無論是何種媒介，都將既時髦又性感。

若有疑問請來信：eztalkQ@gmail.com

瑪丹娜在金髮雄心演唱會上的裝扮

©達志 / UPI PHOTO

Tongue-tied No More

❶ sit up and take notice 刮目相看

sit up 是指「挺起腰桿，打起精神」，sit up and take notice 表現出觀眾忽然坐直注意看的樣子，也就是「刮目相看」。

例 The young actor's performance in the film made critics sit up and take notice.
這位年輕演員在電影裡的表現讓影評人刮目相看。

❷ lie ahead (of) 擺在眼前；面臨

表示前方有東西擺放著，也可表示未來會發生的事。

例 We must prepare ourselves for the challenges that lie ahead.
我們必須為眼前的挑戰做好準備。

Grammar Master

簡化主詞的分詞構句

文中的這一個句子可以拆解成兩句：

1. Hermès continued what Gaultier described as "a dream marriage."
2. Hermès hired him in 2004 to develop its women's wear line.

第一句的簡化步驟：

步驟 1：當主詞相同時，可以簡化其中之一的主詞。

~~Hermès~~ continued what Gaultier described as "a dream marriage."

→ 主詞相同即省略

步驟 2：判斷主詞後的動詞是「主動」還是「被動」，若為「主動」就將動詞改為「現在分詞」；若為「被動」就將動詞改為「過去分詞」。

~~Hermès continued~~ what Gaultier described as "a dream marriage."

→ 因為是動詞在原句中是主動，故改為 continuing

簡化結果：

Continuing what Gaultier described as "a dream marriage," Hermès (真正主詞) hired him in 2004 to develop its women's wear line.

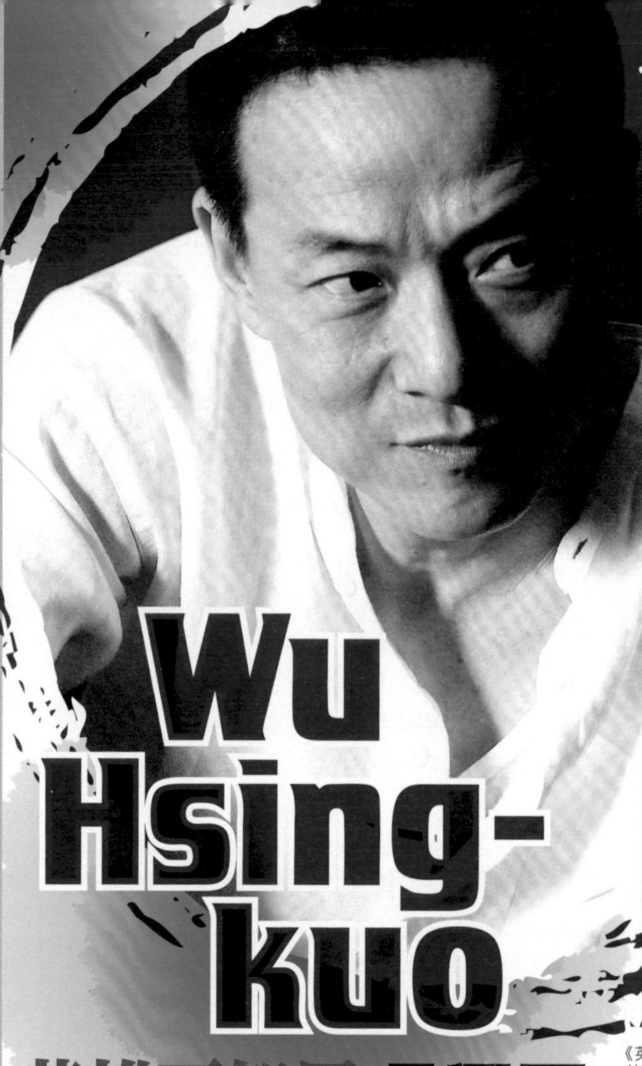

Wu Hsing-kuo
英雄不卸甲吳興國

《英雄不卸甲》一書收錄《慾望城國
特輯及吳興國創辦當代傳奇劇場的心路
（日月文化大好書屋提供）

本單元圖片由當代傳奇劇場提供

朗讀 MP3 226 單字 MP3 227 英文文章導讀 MP3 228

As a young boy, Wu Hsing-kuo lost his father i the Chinese civil war between the Nationalists and th Communists. **1 On the strength of** his singing voic he was accepted to the National Fu Hsing Dramatic Art Academy at the age of 11. Over the next eight years, h received 1) **intensive** training in Beijing 2) **opera**, learning t perform both *wusheng* (male 3) **warrior**) and *laosheng* (ol male) roles. An important part of his training was becomin a 4) **disciple** of Zhou Zheng-rong, one of Taiwan's mos famous Beijing Opera singers. This involved 5) **kowtowing** t the master in a formal 6) **ceremony**, which was attended by group of famous actors who **2 served as** witnesses. Maste Zhou not only taught him acting and singing, but als 7) **disciplined** him and served as a 9) **father figure**.

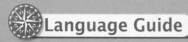

Vocabulary Bank

1) **intensive** [ɪnˋtɛnsɪv] (a.) 加強的，密集的
Craig has signed up for an intensive Japanese course this summer.

2) **opera** [ˋop(ə)rə] (n.) 歌劇
Did you enjoy the opera last night?

3) **warrior** [ˋwɔriɚ] (n.) 戰士
The warrior went to battle with his shield and sword.

4) **disciple** [dɪˋsaɪpəl] (n.) 門徒，追隨者
The disciples listened to the talk given by the Buddhist master.

5) **kowtow** [ˋkaʊˋtaʊ] 卑躬屈膝，叩頭
Brian is always kowtowing to the boss.

6) **ceremony** [ˋsɛrə͵moni] (n.) 儀式，典禮
The wedding ceremony was held at a small church.

7) **discipline** [ˋdɪsəplɪn] (v.) 教訓，懲罰
Sometimes, young children need to be disciplined.

8) **admission** [ədˋmɪʃən] (n.) 入學，進入許可
Betsy gained admission to one of Taiwan's top universities.

進階字彙

9) **father figure** [ˋfɑðɚ ˋfɪgjɚ] (n.) 扮演父親角色的人，父親角色般的導師
The young boy needs a father figure in his life.

10) **choreographer** [͵kɔriˋɑgrəfɚ] (n.) 編舞者
The singer hired a famous choreographer for her new video.

Language Guide

civil war 內戰
civil war 是指一個國家之中因黨派 (faction)、地區 (region) 之間的鬥爭而起的戰爭。文中提到的中國內戰 (Chinese civil war)，是指國民黨 (Nationalists [ˋnæʃənlɪsts]) 與共產黨 (Communists [ˋkɑmjʊ͵nɪsts]) 間的國共內戰。

After graduating from the arts academy, Wu was accepted to the Theater Department at Chinese Culture University. He was among the first group of students to gain [8]**admission** based on performing arts training rather than college entrance exam scores. In university, Wu was exposed to the Western theatrical tradition, studying Shakespeare and other classics. He also ❸ **came to the attention** of famous Taiwanese [10]**choreographer** Lin Huai-min, who invited him to join his Cloud Gate Dance Theater. Wu learned modern dance under Lin's instruction, and eventually became a lead dancer with the troupe. ⒼIt was there that he met his future wife, Lin Hsiu-wei, who was also a lead dancer.

Mini Quiz 閱讀測驗

❶ ____ **Which of the following is true about Zhou Zheng-rong?**
(A) He was Wu Hsing-kuo's father.
(B) He was a famous opera singer in Beijing.
(C) He punished Wu Hsing-kuo.
(D) He was a disciple of Wu Hsing-kuo.

❷ ____ **According to the passage, what is Lin Huai-min's job?**
(A) He takes pictures of dancers.
(B) He creates new dances.
(C) He is a dance teacher.
(D) He designs stage sets.

中 Translation

吳興國還是個小男孩時，父親就在國共內戰中喪生。由於嗓音出色，他在十一歲獲准進入國立復興劇校。接下來八年，他接受密集的京劇訓練，學習扮演武生及老生的角色。他受訓過程其中一件要事是，成為台灣京劇名角周正榮的門生。這包括在正式儀式中向師父叩首，一群知名演員在旁見證。周老師不只教他演技和唱工，也管教他，如師亦如父。

從劇校畢業後，吳興國考上中國文化大學戲劇系。他是第一批以術科演出而非大學聯考成績入學的學生。大學時代，吳興國接觸到西方戲劇傳統，研讀莎士比亞和其他經典。他也引起了台灣知名編舞家林懷民的注意，並受邀加入雲門舞集。吳興國在林懷民的指導下學習現代舞，最後成為舞團的首席舞者。他也在那裡結識未來的妻子，同為首席舞者的林秀偉。

林秀偉

Tongue-tied No More

❶ on the strength of... 因……之故

表示做決定的原因，一般用於有證據支持，或是得到承諾而做的決定。

A: I heard that murder suspect is a free man now.
聽說那個殺人嫌犯現在是自由之身。

B: Yeah. According to the paper, his case was dismissed on the strength of his testimony.
對啊，報上說他的案子因他的證詞而被撤銷。

❷ serve as... 擔任；充當

這個說法用於人，表示「擔任某種職務」；用於物，表示「充當某種用途的東西」。

A: Why does that guy on the TV screen look so familiar?
電視螢幕上那個人怎麼看起來那麼眼熟啊？

B: He served two terms as mayor.
他當過兩屆市長。

❸ come to the attention of.../ come to sb's attention 引起某人注意，某人獲悉

come to the attention of 就如同字面上的含義，當作「引起……注意」，但若是中間插入 somebody，就表示「某人知道、獲悉……」。

A: It's come to my attention that you've been late three times this week.
我有注意到你這星期已經遲到三次了。

B: Sorry. I'll try to be on time in the future.
抱歉，我之後會準時的。

Grammar Master

以 it 為首的強調句型

當我們想強調句子裡某事件、某時、某人等等的時候，可把欲強調事物前面加上虛主詞 it，並將整段話置於句首。

句型 It is/was + 欲強調事物 + that 子句

例 直述句：His words made me angry.
強調句：It was his words that made me angry.
他說的話讓我生氣。

翻譯練習
就是這輛計程車造成車禍。

______

______

翻譯練習解答
It was the taxi that caused the accident.
閱讀測驗解答 ❶ (C) ❷ (B)

Vocabulary Bank

1) **fulfill** [fʊlˋfɪl] (v.) 完成（任務等），執行（命令等）
The manager was fired for failing to fulfill his duties.

2) **accessible** [ækˋsɛsəbəl] (a.) 易被理解的，易被接受的
The author's history books are accessible to a general audience.

3) **contemporary** [kənˋtɛmpə͵rɛri] (a.) 當代的，同時代的
The gallery specializes in contemporary art.

4) **legend** [ˋlɛdʒənd] (n.) 傳奇，傳說
The Loch Ness Monster is just a legend.

5) **script** [skrɪpt] (n.)（戲劇、電影等）劇本
The director turns down most of the scripts he is offered.

6) **costume** [ˋkɑstum] (n.) 戲服，道具服
Do I have to wear a costume to the party?

7) **financing** [ˋfaɪ͵nænsɪŋ] (n.) 籌措（的）資金，提供（的）資金
It was difficult for businesses to obtain financing during the recession.

進階字彙

8) **military service** [ˋmɪlə͵tɛri ˋsɝvɪs] (phr.) 兵役
All Israelis are required to complete military service.

9) **mainlander** [ˋmen͵lændɚ] (n.) 大陸人，（台灣）外省人
Many mainlanders came to Taiwan in the late 1940s.

10) **dwindle** [ˋdwɪndəl] (v.) 漸漸減少
Public support for the war is dwindling.

11) **like-minded** [ˋlaɪkˋmaɪndɪd] (a.) 志趣相投的，看法一致的
Joining a club is a great way to meet like-minded people.

Language Guide

bachelor's degree 學士學位

世界各國學制不同，授予的學位因地而異，無法在此詳述。文中所說的 B.A.（人文科學學士）是 Bachelor of Arts 的縮寫，也可寫做 A.B.，指人文科目 (liberal arts) 、科學 (sciences) 或兩者的大學畢業學位。而專門鑽研科學的學士學位（如理工學院畢業生）為 B.S. (Bachelor of Science)。商學院學士則有偏管理行政的 B.B.A.（Bachelor of Business Administration），或偏數據統計的 B.S.B.A.（Bachelor of Science in Business Administration）。

至於碩士學位 (master's degree)，簡單來說就是把上述的 Bachelor of 改為 Master of（縮寫則把 B 改成 M）即可。而一般所謂的博士學位 Ph.D. 則為 Doctor of Philosophy 的縮寫。

朗讀 MP3 229 單字 MP3 230 英文文章導讀 MP3 231

On completing his B.A. in 1977, Wu joined the Lu Kuang Chinese Opera Company, a traditional opera troup run by the army, to [1]**fulfill** his two years of [8]**militar service**. He would continue performing with the compan for 15 years, and was a three-time winner of the Militar Golden Award for Best Actor. It was during this time tha Wu began to worry about the future of Beijing opera. H noticed that audiences—mostly aging [9]**mainlanders**—were [10]**dwindling**, and realized that in order to keep the a form alive, it had to be made more [2]**accessible** to the younge generation. He made it his life's goal to breathe ne life into Beijing opera, and, fortunately for theater love around the world, ended up succeeding **1** **beyond hi wildest dreams**.

In the early 1980s, actor and dancer Wu Hsing-ku was looking for a way to revive the dying art of Beijin opera, and he and a group of [11]**like-minded** friends bega discussing the possibility of creating an opera base on a Shakespeare play. He chose *Macbeth* ©because reminded him of traditional Chinese opera, renaming

Kingdom of Desire. Because the Lu-Kuang Chinese Opera Company, where Wu was working at the time, turned down his proposal, he and his wife, fellow dancer Lin Hsiu-wei, decided to form their own company, [3]**Contemporary** [4]**Legend** Theater. With no [5]**script**, no [6]**costumes** and no [7]**financing**, the young artists **2 had their work cut out for** them.

Mini Quiz 閱讀測驗

1 Why did Wu Hsing-kuo worry about the future of Beijing opera?

(A) Because fewer and fewer people were attending performances
(B) Because aging mainlanders were losing interest in the art form
(C) Because the younger generation couldn't afford to buy tickets
(D) Because opera troupes were forgetting how to perform it

2 What does the phrase "the young artists had their work cut out for them" mean?

(A) The young artists lost their jobs.
(B) They were each assigned different tasks.
(C) They had a difficult task ahead of them.
(D) The artists decided to quit working.

中 Translation

一九七七年拿到學士學位後，吳興國加入陸光劇團——軍方經營的傳統戲曲劇團——服完兩年兵役。他繼續跟著陸光劇團演出十五年，三度贏得國軍文藝金像獎的最佳男演員獎。這段期間他開始擔心京劇的未來。他注意到觀眾——多半是年邁的外省人——正在凋零，並了解要讓這種藝術形式生生不息，必須更親近年輕一代。他將賦予京劇新生命列為終身志業，而且讓全球戲劇愛好者感到慶幸的是，他最後的成就遠超過他的想像。

一九八〇年代初期，演員兼舞者吳興國努力尋找途徑振興垂危的京劇藝術，他和一群志同道合的朋友開始討論以莎士比亞戲劇為藍本來創作京劇的可能性。他選擇了《馬克白》——因為這部劇本讓他想起傳統的中國戲曲，並改名為《慾望城國》。因為吳興國當時服務的陸光劇團拒絕了他的提案，他和同為舞者的妻子林秀偉遂決定成立自己的劇團：當代傳奇劇場。在沒有劇本、沒有戲服又缺乏資金之下，這群年輕藝術家面臨極大的挑戰。

Tongue-tied No More

1 beyond one's wildest dreams 超乎某人的想像

wildest dreams 是指想像不受限、期待無上限的事物，經常會說 beyond one's wildest dreams 即「超乎某人的想像」。另一個類似的說法是 never in one's wildest dreams「想都沒想過，連想都不敢想」。

A: If you could have one wish, what would it be?
如果你可以許一個願望，你會許什麼？

B: I'd want to be rich beyond my wildest dreams.
我會想要有錢得不得了。

2 have one's work cut out for one 有苦差事等著某人

這個說法一般都用於描述未來要發生的事情。

A: I have three finals next week and I haven't started studying yet!
我下星期有三科期末考，我都還沒開始念書！

B: Sounds like you have your work cut out for you.
看來你有得拚了。

Grammar Master

because 的用法

中文經常說「因為……，所以……」，但要注意 Because + S +V..., S +V ... 句型的主要子句不加 so。because 的使用幾個重點：

- because 在句首或句中，用來修飾主要子句。放在句首的時候，與主要子句要以逗號相隔，放在句中時則不用。

例 Because he is shy, he can't make friends easily.（主要子句：he can't make friends easily）

= He can't make friends easily because he is shy.
因為他很害羞，他不容易交到朋友。

- 若表原因的不是一個句子，而是一個片語或名詞，則用 because of。

例 Our flight was delayed because of bad weather.
我們的班機因為天候不佳延遲了。

翻譯練習

我們不能參加派對，因為我們要出城去。

____

____

翻譯練習解答
We can't go to the party because we'll be out of town. / Because we'll be out of town, we can't go to the party.
閱讀測驗解答 1 (A) 2 (C)

Vocabulary Bank

1) **recruit** [rɪˋkrut] (v.) 招募，招收
The company recruited new employees at the job fair.

2) **premiere** [prɪˋmɪr] (v./n.) 初次上演；首映會
The final season of the series premieres next week.

進階字彙

3) **virtuous** [ˋvɝtʃuəs] (a.) 有道德的，貞潔的
Christians believe that only virtuous people go to heaven.

4) **ovation** [oˋveʃən] (n.) 熱烈鼓掌
The crowd gave the singer a standing ovation at the end of the concert.

5) **full house** [fʊl haʊs] (phr.) 客滿
The show's organizers are expecting a full house on opening night.

6) **cross-dressing** [ˋkrɔsˋdrɛsɪŋ] (n./a.) 穿異性服裝（的）
(v.) cross-dress [ˋkrɔsˋdrɛs]
The woman was disturbed by her husband's cross-dressing.

7) **absurdist** [əbˋsɝdɪst] (a./n.) 荒謬主義的，荒謬主義者
Frank had a hard time understanding the absurdist play.

Tongue-tied No More

1 a labor of love
甜蜜的負荷

a labor of love 是指「做起來艱苦又得不到實質回饋，但仍讓人甘之如飴，心甘情願去做的事」。對話中 Carol 是在玩 labor 的雙關語（表示「苦勞」，同時也是「生產」）。

A: Does Daniel get paid for coaching the little league soccer team?
丹尼爾指導兒童聯盟足球隊有支薪嗎？

B: No. It's a labor of love.
沒有。很辛苦，但他樂在其中。

朗讀 MP3 232 單字 MP3 233 英文文章導讀 MP3 234

They eventually found a graduate student wh was willing to adapt Shakespeare's script, which took year, and [1]**recruited** volunteers to produce the sets an costumes. It was a **1 labor of love** for everyone involve With Wu cast in the lead role, all they needed now wa a Lady Macbeth. They offered the role to Wei Hai-min, leading performer of *qingyi* ([3]**virtuous** lady) roles—bu without pay. Luckily, she accepted, and after three year of hard work, *Kingdom of Desire* was finally ready for th stage in 1986. The players were all nerves on openin night—they were doing something totally new, and ha no idea how the audience would react. They needn't hav worried. At the end of the final act, as Wu fell to the stag from a high wall, body full of arrows, the audience gave standing [4]**ovation**.

With the success of *Kingdom of Desire*, Contemporar Legend Theater became a huge sensation. After playin to [5]**full houses** in Taiwan, they brought *Kingdom* t 26 cities around the world in the 1990s and beyonc The company went on to produce more adaptations c Western classics, including Shakespeare's *Hamlet* and *Th*

Tempest, and Greek tragedies like *Medea* and *Oresteia*. Amazingly, Wu decided to take on *King Lear* all by himself, playing 10 different roles, both male and female ([6]**cross-dressing** is a tradition in Beijing opera). The company has also taken on more contemporary material, including *Waiting for Godot*, an [7]**absurdist** play by Samuel Beckett. Contemporary Legend's latest work, *Run! Chekhov!*, a multimedia production based on Chekhov's short stories, will [2]**premiere** at the National Theater Concert Hall in October.

Mini Quiz 閱讀測驗

1. **How did the audience react on the opening night of *Kingdom of Desire*?**
   (A) They stood up and clapped.
   (B) They were on the edge of their seats.
   (C) They walked out quietly.
   (D) They jumped up and cheered.

2. **What does the term "cross-dressing" mean?**
   (A) Wearing women's dresses
   (B) Wearing men's and women's clothing at the same time
   (C) Wearing different clothes for different roles
   (D) Dressing in clothes usually worn by the opposite sex

中 Translation

他們最後找到一名研究生願意改編莎士比亞的劇本，歷時一年完成，並召募志工製作布景和戲服。對於每一個參與的人來說，這都是完全出於喜愛、不計報酬之事。既然有吳興國擔綱主角，現在只缺一位馬克白夫人。他們去找頂尖的青衣（貞潔女性）魏海敏，希望她演出該角——但沒有酬勞，幸好她欣然接受，經過三年的努力之後，《慾望城國》終於在一九八六年搬上舞台。首演當晚，演員們無不緊張不安——他們做的是全新創舉，完全不知觀眾會有什麼樣的反應。他們的擔心是多餘的。最後一幕結束時，當萬箭穿身的吳興國從一面高牆墜落舞台，觀眾紛紛起立鼓掌。

《慾望城國》成功後，當代傳奇劇場也隨之爆紅。在台灣場場滿座之後，他們從一九九〇年代起將《慾望城國》帶到世界二十六座城市。該劇團隨後製作更多西方經典改編戲劇，包括莎士比亞的《哈姆雷特》和《暴風雨》，以及《米蒂亞》和《奧瑞斯提亞》等希臘悲劇。令人驚訝的是，吳興國決定一肩挑起《李爾王》的演出，扮演十個不同角色，男女皆有（反串是京劇的一項傳統）。劇團也挑戰較現代的題材，包括山繆爾貝契特的荒謬劇《等待果陀》。當代傳奇劇場的最新作品《歡樂時光——契訶夫傳奇》是根據契訶夫短篇小說改編的多媒體作品，將於十月在國家兩廳院首演。

若有疑問請來信：eztalkQ@gmail.com

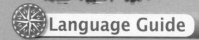

Language Guide

當代傳奇劇場經典演出

***The Kingdom of Desire*《慾望城國》**
改編自莎翁劇 *Macbeth*《馬克白》

***War and Eternity*《王子復仇記》**
改編自莎翁悲劇 *Hamlet*《哈姆雷特》

***The Tempest*《暴風雨》**
改編自同名莎翁劇

***King Lear*《李爾王在此》**
改編自同名莎翁劇

***Medea*《樓蘭女》**
改編自同名希臘悲劇

***Oresteia*《奧瑞斯提亞》**
改編自同名希臘悲劇

Waiting for Godot《等待果陀》

是一九六九年的諾貝爾文學獎得主 Samuel Beckett（山繆爾貝契特，1906-1989）最有名的劇本，為荒謬派戲劇 (absurdist play) 的經典。荒謬劇是一九四〇至六〇年代興起於歐洲的戲劇流派，刻意摒棄傳統戲劇的語言情節邏輯性，以象徵、暗喻來表現主題，常常用荒誕可笑的對白、光怪陸離的形象、甚至雜耍，來否認人類存在的意義，表達對世界悲觀的態度，因此時常被稱做「黑色喜劇」black comedy。

Run! Chekhov!《契訶夫傳奇》

由俄國劇作家 Anton Chekhov（安東契訶夫，1860-1904）的十四篇小說交錯連貫而成，台灣知名作家張大春改編。Chekhov 的祖先世代為農奴，至一九四一年祖父才贖回一家自由之身。由於父親經商失敗，就讀莫斯科大學醫學院的 Chekhov 開始寫作賺取稿費貼補家用。Chekhov 的作品主要是短篇小說及劇本，忠實反映俄國一九〇五年大革命前夕資產階級知識分子的苦悶，是十九世紀末偉大的現實主義作家。

- 詳細劇情及精美劇照請見當代傳奇劇場網站
  http://www.twclt.com/

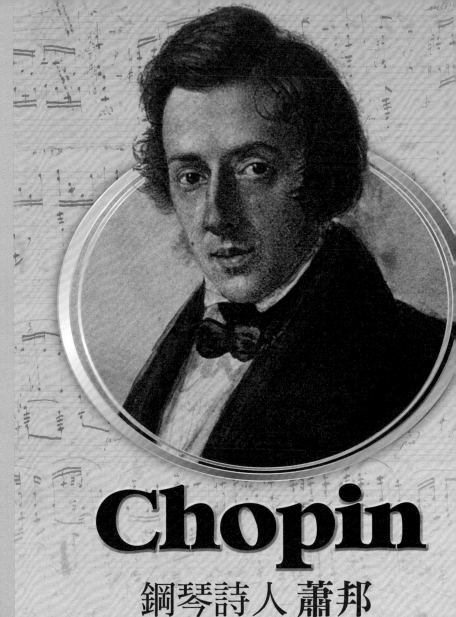

Vocabulary Bank

1) **compose** [kəm`poz] (v.) 作曲，創作（音樂、詩）
(n.) composition [͵kɑmpə`zɪʃən]
Who composed the music for this film?

2) **surpass** [sɚ`pæs] (v.) 勝過，超越
The athlete's record has never been surpassed.

3) **proceed** [prə`sid] (v.) 開始進行，繼續進行
Mary sat down and proceeded to tell me about her weekend.

4) **head** [hɛd] (v.)（朝特定方向）前往
Where are you headed?

5) **disturb** [dɪ`stɝb] (v.) 使憂慮，使不安
Some people may be disturbed by the violence in the film.

6) **patriot** [`petriət] (n.) 愛國的人
John Wayne was a true patriot.

7) **frail** [frel] (a.) 虛弱的，不堅實的
The man became frail in his old age.

進階字彙

8) **conservatory** [kən`sɝvə͵tɔri] (n.)（音樂或戲劇）專科學校
Erika studied violin at a conservatory in Vienna.

9) **acclaim** [ə`klem] (n./v.)（尤指對藝術成就的）稱譽，高度評價
(a.) acclaimed [ə`klemd] 受到讚揚的
The director's films have earned international acclaim.

Language Guide

polonaise 波蘭舞曲

polonaise [polə`nez] 的法文意思是「波蘭的」，是一種四分之三拍子，中等或偏慢速度的舞曲。典型的特徵是每小節的第一拍通常會有十六分音符。原本是十六世紀後半波蘭宮廷的舞蹈，後來也成為民族舞蹈且廣泛在節慶上使用。由於瑞典國王齊格蒙特三世 (Zygmunt III Waza) 曾經兼任波蘭國王，波蘭舞曲和瑞典的民俗舞蹈 polska（波爾斯卡）十分相似。而蕭邦的波蘭舞曲通常是三段或是迴旋曲式的鋼琴獨奏曲，最著名的為降 A 大調波蘭舞曲 op. 53（又名《英雄》，本頁蕭邦畫像的底圖即為《英雄》手稿），強烈的節奏表現出蕭邦對祖國波蘭的熱愛。

concerto 協奏曲

concerto [kən`tʃɝto] 是指一件或數件獨奏樂器（如鋼琴、小提琴等）和樂團協同演奏，既有對比又相互交融的作品。通常由三個樂章組成，第一章為奏鳴曲式，一般為快板且富戲劇性，先是樂團演奏，再由獨奏樂器與樂團合奏。第二樂章通常為柔板、慢板或行板的三部曲式，而迴旋曲式的第三樂章則為急版，常具有節慶的氣氛。協奏曲結合了獨奏的樂器技巧和樂團的交響性，可以同時滿足聽眾兩種不同的需求。

Chopin

鋼琴詩人 蕭邦

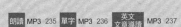

朗讀 MP3 235 單字 MP3 236 英文文章導讀 MP3 237

Frédéric Chopin was born in Zelazowa Wola, a small village near Warsaw, on February 22, 1810 to a French father and a Polish mother. He spent his childhood living at the Warsaw Lyceum, where his father Nicolas taught French. Chopin began playing the piano when he was just four years old, and by the age of six he was creating his own melodies. Recognizing his talent, his parents hired a professional piano teacher, Wojciech Żywny, who introduced him to the Classical works of Bach and Mozart. Just one year later, Chopin began 1)**composing** polonaises and giving public performances. He soon 2)**surpassed** his teacher, and 3)**proceeded** to pursue formal music studies at the Warsaw

Lyceum and later at the Warsaw [8]**Conservatory**. By the age of 15, Chopin was considered the best pianist in Warsaw.

After finishing his studies, like many young musicians of his age, Chopin [4]**headed** to Vienna, the musical capital of Europe, in 1829. He made his debut at the prestigious Royal Court Theater, where he performed several of his own compositions to great [9]**acclaim**. He then returned to Warsaw, where he debuted his two piano concertos, which were influenced by Polish folk music, at the National Theater, and began working on his famous études. [5]**Disturbed** by rumors of a coming war between Poland and Russia, Chopin's family [G]convinced him to leave the country for his own safety. Although he was a [6]**patriot** and wanted to fight for his country, his [7]**frail** health wouldn't allow it. And so, in November 1830, Chopin left for Vienna carrying a silver cup filled with soil from his native land.

Mini Quiz 閱讀測驗

1. **According to the article, how many schools did Chopin study music at?**
   (A) one
   (B) two
   (C) three
   (D) four

2. **Why did Chopin leave Poland for the second time?**
   (A) To debut several of his compositions
   (B) To seek medical treatment for his frail health
   (C) Because his parents feared that war was coming
   (D) Because he wanted to fight for his country

中 Translation

蕭邦一八一〇年二月二十二日出生於華沙附近的小村落澤拉左瓦沃拉，父母親分別為法國人及波蘭人。他的童年在華沙中學度過，父親尼可拉斯在那裡教法語。蕭邦四歲就開始彈鋼琴，六歲便會自己作曲。雙親看出他的才華，於是聘請專業鋼琴老師齊微尼，教他彈奏巴哈和莫札特的經典名曲。短短一年後，蕭邦便開始創作波蘭舞曲，並公開演出。他很快青出於藍而勝於藍，先後進入華沙中學及華沙音樂學校繼續接受正規音樂教育。十五歲的時候，蕭邦就被視為華沙最傑出的鋼琴家。

學校畢業後，一如許多同時期的年輕音樂家，蕭邦在一八二九年前往歐洲音樂之都維也納。他在名聞遐邇的皇家音樂廳首度登台，演奏數首自創曲，大獲好評。接著他回到華沙，在國家戲劇院首次發表兩首具有波蘭民謠風味的鋼琴協奏曲，並開始創作他知名的練習曲。因波蘭與俄羅斯即將開戰的謠言感到不安，蕭邦的家人說服他為安全起見離開波蘭。雖然他很愛國，想為祖國奮戰，但他虛弱的身體不允許。於是，一八三〇年十一月，蕭邦帶著一個裝滿故鄉土壤的銀杯前往維也納。

Language Guide

étude 練習曲

étude 在法文中是「學習」的意思，通常是用來訓練某種樂器特定技巧的音樂作品。在十九世紀早期鋼琴開始普及時，練習曲也陸續出現。練習曲是利用反覆單純的技巧彈奏做為練習，以打下演奏基礎，但是也有難度較高的練習曲，當作演奏會曲目也完全不遜色，蕭邦的練習曲便屬於此類。

蕭邦年

二〇一〇年恰逢偉大的音樂家蕭邦誕辰二百周年，波蘭政府為紀念這位名垂千古的鋼琴詩人，在波蘭華沙舉辦了為期一年的「蕭邦年」紀念活動。擔綱在蕭邦的故鄉波蘭舉辦的「蕭邦年」開幕音樂會的正是來自中國的鋼琴家郎朗，他也是唯一被邀請在「蕭邦年」開幕音樂會上演奏的鋼琴家。二月二十八日在克拉科夫教堂由大主教主持莊嚴彌撒，舉行安放蕭邦紀念徽的儀式。八月舉行的「蕭邦和他的歐洲」Chopin and His Europe 國際音樂節中，舉辦了五十個不同的活動，超過千餘位表演者參與交響音樂會、爵士音樂會和廣場音樂會等不同表演。
十月則將舉行第十六屆「蕭邦國際鋼琴比賽」。比賽期間將會有紀念蕭邦逝世一百六十一周年的紀念活動，活動的最後也會演奏莫扎特的《d 小調安魂彌撒》，實現蕭邦臨終前的遺願。

Grammar Master

convince 的用法

convince 是「說服，勸說」的意思，文中使用的句型為 convince sb. + to V 也就是說服某人去做某事。

例 I convinced Jerry to lend me his camera.
我說服傑瑞把他的相機借給我。

- 後面接名詞的句型為 convince sb. of N

例 The defendant convinced the jury of his innocence.
這個被告說服陪審團相信他是清白的。

- 後面也可接子句，句型是 convince sb. + that S + V.

例 Jacky convinced me that she was telling the truth.
傑奇說服我相信她說的是實話。

翻譯練習

Dan 的父母說服他申請大學。

____

____

翻譯練習解答
Dan's parents convinced him to apply to the university.
閱讀測驗解答
1 (B) 2 (C)

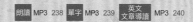

朗讀 MP3 238 單字 MP3 239 英文文章導讀 MP3 240

Warsaw fell to the Russians soon after Chopin's [1]**departur** and the young [11]**virtuoso** decided to settle in Paris, whic was becoming home to a growing community of Polis [2]**exiles.** Chopin became prominent in Parisian artistic circle making friends with authors like Victor Hugo, painters lik Delacroix, and wealthy art [3]**patrons** like the Rothschild Along with other young composers like Liszt, Berlio and Mendelssohn, he became a leading member of th Romantic movement, which sought freedom from Classic [4]**restrictions** and emphasized emotion over reason. Becaus his [5]**delicate** playing style wasn't suited to large concert Chopin played mostly at private [12]**salons**, and supporte himself by giving piano lessons to the daughters of wealth [13]**aristocrats**. He became a French citizen during this period, and would never again return to Poland.

喬治桑
（繪於一八三八年）

巴黎拉雪茲神父公墓中的

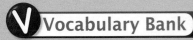

Vocabulary Bank

1) **departure** [dɪˋpɑrtʃɚ] (n.) 出發，離站
(v.) depart [dɪˋpɑrt]
Our departure was delayed by bad weather.

2) **exile** [ˋɛgzaɪl] (n.) 流亡國外（者），離鄉背井
Many Cuban exiles live in Miami.

3) **patron** [ˋpetrən] (n.)（藝術家的）贊助人，資助者
The billionaire is a well-known patron of the arts.

4) **restriction** [rɪˋstrɪkʃən] (n.) 限制
Cheap air tickets usually have lots of restrictions.

5) **delicate** [ˋdɛlɪkət] (a.) 細膩的，精細的
The dress was decorated with delicate lace.

6) **damp** [dæmp] (a.) 潮濕的
We dried our damp socks by the fire.

7) **symptom** [ˋsɪmptəm] (n.) 症狀
The symptoms of food poisoning include stomach pain and fever.

8) **tuberculosis** [tʊˏbɝkjəˋlosɪs] (n.) 結核病
Some types of tuberculosis are resistant to drugs.

9) **productive** [prəˋdʌktɪv] (a.) 多產的，有生產力的
Some employees are more productive than others.

10) **estate** [ɪsˋtet] (n.) 地產，莊園
The estate includes a big house, a tennis court and swimming pool.

進階字彙

11) **virtuoso** [ˏvɝtʃuˋoso] (n.) 藝術或音樂的行家、大師
Yo-Yo Ma is a cello virtuoso.

12) **salon** [səˋlɑn] (n.) 沙龍（舊時作家、藝術家等在名流家中定期舉行的聚會）
The writer was a member of a literary salon.

13) **aristocrat** [əˋrɪstəˏkræt] (n.) 貴族
Many aristocrats were killed in the revolution.

In 1836, at a party hosted by Liszt's mistress, Chopin met George Sand, a French Romantic novelist who dressed like a man and smoked cigars. She became his lover and patron, and decided to take him to Majorca in the winter of 1838, thinking the warm weather would be good for his health. It turned out to be cold and [6]**damp**, Ⓖhowever, and Chopin began showing [7]**symptoms** of [8]**tuberculosis**. ⒼNevertheless, he managed to compose his famous 24 preludes while on the island. Chopin spent happy, [9]**productive** summers at Sand's [10]**estate** at Nohant in the early 1840s, but the couple broke up in 1847, and his health continued to deteriorate. He gave his final concert the following year, and passed away in October 1849 at the age of 39. **1 In accordance with** his will, Chopin's heart was removed and returned to Poland.

Mini Quiz 閱讀測驗

1. **Which of the following is true about George Sand?**
   (A) She was Chopin's mistress.
   (B) Sand helped Chopin compose music.
   (C) He liked to wear woman's clothing.
   (D) She owned property in Nohant.

2. **How did Chopin make a living in Paris?**
   (A) By playing at salons
   (B) By associating with wealthy art patrons
   (C) By giving large concerts
   (D) By teaching piano

中 Translation

蕭邦離開後不久，華沙便淪入俄羅斯之手，這位年輕的音樂好手決定定居巴黎，那裡逐漸成為人數日增的流亡海外波蘭人的家園。蕭邦在巴黎藝術界嶄露頭角，結交雨果等作家、德拉克洛瓦等畫家，以及羅斯契爾德等藝術贊助富豪。連同李斯特、白遼士和孟德爾頌等年輕作曲家，他成了浪漫運動的領導成員——一項力求擺脫古典束縛、強調情緒重於理性的運動。他的演奏風格細膩，不適合大型音樂會，於是蕭邦大多在私人沙龍演奏，教授富裕貴族的女兒鋼琴維生。他在這段期間成為法國公民，此後再也沒回波蘭。

一八三六年，在一場由李斯特的情婦舉辦的派對上，蕭邦遇到法國浪漫主義小說家喬治桑，她穿著像個男士、抽著雪茄。她成了他的情人兼贊助人，並在一八三八年冬天決定帶他前往西班牙馬略卡島，認為那裡溫暖的氣候對蕭邦的健康有益。結果那裡既冷又濕，蕭邦開始出現結核病的症狀。儘管如此，他仍在旅居馬略卡島期間譜出他著名的二十四首前奏曲。一八四〇年代初期，蕭邦在喬治桑位於諾安的莊園度過愉快而多產的夏日，但這對情侶在一八四七年分手，而蕭邦的健康持續惡化。隔年他舉辦個人最後一場演奏會，然後於一八四九年十月逝世，得年三十九。遵照他的遺願，蕭邦的心臟被取出，送回波蘭。

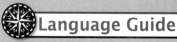

Tongue-tied No More

1 in accordance with 依照，與……一致

accordance [ə`kɔrdəns] 是「依照，依據」的意思，而 in accordance with 是比較正式的用法。

例 Please complete this form in accordance with the instructions.
請依照指示填好表格。

Language Guide

Romantic movement 浪漫主義運動

浪漫主義運動肇始於十八世紀晚期至十九世紀初期，由歐洲許多藝術家、詩人、作家、音樂家、以及政治家、哲學家等各種人物所推動。許多知識分子和歷史學家將浪漫主義視為對啟蒙運動的反彈。啟蒙時代的思想家強調演繹推理的絕對性，而浪漫主義則強調直覺、想像力、和感覺，以具有強烈情感的藝術和文學來反抗，突破了藝術的傳統定義，甚至被評為「非理性主義」。

prelude 前奏曲

prelude [`prɛlud] 沒有固定曲式，是一種短樂曲。通常用在曲子開始前，當作引子先隱約披露主旋律或動機，功用等同書的前言。但到了浪漫主義時期，蕭邦的二十四首鋼琴前奏曲就沒有遵照這個模式，而是具有浪漫與幻想風格的獨立作品。

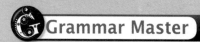

Grammar Master

連接性副詞

與只能連接「子句」的「副詞連接詞」(because、unless、if ……等）不同，「連接性副詞」的用法和意思比較接近「對等連接詞」（and、but、or ……等），可以連接兩個獨立的「句子」。此類副詞前的句子要有分號相隔，或直接打句點；與後面的句子則以逗號相隔。注意唯 howerver 可插入句中，前後以逗號相隔。nevertheless、however 、nontheless 都是具對等連接詞「but」意味的連接性副詞。

例 You're well qualified for the position. Nevertheless, we've decided to hire another candidate.
你有資格擔任此職位，不過我們決定要雇用另一位候選人。

翻譯練習

我們的旅行每一天都下雨，不過我們還是玩得很高興。

____

____

翻譯練習解答
It rained every day on our trip. Nevertheless/However/
Nonetheless, we still had a good time.
閱讀測驗解答 1 (D) 2 (D)

V Vocabulary Bank

1) **estimated** [ˋɛstə͵metɪd] (a.) 估計的
Warren Buffett has an estimated wealth of $50 billion dollars.

2) **tune in** [tun ɪn] (phr.) 選台收看、收聽，鎖定
Be sure to tune in tomorrow for the final episode.

3) **critically** [ˋkrɪtɪkli] (adv.) 評論上
Most of the director's films have been critically successful.

4) **strip** [strɪp] (v.) 脫衣，表演脫衣舞，strip club 即「脫衣舞俱樂部」
Everybody stripped and jumped into the lake.

5) **rhythm** [ˋrɪðəm] (n.) 節奏，韻律
You need a good sense of rhythm to dance well.

6) **bass (guitar)** [ˋbes] (n.) 貝斯吉他，低音提琴
The band's lead singer also plays bass.

7) **session** [ˋsɛʃən] (n.) 一段（用來進行特定活動的）時間
How long did your massage session last?

進階字彙

8) **hone** [hon] (v.) 磨鍊
Patrick is going to a cram school to hone his math skills.

9) **repertoire** [ˋrɛpɚ͵twɑr] (n.)（某人、樂團等）全部作品、技藝、表演項目
The band has added several new songs to their repertoire.

10) **cover** [ˋkʌvɚ] (n.) 翻唱的曲子，翻唱
The band started out playing Rolling Stones covers.

11) **groom** [grum] (v.)（為了特定目標）培養，訓練
Robert is being groomed for a management position.

口語補充

12) **fab** [fæb] (a.) 超棒的，是 fabulous 的縮略
Becky looks fab in her new outfit.

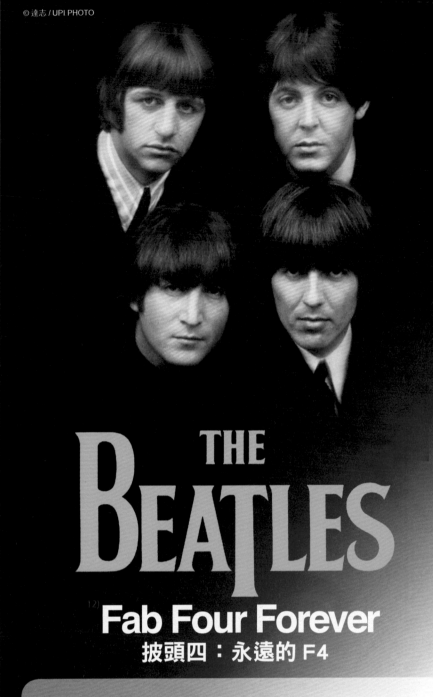

THE BEATLES

[12] Fab Four Forever
披頭四：永遠的 F4

朗讀 MP3 241 單字 MP3 242 英文文章導讀 MP3 243

On February 9, 1964, four young men with mop-top haircuts from Liverpool, England performed live on *The Ed Sullivan Show* in New York. It was their first American appearance, and an [1] **estimated** 74 million viewers—40% of the population—[2] **tuned in**. During the U.S. concert tour that followed later that year, fans screamed so loud that nobody could even hear the music. Beatlemania had 1 **crossed the pond**, and the "British Invasion" had begun. Pop music and pop culture would never be the same again.

The Beatles, arguably the most successful and [3]**critically** acclaimed group of all time, had their beginnings in the late 1950s, when teenage friends John Lennon, Paul McCartney and George Harrison began playing music together in Liverpool. The three sang and played guitars with various drummers and bass players, and in 1960 they were invited to play at a [4]**strip** club in Hamburg, Germany, where they [8]**honed** their [9]**repertoire** of Chuck Berry and Buddy Holly [10]**covers**. While playing at the Cavern Club back in Liverpool, the Beatles caught the eye of record store owner and music critic Brian Epstein, who [11]**groomed** them and got them a recording contract with EMI's Parlophone label in 1962.

After the release of their first single, "Love Me Do," Lennon ([5]**rhythm** guitar), Harrison (lead guitar) and McCartney ([6]**bass**) were joined by Ringo Starr (drums) for the Beatles' debut album, *Please Please Me*. Recorded in a single 10-hour [7]**session** on February 11, 1963 at London's Abbey Road Studios, the album reached No. 1 in the U.K., and marked the beginning of their rise to pop stardom.

中 Translation

一九六四年二月九日，四個來自英國利物浦，留拖把頭的年輕男子（編註：整片留海齊眉蓋住額頭的中長髮型），在紐約《蘇利文秀》節目現場演出。這是他們第一次在美國亮相，估計有七千四百萬人—占總人口四成—收看。在同年稍後的美國巡迴演唱會上，樂迷的尖叫聲大到根本沒人聽得見音樂。披頭四狂熱席捲大西洋彼岸，「英倫侵略」已然展開。自此，流行樂和流行文化永遠改變。

堪稱史上最成功、最受好評團體的披頭四，在一九五〇年代晚期發跡，當時約翰藍儂、保羅麥卡尼和喬治哈里遜這三位青少年好友開始在利物浦一起玩音樂。三人自彈吉他自唱，搭配過多名鼓手和貝斯手，後於一九六〇年應邀至德國漢堡一家脫衣舞俱樂部演出，在此磨練查克貝瑞和巴迪霍萊（編註：兩者均為美國搖滾樂先驅）的曲目。後來三人回到利物浦，在洞穴俱樂部演出時獲得唱片行老闆兼樂評人布萊恩艾普斯坦的青睞，他訓練他們，讓他們在一九六二年取得科藝百代旗下帕洛風公司的唱片約。

在推出首支單曲〈好好愛我〉之後，林哥史達（鼓手）加入藍儂（節奏吉他手）、哈里遜（主吉他手）和麥卡尼（貝斯手）的陣容，一起錄製披頭四首張專輯《請取悅我》。這張專輯於一九六三年二月十一日在倫敦修道院路錄音室僅花十小時就一次錄製完成，一舉登上英國排行榜冠軍，也成為他們崛起為流行巨星的起點。

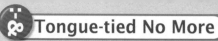

Tongue-tied No More

1 cross the pond 到大西洋彼岸

這個片語將分隔英美兩個英語區的大西洋 (Atlantic Ocean) 比喻成小水池，是戲謔的說法。cross 是動詞「越過」，如果改成介係詞 across，就是「在對岸」的意思。

例 Many British actors are more successful across the pond.
很多英國演員在美國比較紅。

Language Guide

The Ed Sullivan Show

《蘇利文現場秀》是美國最具代表性的綜藝節目之一，從一九四八開始至一九七年，是少數在同個頻道上播映超過二十年的節目。這個從歌劇、流行樂、即興喜劇、芭蕾…等，甚至連馬戲團表演都有的綜藝節目，混合著前一個世代的輕歌舞劇 (vaudeville) 元素，搭配主持風格古拙的主持人，形成節目的一股奇特魅力。

曾在這個綜藝節目上表演的傳奇巨星如貓王 (Elvis Presley)、滾石合唱團 (The Rolling Stones)、傑克森兄弟 (The Jackson 5) ……等比比皆是。一九六四年二月九日披頭四合唱團 (The Beatles) 初次在美登台的《蘇利文現場秀》更是創下收視紀錄，至今仍是電視史上單集收視率最高的節目之一。

Beatlemania

一提到「披頭四狂熱」，大批高聲尖叫得幾乎進入歇斯底里狀態的青少女馬上就會浮現腦海，因為 Beatlemania 正是 The Beatles（披頭四）和 mania（瘋狂、狂熱）兩字結合而成。當時披頭四樂團風靡全英國，首次跨海從英國抵達美國甘迺迪機場，即被一群瘋狂迷妹包圍，當晚在《蘇利文現場秀》表演之後，「披頭四狂熱」便正式席捲美國，不論是演唱會或披頭四出現的旅途上，都會發現這群超級追星族的身影與尖叫聲。

字尾用 mania 來形容某種狂熱、迷戀的字眼，Beatlemania 並非先例。早先古典音樂風行歐洲時，鋼琴家李斯特 (Franz Liszt) 就已引起一陣 Lisztomania（李斯特狂熱）。這種將流行人物與英文字結合的用法也並專屬披頭四樂團，最近的 Linsanity「林來瘋」便是另一個絕佳例子；但當然，Beatlemania 蔚為奇觀的極度痴迷，絕對是空前絕後，無人能及。

British Invasion

一九五〇年代，美國搖滾歌手在全球掀起一陣旋風，英國青年爭相模仿美國搖滾重節奏又帶著叛逆色彩的音樂風格。六〇年代中期，搖滾樂在英國產生了全新風貌，披頭四樂團、滾石合唱團、奇想樂團 (The Kinks) 以排山倒海之氣勢將英國搖滾樂帶入美國，開啟英國樂團在美國音樂及娛樂市場之大門。這股在當時遍及美國及加拿大、澳洲等地樂壇的「哈英」風潮即稱為 British Invasion。

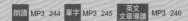

朗讀 MP3 244 單字 MP3 245 英文文章導讀 MP3 246

Over the next few years, the Beatles toured the world and recorded hit singles like "I Want to Hold Your Hand" and "Can't Buy Me Love." In April 1964, the latter became the first single ever to top the U.K. and U.S. charts 1) **simultaneously**. The world just **1** **couldn't get enough of** the Fab Four. In addition to putting out hits, the Beatles also starred in movies like *A Hard Day's Night and Help!*, and were heavily 2) **merchandised**. Fans could buy anything from Beatles dolls and lunchboxes to clothing and 3) **wigs**. There was even a Beatles cartoon that aired in the U.S. from 1965 to '69.

There was more to the Beatles, however, than just love songs and 7) **teenyboppers**. A meeting with Bob Dylan in 1964 led them to experiment with different musical styles (and drugs) and develop a more mature sound, which can be heard on 1965's *Rubber Soul*. Controversy 4) **erupted** in 1966 when Lennon told a British reporter, "Christianity will go…we're more popular than Jesus now." While the comment 5) **went unnoticed** in England, the band began receiving death threats in the U.S., and radio stations in the Bible Belt stopped playing their songs.

The Beatles stopped touring in August 1966, but produced their most groundbreaking music in the subsequent years before breaking up in 1970. Their 1967 concept album, *Sgt. Pepper's Lonely Hearts Club Band*, was hailed for its innovative sounds and deep lyrics. Their influences had expanded to Eastern 8) **spirituality** and psychedelic drugs, evident in songs like "Lucy

Vocabulary Bank

1) **simultaneously** [ˌsaɪməlˋteniəsli] (adv.) 同時地
Everyone in the room was talking simultaneously.

2) **merchandise** [ˋmɝtʃənˌdaɪz] (v.) 推銷，在此指「做周邊產品」
The Star Wars movies were merchandised into toys, games and comic books.

3) **wig** [wɪg] (n.) 假髮
Judges in the U.K. still wear white wigs.

4) **erupt** [ɪˋrʌpt] (v.) 爆發，噴發
Police are afraid the demonstration will erupt into violence.

5) **go unnoticed** [go ʌnˋnotɪst] (phr.) 沒被發現，沒被注意
I hope all your hard work won't go unnoticed.

6) **defining** [dɪˋfaɪnɪŋ] (a.) 關鍵的，代表性的
The Berlin Wall was the defining symbol of the Cold War.

進階字彙

7) **teenybopper** [ˋtiniˌbɑpɚ] (n.) 趕流行、追星的青少年，尤指少女
The boy band is popular with teenyboppers.

8) **spirituality** [ˌspɪrɪtʃuˋæləti] (n.) 靈修，宗教信仰
Religious leaders are worried about the decline in spirituality.

in the Sky with Diamonds." Forty years later, the Beatles remain the best selling act of all time, and the [6]**defining** group of the 20th century.

中 Translation

接下來幾年，披頭四巡迴世界演出，並錄製〈我想牽你的手〉和〈愛情無價〉等暢銷單曲。一九六四年四月，後者成為史上第一支同時榮登英美排行榜冠軍的單曲。全世界都為 F4 著迷。除了推出膾炙人口的歌曲，披頭四也主演《一夜狂歡》和《救命！》等電影，並大舉推出授權商品。樂迷可以買到各式各樣的披頭四商品，從披頭四娃娃、便當盒到服飾和假髮都有。一九六五至六九年，美國甚至播出一部披頭四卡通。

但披頭四的世界並非只有情歌和少女粉絲。一九六四年和巴布狄倫碰面後，他們開始嘗試不同的音樂類型（及毒品），並發展出更成熟的聲音，可從一九六五年的《橡皮靈魂》聽出來。一九六六年爆發爭議，當時藍儂告訴一位英國記者：「基督教一定會式微……現在我們比耶穌更受歡迎。」雖然這句話在英國未獲注意，披頭四卻在美國收到死亡威脅，保守派基督教徒較多的南部地區更停止播放披頭四的歌曲。

披頭四在一九六六年八月停止巡迴演唱，但在接下來幾年創作出他們最具突破性的音樂，而後於一九七〇年解散。他們一九六七年的概念性專輯《比伯軍曹寂寞芳心俱樂部》以創新的樂音和深刻的歌詞備受讚譽。他們的靈感來源已拓展至東方靈修和迷幻藥物，這在〈鑽石天空中的露西〉等歌曲中歷歷可見。四十年後，披頭四仍是史上最暢銷的樂團，也是二十世紀最具代表性的團體。

Tongue-tied No More

1 can't get enough of sth.
再多也不夠

形容非常非常鍾愛某樣東西，怎麼樣也不會膩、不嫌多。

A: Do you watch *Grey's Anatomy*?
你有看《實習醫生》嗎？

B: Of course! I can't get enough of it!
當然有！看再多都不會膩呢！

Language Guide

Rubber Soul 橡皮靈魂

《橡皮靈魂》是披頭四樂團的第六張專輯，也是第一次他們的唱片封面擺脫大大的「披頭四」字樣，真正展現樂團音樂性才華與深度的里程碑專輯。《橡皮靈魂》不但是披頭四另一張暢銷專輯之一，也廣受音樂評論家推崇。2012 年《滾石雜誌》評選該專輯為「史上最傑出 500 專輯」的第五名。

Bible Belt 聖經地帶

「聖經地帶」一般是指美國東南部及中部以保守福音派基督教為社會主導的地區。這區人民篤信浸信會，上教堂的比例遠高於美國其他地區，幾乎每個人都是基督徒是一個宗教氣息濃厚且民風保守的地帶。要注意的是 Bible Belt 一詞並非正式名稱，而是反對此地區過度將宗教與社會事務攪和在一起的人給的名稱，是帶有點貶意的。

Sgt. Pepper's Lonely Hearts Club Band 比伯軍曹寂寞芳心俱樂部

被《滾石雜誌》評為「史上最傑出 500 專輯」第一名的《比伯軍曹寂寞芳心俱樂部》無疑是搖滾樂迷及樂評心中最有影響力的一張專輯，也是迷幻搖滾 (psychedelic rock) 的代表大作。這張專輯在音樂複雜度、曲目編排、錄音技術甚至是封面設計等方面，在當時皆為前衛創舉。《比伯軍曹寂寞芳心俱樂部》收錄曲目多達 13 首，曲曲相扣、一氣呵成，被某些樂迷喻為世界第一張「概念專輯」(concept album)，堪稱為披頭四樂團華麗極致的高峰作品。

Vocabulary Bank

1) **protest** [ˋprotɛst] (n./v.) 抗議，反對
A group of students held a protest in front of the American embassy.

2) **accomplished** [əˋkɑmplɪʃt] (a.) 熟練的，有造詣的
Professor Adams is an accomplished scholar.

3) **commentator** [ˋkɑmən͵tetɚ] (n.) 評論家，（實況）播音員
The political commentator has a weekly column in the paper.

4) **immigrant** [ˋɪmɪgrənt] (n./a.) 移民（的）
Carlos is the son of Mexican immigrants.

5) **cut off** [kʌt ɔf] (phr.) 切斷，中斷
The phone company cut off my phone service because I didn't pay the bill.

6) **nod** [nɑd] (n./v.) 點頭，致意，同意；點頭
In a nod to the locals, the star said a few words in their language.

7) **freshman** [ˋfrɛʃmən] (a./n.)（高中、大學）一年級生（的）
I can't believe you failed freshman English.

8) **favorable** [ˋfevərəbəl] (a.) 稱讚的，贊同的，有利的
Response to the proposal has been mainly favorable.

進階字彙

9) **dabble (in)** [ˋdæbəl] (v.) 淺嘗，涉足
Ross dabbles in photography in his spare time.

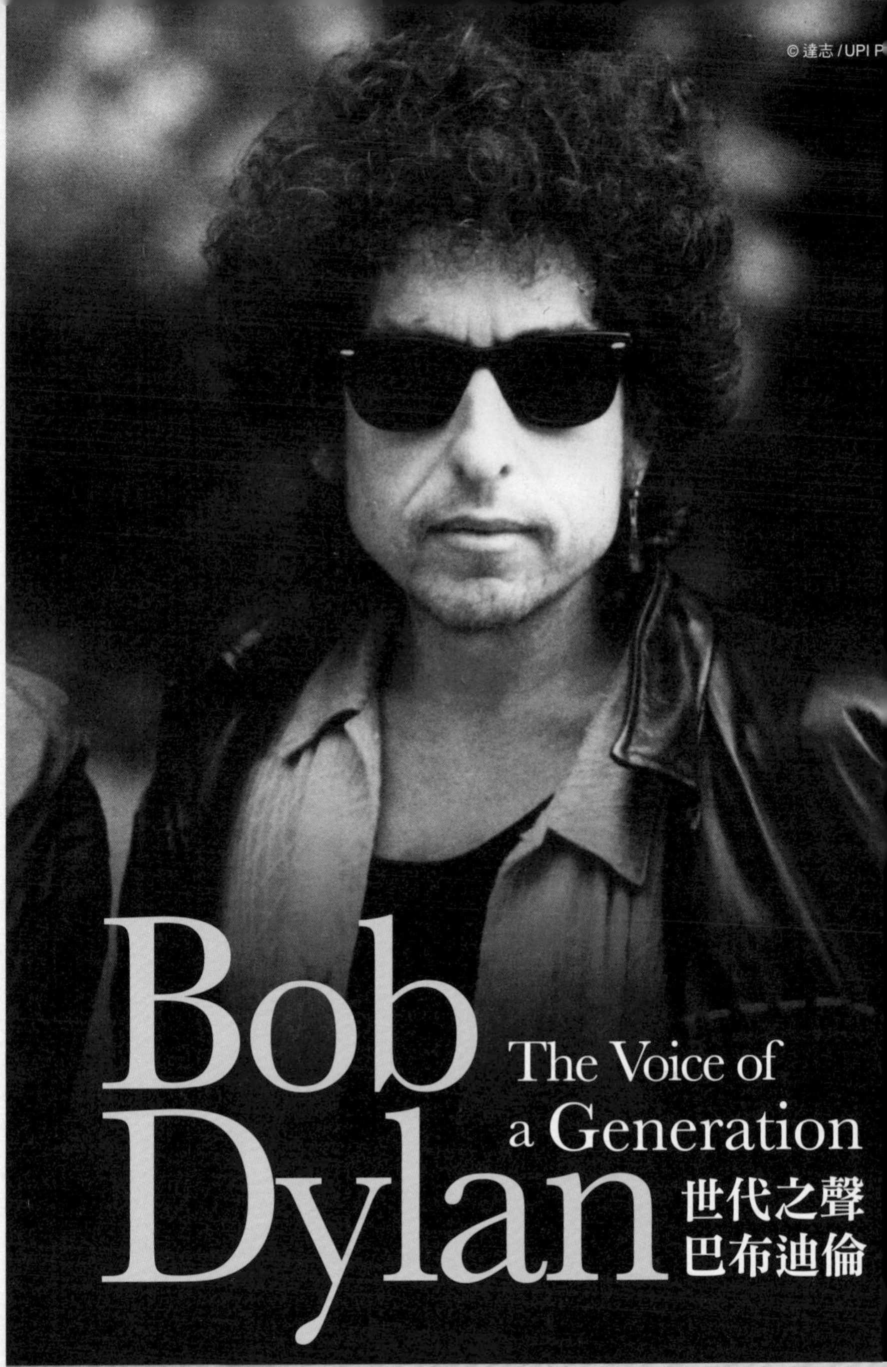

Bob Dylan
The Voice of a Generation
世代之聲 巴布迪倫

朗讀 MP3 247 單字 MP3 248 英文文章導讀 MP3 249

"How many roads must a man walk down before you call him a man?" asks singer-songwriter Bob Dylan in his classic 1963 song "Blowin' in the Wind." Over the course of his 50-year musical career, Dylan himself has walked down many roads: he **1 gave voice to** the [1]**protest** movements of the 1960s; he pushed the limits of folk and popular music in the mid-'60s and beyond; and he even [9]**dabbled** in Christianity in the late '70s and early '80s. An [2]**accomplished** artist, Dylan has also published several books of his drawings and paintings. Today, at 70, Dylan continues his journey as an artist, social [3]**commentator** and, of course, musician.

Bob Dylan was born Robert Allen Zimmerman on May 24, 1941 in Duluth, Minnesota. The grandson of Jewish [4]**immigrants**, he began playing and singing in rock 'n' roll bands in high school. At one talent show, his band was so loud that the principal [5]**cut off** their microphones. After graduating, he attended the University of Minnesota, where he began performing folk music in coffee shops as Bob Dylan, a [6]**nod** to the poet Dylan Thomas. On the shift from rock to folk, Dylan called the latter "more of a serious type of thing" that was capable of expressing deeper feelings. He dropped out of college after his [7]**freshman** year and headed to New York City, where he hoped to play music and meet his idol Woody Guthrie. Dylan began performing in Greenwich Village clubs in 1961, and after a [8]**favorable** review in the New York Times, he was signed by Columbia Records.

中 Translation

「一個男人必須走過多少路，才會被稱為男子漢？」創作型歌手巴布狄倫在他一九六三年經典單曲〈在風中吹響〉中問道。在他五十年的音樂生涯，狄倫自己就走過很多路：他為六〇年代的抗議運動發聲；他在六〇年代中期以及日後突破民謠與流行樂的限制；他甚至在七〇年代晚期至八〇年代初期涉獵基督教。身為造詣深厚的畫家，狄倫也出版了數本素描和畫作的書籍。如今，年已七十的他，仍繼續他身為畫家、社會評論家，當然還有音樂大師的旅程。

巴布狄倫本名為羅伯特艾倫齊默曼，一九四一年五月二十四日生於明尼蘇達州杜魯市。身為第三代猶太移民，他高中時加入搖滾樂團玩樂器及演唱。在一場才藝表演中，他的樂團因聲音過大，被校長關掉他們的麥克風。高中畢業後，他就讀明尼蘇達大學，開始在咖啡廳以巴布狄倫的藝名表演民謠，取這個名字是為了向詩人狄倫湯瑪士致意。對於捨搖滾就民謠一事，狄倫說後者是「比較嚴肅的東西」，能夠表達更深層的情感。他念完大一便輟學，前往紐約市，希望在那裡玩音樂並結識他的偶像伍迪葛瑟瑞。一九六一年，狄倫開始在格林威治村的夜店演出，《紐約時報》刊出一篇對他讚譽有加的評論後，他被哥倫比亞唱片公司簽下。

Woody Guthrie 和他的著名的吉他，上面的標語是 This Machine Kills Fascists. 意思是這把槍（指吉他）能打敗法西斯.

Tongue-tied No More

1 give voice to 發聲，表達情緒

照字面翻譯是傳達聲音，to 後面加正面的字可解釋為「為……支持、發聲」，加一些情緒的字就有「表達感覺」的意思。

例 The protesters gave voice to their anger at the demonstration.
抗議人士在遊行中表達他們的憤怒。

Language Guide

folk 民謠

這裡指的是現代民謠音樂 (contemporary folk music)，是從傳統的民謠音樂演變而來。在 1960 年代，因為搭上美國人權主義和反戰訴求興盛，而大為流行。內容變成以歌詞傳達政治理念和反戰意識。代表歌手有：瓊拜雅 (Joan Baez)、彼得席格 (Pete Seeger)、巴布狄倫等。

Woody Guthrie 伍迪葛瑟瑞

美國傳奇民謠歌手——伍迪葛瑟瑞，於三〇年代經濟大蕭條時期，隨著大批找尋工作機會的失業工人一起遷徙至加州，這段經歷啟發了他的許多創作。葛瑟瑞於一九四〇年遷居紐約市，寫出 This Land Is Your Land，這首被譽為美國地下國歌的愛國歌曲，從此成名。他的歌詞淺白，為勞工階層發聲，關注社會正義，多位民謠歌手如巴布迪倫、布魯斯史賓史汀 (Bruce Springsteen) 都宣稱深受他的作品影響。

Greenwich Village 格林威治村

格林威治村，也稱做「the Village」，是美國紐約曼哈頓 (Manhattan) 西區以華盛頓廣場公園 (Washington Square Park) 為中心的一個區。住在這裡的多半是作家或是藝術家，聚集著各種各樣的藝術工作者和社會運動人士，因此有許多重要的社會文化運動都在這裡蓬勃發展，像是二十世紀的婦女爭取選舉權，到五〇年代的「垮掉的一代」(Beat Generation)，六〇年代的反戰，六〇年代的性解放運動，婦女解放運動，同志權益運動…等等。

近年來，格林威治村被細分為二，以第六大道 (6th Avenue) 為分界，以西變成具有同性戀色彩的西村 (West Village)；以東則有嬉皮色彩的中產階級知識份子聚集的地方。這裡還保存了一些早期古老美麗的建築物，許多有趣的古董店和小酒館、咖啡館，其中以華盛頓廣場最為出名。

華盛頓公園西側著名的 MacDougal Street，從 West 8th Street 到 Bleecker Street、Prince Street，這一帶幾個街區，吸引許多當代藝術家們進駐。而文人墨客在咖啡廳酒吧流連，這些咖啡廳酒吧們也因為他們而聲名大噪，發展出了一個藝術聚集。

Vocabulary Bank

1) **trademark** [ˋtred͵mɑrk] (n.) 招牌，代表性物品
The country singer wore his trademark cowboy hat.

2) **harmonica** [hɑrˋmɑnɪkə] (n.) 口琴
Learning how to play the harmonica is easy.

3) **nuclear** [ˋnukliɚ] (a.) 核子的，原子彈的
Many experts believe that Iran is trying to develop nuclear weapons.

4) **motivated** [ˋmotɪ͵vetɪd] (a.) 受…激發、驅使的
Rape is seldom a sexually motivated crime.

5) **spokesperson** [ˋspoks͵pɝsən] (n.) 發言人、代言人，複數為 spokespeople
A government spokesperson announced the new tax plan.

6) **transition** [trænˋzɪʃən] (n.) 轉變，變革
The country made a smooth transition to a market economy.

7) **core** [kor] (a./n.) 核心（的），基本（的）
Beijing has stated that the South China Sea is a core national interest.

進階字彙

8) **politicize** [pəˋlɪtə͵saɪz] (v.) 把…政治化
The debate over global warming has become highly politicized.

9) **topical** [ˋtɑpɪkəl] (a.) 時事主題的，切題的
Guests on the talk show discussed a variety of topical issues.

10) **nasal** [ˋnezəl] (a.) 鼻音的，鼻子的
This nasal spray will relieve your allergy symptoms.

11) **acoustic** [əˋkustɪk] (a.) 不插電的（樂器），聲學的，acoustic guitar 即「木吉他」
The band members all play acoustic instruments.

12) **subterranean** [͵sʌbtəˋrenɪən] (a.) 地下的，隱蔽的
The ants live in subterranean nests.

13) **reinvent** [͵riɪnˋvɛnt] (v.) 改造，重新發明、創造
The chef is famous for reinventing traditional dishes.

口語補充

14) **folkie** [ˋfoki] (n.) 民謠歌手、樂手
Lots of folkies play at that club.

朗讀 MP3 250 單字 MP3 251 英文文章導讀 MP3 252

Dylan's 1962 self-titled debut album consisted of familiar folk, gospel and blues songs. It was hardly a success, selling just 5,000 copies during its first year. His second and third albums, *The Freewheelin' Bob Dylan* and *The Times They Are A-Changin'*, however, perfectly captured the spirit of the '60s with their [8]**politicized** lyrics, producing a number of popular protest songs. These [9]**topical** songs, which Dylan sang in his [1]**trademark** [10]**nasal** voice while playing [11]**acoustic** guitar and [2]**harmonica**, were about issues like school integration, [3]**nuclear** war and racially [4]**motivated** murders. In 1963, he performed with fellow [14]**folkie** Joan Baez at the March on Washington (where Martin Luther King, Jr. gave his famous "I Have a Dream" speech) and visited student civil rights activists in Mississippi. But just as quickly as he became a voice for the civil rights and anti-war movements, he seemed to reject his status as their [5]**spokesperson**.

Dylan's mid-'60s albums—*Bringing It All Back Home, Highway 61 Revisited* and *Blonde on Blonde*—marked his [6]**transition** from folk singer-songwriter to pop star. He began performing and recording with electric instruments, angering his [7]**core** folk audience. However, songs like "[12]**Subterranean** Homesick Blues" and "Like a Rolling

Bob Dylan 和 Joan Baez 在「向華府進軍」中演出

Stone" suggested a bold, innovative direction for popular music. Over the following three decades, Dylan would continue to [13]**reinvent** himself. He became a born-again Christian in the late '70s, and won his first Grammy for "Gotta Serve Somebody," a single from his 1979 Christian rock album *Slow Train Coming*. These days, he continues to make music and tour—including shows this year in Taiwan and China. What's next for the great Bob Dylan? The answer is blowin' in the wind.

中 Translation

狄倫在一九六二年推出的首張同名專輯收錄了大家熟悉的民謠、福音與藍調歌曲。這張處女作並未一舉成功，第一年只賣了五千張。但他的第二張和第三張專輯《自由自在的巴布狄倫》和《蛻變時節》，就以政治化的歌詞完美捕捉六〇年代的精神，創造出數首備受歡迎的抗議歌曲。這些反映時事的歌曲—狄倫以其招牌鼻音演唱，並用木吉他和口琴伴奏—係探討消弭學校種族隔離、核子戰爭和種族歧視引起的謀殺案等議題。一九六三年，他和民謠同好瓊拜雅茲在「向華府進軍」的示威活動中演出（小馬丁路德金恩博士著名的「我有一個夢」演說就是在此活動中發表），並到密西西比拜訪學生民權運動人士。但一如他迅速成為民權及反戰運動的代言人，他似乎也很快就拒絕擔任他們的發言人。

狄倫在六〇年代中期的專輯—《全帶回家》、《再訪六十一號公路》和《金髮美女》—記錄了他從創作型民謠歌手轉變為流行巨星的過程。他開始用電子樂器表演及錄音，觸怒了他的死忠民謠粉絲。然而，〈地下鄉愁〉和〈像顆滾石〉等歌曲也為流行音樂啟發了一個大膽、創新的方向。接下來三十年，狄倫仍不斷重新改造自己。他在七〇年代晚期成為重生的基督徒，並以一九七九年基督搖滾專輯《慢車來了》的單曲〈為人服務〉贏得他首座葛萊美獎。近年來，他繼續創作音樂及巡迴公演—包括今年到台灣及中國的演出。偉大的巴布狄倫下一步會怎麼走？答案就在風中吹響。

Language Guide

school integration 學校種族融合

美國在南北戰爭後雖然廢除奴隸制度，種族隔離 (segregation) 制度在南方其實還是存在的，比如各種公共設施，旅館，學校，公車，火車，餐廳，醫院等，都是黑白種族分開使用。所以根據種族隔離的法律條款規定，白人和黑人必須就讀不同的公立學校，黑人的各種設施都比較差。這樣的現象在布朗訴教育局 (Brown v. Board of Education) 案子出現時才破除，這個判例反對之前教育上的種族隔離，主張不得因為種族因素拒絕學童入學，終止了長久以來黑白種族隔離教育。integration 是「整合，融合」之意，這裡特別指種族上的融合。

March on Washington 向華府進軍

五〇至六〇年代是民權運動對抗種族隔離制度的動蕩時期，示威活動在一九六三年的華府遊行達到最高潮。從華盛頓紀念碑 (Washington Monument) 至林肯紀念堂 (Lincoln Memorial)，美國史上最大的人權政治集會就在此舉行，目的為爭取非裔美國人的政治和經濟權力。遊行活動還包括林肯紀念堂前的集會節目，像是歌手振奮人心的歌曲和領導人極具凝聚力的演說，其中以小馬丁路德金恩 (Martin Luther King, Jr.) 的《我有一個夢想》(*I Have a Dream*) 最為有名。這場示威活動促成隔年主張廢除種族隔離的民權法案 (Civil Rights Act) 和一九六五年投票權法 (Voting Rights Act) 的通過。

anti-war movement 反戰運動

第二次世界大戰 (WWII) 後，美國面臨到共產赤化世界的威脅。在越戰 (Vietnam War) 前美國積極對抗，提供物資或是軍力交流，杜絕各自由主義國家有被赤化的可能。因此決議軍援南越以對抗共產勢力。

反越戰運動從一九六五年的美國大學校園開始萌芽，一九六八年時反戰情緒最為高漲。反越戰運動主要以學生運動為主軸，當時有人認為美國參與越戰，是帝國主義 (colonialism) 的一種行為因而反戰，另一派則是支持社會主義 (socialism) 的左翼份子。

當時，反戰情緒的高資助漲還有另一個很大的因素，美國人民常在電視上看見美國士兵棺材運回的情形，年輕生命戰死異鄉，消逝在無意義戰火裡，使得許多大學生害怕從軍，紛紛逃往加拿大以躲避徵召，反戰意識更加濃烈。最慘烈的抗議事件發生在一九七〇年俄亥俄州肯特州立大學 (Kent State) 校園裡，反戰學生被國民兵 (National Guard) 掃射斃命。

屏東 國賓影城
盛大開幕!!
國賓影城
AMBASSADOR THEATRES
網路訂位
使用『國賓A+卡』訂票張數超彈性！
會員專屬網路訂位服務，新增儲值金額交易機制，
訂票張數增加，使用更便利！
購票優惠
使用『國賓A+卡』票價最優惠！
使用國賓A+卡，
立即享有會員優惠票價！
國賓A+卡
禮遇優惠多更多
餐飲折扣
使用『國賓A+卡』消費最超值！
使用國賓A+卡，
立即享有影院販賣部可樂、爆米花5折，
其他單品8折優惠！
紅利回饋
聰明消費別忘了『國賓A+卡』！
先現金儲值再消費，累積紅利點數換贈品，
讓您儲值娛樂，積點好康A更多！
A+ AMBASSADOR
Enjoy Movie! Enjoy Life!
便捷取票
使用『國賓A+卡』付款，取票機制更快速！
會員運用儲值金額交易機制訂票，
可利用現場會員售票窗口，取票更快速！
專屬活動
擁有『國賓A+卡』獨享貴賓禮遇！
每週會員電子報，不定期專屬活動，
讓您限量電影贈品手到擒來！

The Divine Michelangelo
完整看見最眞實的米開朗基羅
錯過這次，再等500年
以不同角度剖析米開朗基羅的個性、生活、
藝術成就，以及大師工作室的學習實況
天堂・審判・重生
米開朗基羅
文藝復興巨匠再現
2013 01/SAT 26 » 05/SUN 12
週一至週日・0900~1800・除夕休館
國立歷史博物館
(台北市南海路49號)
粉絲團 米開朗基羅
洽詢專線 02-6630-8288
www.mediasphere.com.tw/michelangelo
國立歷史博物館 National Museum of History
時藝多媒體
JING KAI
台灣啤酒 TAIWAN BEER
中華電信
廣達文教基金會
EVA AIR 長榮航空
GARDEN HOTEL 台北花園大酒店
CHAMPTRON

國家圖書館出版品預行編目 (CIP) 資料

歷史名人堂 Hall of Fame : EZ TALK 總編嚴選閱讀特刊 / EZ 叢書館編輯部作 . -- 初版 . -- 臺北市 : 日月文化 , 2013.02
188 面 ; 21x28 公分
ISBN 978-986-248-304-6(平裝附光碟片)
1. 英語 2. 讀本
805.18 101025720

EZ 叢書館

歷史名人堂 Hall of Fame : EZ TALK 總編嚴選閱讀特刊

總　　編：顏秀竹
主　　編：王廼君
執行編輯：黃鈺琦
美術設計：管仕豪、徐歷弘
排版設計：健呈電腦排版公司
錄 音 員：Sara Zitter、Michael Tennant 、Meilee Saccenti 、Jacob Roth

發 行 人：洪祺祥
法律顧問：建大法律事務所
財務顧問：高威會計師事務所

發　　行：日月文化出版股份有限公司
出　　版：EZ 叢書館
地　　址：台北市大安區信義路三段 151 號 9 樓
電　　話：(02) 2708-5875
傳　　真：(02) 2708-6157
網　　址：www.ezbooks.com.tw
客服信箱：service@heliopolis.com.tw

總 經 銷：聯合發行股份有限公司
印　　刷：科樂印刷公司
出　　版：2013 年 2 月
定　　價：350 元
I S B N：978-986-248-304-6

日月文化集團 HELIOPOLIS CULTURE GROUP　EZ TALK　EZ Japan　EZ Korea　EZ 叢書館